"One of the reasons I love the Lauren Holbrook series is the fact that your books are unpredictable and always have a unique touch to them."

—LEXI N.

"The dialogue is nonstop, and the humor is laugh out loud. Laurie's faith is strong, and the message of salvation is evident . . . there's a really cool conversion conversation that just flows like water in this one. I would LOVE to be a part of this wacky, wonderful circle of friends."

—DEENA P.

"What I want to say is this: *Miss Match* was fabulous. Such a fun read! I can't wait to dive into *Rematch*!"

—MELISSA O.

Also by Erynn Mangum

A LAUREN HOLBROOK NOVEL: *Miss Match*

A LAUREN HOLBROOK NOVEL: *Rematch*

NAVPRESS THINK

MATCHPOINT

erynn mangum

a lauren holbrook novel book 3

NavPress is the publishing ministry of The Navigators, an international Christian organization and leader in personal spiritual development. NavPress is committed to helping people grow spiritually and enjoy lives of meaning and hope through personal and group resources that are biblically rooted, culturally relevant, and highly practical.

For a free catalog go to www.NavPress.com or call 1.800.366.7788 in the United States or 1.800.839.4769 in Canada.

© 2008 by Erynn Mangum

NAVPRESS, the NAVPRESS logo, THINK, and the THINK logo are registered trademarks of NavPress. Absence of ® in connection with marks of NavPress or other parties does not indicate an absence of registration of those marks.

ISBN-10: 1-60006-309-8
ISBN-13: 978-1-60006-309-1

Cover design by Arvid Wallen
Cover images by Shutterstock
Author photo by Portrait Innovations
Creative Team: Rebekah Guzman, Amy Parker, Kathy Mosier, Darla Hightower, Arvid Wallen, Kathy Guist

This novel is a work of fiction. Names, characters, places, and incidents are either the product of the author's imagination or are used fictitiously. Any resemblance to actual events, locales, organizations, or persons, living or dead, is entirely coincidental and beyond the intent of either the author or publisher.

Unless otherwise identified, all Scripture quotations in this publication are taken from the HOLY BIBLE: NEW INTERNATIONAL VERSION® (NIV). Copyright © 1973, 1978, 1984 by International Bible Society. Used by permission of Zondervan Publishing House. All rights reserved.

Library of Congress Cataloging-in-Publication Data

Mangum, Erynn, 1985-
  Match point : a Lauren Holbrook novel, book 3 / Erynn Mangum.
      p. cm.
  ISBN-13: 978-1-60006-309-1
  ISBN-10: 1-60006-309-8
  1. Holbrook, Lauren (Fictitious character)--Fiction. 2. Dating (Social customs)--Fiction. I. Title.
  PS3613.A53673M38 2008
  813'.6--dc22

                                    2007051981

Printed in the United States of America

2 3 4 5 6 7 8 9 10 / 12 11 10 09 08

To Nana, a.k.a Eloise Terry, for calling me about the characters in this series, correcting drafts, having suggestions, and giving me the most amazing example of what marriage looks like. I love you so much!

To my husband, Jonathan Ryan O'Brien, I never expected my Ryan to be literal. God definitely has a sense of humor! Thank you for always supporting me and encouraging me in this—even when I'm crabby and on a deadline. I love you!

Acknowledgments

To Christ, my Savior, my first love: Lord, how can I possibly ever thank You even for the family and friends You've given me, much less the opportunity to do what I love best for a career? Thank You for holding my hand and not letting go, even when I get tired and overwhelmed. I love You, Lord! To You alone be all the glory.

Here are a few of my favorite people and why:

My mom, because she giggles with me at chick-flicks, corrects thousands upon thousands of pages of drafts, makes birthdays and holidays special, quotes *While You Were Sleeping*, and gave me her love of shopping. I'm so blessed you're my mother, but I'm very glad you're my friend. ☺

My dad, because he grills the best steaks ever, provided so I could travel places with my writing, taught me about cars and finances and other mysteries of life, tells the funniest stories, and tries to help me think logically. I'm so proud to be known as the daughter of a man with such high integrity. ☺

Jon, because he gives the best hugs ever, holds my hand and lets me talk when I'm upset, takes care of me and protects me, watches late-night movies, is a man of prayer, makes me laugh so hard I cry, and works at everything with diligence. I'm very proud of you for who you are and what you've accomplished.

Bryant, because he always puts aside everything to talk to me, worships when he plays the guitar, helped me with my math (thanks!), and can always cheer me up on a bad day. I can't believe God gave me such an amazing brother!

Caleb, because he works hard to make everyone happy, can make almost anything seem funny, rocks out on the drums, is amazing with little kids, and is always good for a big hug. I think you're awesome!

Cayce, because she sat on my bed and talked girl-talk for hours really late at night, watches our yearly "Worst Movie Ever" and likes it, gets into giggling fits and can't stop, and is the bravest girl I know. You're my sister, but you're also my best friend.

Nama, because she bakes peach and apple pies, daily lives the hardest example of true love I've ever seen, took me out for Nama-and-Erynn alone time when I was little, and shares wisdom over the phone. Thanks for being the most heroic grandmother out there!

Grandad, Grandmom, and Tapa—I wish each of you could share in this with me, since so much of my life was shaped by your faith and influence. I love the memories I have of you!

My aunts, uncles, and cousins who put up with a dorky twelve-year-old and performed in or watched the plays I wrote and loved me even in spite of it. I love you all!

My friends who have prayed, laughed, celebrated, cried, and been the most amazing support out there, especially Steve, Elaine, Chris, Laura, and Caleb Wright, Jonathan Schmidt, Shannon Kay, Kaitlin Bar, Ellyn Thompson, Elisa Wingerd, Sarah Chancey, Eliya Schmidt, and Jessie Warwick.

NavPress is a fabulous publisher and here's why it is: Kris Wallen and Rebekah Guzman—I think I've bugged you on a weekly basis for . . . how long have you been my publisher? 😊 Thank you for always answering my hundreds of questions, celebrating with me and being there to calm me down. Arvid Wallen, you make the bestest covers in the business. Amy Parker, Kathy Mosier, and Darla Hightower, thank you for making this book the best it can be.

The Christian Writers Guild—thank you for guiding this extremely naïve kid through this journey and making it fun!

And finally, three very important items that got me through writing this book: Starbucks French Roast, to get the brain cells moving; Dentyne Ice gum, to give my ADD something to do while I typed; and the treadmill in the basement, where I vented my frustrations and saved my hair from being pulled out by the roots.

Chapter One

An Ode to Weddings
by Lauren Emma Holbrook

What light through yonder window brings?
It is the sound of dear ones' weddings.

The sounds of joy, the sounds of tears,
The sounds of music, the sounds of fears.

The smell of flowers, the taste of cake,
The look of elegance and that touch of lace.

Of kisses and curling irons and mothers' loud crying
Of doorbells and gifts brought and plants now dying.

Of weekends and ribbons and endless thanks to send,

This is the ode to weddings we give.

"So what do you think?" I ask Hannah, holding my hands over my head.

She looks up, her nose wrinkling. "Uh, no offense, Laurie, but I'd stick to photography."

"It's not *that* bad."

"Laur, *send* and *give* don't rhyme."

"Well, that's a haiku, or whatever they're called. You know. The poems that don't rhyme."

She waves the paper at me. "Yeah, but the rest of it *does* rhyme! Okay, maybe not the bit about cake and lace."

I grin at her.

"And why are you holding your arms up like that?"

I keep them on my head. "Because the lace around the sleeve line itches."

She rolls her eyes and walks away, taking my poem with her. No doubt to show whatever high-up-in-Hollywood producer may be here.

Someone makes a loud announcement, and I turn to grin at my dad and his blushing bride of thirty-seven minutes coming through the double doors. The Hyatt is bustling, tuxed-out waiters and waitresses scrambling, guests applauding, and all my little nieces and nephews yelling.

And Dad's grinning like I haven't seen in . . . come to think of it, I haven't *ever* seen him smile like that.

Joan Abbot Holbrook, my new stepmom, sends me a wink

and turns to hug her daughter, Ruthie.

This wedding clinches it for me. I have now been a bridesmaid three times: first at my sister Laney's wedding, next at my good friend Ruby's wedding, and now here.

According to the old saying, I will now never be a bride.

Pity.

Maybe being maid of honor twice cancels out two of the bridesmaids. I will have to read up on this. I was maid of honor for my other sister, Lexi's, wedding, and I was maid of honor two weeks ago at a very special wedding between two very special people who had been engaged nearly an entire year and finally tied the knot.

My two best friends, Brandon and Hannah Knox.

Dad comes over, and I wrap my arms around his neck. "Congratulations, Dad," I grin, feeling tears sting the back of my eyes.

Again. I sobbed like a leaky sprinkler head through the entire ceremony, trying to hide it behind the huge bouquet of orange carnations I held.

Yes, I know. *Orange.* And carnations! My new stepmother does not have very good taste in flowers or colors.

But that's another story.

Dad hugs me tight and kisses the top of my head like he used to when I was a little girl. "You look beautiful, Laurie-girl."

"Thank you, Dad." I lean toward his ear and lower my voice. "We have a slight problem."

"Oh dear."

"Um, something has happened to the cake," I whisper. "It's not here."

All through the last six weeks, my dad and Joan couldn't

stop talking about this amazing lime green and orange cake they discovered, which happen to be Joan's favorite colors and subsequently the colors of my living room and study.

Dad pats my cheek. "Not to worry, dear. It's here. It's probably refrigerating."

Note here: I have no experience with wedding cakes other than consumption. This statement seems perfectly normal.

"Oh, okay," I say.

"You'll remember to water my plants while we're gone, right?" he asks.

I smile and reassure him for the seventh time. "Yes, Dad."

"They're very delicate. They need care, Lauren. Don't forget."

"I won't, Dad."

I hate live plants.

Dad and Joan are going on a week-long honeymoon to Baltimore, of all places, to attend a seminar on germ awareness and health consciousness at Johns Hopkins.

How romantic!

Dad and Joan are so excited they can hardly wait.

"Josh will take us to the airport since he's going to be driving back that way anyway," Dad says.

Josh is Joan's son. He and his wife, Kerrianne, are staying here at the Hyatt.

"Sounds good, Dad."

"There was something else I was going to tell you." He frowns at the thought.

And I suddenly realize how different things are going to be from now on.

Very different.

I bite back tears. *Lord, please help me to stop crying!*

Dad sighs, shrugs, and smiles. "I don't remember."

"That's okay, Dad."

He pats my shoulder. "Excuse me, Honey, Joan's calling."

He goes back over to Joan, who is decked out in a long, prom-style ivory dress.

Meanwhile, the bridesmaids are wearing, yep, orange.

I look icky in orange, and if I start crying again, my red nose isn't going to help matters.

I hear paper rustling, and someone clears his throat behind me. Ryan Palmer stands there, brow wrinkling, his bow tie slightly off center. He's holding my poem.

"Did you . . . um, really write this?" he asks.

I glare at him, wiping my wrist under my eyes. "It is not that bad! Sheesh, you and Hannah." I reach over and fix his tie, sniffing.

He grins his little-kid smile at me, and I smile back. Joan was nice and let Ryan be one of the ushers, to his sheer delight — mostly, I think, because the ushers get to wear top hats.

To Ryan, any hat is a chance to smooth down his curly hair.

"Are you crying?" he asks, tipping his head as he looks at me.

"No."

"So the water swimming around in there is what? Rewetting drops?" His expression softens, and he wraps me in a hug.

Drat. Affection. Now the tears are doubling up.

"Okay, enough hugging," I say, pulling away and using my knuckle to dab at the corner of my eye. "I'm trying not to cry. Mascara. Eye shadow. Rudolph noses. Crying is bad. Quick. Distract me," I plead, sniffling.

He gives me a look and then nods. "So where's this cake?" he asks, glancing around. Ryan was there for several of the conversations Dad and Joan had about the cake.

Good. Good change of subject. I blink rapidly and the tears mostly disappear. "I have no idea. I'm a little scared about it."

"Why?"

"Well, first, because we can't find it. Second, because we can't find it. And third, because neither Dad nor Joan like or even support the general idea of sweets."

Ryan's eyebrows go up in understanding. "Ah. I might not have cake."

"Right. It could be made with barley or whatever flour is in their nutritional magazines these days."

He makes a face and I grin, tears gone.

Ruby Amery, who is Ryan's sister, my former coworker, and a new mom of four months, comes over carrying baby Adrienne.

"Hey, guys, Nick and I are heading out pretty quick. I've got to get Adrienne down for the night. Lauren, the wedding was beautiful, and your dad looked great." She smiles, her brown eyes reflecting the candle glow.

Over the last year, she's taken on what I like to call the "New Mom" hairstyle—long, unruly, and in desperate need of a haircut that I guess she hasn't had time to get. Tonight, though, it is up in a bun, a few shorter strands falling around her face.

She looks beautiful.

I take Adrienne from her without asking. "Hi, wittle baby gwirl," I coo, kissing the baby's soft forehead. Adrienne is a tiny little girl with tons of dark, dark, dark brown hair and big brown eyes that are always wide open.

She blinks at me confusedly.

"Get used to that expression, Kiddo," Ryan tells his niece.

"Funny, Ryan."

Ruby kisses my cheek, takes her baby back, and goes to corral her husband, who is the singles' pastor at our church.

Something short slams into my legs, and I look down to see my year-old niece, Allie, tangled in the long mess of tulle and satin.

I heft her up and she grins a baby smile, grabbing my cheeks in her hands. "Dom me goom?" she baby-talks, leaning forward until she is an inch away from my eyeballs.

Allie and her twin brother, Mikey, have three older siblings—the other set of twins, Jack and Jess, now four, and the big sister of them all, Dorie, now a mature six. All of my sister Laney's kids got her blonde hair except Allie and Dorie, who both ended up with beautiful, silky, shiny brown hair from Laney's husband, Adam.

"What are you doing running around unsupervised?" I ask Allie, holding her back a few inches. She likes to invade my circle of space.

She giggles at something behind me, and I turn to see Ryan making faces at her.

"Hey, I am in the middle of a serious discussion," I say to him.

He grins and takes Allie from me, tossing her in the air. She shrieks with laughter.

"Laurie, with you, nothing is a serious discussion."

"Hmph. I want my niece back."

He throws her in the air again. "Mm. No."

"Hey!"

Someone hits a water glass with a knife, silencing Ryan's comeback. He catches Allie and settles her into the crook of his arm. She shoves three fingers in her mouth, staring at her new aunt, Ruthie, who is doubling as maid of honor and wedding coordinator.

"Everyone, may I have your attention?" she says sweetly. "We're now going to bring out the cake and start the toasts, if you would kindly take your seats."

Ryan, Allie, and I sit at the table we are nearest to, and Dad and Joan take their places at the front table.

The door to the kitchen opens, and two waiters carry in the cake.

I slam my hands over my mouth, and Ryan covers his eyes. Allie coos.

"Do not laugh, Laur, do not!" Ryan hisses, his shoulders shaking.

"I can't help it!"

Celery spears and carrot sticks are arranged in the shape of a three-tiered cake, a plastic bride and groom perched precariously on top.

Chapter Two

I walk into work Monday morning, yawning. Dad called at six to remind me, once again, not to forget to water the plants and to tell me good-bye since last night had ended in a flurry.

So there I was at six in the morning, sobbing, my dog, Darcy, trying to figure out what was wrong. I did a good job of soaking the book of Psalms.

Hannah looks up from her desk and does a double take. "What happened to you?"

"My dad got married."

"I thought it was a happy occasion."

I sigh. "Yeah, me too."

She gives me a sympathetic smile.

Florence Porter walks in, and, yes, that is a person.

Ruby left the studio four months ago to give birth, shaking the dust off her shoes and vowing never to work again, leaving us in a bind. Both Brandon and I were booked full-time, and Ty and Newton, already full-timers, were getting run-down too.

So Brandon, being Brandon, went out and hired Florence Porter, a new-to-towner who borrowed Tammy Faye's eyelashes and has moguls of thick, mousy-looking brown hair, a somewhat dumpy figure, and a permanent squeak in her voice.

To quote Brandon, "I don't think she *means* to twitter; she just does."

Mm-hmm. *Right.*

Hannah and I both lambasted him, but what was done was done, and Florence Porter is now a paid worker at The Brandon Knox Photography Studio.

"My nine o'clock is late," she screeches, shoving a long fingernail into her ever-present tower of hair. I watch, oddly fascinated as the tower quivers, shakes, and almost falls before straightening again. One day, it will fall.

And I will be there.

"I'm sure they'll be here soon," Hannah soothes, like a good secretary.

I keep staring at Florence Porter's hair.

"They'd better be. Last week my nine o'clock was twenty minutes late, and that made me twenty minutes late for every appointment the rest of the day." She gives me a look. "What are you looking at?"

"Oh, nothing."

"You look terrible," she tells me.

I can take friends telling me I don't look good, but Florence Porter is not a friend. I smile tightly. "Thanks."

She looks out the window and sighs, her lower lip protruding slightly, and I suddenly have the very strong feeling of watching Mrs. Bennet in that scene where she's staring out the window waiting for Mr. Bingley.

I shoot Hannah a wide-eyed stare, and by her nod, I can tell she sees it too.

"Well, send them back when they get here," she demands and slams the door to Studio Two.

Hannah's mouth drops and she points her pen toward the closed door. "Did you—wow, did you see that?"

"She looked just like Mrs. Bennet!" I shriek.

Brandon's door opens. "Laurie, shut up!" Then it slams.

Hannah presses her lips together and gives me a look. "I think he's paying bills."

"Ah. To quote Jack Sparrow, I think he needs to find himself a girl."

"He has a girl."

"Oh yeah." I grin, shoving my backpack in the cubbyhole behind her. "I'd nearly forgotten."

"Funny, Laurie." Hannah smiles sweetly, rubbing her wedding ring with her thumb like newlyweds do. "I saw you and Ryan sitting together last night," she says.

"Really?"

"He was holding *your* niece."

"Yeah, well, he has a way with women."

She chuckles. "Seriously, Laurie. You and Ryan have been dating forever. How long are you going to put it off?"

I frown. "Put what off?"

"Engagement! Marriage!" She waves her left hand at me. "Rings!"

I sit down in one of the chairs in front of her desk. "Hannah," I say slowly, "first, we've never . . . that is to say, we don't really *date*."

She steeples her fingers. "What do you do?"

"Hang out. We're really just good friends."

"Mm-hmm," she says, not believing me.

"Really, Hannah," I say, leaning forward. "It's true."

"Laurie, your dad is married. On his honeymoon. When is it going to be your turn?"

I shrug. "I'm not in any hurry to get married."

She raises her hands, surrendering. "Fine, fine. All I'm saying is, you need to snatch that boy up before someone else does."

"Who else? Everyone in our singles' class is married!"

She grins.

"Okay, Shawn and Hallie aren't, but that's just a matter of time."

The Harrisons walk in, carrying their three-year-old daughter. "We're Florence's nine o'clock. Sorry we're late," Mr. Harrison says.

Florence bursts out of Studio Two like Lucifer the Cat going after Jaq the Mouse in *Cinderella*.

"Come in!" she squeals. "You, there! You, there!" She points, the door closing behind her.

Hannah raises her eyebrows and shakes her head, at her husband's stupidity, I guess.

The front door opens again, and my nine fifteen comes in. "Hi, Laurie," Mrs. Bell says, holding little Liberty by the hand.

Poor Liberty Bell. Her brother is named Alexander Bell, after the guy who invented the telephone, I can only assume.

At nine forty-five, I had a family of seven. Ten thirty, a family reunion. Fourteen people, two dogs, three cats, and two babies who screamed at a pitch just above bomb sirens.

By twelve thirty, I had had enough.

I bang through Brandon's office door. "You have to hire another person!" I yell, raising my fist for emphasis, like Scarlett O'Hara.

"Shut the door, Laurie."

I do and climb up on his desk, grabbing his face. "I can't handle this!"

"What did Florence do this time?"

"What?" I ask, frowning. "It's not Florence, Brandon. It's the fact that I haven't even had time to go to the bathroom all day! I'm so jam-packed with appointments, I can't even think! And I'm a *part-time* employee!"

"All right, all right, all right!" Brandon shouts. "Just calm down," he says soothingly, yanking my hands away from his face.

"I don't have *time* to calm down!"

"Laurie!"

The door opens, and Hannah sticks her head in. "Honey, is Laur—" She sees me and smiles. "Hey, Laur, your next two appointments are here."

I point wordlessly to Hannah.

Brandon sighs, and a smile flirts with his mouth. "Okay, all right. Point made. I'll start looking for another person to hire."

"No!" Hannah and I yell at the same time.

"But I thought you just said—"

"Why don't you let Hannah hire someone?" I suggest.

He narrows his eyes. "Why? You don't think I'm good at hiring people? May I remind you that I hired both of you?"

"I've known you since second grade, so I don't count. And Hannah was sent from God. Please let her handle it?"

He sighs again, looks at his wife, looks at me, sighs again, and backs down. "I conduct the interviews," he says. "And I have the final decision."

"Good. Works." I slide off his desk and push imaginary sleeves up. "Pardon me, my doom awaits." I scoot past a giggling Hannah, who turns to follow me out into the hall.

"Wait a second, Hannah. Can I see you for a minute?" I hear Brandon ask, his voice tinged with a grin.

The door to his office closes, and I shake my head. Married people should not work together. Particularly newlyweds.

— ❖ —

By the time I finish at six, I am exhausted and hungry, and my contacts are burning like crazy. Probably due to my early morning sob-fest.

"Night, guys," I mumble to Brandon and Hannah, digging my keys out of my backpack.

"Good night, Laurie. Drive carefully," Hannah says.

"See you, Nutsy," Brandon says, wrapping an arm around his wife and escorting her out the door behind me.

I drive home, park in the driveway, and step into the dark, shadowy, very quiet house.

Darcy pads over, wagging his tail, and I rub his ears.

"Just you and me, Baby," I tell him, sighing.

He licks my hand.

I press the button on the answering machine. "No new messages," the mechanized voice says.

I sigh again. Dad hasn't called, so I assume they got to Baltimore okay.

"Want dinner?" I ask Darcy.

He wags his tail.

I open the refrigerator. "Looks like we have celery, carrots, or . . . more celery."

Darcy sits and frowns.

I moan. "I don't want to go back out."

I walk over, collapse on the couch, and prop my feet up on the coffee table. Darcy falls with a *whuff* underneath my legs.

Dad is married, Hannah and Brandon are married, I know Shawn and Hallie will be engaged within a month. . . .

I smile bleakly at Darcy. "What is a matchmaker without couples to match?"

He cocks his head as he thinks.

"I'll tell you. Bored. And tired. And I'm ordering Chinese." I grab the extension from the coffee table and am about to start dialing.

The front door opens. Darcy jumps up and skids into the entryway. "Whoa, hey, Boy," Ryan says. "Laur?" he calls, then walks in and sees me morphing into a permanent part of my couch.

He grins. "You look comfy."

"I had a very, very, very long day at work."

He sits down on the cushion beside me and hands me a bag from Merson's.

"Bless you." I moan, opening the bag and setting the phone down.

I inhale the sweet scent of homemade bread and cookies, feeling life pour back into my bones. I turn my head on the cushion and smile at Ryan. "You can come over as often as you want."

He chuckles. "Shouldn't be too hard. I already do."

I grin and dig out a cookie.

"Dessert first, Laur?"

I wipe the chocolate off my bottom lip. "And here I thought you'd learned not to criticize my eating habits."

"Hey, you'll notice that I didn't say a word about the front door being unlocked." He flicks my arm. "Not safe, Laurie."

I swallow. "Ry, the last burglary we had here was twenty years ago when little Tommy Hutchins stole a crescent wrench from his neighbor's garage to fix his mother's air conditioner."

"Tommy Hutchins. Isn't that the name of the sheriff?" Ryan frowns.

I grin. "And thus is our town."

⎯⎯ ❖ ⎯⎯

Tuesday passes in another blur, and by Wednesday night, my pointer finger is sore from mashing the button on the camera.

I get home, pat Darcy on the head, run upstairs, change shirts, run back downstairs, rub Darcy's ears, and dash back out the door to where my Tahoe is idling.

Nick, Ruby, and Adrienne live within walking distance, but I don't like walking, so I drive. I park behind Ryan's truck and open their front door.

In the last year, the Bible study has multiplied—but not with singles, with married couples. Awhile ago I had a scary premonition that is coming true: Singles' Bible study is going to end up being the Married with Children Bible Study, with a built-in single babysitter.

Me.

Ruby holds baby Adrienne in one arm and pours coffee for Tina Medfield, whose babysitter must have cancelled for tonight, because she's holding baby Sophie in one hand and the coffee cup in the other.

Married Couple Numbers 3–5, 6–7, and 10 are all pregnant, one with twins. I look around at all the maternity clothes present and have to smile.

I guess I've always wanted to be the thinnest person at Bible study.

"What are you grinning at?" Nick asks, standing by the front door, pastor-style.

"When are you going to get child care for this singles' class?"

"Hardy-har-har." He rolls his eyes but smiles. "I'm teaching tonight on the importance of multiplying and replenishing the earth." He pats my arm. "Stick around. I'm sure you'll enjoy it."

"Oh, for the topics that once applied to me!" I clasp my hands together and close my eyes dramatically.

"Excuse me, I see other people I need to talk to."

"Works for me. I'm going to go steal your daughter."

I follow Ruby into the kitchen and take Adrienne without asking. Ruby sighs, relieved, and starts making another batch of coffee, staring at her left hand. "I never fully appreciated working with two hands until I couldn't." She sighs again.

I kiss Adrienne's dark head. "Anytime you need a baby holder, let me know."

Ruby smiles. "Ryan mentioned you're a little stressed with work lately."

I groan. "You're a pastor's wife. Can you please tell Brandon and Hannah to stop stalling and hire someone?" I show her my pointer finger. "Look. I've strained my finger. See? It bends crookedly now."

She snorts. "What about Florence? She's not pulling her weight?"

"No, her weight is fine. It's her personality I can't stand. She's no Ruby. And Brandon keeps getting more clientele from all over the county." I shrug. "It's a no-win situation. Are you sure you don't want to go back to work, and I'll stay here with Adrienne?"

Ruby turns from the coffeepot and nuzzles Adrienne's nose with her own. "No, Mama couldn't spend that much time away from the precious!" she coos.

Eek. Ruby is starting to sound like Gollum.

Ryan comes in then, closing his eyes, groping around blindly, and yelling, "Adrienne! Adrienne!" like Sylvester Stallone in *Rocky*.

I laugh.

Ruby scowls. "Will you quit calling her like that?"

He angles his head at the baby. "Hey, yo, Adrienne!" he drawls, again imitating Stallone.

"Ryan!" Ruby yells.

He grins at me, leaning down to kiss his niece. "What do you think, Laur? Creative or annoying?"

"No offense, Ruby, but I prefer Stallone over Gollum."

"What?" she asks, pouring water into the coffeemaker.

"You know, the bit you just said about the precious."

Ryan makes a face at Adrienne. "Did your mommy just refer to you as an evil ring, Honey? Do you want to come live with your Uncle Ryan?"

He uses two fingers and tips the baby's head forward a few centimeters. "Ruby, she just said yes."

"Honey, if she *said* yes, I'm giving her to the circus, not you."

I gasp and turn Adrienne away from her mother and uncle. "Poor baby. Your mom wants to give you to the circus, and your uncle wants you to be a boxer's wife. You want to come live with your favorite Auntie Laurie, don't you?"

Adrienne lets out a little mew, her big eyes wide.

"Ha!" I shout to Ryan.

Ruby finishes measuring the coffee, turns the maker on, brushes her hands on her jeans, and squints at the clock.

"All right, baby girl, time for bed."

"But, Mommy, it's only seven thirty!" I squeal, shaking one of the baby's fists gently at Ruby.

"I want to stay up and watch *Rocky IV*!" Ryan tries to squeal, his voice cracking, pulling Adrienne's fingers into the number four.

Adrienne's little mouth works like she is drinking an invisible bottle, her eyes wide as she stares at her mom.

"Great, Ruby, great," Ryan bursts. "The kid is seeing bottles that aren't there now. What *A Beautiful Mind* thing to do."

Ruby chuckles and takes Adrienne from me. "She's hungry. It's time for her bedtime snack. Wave good-bye to Auntie Laurie and Uncle Ryan," Ruby croons, waving one of Adrienne's fists at us.

Adrienne starts whimpering.

"See? See? She wants to stay with us," Ryan calls as Ruby leaves the room with the baby. He turns and grins at me. "Know why that baby is cute, Laur?"

"Um, because she's a baby?"

"A *cute* baby," Ryan corrects. "I saw some of those babies in the church nursery last week. They are not cute at all."

"Ryan!"

"Well, they aren't!" he protests. "Now, take Adrienne. Cute curly hair, cute chubby cheeks, cute Shirley Temple eyes . . . she's just cute all over. Not like the bald, wrinkled little kids in the nursery."

"You are not a very nice person," I lecture.

"The reason she's cute," Ryan continues, "is because of the Palmer family genes."

"The Palmer family genes," I echo.

"Exactly," Ryan says, nodding. "Ruby was a very cute baby; I was a very cute baby. My dad was a very cute baby. See? Having cute babies runs in the family."

I cock my head at him. "So then your job would be to marry someone who also has cute genes and then you could win five thousand dollars in the county Cute Baby contest."

He grins widely. "Precisely."

I shake my head, smiling. "Yeah. Good luck with that. I can just see you on your knee, proposing, and right before you pop the question, you ask the poor girl for her baby pictures."

"You never know." He wraps an arm around me and escorts me into the living room. "You still have to admit it."

"Admit what?"

"Adrienne is the cutest baby you've seen."

"Of course she's the cutest baby I've seen. That's why I'm her Auntie Laurie. With toddlers, though, I'm going to have to say little Allie is the cutest."

Ryan spreads his free palm, eyes wide. "Well, yes! That's why I'm her Uncle Ryan." He grins, leans over, kisses my cheek, and points to two free places on the couch next to Hannah. "Save that other spot for Ruby. I'll sit on the floor in front of you."

I sit on the sofa, laying my Bible on the seat beside me. Ryan falls to the ground and leans back against the couch.

Hannah looks at me and raises her eyebrows toward Ryan.

I sigh.

She grins.

Keller Stone, perfect specimen of maleness, complete with the English accent, takes his place in the front with his guitar.

"Evening, everyone." He smiles, tweaking his guitar.

Baby Sophie starts bawling. Tina apologizes and goes down the hall.

Keller watches her go, looks at all the pregnant bellies and all the married couples, and then looks at me.

I shrug and grin, knowing what he is thinking.

And this is a singles' Bible study?

He returns the smile and scrapes his pick down the strings, the first chord of "As the Deer" miraculously coming out.

I tried strumming a guitar one time and realized that not only do I not have any musical talent at all, but I also don't have the desire to have musical talent.

I do, however, have a healthy respect now for those who play musical instruments.

Ruby appears in the doorway, and I wave to her saved seat. She picks her way across the spread of beanbag chairs and people sitting, tripping over Ryan, and barely landing on the couch, giggling hysterically and trying to hide it as people start singing.

She regains her composure by the time Keller sets the guitar down. "All yours, Pastor Nicholas." He grins.

Nick stands, one brow raised. "Thanks . . . uh, Brother Keller."

The class twitters.

"All right, Kids, open *sus Biblias* to Philippians." He grins. "Now you can all return to your homes and remember how I taught you this passage bilingually."

Nick prays in dismissal forty-five minutes later, and Ruby calls, "Snacks in the kitchen!"

The majority of the crowd goes that way, Ryan and Ruby included. I look over at Hannah.

"So what can I bring to the family lunch on Sunday?" she asks as I kick my sandals off and tuck my feet underneath me.

"Nothing. I'm getting barbecue from Smith Valley and a

cheesecake from Shawn."

She cranes her neck. "Speaking of which, where are Shawn and Hallie?"

"They came in late. I think they're getting snacks."

"What time does your dad and Joan's flight get in?"

"Sunday at noon."

She nods. "Short honeymoon."

I look at her. "Long engagement." She and Brandon were engaged a year before they finally got hitched.

She rolls her eyes.

"Hey, Laurie." Keller stands in front of us, holding his guitar.

"Hi, Keller, how are you?" I ask.

"Good, thanks. And you?"

"Fine. I'm about to go get some of those snickerdoodles that Holly brought. I think they're still warm." My mouth starts watering.

Keller props his guitar against the couch. "You look too comfortable to move. Stay there. I'll get them for you. Hannah?"

"No thanks." She smiles politely.

Keller leaves.

Hannah watches him go and then looks at me, eyebrows raised. "Laurie, you don't think—" she starts.

"Not often," I agree.

"Funny." She squints at Keller's back before it disappears into the kitchen. "He's getting you cookies."

"I know, Hannah. I was here." I yawn and lay my head against the cushions, closing my eyes.

I never sleep well when Dad is gone. Combine that with the past three days of total craziness at work, and I am one tired puppy.

"Laurie?" Hannah whispers.

I keep my eyes closed. "Mm?"

"What if Keller *likes* you?"

I shift positions, squishing deeper into the sofa. I might stay here tonight. "What are you talking about?" I mutter.

"I think he likes you!" she hisses.

"So? I like him. He's nice."

"What about Ryan?" she says in a low voice.

"What about him?"

"You're his girlfriend!"

"We've been through this, Hannah." I yawn again, crossing my arms over my chest and sighing. "This is a very comfortable sofa."

"Laurie, what if Keller asks you out?"

I open one eye and frown at her. "What?"

She opens her mouth just as Keller reappears with the cookies. "Here you are, Laurie. I remembered you like coffee, so I brought you that as well."

I sit up and take the Styrofoam cup and napkin from him. "Thanks, Keller." I smile.

He dimples. "Not a problem." He takes his guitar, goes back to the front of the room where his chair sits, and starts strumming.

Hannah leans over and stares at my cup. "Laurie."

"These are good cookies."

"Oh my gosh."

"Holly should market these."

"Laurie, he fixed your coffee for you!" she whispers, chin dropping.

I sigh and look at her. "Obviously, Hannah, he has realized that I like tan-colored coffee. It's a hard fact to miss! Sheesh. Lay off it, will you?"

I sip the coffee, pleasantly surprised. Exactly the right amount of sugar and milk. Amazing. That ratio has taken me almost a decade to perfect.

I look over at Keller, who smiles at me and keeps strumming.

"Hey, Laurie, I brought you—"

Ryan stops, seeing the cookies in my lap and the coffee in my hand. "Guess someone beat me to it," he says, a weird expression on his face. Mouth full of cookie, I nod and smile close-mouthed.

Hannah glares at me, then smiles brightly at Ryan. "I'll take them, if you're offering," she says sweetly.

Ryan smiles and gives her the cookies and coffee. He turns, looks around the room, sends me another strange look, and goes back into the kitchen.

Hannah covers her eyes. "Oh, Laurie, did you see his face?"

I swallow. "Confusion."

"Not confusion! The man is heartbroken, Laurie!"

"He is not!" I argue. "We're friends, Hannah! Just good friends! All right? Okay?" I sigh, block a yawn, drain the rest of the coffee, and stand, using Hannah's shoulder. "I have to move, or I'll never get off this couch."

"Where are you going?" she asks, worry skittering through her eyes.

"I've got to go find Steve."

"Who?"

"My fiancé."

She gives me a look and shakes her head. "Fine, be difficult," she says, popping a cookie in her mouth.

I laugh and walk into the kitchen.

Ruby holds a hand out to me, and I walk over. "I'm about to fall asleep on your couch," I tell her. "I might stay the night."

She wraps an arm comfortably around my waist. "That's fine,

Honey. Then you can get up with the baby."

I chuckle. "I don't think I have what she'd want."

Ruby rolls her eyes. "They invented bottles, you know."

"I think I'll pass, Ruby."

"Smart girl. Get all the full nights of sleep that you can."

"You know, you've become quite the doomsayer since you were impregnated."

She grins. All through her nine months of pregnancy, she told me and Hannah how we should never take for granted breakfast, slim jeans, or tying our own shoes ever again.

I kiss her forehead and pull away. "I'm going home."

"Did you walk? Let Ryan drive you home."

"I drove."

"Oh. Well, drive safely then." She squeezes my hand and turns to one-half of Married Couple Number 2.

I go back into the living room and find Ryan and Hannah talking. Keller is still strumming his guitar.

I dig my backpack out from under Hannah. "Okay, guys, I'm leaving."

"What are you doing tomorrow, Laur?" Ryan asks.

I sigh. "What else? Working. I have no life."

"I thought you were just part-time."

"So did I." I smile at him and then squeeze Hannah's shoulder to let her know all is well in paradise and to stop worrying.

"Love you. See you tomorrow." She grins.

"Love you too. Bye."

"I'll walk you out," Ryan says, catching my elbow.

"Okay."

"Bye, Laurie!" Keller calls.

I wave. "See you, Keller!"

Ryan closes the front door behind us and looks at me, that same weird expression on his face.

"So I was thinking," I say, walking toward my car. "How does this sound for a country song: 'Your Bowling League Strike Strikes Fear in My Spikes'?"

He laughs, the expression melting off. "What are you doing for lunch tomorrow?"

"Probably what I did the last three days. Grab a cheeseburger from Bud's and eat it on the way back to the studio."

"You know, if you had a lunch date, Brandon would probably let you leave."

I grin evilly. "You are a genius."

"Thank you for finally noticing," he says, eyes twinkling.

"Now where could I find someone to ask me to lunch?" I smirk.

Suddenly the expression is back. "Probably several places," he says seriously.

I bite back the sigh. Just when things started to feel normal . . .

"However, I do know of someone who would like very much to take you," he says. His tone sounds forced.

"Good," I say weakly.

"I'll pick you up at noon."

"Okay." I climb in the Tahoe, smile, and shut the door. I wait until I am driving down the street to let out the aggravated huff.

What is *wrong* with everyone these days?

I pull my Bible over onto my lap. It's nearly midnight, my room is lit only by my lamp, and Darcy is snuggled on the foot of the bed, snoring softly.

I rub my finger on the pages, smiling slightly at the highlighting. I tend to highlight based on the study. First, there's blue pen all over the references to sovereignty. Then I used a green pen last year when I studied Psalms. I'm starting a new study in James tonight. The only color left in the three-pack I bought is a boring yellow.

I open the Bible to James and then pause. And sigh.

Darcy cocks his eyes open at me.

"It's just getting annoying, that's all," I tell him. "I mean, people just can't seem to get that I don't know . . . I'm not sure what I feel about Ryan."

Darcy licks his chops and then closes his eyes again. Understanding dog, my foot.

"Darce. Darcy."

He moans.

"It's not that I don't like him. I just don't know if I love him. Especially in, you know, like, the forever-I-do way. Darcy, are you listening?"

He calmly ignores me, his snoring returning. I look down at the Bible. "If any of you lacks wisdom, he should ask God, who gives generously to all without finding fault, and it will be given to him."

Okay then, Lord. Apparently You are listening even when man's best friend is not. What do You think about Ryan?

There's no audible answer, but I haven't ever had that happen before. I'm not sure I'd ever want that to happen anyway. I think I'd wet my pants, and changing the sheets this late at night would be a pain.

Chapter Three

Late Thursday morning I walk out of Studio Three, ushering a family of five out the door. Hannah waves me over, pointing to a young brunette studying the life-sized portrait of Tina and her husband, Kyle.

"Claire Raleigh," Hannah whispers. "She's got an eleven o'clock interview with Brandon."

"What's she like?"

Hannah smiles.

I look over at her again. Brunette. Slender. Pretty. Available?

I straighten as Claire Raleigh turns. "Hi," I say, smiling politely. "I'm Laurie. I'm a photographer here."

She steps forward and clasps my hand in a firm shake. "Hi. Claire Raleigh."

I notice the sparkly diamond on her left hand and feel all hopes fall. "Good to meet you," I say as Brandon opens his office door.

"Come on in, Claire." She follows him in. He leaves the door open.

Hannah tips her head at me. "What do you think?" she asks in a low voice.

"She's engaged." I sigh, falling into a chair in front of her desk.

"So?"

"So? Hannah, I'm going stir-crazy! Everyone is engaged! Isn't there someone unattached that I can attach?"

She grins. "What about Ryan?"

"Don't start," I say, covering my face.

"You know he likes you, Laurie."

"You don't match someone up with yourself. It's against the rules."

"I wasn't aware that there were rules."

"Well, there are."

She waits until I look back up at her. She smiles, reaches over, and pats my hand. "I'm sure someone unattached will come along."

The front door opens and Florence walks in, pushing her wide sunglasses up into her tower of hair. She squeaks something that could have been hello and marches into Studio Two.

Hannah watches her and then turns to me, brows raised. "See? Someone unattached just came your way," she says in a low voice.

"Right, right. Match Mrs. Bennet." I let my breath out. "Hannah, there is only one Mr. Bennet, and I'm afraid he just existed in print."

She grins.

Claire and Brandon come out of his office. Both smiling.

"I'll assume the interview went well," Hannah says. She hands her husband an employment application and tax forms before he even asks.

He sends her a special smile and then turns to Claire. "It will be good having you working here, Claire."

"Thanks. I'm looking forward to it." She smiles. He goes back to his office.

She has a nice smile, cute dimples. She pushes her straight, short, brown hair behind her ear with her left hand, and that annoying engagement ring flashes again.

"Laurie, right?"

"Yeah, that's it."

"And Hannah?"

Hannah nods toward the chair. "Good to have you on board, Claire."

"You're Brandon's wife, right?"

"Right."

She looks at me. "And you're Brandon's . . . he said something about a sister."

I grin. "Shirttail in-laws."

"Got it."

Hannah shrugs. "It's all in the family."

"That's good, though. Nice."

"What about you, Claire? You lived here long?" Hannah asks, shuffling some papers around on her desk.

Claire pauses filling out the tax form. "About four years. I came here originally to work as a psychologist."

I blink at Hannah. "A shrink?" I clarify.

"That's the slang for it, I hear." Claire grins. "That's where I met my fiancé, actually."

"Is he a psychologist too?" I ask, trying to hide my horror. I hope these two aren't planning on procreating. Two shrinks for parents! The kid will be a freak show.

"No, no. He was a patient of mine."

"What was his ailment?" Hannah asks, frowning.

Claire grins at her nosiness. "Mass murder. Don't worry, I think I cured him. I don't think he *really* wanted to hurt those people. He was just dealing with a lot of anger."

My chin hits my left foot. Hannah's eyes are bigger than E.T.'s.

"Relax." Claire chuckles. "I'm kidding. No, he actually came in to talk about—and this is bad—he came to talk about whether or not he should marry his girlfriend." She bites her lip, grinning.

"Oh, Claire," I say accusingly.

"Isn't it terrible? It's awful!" She rubs her head. "I really don't know how it happened. Anyway, the office where I worked had a significant loss in clientele and let me go. I've always liked photography, actually minored in it, so when I saw the ad, I thought this sounded good."

She smiles, and Hannah returns it.

I, meanwhile, am thinking. "What was the name of your fiancé's old girlfriend?" She is probably still single.

"What? Oh, um . . . Isabel. Why?"

Hannah must've read my expression because she groans. "Laurie, stop it!" She looks at Claire. "Claire, it's a good thing you're engaged, because Laurie is an insane, out-of-control matchmaker, and she can't stop for the life of her."

Claire crosses her legs, balances her clipboard on her knee, and looks at me, head tipped, mouth relaxed, eyebrows slightly bunched. "Really, Laurie? And when did you start feeling this way?"

Here's what's going on: I am getting *psychoanalyzed*!

Dad has threatened me with this for years.

"Da-um, feeling what way?" I stutter, straining back from that see-all expression she has on.

"Stressed. Rushed. Incomplete. Bored, perhaps? Tell me, Laurie, has there been any change in your diet recently?" she asks, her voice a soft cadence, her eyes in an "It's okay, I'm your friend" look that all those aliens have before they blast the innocent dog-walker with their laser guns in the movies.

I am beginning to whimper.

"Well, um, you see, I don't diet," I whine, trying to scoot my chair back without being obvious.

Scoot my chair back? What am I thinking? I should be running for the treetops hollering like Chicken Little!

Claire's eyes narrow just a fraction of an inch and she nods doctor-like. "I see. Is someone in your life making you feel pressured?"

Hannah starts hacking.

Claire rolls her wrist as she talks to me like any sanity I had leaked out into my lunchbox when I was in third grade. "What I mean is, are there people in your life telling you to do things or expecting you to do things that you don't want to do?"

I blink at her. "Yes, there is," I say in a low voice, staring at my hands.

"Go on, Laurie. You are in a friendly environment."

I exhale. "There's a lot."

"I have time," she says softly. "Go on."

I keep looking at my hands. "The people at the zoo won't let me feed the koalas grape juice. The electrician didn't let me electrocute the cricket I found while he was at my house." I look up at Claire, my eyes big and sad, hers very confused. "Whitney Houston will never play me in a movie about my life."

Hannah covers her face.

Claire looks at me, half of her mouth tipped up. "You are

ducking the question, and I'll let you get away with it for now."

"Thanks, Claire, I appreciate the assessment, but I'm fine, really. Hannah has a tendency to exaggerate." I glare at her. "Make that a habit."

"Really, Hannah? Why do you think you do that?"

Ha!

I grin at Hannah's tortured look and slap my hands on her desk. "Well, ladies, if you'll excuse me, I have a lunch date. Nice to meet you, Claire. Good-bye, Hannah," I sing.

Claire sends me a smile. Hannah shoots cattle prods.

Ryan opens the front door as I sling my backpack over my shoulder.

"Ready for lunch, Darling?" I ask, batting my eyelashes.

He pauses. "Rethinking it, actually."

"Very funny."

He grins, leans over, kisses my cheek, and waves to Hannah. "Hey, Hannah."

"Ryan! Come meet our new photographer!"

He frowns at her but smiles politely at Claire. "Hi there."

"Hi," Claire says nicely.

"Claire was once a psychologist," I tell him.

Why can't people have expressions like that in front of a camera?

He blinks repeatedly, lips together, before finally smiling. "Interesting." He grabs my hand. "We're actually running late for lunch. Reservations, you see."

"But don't you want to — " Hannah starts as Ryan waves, pushes me out the door, and sprints for his truck.

I climb through the passenger's door he holds open.

He slams his door a second later.

"Well?" he asks, looking at me.

"Well what?"

"Aren't you going to thank me?"

"For lunch?"

"No, for getting you out of that office before she had a chance to analyze something. She looked ready for it."

I grin. "She had already finished with me."

He winces. "And?"

"And now I feel much more secure . . . relaxed . . . refreshed. . . ."

"Shut up, Laurie."

I laugh. "I told her I wanted to feed koalas grape juice."

He sighs and then grins. "The two of you working together could be quite the experience."

"Yes, well, such is life." I give him a sideways glance. "Do you really have lunch reservations?"

"Yep."

"Oh. Where?"

"Vizzini's."

I nod. "Good idea." Last time we went there for an impromptu lunch, we had to wait forty minutes for a table.

When all you've got is an hour lunch break . . .

He parks, opens my door, and pushes me through the lunch crowd. "Two for Ryan?" he asks the hostess, a pretty, blue-eyed girl twirling a long lock of brown hair around and around her finger.

She looks up at Ryan, glances obviously at his bare left hand, and smiles cattily. "Yes, of course. Right this way." She leads us to a table in the far back corner, slaps my menu on the table, and slowly gives Ryan his.

I raise my eyebrows at Ryan as she leaves. "Seems like you found an admirer."

"In a town this size, I think any single guy is met with . . ." He shakes his head, not finding the word.

"Pandemonium?"

"I was thinking more along the lines of competition." He grins.

"Same thing."

"Not into sports, hmm?"

"I have never understood the concept of sacrificing the ability to see your grandchildren for a piece of sewn leather."

He smirks. "You played soccer as a kid, didn't you?"

I scowl. "First and second grade. Mom made me. She was really athletic. Laney and Lexi, they're really girly. So when Mom saw I wasn't into the whole pink thing, I think she got grand ideas that didn't pay off." I balance my chin on my hand. "She died before the next season. Dad didn't make me go back."

"Speaking of your father . . ."

I shake my head.

"Not a word?" Ryan asks, aghast.

"I know! I even went online and checked to make sure their flight was in because I was so freaked out."

"Wow," he says slowly. "I guess the anti-germ conference is more enthralling than we gave it credit for."

"Yeah, well, then I started thinking about how many people I know who call their grown children while they are on their honeymoon."

"You're calling yourself grown?"

"And organic."

He snorts. "With what you eat? You're not even biodegradable. In two hundred years, someone will accidentally stumble onto your grave and you won't even have started decomposing."

I frown in thought. "Think I should look into cremation?"

He starts laughing.

I grin and sigh. "I'm thinking I should look into it sooner rather than later. After Dad and Joan get back, I'm never going to be let outside our bacterially safe home again. When will I get chocolate? When will I buy coffee? Who will comfort me in my distress? Not Dad or Joan, they'll be sanitizing."

"What about me?"

"Are you kidding? You work at a construction site!"

He raises an eyebrow. "So?"

"So it's the definition of dirt. I've seen you when you're fresh from work. You reek of bacteria."

"Well, thank you very much." He grins.

"I guess we should consider this our farewell lunch," I say, doleful.

"Guess so," Ryan says, matching my tone. "It's been a nice couple of years, Laur. I will miss you."

I cover a grin, feeling relief. He hasn't displayed any of those weird expressions like last night so far today. It's not that I dislike him being envious of other guys—everyone likes to feel wanted—but it's the fact that he feels possessive.

Whatever Hannah says, I'm convinced we're mostly friends.

If anything, this lunch proves at least that much.

Right?

Don't get me wrong—there have been times when I've felt a little squirmy around him. And I *like* Ryan more than anyone. I wouldn't be basically dating him if I didn't.

I just don't love him.

I look over the edge of my hand at him. He has that cute

smile on his face, and his brown eyes are twinkling conspiratorially at me.

I don't *think* I love him.

Wisdom. Wisdom. Wisdom. This is me asking for it. Ryan breaks eye contact and sips from his straw.

It's best if everyone just starts acting normally again.

Chapter Four

I stand in a line at Smith Valley Barbecue that stretches all the way out the door and partially around the building. The Sunday afternoon crowd is there in full.

I should've gone home to change out of my church clothes first. I hate skirts.

Dad and Joan should be on their way to the house at this precise moment, and if this line doesn't hurry, I won't be there to greet them.

The woman in front of me gets called up to the next open register, and I watch carefully.

"Next!" a young kid with a scratchy voice yells.

I run over. "Call-in order for Laurie."

"Name?"

I blink at him. "Laurie," I enunciate.

He squints as he flips through the order slips. "That's L-A-R-?"

"L-A-U-R-I-E."

"Oh, *Laurie*. I thought you said Larry." He yanks out a yellow slip of paper. "All right. Four pounds of shredded beef and two pounds of sliced turkey?"

"And a pound of barbecue beans and another of creamed corn."

He clears his throat and squints at me. "Um . . . okay."

I know what he is thinking.

Vanity, vanity.

"It's not all for me," I burst.

"Mm-hmm."

"It's not! We're having a family lunch, and I drew the short straw."

He looks up and grins. "I know, I know. I heard that excuse earlier today. That'll be twenty-eight sixty. Uh, not including the tip."

I count out exactly twenty-eight dollars and sixty cents and slap it on the counter. "Here's a tip," I say, hefting the big paper sack off the counter. "I wouldn't insult your customers anymore."

He grins again, and I roll my eyes.

"You like this job, don't you?"

"Yes, I do."

I shake my head. I leave, and the graying man behind me immediately starts ordering.

I drive home—the tantalizing smell of barbecue hanging heavy in the car—and end up parking on the street because Lexi and Laney have both parked in the driveway, blocking my way to the garage.

Brandon's car is there, as is Ryan's. And Dad's baby SUV is driving up the other side of the street.

I grin, laugh, jump out of the car, and wait by the driver's side for Dad to stop.

He climbs out and grabs me in a hug. "Laurie-girl, I've missed you!"

"Hi, Dad!" I pull back a few inches and look at him. He looks good, very healthy.

Uh-oh.

He grins. "How have you been, Honey?"

"Busy. Brandon finally hired someone to tame my job back to part-time, but she's a shrink."

Joan climbs out the passenger's side and comes over.

"Hi, Sweetheart."

I give Joan her own hug. I have known this woman only a year, but I feel like I've known her a lot longer.

"Hi, Joan."

She looks around at the used-car-lot mess of vehicles, and grins. "Looks like we've got a full house."

Dad pulls a pocket-sized hand sanitizer from his khakis, squirts a big blob in my palm, and, still smiling, rubs it in for me.

My hands say, "NOOOO!"

This Is Bad.

He hasn't even been back for three minutes, and he's already cleaning.

"Uh, let's get the barbecue in," I say, squirming away, the fresh air around me tainted by the lingering stench of anti-bacterial gloop.

Here's what I like to do: Make up words.

Gloop: (*n*) Yucky, slimy, gel-like substance.

"Barbecue, barbecue, barbecue," Dad mutters, looking off into the distance. His eyes are all squinty and Clint-Eastwood-cowboy-ish. He turns to Joan. "Honey? Was barbecue on The List?"

"The List?" I parrot. "What's The List?" I'm envisioning a list similar to the one the Nazis used.

What's that, a Milky Way? Ooo. That is on The List. *ELIMINATED!*

Joan digs into her massive purse and pulls out her glasses and a blue booklet that is titled, "Health Helps: How to Keep You and Your Family Healthy, Safe, and Germ-Free."

She thumbs through it, and I don't miss the fact that it looks well-used.

My life as I know it is over.

Worries about love aside, I wonder if Ryan could be talked into elopement? Or if Ruby and Nick would be willing to adopt me?

"Ah, here we go," Joan says, running her index finger along a passage. "'Barbecue sauce contains additives, preservatives, and quite frequently, large amounts of salt.'" She looks up at us over her bifocals. "It's on the Avoid-If-Possible List."

"But not the Avoid-At-All-Costs List?" Dad asks.

"Not that I can see."

"Hmm."

I stand there holding the gargantuan sack of barbecue tightly. Barbecue is lunch, and since it has just been me and my dog all last week, and since I'm perfectly happy with takeout, and Darcy is A-OK with dog food, I did not go grocery shopping.

Barbecue is more than lunch; it is all the food in the house at the moment.

I start up the walk, Dad and Joan behind me, discussing whether or not they should risk the additives, preservatives, and high blood pressure.

I open the front door.

Allie and Mikey are lying flat on their backs on the entryway floor, Lexi kneeling over them, blowing a huge gum bubble right at their faces. The bubble explodes, and Allie and Mikey roll over laughing.

I grin.

Dad and Joan look horrified.

"Dad!" Lexi grins, peeling gum off her face, standing.

"Lexi, what on earth—" Dad starts.

"Welcome home!" Lexi yells.

My sister is the Queen of Shirking Punishment. I used to watch her with awe growing up. Where I would be so ridden with guilt I had to confess my crime, Lexi would simply change the subject and wait for Dad to forget.

"Lexi, do you have any idea what kind of bacteria is in that gum?" Dad says, aghast.

"It's Doublemint, Dad. Twice the freshness!"

Yeah, it's time for me to leave. I step over the twins and go into the kitchen, where Laney and Hannah are talking.

"Hey, guys."

Laney looks up, pushing her long, brown-blonde hair behind her ear. "Did I hear Dad, Laurie? Are they home?"

"They're home." I set the huge brown bag on the counter. "I wouldn't go in there just yet. They caught Lexi blowing gum at your kids and spazzed about germs."

Spazzed: (*v*) Freaked out.

Hannah grins and helps me unload the barbecue. "Your life could become . . . interesting," she whispers.

I sigh woefully.

Brandon wanders in, looking back over his shoulder at the entry. "Hey, has Lexi *ever* gotten razzed for something before?" he asks me and Laney as he stands behind Hannah and wraps his arms around her waist.

Laney and I frown at each other.

"She didn't lock her car doors when she was a . . . junior?" Laney asks me.

I nod. "Around there."

"Dad got on her for that. Otherwise . . ."

Ryan comes in the kitchen, Jack perched on his shoulders and Jess around his right leg.

He grins at me and winces as Jack yanks his hair. "Ouch. Watch the pulling, Bud," he tells him.

Jack giggles. "Your hair is weird."

"Thanks," Ryan says wryly. He shoots me a glance that says, *Help!*

I tug Jess off of Ryan's leg and heft him up on my hip. "You haven't given me a hug yet, mister."

Jess grins, one front tooth missing, and wraps his arms around my neck.

"Guess what, Auntie Lauren," Jess says.

"You're buying me a Mustang? Aw, Jess, you're too sweet."

He wrinkles his little nose at me. "What's a Mustang?"

"My future car, Kiddo."

"That's not what you're supposed to guess."

"What?"

"Uncle Ryan's taking us to a baseball game!" he shouts.

We all look at Ryan, who shrugs. "The high school is in the championship. I thought the boys would enjoy it."

Laney smiles sweetly. "That's so nice, Ryan!" She looks at me, eyebrows raised.

Brandon grins. "If you want company—"

"Yes," Ryan interrupts, stopping abruptly as Jack again catches his hair.

I set Jess down and lay out plastic forks and knives. "Well, lunch is ready."

"Looks good, Laur," Brandon says.

"Thank you. I slaved over it."

Lexi comes in looking chagrined, carrying Allie, followed by her husband, Nate, carrying Mikey. Dad and Joan are right behind them. Laney's husband, Adam, and her oldest daughter, Dorie, bring up the rear.

Those who haven't already said hi to Dad and Joan welcome them back, Dad prays, and Laney starts going through the buffet-style line, making a plate for each of her kids.

"Adam? Where's Mikey and Allie's food?"

"In the fridge."

"I'll get it," I say. I pull out the two jars of baby food and read the label, mashing my lips together.

"What is it?" Ryan asks from behind me, free of Jack.

"Chicken pot pie." I pop the lid, inhale, and gag. "Oh, Laney, how can you feed them this stuff?"

"Easy. They love it, Laurie."

I take one of the rubber-shrouded baby spoons from the counter and swirl it around in the beige-colored substance, and this time Ryan and I both gag.

"It's gloppy." I grimace.

"That is disgusting," Ryan says.

Laney gives us a look and plops barbecue on the three older kids' plates. "Cut it out, you two. It happens to be very healthy food for the babies."

Dad's forehead creasings lift. "Wonderful, Laney. I'm glad you're starting them early."

"Why, thank you, Dad," Laney says proudly.

I look at Ryan and roll my eyes. What Dad doesn't know is that just the younger twins eat healthily. The older kids usually eat whatever they want. I've been over there when Jess and Jack have had Lucky Charms for all three meals.

Ryan grins.

We finish lunch in our usual loud, unorganized fashion, and then Laney's kids all take off for the guest room we keep filled to the brim with toys.

Dad and Joan settle on the love seat, Brandon, Hannah, and Adam take one couch, and Laney, Lexi, and Nate take the other.

Ryan and I, as the only singles, get the floor.

Like usual.

"So my cousin Dave is visiting next week," Nate says loudly, stretching one arm around Lexi. Nate and Lexi cannot say anything quietly.

I bite back a grin at Lexi's grimace.

"What's wrong with Dave?" Ryan asks innocently.

"Oh, let's just say he's unique," Lexi says.

Adam chortles, and Laney starts laughing and pokes Lexi in the ribs. "Remember at your wedding?" she screeches.

Even Dad grins. "He likes to make a statement," he tells Joan, who shares Ryan's and Hannah's confused expression.

Brandon smirks. "He cooked the rice before he threw it," he tells Hannah.

"Oh, that's terrible!" Hannah gasps.

Lexi nods wearily. "Yes, it was."

Laney cocks her head. "Wasn't he also the one who disconnected the battery in your car?"

Lexi nods again. "Yes, he was."

Adam laughs so hard he has to wipe away tears. "Oh, you should have seen it," he tells Ryan, who is grinning. "Lex and Nate just sat there, trying to get the car to start for like fifteen minutes—"

"In my dress with gross, clumpy rice sticking to the back of my neck—"

"And so Brandon finally pops the hood and we realize what happened—" Adam laughs.

"And he had not only disconnected the battery, he'd taken the radiator cap," Lexi says, disgusted.

Nate offers, "Dave's a bit of a car junkie. Likes to take them apart and put them back together."

Lexi shakes her head. "He could have picked a different car!"

"They ended up using our car," Adam says, still rolling.

Laney grins across the room at him. "Yeah, our '96 forest green minivan."

Joan laughs. "What memories!"

"Not pleasant ones. I'm scared to death to think what he will do to our house." Lexi groans.

"How old is he?" Brandon asks.

Nate looks at Lexi, who shrugs. "I don't know," Nate says. "Thirty. Thirty-one. Somewhere in that neighborhood."

"Hey, is he still single?" I ask.

"Laurie, for the love of Mike!" Hannah yells.

Little Mikey toddles in, baby-talking. Joan swipes him up and kisses the top of his head. "Not you, baby boy," she coos.

"We could set him up with Florence!" I shout.

Hannah covers her eyes. Lexi brightens immediately. "That

lady you work with? That would be perfect!"

"Have you met that woman?" Nate asks. "She's worse than scary!"

"That's why I think it's perfect!"

"You are not a nice person, Lexi," Ryan tells her.

Lexi sticks her tongue out at him.

Here's the thing about Ryan, Lexi, and Nate: Nate and Ryan hit it off from the beginning, and so Ryan spends a lot of his free time hanging around their house. Because of that, my sister is more comfortable with him than she is with most people. Ryan's been there when she's been in her pajamas, when she had the flu, when she's covered in paint. . . .

Ryan even has one of the spare keys to their house.

Joan smoothes Mikey's hair. "Well, I think it would be divine. Men don't usually grow up until they marry." She kisses Dad's cheek. "Save you, Darling."

I rub my hands together, so excited I can't sit still. "Ah, my toughest assignment yet."

Ryan looks at me and raises one eyebrow. "You need a life."

"I have a very nice life, thank you."

"Stop doing that with your hands, Baby. You look like Scrooge," Lexi says, frowning at me.

I grin at Lexi. "Want to help?"

"No. I don't want to be near that man any more than I have to."

"Hey, Hannah?"

"No, Laurie. I do not want to help," Hannah says, tucking her feet up underneath her and leaning against Brandon.

"Bran—"

"Nope," he interrupts cheerfully. "Sorry, Nutsy. I draw the line at setting up employees."

I sigh and look at Ryan. "Please?"

He looks at me for a long minute and then grins. "Sure, why not?"

"Yay!"

"But you have to recognize that even though I'm helping, I am not condoning this behavior," he lectures, pointing his finger in my face.

"Yeah, sure, whatever." I grin, wrapping my arms around his neck in a quick hug.

I pull away and Ryan looks at my sisters.

"I'm going to regret this, aren't I?" he asks, flinching.

"Yep," Laney says.

"Most definitely," Lexi agrees.

Ryan moans and covers his face.

———— ⚜ ————

"There's a loophole!" I yell later that night.

Dad pokes his head in my bedroom door. "Did you say something, Honey?"

I jab at the Bible. "It says ask for wisdom. So I do. But then I keep reading, and it says 'without doubting.' Loophole! Loophole, ladies and gentlemen."

Dad grins and comes all the way into the room. He's wearing his scrub-resembling pajamas and carrying a folded-up magazine and a mug of hot lemongrass tea.

Blegh. There is one smell I didn't miss having around for a few days.

He settles on the foot of my bed, nudging Darcy over a few

inches. "What are you reading?"

"James."

"And you're wanting wisdom?" he asks, sipping his tea. "About what, Sweetie?"

I open my mouth to spill it and then pause.

Here's the thing: I love my dad. I really do. But my dad tends to, um . . . freak out over things that don't need to be freaked out over. Like this tiny question of loving Ryan or not. Why worry Dad, right?

"Uh," I say instead.

Dad gives me another Clint Eastwood squint.

"Did you watch westerns or something on your honeymoon?"

He brightens. "Why, yes. Actually, we watched *High Noon*. How did you know?"

"Just a theory."

"Mm. Well, sleep tight, Laurie-girl." He pats my leg and stands, careful to keep his tea from sloshing out of the cup.

"I'm glad you're back, Dad." I smile at him.

"Love you, Laurie-girl. Sweet dreams."

Chapter Five

Monday morning my alarm goes off and I interrupt a yawn to inhale.

Bacon?

I frown, mash the button on my alarm clock, brush my teeth, and cautiously go partway downstairs. Joan stands in her robe in front of the range, pushing what appears to be strips of bacon around in a skillet.

I sit down on the fifth step from the bottom and pinch the back of my arm.

Bacon? Bacon is *healthy*?

Dad looks up from the breakfast table, sees me, and smiles over his lemongrass tea.

Blegh.

"Morning, Honey," he says, sipping the rind-infested sludge. "We made you coffee."

"Bacon?" I ask, incredulous.

He smiles. "Why not? It's our first morning in our home with our daughter."

Joan turns then from the skillet and smiles sweetly. "Good

morning, Darling. Did you sleep well?"

"Mm. You're making bacon?" I ask again.

"And eggs." She chuckles at my look. "You eat cereal every morning, Laurie. Let someone spoil you for once."

I trip down the remaining steps and fall into one of the kitchen chairs, eyebrows raised.

Well, well. Perhaps the health awareness seminar didn't have as much of a negative effect on them as I had originally thought.

I smile as Joan sets a big mug of coffee in front of me, ruffling the back of my hair. "There you are, Dear." She pauses, running her fingers through my hair. "You know, Honey, I used to cut Ruthie's hair when she lived with me. Would you like me to trim yours?"

"That would be great, Joan." I grin, picking up the tan-colored, steaming drink.

She goes back to the skillet.

Dad looks back at his newspaper.

I sip the coffee.

And just about spit it out.

ACK! ACK! ACK!

I choke it down, my stomach revolting, my esophagus trying to push the liquid into my lungs so my stomach doesn't have to hold it.

I gasp and the mug almost falls from my hands.

What on earth?

Someone has tampered with my coffee!

They didn't! They couldn't!

I clear my throat, hacking, and look at Dad, my eyes stinging, tears falling down my cheeks. "What . . . um, is this?"

He looks up calmly from his newspaper. "It's a coffee substitute, Laurie-girl." He sips his tea.

Coffee substitute.

The words ping my brain and I shake my head, afraid I've misunderstood.

"I'm sorry?" I say.

"It's good, isn't it?" Joan croons, setting a plate of bacon and eggs in front of me. "We heard about it at the conference. No preservatives, no additives, and the best part is, it's free from the chemicals used to make decaf while still being naturally caffeine-free."

I sit there, mouth open, staring at my beautiful Minnie Mouse mug that is holding this monstrosity.

"It's called Soyee. It's made completely with soybeans." She pats my shoulder, smiling. "Isn't it amazing how much it tastes like real coffee?"

I cough.

"And that's wood sugar in the coffee," Dad says. "It looks identical to regular sugar, but this stuff is amazing. It fights cavities and gum disease, and it's a natural antibiotic, meaning that it counteracts bacteria and viruses."

I have to shove my fist in between my teeth to keep from screaming.

"Eat up, Honey. You need to be at work at nine, right?" Dad says.

I take my hand out of my mouth and inhale harshly, grabbing my fork.

I scoop up a spoonful of the scrambled eggs and freeze right before I put it in my mouth.

Dad and Joan are both staring at me, smiling encouragingly.

"What are these?" I whisper.

"It's a wonderful new egg substitute made entirely from 100 percent olive oil," Joan says.

"And that is turkey bacon." Dad points.

"Ninety-seven percent fat free!" Joan smiles.

I can hear myself breathing. I set the fork down, my hands shaking. I try pinching my leg, but I don't wake up.

"I . . ." I breathe. "I have to go . . . get dressed."

I bolt from the table, run up the stairs, into my room, into my bathroom, and stick my head under the faucet in the tub.

Breathe in. Breathe out. Good girl.

Thirty minutes later I open the door to Merson's and stumble over to the counter, blinking.

Shawn Merson stares at me, slowly wiping his hands on a towel. "Laurie?"

I breathe. In and out. In and out.

"Laurie, I've never seen you stand that straight," Shawn says.

I blink at him.

He leans across the counter, staring at me. "Laurie? Your pupils . . . they're going in and out," he says slowly. "They're getting bigger and smaller." His eyes get big and he drops the towel, running around the counter. "Laurie! Sit!" he shouts, pushing me into a chair.

Hallie Forbes runs in from the back room. "Laurie? What's wrong?"

"I need coffee," I mutter.

"Toss me that rag," Shawn says to Hallie, keeping one hand on my shoulder.

I lean forward until my forehead hits the counter. "I just

need coffee," I moan.

Shawn pushes my hair to one side and presses the rag to the back of my neck. Hallie pours a big cup of coffee and slides it right in front of me. "Here. Drink," she commands.

I lift my head a few inches and slurp.

The rich, bold taste of freshly roasted coffee beans wash any remnants of that other stuff away. I moan and keep drinking.

Shawn stops wiping me with the rag and watches, shaking his head. "Addict," he pronounces. "Addict in the worst sense of the word."

I drain the cup, set it down, and pass it to Hallie, who refills it. "They gave me soybean coffee!" I wail, holding my head.

"They gave you what? And who is they?" Hallie asks, handing me the mug.

"Dad and Joan."

Shawn and Hallie share a smirk. "They learned about it on their honeymoon?"

"It's *healthy*." I close my eyes and drain the second mug. I lick my lips and set the empty mug down. "With *wood* sugar in it! And olive oil eggs! And turkey bacon!"

Hallie holds up her hand. "Okay, I've tried turkey bacon, and I have to say, it's better than buffalo burgers."

Shawn and I both stare at her, noses wrinkled.

"My aunt is kind of a health nut."

I groan. "They came home with The List."

"The List?" Shawn echoes.

"It's a book with what they can and cannot eat." I cradle my head in my hands. "My life . . . my beautiful life . . . is over."

Shawn pats my back and goes back around the counter. "No offense, Laur, but I think you might be exaggerating."

"No, I'm not! I looked! They replaced *all* the food in the pantry!"

Hallie grimaces. "Ick."

"Sorry, Laur," Shawn says. He pours coffee into an extra-large to-go cup, adds sugar and milk, and pops the plastic lid on. "Here. On the house. Sorry," he says again.

I slide off the barstool and smile weakly at them. "Thanks, guys."

❖

Fifteen minutes later I push open the door to the studio. Hannah looks up from her desk, cradling her own cup from Merson's.

"Hey, Laur." She squints. "You look pale."

"Well, soybeans are white, right?" I set a bulging white grocery bag on the floor beside me.

She frowns. "What's in the bag?"

I untie the top and dump the contents on her desk.

"Laurie, for heaven's sake!" Hannah mutters, shaking her head.

Milky Ways, Butterfingers, Snickers, and Three Musketeers bars litter the desk. For good measure, I'd also tossed in a couple of bags of Hershey's Kisses.

The door opens behind me, and Keller Stone walks in, pulling a pair of sunglasses off his perfect face.

Confession: I always feel a little homely standing next to someone that gorgeous.

He smiles at me. "Laurie, good. I'm glad I caught you without clients."

I look at Hannah, who has one hand over her mouth, her

eyes wide.

"Hi, Keller," I say, sipping the coffee.

He angles his head at me. "Are you okay? You look . . . jittered."

I manage a bleak smile. "It will pass. I just have to find a new home is all."

His forehead creases in a frown, but he doesn't comment.

"What are you doing here?" I ask, leaning up against Hannah's desk.

"Well, I just wanted to talk to you . . . privately," he says slowly, fiddling with his shades.

"Okay. Go on," I say.

He looks pointedly at Hannah, who jumps and then goes down the hall to her husband's office, apologizing.

Keller waits until the door closes behind her and then looks back at me, smiling again.

"Tell me about Ryan," he says suddenly.

"Ryan," I parrot. "Why?"

"I'm just curious about him . . . uh, dating."

"Why?" I say again. "Are you interested?"

"In what?"

"Dating him."

Keller chokes. I grin.

He points his finger at me. "Very funny."

"Thanks."

"No, it's just, you two seem pretty close."

He is looking for an explanation, but I'm not going to give it to him. "Mm," I say, sipping my coffee.

"Are you . . . that is to say, are you two . . . dating?"

I open my mouth to answer when Hannah comes out of

Brandon's office, yelling back into the office. "Yes! Yes! Yes!" she screams and marches down the hall.

I bite back a grin.

"Um, Hannah?" Keller asks.

"Yes?" she says, looking up.

"Is something wrong?"

"Yes. Yes, yes, yes." She sends me a look that could solder a C-drive, grabs a yellow sticky pad from her desk, and stalks back into Brandon's office.

I catch Keller's confusion and sigh silently. For all his perfection, Keller doesn't have the quickest wit. Ryan would have caught Hannah's answer to Keller's question in a microsecond.

"Yeah, Keller, Ryan and I are dating," I say, loud enough for Hannah to hear through Brandon's door.

Keller looks down at his sunglasses, nodding. "Okay. Well, I just thought I'd check." He looks back up at me and smiles Mr. Darcy-like. "He's a lucky guy."

I grin, touched. "That's really sweet, Keller."

"Let me know if it doesn't work out." He slides his shades back on and slips out the door.

I sip my coffee and then yell, "You can come out now!"

Hannah opens Brandon's door. I hear Brandon laughing.

Hannah, all smiles now, fairly skips down the hall and settles lightly in her chair.

"You are pitiful," I tell her.

"I'm pitiful? You're the one who can't admit you love him!"

"Keller?"

She sighs loudly and rolls her eyes. "Ryan, you dolt!"

I sit down in one of the chairs in front of her and lean forward. "Listen, Hannah," I say, lowering my voice. "I like him." I pause, thinking. "I like him a lot."

She nods, grinning. "We know."

"But, I don't . . . think . . . I love him," I say slowly.

She narrows her gaze at me, shaking her head. "You know what your problem is, Lauren Holbrook?"

"There's only one? Swell!"

She ignores my comment. "In doing all this matchmaking, you've come up with something that you *think* is love." She leans closer, touching my hand. "But it's not."

I frown.

"You think love is something fuzzy and tingly that makes you stand crookedly when he walks in the door." She shakes her head. "That's not love, Laur."

I hold my cup like I'm going to take a drink, sneaking in a deep breath before sipping. My heart is starting to pound harder.

I am Lauren Holbrook, right? The local matchmaker? The love expert? People come to me with questions and I give them answers.

Have I been giving people the wrong answers?

Hannah smiles at me sympathetically before shoving candy bars out of the way, digging around in her desk drawer, and coming out with a small New Testament. "John is probably my favorite writer in the Bible," she says, flipping to the back of the book. "He writes a lot about love. In 1 John chapter 4, verse . . ." She skims the page and stops, underlining the verse with her finger. "Verse 7. It says, 'Dear friends, let us love one another, for love comes from God.'"

She looks up at me, her forehead creased in thought. "See, Laur? Love is . . . love is so much more than *feelings*."

"Doesn't John say to love with actions?" I ask, tentatively.

"Yeah. It's a *command* to love each other, Laurie." She squints at me. "Do you get it?"

I look down at my cup, turning it around and around in my hands. I bite my lip. "So you think . . ." I say heavily. "You think me and Ryan . . ."

She smiles, her eyes sparkling. "All I'm trying to do, Laurie, is get you to think a little differently."

Ryan.

I sigh and lob my empty coffee cup into Hannah's trash can.

She smiles at me again. "And now you can clean up my desk." She tosses a Milky Way at me.

I did ask for wisdom, didn't I? Maybe God is talking through Hannah.

I catch the Milky Way as the door opens and the Morrison family comes in. "Hi, Laurie." Mrs. Morrison smiles. "I think we're your ten o'clock."

I nod and stand, squeezing Hannah's shoulder and unwrapping the Milky Way. "I think you can live with the chocolate for a few minutes." I grin. Hannah eats one piece of chocolate a day for her sanity and then goes out and exercises.

"Darn it, Laurie! I'll just sit here and eat it!"

"Well, then you'll owe me money."

The Morrison kids have the same look Aladdin had on his face when staring at the treasure cave as they stare at the mountain of candy.

I grin wider. "Come on back, guys. We're in Studio Three."

Chapter Six

Hannah's little sermon rankles my nerves the entire morning, and over a hamburger at Bud's, I finally do something about it.

Ryan answers his phone on the second ring.

"Hey, Ry," I say, chewing a french fry.

"Hey, Laurie. What's up?" I can hear the grin in his voice.

"I need to get dinner out tonight." The Lord only knows what Dad and Joan will come up with for the biggest meal of the day. I am scared to go home.

"You need to?" Ryan questions.

"Make that have to. Must. There aren't words to describe how essential it is to eat out tonight."

He starts laughing. "Could your dad and Joan possibly have something to do with this?"

"Quite possibly."

"Were you looking for company?" he hedges.

I smile. "Yes, I was."

I hear relief. "Where do you want to go?"

I take a deep breath. "I was thinking Krispy Kreme, then Vizzini's, then Merson's for coffee and dessert, and we can drop by the candy aisle in the grocery store so I can restock my bedroom."

"Mm-hmm. Mm-hmm," Ryan says. "Oh! Wait a second, Laurie," he says in a low voice. "What if they frisk you when you walk through the door?"

"I did not even think of that," I moan. I brighten. "Hey! You can carry the candy into the house. They won't search you."

"Um, no, I don't think so."

"Why not? I'd do it for you."

"I'm trying to stay on good terms with your father, Laur. He'll love you regardless. Me? I have to earn my way."

I grin. "You're pretty smart."

"At least you recognize it."

"The coffee problem will be harder to solve."

"Coffee problem?"

"They got rid of all my coffee." I sigh.

"You're kidding. They've obviously never seen you without caffeine."

"I'd rather they didn't. I tend to be a little homicidal without caffeine. But don't worry. Claire and I are working through it." I grin.

"Really?" Ryan chuckles. "Whose fault is it?"

"The caffeine addiction or the homicidal tendencies?"

"Both, I guess."

"I'm going to blame my mom for the caffeine. She introduced me to coffee when I was in second grade."

"Second grade?" Ryan asks, incredulous.

"And as for the tendencies, I'm saying Dad and Laney. They both tried to break my addiction after Mom died."

"I guess we know it didn't work," he says dryly.

I fiddle with a fry, smiling.

"So dinner," he says. "I'll probably be done here around five-ish."

"How's the house building going?"

"We're doing drywall today. Loads of fun. Wish you were here."

I grin at his sarcasm.

"Say I pick you up about five thirty?" he asks.

"I pick you up about five thirty."

"What?"

"You told me to say that."

"Good-bye, Laurie," he singsongs. "Go find someone else to make a mental case."

"If you hated it so much, you wouldn't stick around. And besides, now I know a shrink. Maybe we can keep the mental case counts down with her around."

He laughs. "See ya."

I hang up, wad up the greasy paper I ate off of, shove it into the greasier paper sack, and throw them in the trash, waving to Bud as I leave.

There are days I can hear the pores of my skin cells pleading for mercy when I walk into that place.

The Brandon Knox Photography Studio is three doors down from Bud's, so I walk back, waving to the Swedish owners of Wong Hu's, a Chinese restaurant.

Don't ask.

Hannah and Brandon went to lunch, and Claire isn't taking over for me until one o'clock, so it is just me and Florence here.

Bad news bears. We don't, um . . . click, as it were.

She sits in one of the chairs in front of Hannah's desk, calmly eating a grilled chicken sandwich minus the bread and reading a magazine. I lean over her shoulder.

The heading at the top of the page says, "To Diet or Not to Diet?"

I glance down at Florence's frumpy figure shrouded in what Laura Ingalls Wilder would have called *calico*.

"Thinking about starting a diet?" I ask, going around the desk to sit in Hannah's chair.

Florence looks up, eyes narrowed. "Perhaps," she says, then goes right back to her reading.

I push aside a framed picture of Hannah's parents and pull two of the three Milky Ways from behind it. It's an odd place to hide the candy, but Brandon won't look there.

Brandon doesn't approve of candy stashed around the office. He freaks out about mice.

The trick is to spread the candy in a variety of places so if he does find a stash, at least he won't have found all of it.

I open the candy bar, reading Florence's magazine upside down.

"What's the North Shore diet?" I ask, biting into the Milky Way. "I thought that was a TV show."

She looks up, sighing, her tower of hair slightly off center.

"You focus primarily on eating proteins," she says, her voice screeching. She goes back to her magazine.

"Sounds like Atkins."

"Well, it's not. It's the North Shore diet."

"So what's the end result? You follow the diet, you end up looking like Lori Loughlin?"

Florence sighs heavily and glares at me. "It is impossible for you to be quiet for more than thirty-seven seconds, isn't it?"

I hold up a hand, licking caramel off my lip. "Actually, the longest I've gone is seventeen minutes, and that's when I had just gotten my wisdom teeth removed." I take another bite, a few bits of chocolate landing on my shirt.

Florence glowers at me. "Could you possibly eat that somewhere else?"

I swallow. "Well, I'm actually waiting for my twelve thirty client."

"Wait in the studio."

"Yeah, but then I won't be able to see them coming." I bite into the bar again, a long tail of caramel smearing on my chin. Florence watches, her hair tower quivering, her eyes shooting off sparks. I brace myself for a blow.

"You have no idea how distracting it is to watch you eat that while I'm trying to read!" Florence shrieks, banging her hand on the desk.

I jump. "Sorry, sorry," I apologize. "I'll just . . . lean against the wall, then."

"Good! Thank you!" she says, her voice squealing like bad brakes on a Chevy.

Eek.

She settles back with her magazine, finishing off her breadless sandwich.

I don't think they should even be called sandwiches if the contents aren't between two slices of bread.

So far I've been able to ignore the whole diet mania sweeping the nation simply because I'm oblivious in grocery stores and I'm too lazy to diet. I don't think I would survive for very long on a diet.

Plus, I heard that my metabolism will never be as high as it is at this point in my life, so I figure, why mess with a good thing?

But now with Dad and Joan around . . .

I'm thinking that I'll have to die of starvation before they let me eat normally again.

The Washingtons open the front door, shoving their two little boys ahead of them. "We've got an appointment with . . . uh, Lornie."

"It's *Laurie*, and that's me." I smile, tossing the empty Milky Way wrapper in the trash can.

Mr. Washington nods. "Great, great. Nice to meet you, Lornie. This is my wife, Ada, and our kids, Tom and Bobby."

I notice the corner of Florence's mouth crease in a smile as they get my name wrong the second time.

—⊕—

I leave at one, waving to Claire, who is heading into the studio I just vacated. Hannah catches my sleeve as I pass her desk.

"You want to join me and Brandon for dinner?" she asks, her voice tinged with pity for my situation regarding food.

I grin. "No, thanks. I've actually got plans."

"Plans?" she says, drawing out the word, grinning.

"Yes. It's when you schedule something for a set time in the future."

"Mm-hmm." She flutters her eyelashes. "Tell Ryan hello for me."

I stick my tongue out as I step outside.

—⊕—

Ryan rings my doorbell at exactly five thirty. I run down the stairs, kiss Dad and Joan good-bye, wish Darcy luck, and cannonball through the door.

Ryan frowns at me. "You're weird."

"And you're punctual."

"So?"

"Same thing."

He holds the passenger's door of his truck open for me and I heft myself in, noting with worry the rust holding the hood down.

"When are you going to get a new truck, Ry?"

"When this one dies."

He climbs in and I wrinkle my nose at the bungee cord keeping the glove compartment closed.

"I think it already did and got resurrected against its will."

He gapes at me. "Don't talk about her that way." He rubs his hands over the steering wheel soothingly.

"Her? Your truck has a gender?" I laugh. "Just as long as it doesn't have a—"

"Alice has always been a reliable truck," Ryan interrupts sternly.

"Name," I finish, rolling my eyes.

He turns the key and the truck sighs.

"Want me to get out and try cranking it?"

"Shut up, Laurie. Don't listen to her, Alice."

He jiggles the key again, and I swear the truck groans in her death throes.

"You could try baby talk. It works in the movies."

"Laurie, what did I say about being quiet?"

"Dis oo a gwood wittle twuck?"

"Laurie!"

He shouts, but I see his mouth curve.

"Or, another popular trick is to kick the tires," I say. I undo my seat belt.

"Do not kick my truck, Lauren Emma Holbrook." He unlatches his seat belt, sighing. "I'm going to look under the hood. Stay here. And if you blow the horn, death will be swift."

I grin.

He yanks the lever for the hood, and the truck shudders, rocking from side to side on its wheels.

"That's it. I'm getting out. This truck is giving me the willies."

"Laurie!"

I hop out and meet him in front of the truck, watching his biceps bulge, filling out the sleeves of his T-shirt, while he tries to lift the rust-encrusted sheet of metal.

"Want help?"

"No," he mutters through clenched teeth.

"Try tightening your abs."

He turns and stares at me.

"Well, at least you'll be getting a good workout then."

He closes his eyes, mumbling, then mashes his lips together and jerks. The rust snaps and the hood pops open.

"Good job, Honey!" I squeal, patting his shoulder.

"Go away from me."

"Do you want a flashlight?"

"Laurie, it's broad daylight out here. Why would I want a flashlight?"

I shrug. "The guys at the car dealership always have one." I squeeze his arm, batting my eyes up at him. "Makes them look manly."

"Leave me alone, or I swear I'll let you eat dinner here with your father and Joan."

He grins as he says it, so I'm not too worried, but I do back off just to be safe.

He leans over the engine, tweaking wires, rubbing his fingers over a big black box, and tapping assorted containers and tubes.

I know squat about cars, in case you are wondering.

A couple of minutes later, he sighs contentedly and brushes his hands off business-like.

"Did you fix it?" I ask.

"Yep. Plug wire was loose." He grins and slams the hood back down. "That's all there is to it, Laur. Just got to know what the truck wants and give it to her."

"Well, what do you know? Trucks are somewhat similar to marriage, then."

He rolls his eyes and goes back around to the driver's side, turning the key.

The truck bounces, sways, does a couple of low dips, and then rumbles to life.

"Hop in, Laur."

"Can't. I'm scared."

"Alrighty then. Stay here and eat who knows what kind of casserole for dinner."

I am in and buckling my seat belt before he finishes the sentence.

He starts laughing. "You, Laurie, are something else." He leans across the bench seat and kisses my cheek.

I smile at his profile as he shifts the truck into drive and pulls out of my driveway. I've decided something. I like it when Ryan kisses my cheek. His face is never shaven super clean, and so his whiskers always rub my face. It kind of tickles.

He looks over at me and grins as he turns the corner. "What?" he asks, reaching over and picking up my hand.

I squeeze his hand and shake my head. "Nothing." Then I push his hand away. "But you could keep both hands on the wheel."

"Why?"

"Because if Tracy bucks the system, I want you to be able to corral her."

He snorts and laughs again. "Alice, Laurie. Her name is Alice."

I grin. "Whatever."

———⊗———

Four hours later, after dinner, dessert, and coffee, I stand, arms crossed, staring at the candy aisle, deep in thought.

"Hey, Laur?"

"Shh." I hold a finger to my lips, not looking at Ryan. "I'm thinking."

"What if you just bought the bag of assorted minis?"

"Mm. No. Peanut M&Ms. Yuck."

He grabs the bag. "What's wrong with Peanut M&Ms?"

"Protein. That's a nutrient."

He frowns. "So?"

"So that makes them *healthy*. We're trying to avoid healthy. Now. Shhh," I shush him again.

I frown as I study the aisle. It is at least a foot shorter than it was yesterday.

Carb-Free-Fat-Free People are taking over this earth.

I close my eyes. *May it never be, Lord.*

"You pray over the chocolate?" Ryan asks incredulous, once

again reading my mind.

Confession: I hate it when he does that.

"You pray over your truck."

"Totally different!"

"It is not and be quiet!"

I finally pick up three Twix bars, four 3 Musketeers, seven giant Milky Ways, and a couple of plain Hershey bars.

Ryan shakes his head as I pile them into his hands. "Anything else, Dear? Like blood thinner to ward off your heart attack for a few months?"

I smile cheekily. "Funny." I lead him to the appliance aisle and stop in front of the coffeemakers. "We haven't solved the coffee problem yet."

"Oh yeah, right," Ryan says, blocking a yawn with his shoulder. "Um, what about those little guys? Those are cute." Since his hands are full, he uses his head to motion to a line of baby coffeemakers with tiny four-cup pots like they keep in hotel rooms.

I pick the blue one up, pursing my lips. "This pitcher is the size of one of my mugs."

"Easier to hide, Laur. You can make it in your bathroom cabinet and get more coffee from Shawn later."

I look up at Ryan and grin. "I knew there was a reason I liked you."

"Because I let you slowly kill yourself?"

"Something like that."

I stand back and study the shelf. "So what color?"

He squints. "Mm. Green."

"No, no. That wouldn't work. My bathroom is blue and yellow."

He sighs. "Okay. Blue."

"That's not the same color blue."

"What difference does it make? It'll be in the cabinet!"

"It should still match! My bathroom is a *cornflower* blue. That one is *metallic* blue. I'll buy that one when I get my metallic blue Mustang."

Ryan rolls his eyes. "There couldn't just be *one* shade of blue, could there?"

"How boring would that be?" I grin, rubbing his shoulder. "Okay. I'll get the yellow. Joan always says that bright colors invigorate the mind."

"Is that why your living room is green?"

"*Lime* green. And yes."

"There are different shades of green too?" he bursts.

"You know, I find it very amazing that you actually learned to dress yourself."

He grins. "In jeans and flannel shirts?"

I find the box for the yellow coffeemaker and pause. "Then again, baby Allie could probably match those."

I pay for the candy, a couple of bags of coffee, real sugar, miraculous little cups of cream that needs no refrigeration, and the coffeemaker, and Ryan puts his arm around my shoulders as we walk back to the truck, his other hand swinging the grocery bag.

"Thanks for inviting me to dinner, Laur."

"Thanks for paying for dinner." I smile.

"Anytime." He grins.

"Okay. What are you doing tomorrow night?"

He laughs.

Dad and Joan are already in bed when I get home, so sneaking the contraband in is easy. I have to giggle, though, as I stuff it in my bathroom cabinet. Here I am, a grown woman, sneaking candy in under her father's nose.

It would be funnier if it weren't so painful.

"Hey, Laur." Ryan's half-whispering when I come back downstairs. He gestures to the TV with the remote. "*Gilligan's Island* is on."

"With the Skipper too?" I squeal quietly, grabbing his arm. "I haven't seen this show in forever! Want to watch it?"

"Sure."

We settle on the couch in front of the TV. I pull my knees to my chest, wrapping my arms around them. A minute later, Ryan slides his arm around my shoulders.

He smiles at me when I look over at him.

"I like you, Ryan Palmer."

A weird look goes across his face for the briefest second, but then he squeezes my shoulders and presses a kiss to my forehead. "It's mutual, Kid."

———— ❖ ————

"Everyone should be quick to listen, slow to speak."

I purse my lips at the book of James. Can anyone say impossible? I stroke the scruff of Darcy's neck, looking at the words. Maybe this goes in tandem with wisdom.

If this is the case, I'm never attaining wisdom. My vocal box is way too developed to ever stay silent.

Chapter Seven

I squish down into the love seat contentedly, unwrapping another Hershey's Kiss. Brandon and Hannah had kindly invited me over for dinner when I'd walked into work Tuesday morning, and I took them up on it.

Hannah grins at me from the sofa. It is now past midnight, and we are only halfway through *The Prince & Me*. Brandon is next to his wife, one arm around her, his head back, eyes closed.

"I think Brandon's asleep," I tell Hannah.

"I know. His shoulder is digging into my arm." She nudges him. "Go to bed, Honey."

"Mm." He sighs. "I'm awake." He shifts away from her, then lies down, his head in her lap, his feet on the end of the couch.

She rolls her eyes.

"Thanks for feeding me, Hannah."

"Sure, Laur."

I lay my head back, watching Luke Mably bend down and gently kiss Julia Stiles for the first time.

"Hey, Hannah?"

"Mm?"

"What made you fall in love with Brandon?"

She purses her lips, watching the movie as she thinks.

"I heard my name," Brandon mumbles, rubbing his face on Hannah's jeans, keeping his eyes closed. "Whatever it was, I didn't do it."

"Look, seriously, Honey. Go to bed."

He yawns. "I'm fine."

"You're half-asleep."

"Well, you're comfortable."

"And you have a hard head." Hannah shifts, grimacing. "It's digging into my thighs."

His mouth curves, his eyes still closed. "Mm. I love you too."

"Brandon, you really should just go to bed," I say, popping the Kiss in my mouth.

He forces his eyes open. "But I'm watching the movie."

"You *hate* this movie," Hannah says, incredulous. "You always tell me that Eddie is a psycho-babbling softie and that no real guy would ever act like that."

"Guess that's true," he says sleepily. He stretches, rolling to his back and nearly hitting Hannah in the face. "True of almost every romantic comedy you two watch."

I throw a Kiss at him, and it whacks him in the head. "Go to bed."

Brandon makes a noise and rubs his forehead. "Ow."

"You know, Eddie would stay awake if he ever watched a movie with Paige," Hannah lectures.

"That's because Eddie is a psycho-babbling softie." Brandon sits up with a groan.

I throw a 3 Musketeers this time, harder. "Eddie is sweet."

"And *sensitive*," Hannah adds.

"And he cares about what Paige cares about," I say and nod.

"And he worries about her feelings."

"And he cured world hunger," Brandon mimics, his voice an octave higher. "And he solved the oil crisis. And he single-handedly built a fireplace so Paige could roast marshmallows like she always wanted to."

Hannah covers her eyes as Brandon pushes himself off the couch.

"Good night, ladies. I leave you to your fantasies."

"At last!" I rejoice.

He leans down, lifts Hannah's chin, and smirks at her. "Night, Love." He gives her a kiss, then flicks her nose as he straightens, ruffling my hair before going down the hall, yawning.

Hannah sighs. "What did you ask me?"

I giggle. "What made you fall in love with Brandon?"

She grins, stretching out on the couch on her stomach, tucking a pillow under her. "Well, it wasn't his taste in movies."

"You mean it doesn't just send shivers down your spine that he loves *The League of Extraordinary Gentlemen*?"

"Not particularly, no." She yawns. "I don't know, Laur. It was a lot of things."

"Like what?"

"Well, like he's got a lot of integrity. You know? I didn't come from a Christian family, so that whole concept was new to me. And he really cared about my salvation. He talked with me a lot about faith and God and things like that."

I nod. "We prayed for you every day."

She dimples. "Yeah, he told me." She glances at the TV. "He was different from other guys I knew. He didn't just see me as another blonde."

I look over at her. Her hair is pulled up in a half-hearted knot, and she wears a beat-up sweatshirt and jeans that have definitely seen better days. Even so, she is gorgeous.

"Hannah?"

"Mm-hmm?"

"I'm glad Brandon married you."

She smiles slowly. "Thank you, Laurie." She angles slightly away from the movie. "So why all the questions?"

"Just curious." I fiddle with a Milky Way wrapper, watching Eddie try to apologize to Paige.

"You never told me how dinner was last night with Ryan." She bites into a Snickers bar.

"It was fine."

"Just fine?"

"We bought a coffeemaker."

She chokes on the chocolate. "You bought a coffeemaker?" she repeats. "Is that like buying a blender?"

"What?"

"That's how you know couples are getting serious."

I frown. "They buy blenders?"

"Sure. No one gives a blender for a wedding present, so they go buy it themselves." She waves her hand, finishing off the Snickers. "It's a common fact, Laur."

"I have never heard of that fact."

"Well, it is one."

"And, no, *I* bought the coffeemaker, and it's a little four-cup mini thing for me to hide in my bathroom cabinet."

Hannah snorts. "How did you get that inside?"

"By the time I got home last night, Dad and Joan were already in bed."

"Does it work?"

"Like a charm." I grin at Hannah. "I'm still holding my breath, though, because like Solomon says, 'Charm is deceitful.'"

Hannah nods. "'And beauty is vain.'"

"You know, when I was little, I used to be ticked that Proverbs didn't mention the Beast. I mean, if Beauty was vain, she hid it well. But the Beast? He was just downright mean."

She laughs.

I smile and stretch as the credits start. "Well, Lovely, I should go."

"Mm. I'm glad you came over. I miss our girls' nights."

"They're harder when there's a guy here."

"The downfall of marriage." She yawns.

I gather all the empty wrappers, find my backpack, and hug her good night. "You're off tomorrow, right?" she says, walking me to the door.

"Yeah. But I'll be at Bible study."

She steps outside with me, hugging her arms around herself. "Hey, Laur?" she asks as I'm halfway to my car.

I stop and look at her. "Yeah?"

"Why did you ask me about falling in love?"

I bite my bottom lip. "Mm. Just curious."

Her eyes are sparkling, but I can't tell if it's mischievousness or the moonlight.

"Okay. Well, drive carefully."

I wave and leave, breathing a sigh of relief that she didn't press me on that one. I'm the matchmaker here. There's only room for one.

—❀—

Dad wakes me up at six Wednesday morning.

"Laurie?" he whispers, shaking me.

"Mmphg."

"Are you awake, Honey?"

I open my eyes a fraction of a centimeter. He stands over my bed, smiling. I close my eyes again, sighing.

Good grief, it isn't even light out!

"No," I mumble.

"Laurie, it's a beautiful morning out there!"

I roll over, facing the wall, pulling the covers over my head.

"Laurie? Laurie?"

I moan.

"Come take an early morning walk with me, Laurie-girl. We can catch the last part of the sunrise!"

I have to be adopted. Either that, or Mom must have had a sordid affair with the newspaper delivery guy. Having known my mother, though, I'm going with the adoption theory.

I roll back over, my eyes closed. "Go get Joan," I say and sigh.

"She's got her Bible study this morning. She already left."

This is the difference between singles' Bible studies and married people's: The time they take place.

Who can possibly study—or for that matter even read—this early in the morning?

I decide that Joan and all the women in her little breakfast group are crazed mutants taking over the world.

"Laurie?"

I groan, half-crying. "What?"

"Please, Honey? Walking is wonderful exercise, and it's been awhile since it was just the two of us, and I miss talking to you."

Awww.

I squint through one set of eyelashes at him, see his pleading expression, and sigh.

It was one fifteen before I got to bed last night. One thirty-five before I finished reading in James.

I push the covers off and stumble past Dad to the bathroom, eyes closed.

I hope Dad realizes what a saint he has in his youngest daughter.

"Just give me a minute to shower," I mumble.

"Oh, thank you, Sweetheart! I'm so happy. I'll go make you some Soyee coffee."

"Why? There isn't any caffeine in it."

Dad pauses. "Oh. True. Never mind then. I'll change into my walking shoes."

I dump half a bag of coffee grounds into the coffeemaker in my cabinet, silently thrashing Ryan for suggesting the diminutive maker. I should have bought the restaurant-style twenty-cupper and ditched the whole under-the-counter idea!

I'm never buying anything because it's cute again.

———— ❖ ————

Fifteen minutes later I am dressed, my hair is wet, I wear no makeup, and I've drunk the coffee directly from the tiny pitcher, draining the thing dry.

Dad is waiting downstairs by the front door. Darcy is lying at Dad's feet, fast asleep. Dad holds his leash.

"We're taking Darcy?" I ask.

"Isn't that a good idea? He needs the exercise too. We'd better go, Laur. We already missed the sunrise."

Oh, rats.

Darcy lifts one eyelid at the sound of my voice and shoots me a glare that could freeze kryptonite.

Great. Now my dog hates me, and it's not even my fault.

"Come on, Boy, get up," Dad coaxes, opening the door and dragging Darcy down the steps.

Dad starts off down the street at a good clip, and I struggle doubly—first to keep up and second to keep my eyes open.

Poor Darcy slinks along like he is drugged.

Dad inhales deeply, grinning. "Ah! I love this time of day! The birds chirping, the air just beginning to warm, the smell of the dew . . ."

And on and on he rambles, talking about how blue the sky is and how green the grass is and how pretty our neighbor's roses look and how fresh air revitalizes the lungs and gets more oxygen to the brain and how walking this fast this early in the morning is good not only for your heart but also for your muscles, brain waves, abdomen, liver, white blood cells, bone marrow, and corneas.

Then he looks at me. "So, Laurie-girl, tell me how you're doing."

Darcy still hasn't lost that vicious-pirate look, so to be perfectly honest, I am a little freaked out about what will happen the next time I'm in the house alone with this dog.

I don't tell Dad that. "I'm doing good, Dad."

"You didn't get in until late last night."

"Hannah and I were watching a movie and talking."

"Where was Brandon?"

"Sleeping."

Dad nods approvingly. "The boy knows what is good for him. Sleep, Laurie. Sleep is the best thing for your body at your age."

Then why did you wake me up before the condensation in the air had a chance to evaporate? I wonder.

"Yes, early to bed and early to rise!" Dad keeps going.

I decide silence is best.

"Mornings, Honey, are the most fruitful part of the day. You can get more done before six than you can get done all day."

I *hate* this saying. It's not even possible!

To quote Doc Brown from *Back to the Future*, "It disrupts the time/space continuum!"

Dad pats my hand. "I'm so glad you came with me. Walks are so much nicer with another person."

"Mm-hmm." I yawn. Then I say something really stupid, which I can only attribute to lack of sufficient sleep. "Anytime, Dad."

Dad keeps walking, dragging Darcy along with him, the dog staring fiercely back at me, plotting my grisly death. "I'm glad you said that, Honey. We should do this every day before you go to work."

I stop walking completely, staring at my father's back as he keeps marching away from me, avoiding my dog's murderous gaze.

Oh no.

Here's something I will never learn: How to keep my mouth shut.

"Uh, Dad, I didn't actually—I don't think that would be . . ." I stutter, running behind him, trying to catch up to his General Patton pace.

"What a terrific way to brighten your mind before work!"

"Yeah, but . . . sleep! Sleep, Dad, remember?"

"You should go to bed earlier," he says, reverting into lecture mode.

Dad's idea of bedtime is nine thirty.

Bible study isn't even over then!

Darcy shows me his teeth, and I wince.

We make a circle around the block and walk back to the house. I rub my head, blinking, trying to clear my eyes.

"See, Laurie-girl? Wonderful exercise!" Dad exclaims. He stretches. "Ahh! I feel rejuvenated, don't you?"

"Um. Yeah."

He marches up the front steps and thrusts open the door, motioning for me to head in first.

I walk into the quiet house, aiming for the couch. "I'm going to catch a quick nap," I tell Dad. "Wake me up at eleven."

"It's lunch then," Dad chides.

I walk around the corner. "Well, that will be—"

"SURPRISE!"

I fall over from shock, wonking my head on the side of the sofa.

Joan, Hannah, Ruby, and Dad all start laughing.

"We got her! We got her!" Hannah gloats, laughing hysterically, helping me to my feet.

"It's not my birthday," I mumble, staring at all of them like they have ice cubes coming out their ears.

It is then I notice my suitcase calmly sitting against the wall separating the kitchen and the living room.

Joan grins. "Surprise, Laurie! We're kidnapping you!"

"Where?" I ask, wide-eyed.

"Right now!"

"No, I mean, where are you taking me?"

"That's the surprise," Ruby says, shifting baby Adrienne to her shoulder.

I gape from her to Hannah. "You two are in on this?"

Hannah snorts. "Honey, we three cooked this up together."

"We three?"

"Me, Ruby, and Hannah," Joan explains, still grinning. "Your father helped some. Come on, Honey, we need to get to the airport."

"Airport?" I gasp.

"For our flight," Joan says, patting my cheek, smirking at my shock.

"Ha ha ha!" Hannah laughs evilly, rubbing her hands together.

They push me out to the car, shove my suitcase on my lap, pile in themselves, and slam the car door.

All while I sit there, still in shock, my mouth partially open, my eyes big.

"Laurie, will you *relax*?" Hannah says, buckling her seat belt. "Sheesh. No trust at all."

"I promise you'll have fun." Ruby smiles.

I feel myself start to calm down and my mouth tips.

"There you go," Hannah says.

Joan looks back at me from the passenger's seat. "Are you excited, Sweetie?" she trills, squeezing my knee.

"Uh-huh," I say, not quite convinced. "I'll be more when we get there."

Joan turns back to the front grinning knowingly. "Mm-hmm. You'll find out soon enough."

I do not like that tone.

—⟨❖⟩—

"Phoenix?" I ask a little later.

"Shopping, entertainment, great hotels," Hannah rattles off, sounding like a travel agent.

They'd stopped at this particular gate a few seconds earlier, declaring this the one. Ruby drops the handle of her rolling suitcase and rubs Adrienne's back. "This will be Adrienne's first plane ride," she tells me.

Eek.

What if Adrienne is one of those babies who screams the entire flight?

I always assumed one day I'd have to deal with a baby like that, but I guess I also assumed I'd be married.

I force a smile. "Oh, really?"

Ruby laughs at my look. "Don't worry, the doctor gave her some medicine to help her sleep."

"Good." I smile genuinely.

Joan pats my shoulder. "Are you excited?"

"To go to Phoenix? Are you kidding? It sounds great!" I stretch, feeling my muscles loosen. An elderly couple waiting next to us sends me a weird look. "How long are we there?" I ask, trying to ignore them.

"We fly back Sunday," Hannah says. "Four days, basically."

"Great!"

She keeps going. "We'll hit three malls, catch a movie, eat at The Cheesecake Factory—"

"Yay!"

"Swim, go eat out really nice one night, and pretty much just relax," she finishes.

I laugh. "This sounds terrific! One question."

"Go ahead," Joan says.

"Why now? It's July. It's not anywhere near my birthday, Christmas, or any major holiday I can think of. Plus, in Phoenix it's probably a hundred and fifteen degrees," I say, ticking the points off on my fingers.

The elderly woman touches my elbow, and I jump fifteen inches off the ground.

"Oh, I'm sorry to scare you," she says in her little-old-lady voice.

"Not a problem," I huff, pressing my hand to my chest, sure that I've just had a mild heart attack.

"But I couldn't help overhearing your conversation. Actually, it's one hundred and eleven degrees in Phoenix," she says.

Joan, Hannah, and Ruby all nod politely. I smile. "Thanks," I say.

"Anytime."

I look back at Joan, who smiles sweetly. A little too sweetly. "We just thought a girls' weekend would be fun."

I angle my head at them, narrowing my eyes. "And?" I prod.

They just grin.

Uh-oh. Something deep in my gut tells me this has something to do with a boy whose name begins with *R* and ends with *N*. And my gut is rarely amiss in judgment.

"Hello and good morning!" a way overly zealous airline employee shouts into the microphone. "We are getting ready to board! Not *be* bored, but *to* board!"

Hannah snorts and covers her mouth.

I crane my neck trying to see this guy. I want whatever coffeemaker he has.

"So if I could get all you fantastically gorgeous people in a line, that would be superific!"

Now Ruby is giggling too.

I look at Joan. "Superific?" I echo, trying to keep back a grin. She laughs.

A few minutes later, I hand my ticket to a tall, skinny guy with a shock of black hair badly needing a trim. He grins at me, sticking my ticket into a little machine. "Have a great flight, miss!" he shouts.

"What kind of coffeemaker do you use?" I ask.

He hands me my ticket stub, grinning. "I don't drink coffee! Too much caffeine!"

"Smart man," Joan says from behind me.

"Weird." I whistle, shaking my head. "Well. Have a nice day."

"You too!"

Phoenix. Shopping. Movies.

Possibly coffee.

I grin, rolling my suitcase behind me as I walk onto the plane. This could be fun!

Chapter Eight

"All right. Laurie, you and I are sharing that room. Hannah, Ruby, and little Adrienne have the other room," Joan directs as we step into our hotel suite.

The suite is huge! A living room and kitchen are in the middle of the two bedrooms, and I sigh with relief as I see the coffeemaker.

Joan goes into the room she's allocated to us and hefts her suitcase onto one of the double beds.

"Which bed do you want, honey?"

"I don't care."

"I'll take the one by the bathroom then." She rolls her eyes. "Middle age does terrible things to your body."

"Duly noted."

She starts pulling out assorted shirts and pants. "Adrienne did really well on the trip."

"That's because she was drugged."

"Really? Wow. You know, medicine has come so far since I had children."

I grin at her, opening my suitcase. "You calling yourself old?"

"Mature, Laurie. There is a difference."

"In what? Wrinkle quantity?"

"I changed my mind, I'm rooming with Hannah."

I laugh. Then I pull out my very nice, very expensive black dress they packed for me and gasp. "Where on earth are we going? I thought we were shopping!"

Joan looks over at me holding the dress. "That's for dinner out, Sweetheart."

"Where? The governor's palace?"

She smirks, but shakes her head. "Can't tell."

I dig through my bag, pulling out five pairs of jeans and all the pink shirts I own — all of which were given to me by Lexi and still have the price tags attached.

"Who packed this?" I shriek.

Hannah comes in then and leans against the doorway, tossing her head self-importantly. "I did."

"You! You know I hate pink!"

She flutters her eyelashes at me. "Deal with it."

"*Deal* with it?" I screech.

Ruby walks in, waving her hands. "Whoa, whoa, whoa. It's not that big a hotel room, Laurie. Keep it down. Adrienne's sleeping off the drugs." She goes over and sits down at the little useless table all hotel rooms have.

"I have to wear pink!" I complain.

Ruby looks at me. "So?"

"So! I hate pink! Lexi gave me all these shirts!"

Joan looks up from her suitcase. "I guess you could always wear the black dress every day."

"Pink is fine," I say quickly, watching Hannah's eyes light up.

Joan chuckles. "All right, girls, let's freshen up and hit The Cheesecake Factory tonight, what do you say?"

"Aye?" I ask, grinning.

"Sounds good," Hannah says.

"Does freshening include changing shirts?" I ask, twisting a baby pink top into a tight ball.

Ruby laughs. "We'll go easy on you tonight, Laur. Guess I'll go get Adrienne up."

"Can I?"

She looks at me. "Uh, sure, I guess."

I walk across the suite to Hannah and Ruby's room. Adrienne is sleeping on the bed, surrounded by blankets to keep her from rolling off.

I climb on the bed beside her and rub my finger down her cheek. "Hey, Baby, time to get up," I sing. Her cheek is soft and warm, completely smooth. I smile appreciatively at her. God did a good job with Adrienne; she's like the Gerber baby come to life.

Adrienne heaves a sigh and stretches her chubby baby arms over her head, making popping noises with her lips, keeping her eyes closed.

What do you know? This kid takes after me.

"Adrienne? Come on, Honey, time to wake up. We're going to get cheesecake."

Hey, it works for me.

Adrienne obviously doesn't care. She sleeps on.

I cradle her fuzzy dark-haired head under my hand and her little rump under my other hand and lift her up. She squirms, letting out a little aggravated mew.

"Rise and shine, Baby Girl."

Her big brown eyes open slowly and she blinks at me, frowning.

"She up?" Ruby asks, coming in behind me, scrunching her

curls back into place.

"Sort of."

"Hi there, Precious," Ruby coos.

Adrienne smiles at her mother, then looks curiously at me.

"Is my hair really that bad?" I ask.

"Yes," Ruby answers.

"I was talking to Adrienne."

"I was answering for her."

"Telepathic communication?"

"It's a scientific fact. Mothers can understand their baby's thoughts."

I look at little Adrienne, who is waving her fist around. "All right. What are we thinking about now?"

"Dinner," Ruby says, pulling a pair of nice dark-rinsed jeans out of her suitcase.

"Wrong!" I announce gleefully as Adrienne shoves her fist into her mouth. "We were thinking about Brad Pitt, weren't we, Honey?"

Ruby shushes me. "Be quiet, Laurie. Adrienne's not allowed to think about boys until she's thirty-seven."

"Weeks?"

"Years."

"Poor baby." I wink at Ruby, kiss Adrienne's dark head, and slide off the bed with her.

"Hold her for a second."

I bounce the baby while Ruby finishes changing into the jeans and redoes her mascara.

"Okay, thanks." She takes her, kissing her baby cheek. "Are you Mama's wittle precious?"

Wow. Disturbing.

"I'll leave you to your bonding."

"Appreciate it." Ruby chuckles.

Hannah sits on my bed, talking animatedly to Joan.

"So then we had to pick out a mattress, and he's like, 'Hey, my aunt Ernestine has this great mattress she never uses.'"

Joan's eyebrows go up. "Aunt Ernestine?"

Hannah sighs. "Right. We went to her house, and the mattress dates back to 1947." She rolls her eyes. "So Ernestine is telling Brandon all about how his grandfather slept on this mattress as a young man before heading off to war and what memories it has, and I sit down on it, and the middle hits the floor."

Joan bursts into laughter. I grin.

Hannah smiles at me. "Just sharing a few newlywed stories."

"I don't have much there," I say thoughtlessly, digging out a pair of jeans to change into. I'm still wearing the athletic pants I had put on for my early morning waltz with Dad.

"You will someday." Joan smiles.

My trip's itinerary is quickly becoming: (1) Avoid Subject of Ryan, (2) Avoid Subject of Marriage, (3) Avoid Pink.

"Mm. Just how bad is my hair?" I ask, changing the topic as quickly and smoothly as I can, then refill my coffee mug while the coffee is still dripping from the machine.

Hannah tips her head as she looks at me. "I'd wear a hat."

"Swell. Did you pack me one?"

"Nope," she says cheerfully.

"Pull it up in a ponytail," Joan says.

"I also have on zero makeup." I groan and go over to the mirror, flinching.

"Well, Ryan's not here, so who do you have to impress?" Hannah says, batting her eyes.

I glare at her reflection.

She grins cheekily.

I ruffle a hand through my hair, frowning. I hadn't dried it before the walk with Dad, and so it curls willy-nilly all over the place. My hair is weird. It's long—past my bra strap—but unlike the hairstyle magazines proclaim, the length doesn't pull the curl out at all.

Here is what I think about long hair: If one part looks bad, it all looks bad. With short hair, you can just comb it down, and it looks fine.

I lean closer to the mirror, squinting. My eyes look dry and splintery, and they've got big black circles underneath them. And squint-wrinkles. I immediately widen my eyes.

"Blegh!" I declare.

"Oh for heaven's sake, Laurie, it's not that bad. You're twenty-four! Your skin is still babylike." Joan grins.

"I need calcium," I state, popping open the makeup kit Hannah packed. "I think I'll have to get cheesecake for dinner and dessert."

Joan sends me a look. "Do you know how many calories are in just one slice?"

Hannah groans. "I don't even want to know."

"But there's calcium in cheesecake," I point out.

"And fat. Lots of fat!" Joan nods.

"And protein."

"And carbs." Joan moans.

"Come on, Joan. You have to have a slice." I layer on the concealer under my eyes. "It's a girls' weekend; you can't count calories."

She wrings her hands, fretting. "Do you know what your father would say?"

I turn from the mirror, grinning at her. "Who said we have to tell him?"

Her forehead creases as she worries about it. "Just a second," she mumbles, digging through her purse and coming out with something resembling a palm pilot.

"What's that?" Hannah asks.

"It's a calculator of sorts," Joan says, pushing a button.

"Wel-come," a male computer voice says.

Joan pushes more buttons, and then her mouth goes slack and she starts fidgeting. "OH MY GOSH!" she finally shrieks.

"What?" Hannah and I exclaim.

"For just a small, just a *small* slice of plain cheesecake, I'll have to walk two hours and twenty-eight minutes to burn the calories!"

"Which you'll be doing tomorrow," I tell her calmly. "At the mall."

"For a *small* slice!"

"Can I have that?" I ask, taking the calculator from her. I turn it off, flip it over, yank out the batteries, and pocket them.

"Hey!" Joan squeals.

"You'll get them back on the way home. No counting, Joan! It's the rule!"

Ruby comes in then, holding Adrienne in her car seat.

"Ready?" she asks.

Joan stares at her, big-eyed. "Do you know how long we'll have to walk to work off a small slice of cheesecake?"

Ruby frowns. "This is a girls' trip, Joan. You aren't allowed to count calories."

"Ha!" I yell. "See?"

Joan breathes, covering her face for a minute.

"Oh, good going, Laur. We're giving Joan a heart attack and we haven't even been here an hour," Hannah drawls.

Joan pulls her hands away and shakes her head at me. "You have serious problems with authority, young lady," she says, but her eyes are twinkling again, so I decide I am forgiven.

"Funny. That's what all my grade school teachers said."

I slap on some mascara and a little bit of sparkly stuff on my eyes, flip my hair into a bun, and decide that will have to do.

Adrienne frowns at me as I grab my backpack, and I tickle her chin. "What is it this time?" I ask her.

"She's just hungry," Ruby says. "I guess you resemble a bottle to her."

"Terrific." I sigh.

⁓ ⊕ ⁓

Joan drives us to The Cheesecake Factory, and a black-and-white-clad waiter seats us at a huge table. Ruby shoves little Adrienne's car seat across the bench seat, and I follow her in. Joan and Hannah sit opposite us.

"Something smells really good!" Hannah sighs, closing her eyes and inhaling.

The waiter, a tall scrawny guy with really curly brown hair, leans down close to Hannah's gorgeous head. "It's the bread," he murmurs in her ear.

Hannah gasps.

I have to bite my bottom lip hard to keep from laughing.

"Oh, oh, I'm sorry," she stutters. "I didn't know you were right there!"

The waiter blushes four shades of red, ending with a hue close to purple. "No, I apologize, miss. I'm George, by the way."

"Hi," Hannah stammers.

He smiles a gawky smile at her. "What's your name?"

"Um. Hannah."

"Hi," he says softly.

I put my elbows on the table, cupping my chin as I watch the waiter fall in love with my married coworker.

Joan clears her throat. George jumps. "Right, right. Can I start you with beverages?" he asks.

"A bottled water," Joan orders.

I look at Ruby and Hannah, who both nod. "And three Dr. Peppers."

George writes it down. Slowly and glancing at Hannah after every letter.

Hannah lays her left hand on the table in an attempt to politely discourage him. George doesn't even notice the diamonds.

"I'll give you a minute to decide on the main course and bring back some bread."

He leaves.

Joan sighs. "Bread," she moans. "I'm not supposed to eat bread!"

I shrug. "You don't have to eat it."

Ruby grins. "Yeah, you can just watch the rest of us inhale it. I've been here before. Hot, sweet, buttery . . ."

"Stop!" Joan shouts, covering her ears.

Hannah's mouth is open. "Did you see that?" she demands.

"You mean your boyfriend?" I taunt.

"Yeah, Hannah, really. I had you pegged as a totally different kind of girl." Ruby grins, uncapping Adrienne's bottle.

"He didn't even notice my ring!"

"Honey, he didn't notice much of anything after he saw you."

Joan smiles.

"This is terrible!"

"Why?" I ask.

"Do you know what Brandon would have done to him?" she shrieks.

"Laughed?" Ruby asks.

"Hannah, the kid's like fifteen. You're obviously the most attractive customer closest to his age and without a baby, so give him a break," I say.

"Take it from someone who gets to work with teenage boys a lot," Ruby says, pulling on her pastor's wife voice. "Fifteen-year-old boys fall in love at a rate of six times an hour."

I laugh.

"You know, I went to high school with a fifteen-year-old kid named George," Joan says thoughtfully.

"Oh yeah? What was he like?" I ask.

"Annoying."

"Follow you around?" Ruby grins, holding the bottle for Adrienne, whose mouth is working like a little plunger.

"Like a puppy." Joan smiles. "Used to drive me insane."

"Why?" I ask.

"I was a senior. He was a sophomore. It wasn't cool."

"So what happened to him?"

"Oh, he went into show business," Joan says offhandedly. "Have you ever heard of George Clooney?"

My chin hits the table.

Hannah gasps.

Ruby grins. "You're kidding," she says.

"Oh . . . my . . . gosh!" Hannah screeches.

"You went to high school with . . ." I inhale harshly. "George

Clooney!"

Joan nods, grinning. "Surprise you?"

My mouth is still open.

George the waiter comes back with the bread.

"Are you okay?" he asks me, a frown wrinkle appearing between his eyebrows.

What an entirely aged look for one so young.

I nod, using my fist to close my mouth.

"Here's your bread. Your drinks will be out shortly."

Hannah and I both stare at him blankly.

Ruby smiles politely. "Thanks. Don't mind them; they've just had startling news."

"I hope it wasn't bad news," George says, sneaking another look at Hannah before leaving.

"I've never understood why it takes them so long to fill a couple of glasses and bring a bottle of water," Joan says to the booth next to us.

"Over here, Joan," Hannah says, shaking her head to clear the thoughts of Mr. Clooney.

"I can't look at the bread."

"It's okay. It doesn't bite." I pull a hunk off of the steaming loaf, spreading butter on it quickly.

Joan groans, covering her eyes.

Adrienne coos.

"You're still a bit small for this, Precious," Ruby tells her, buttering her own piece.

Hannah tears off a piece and then sweetly passes the bread to Joan.

"No, no, no!"

"Jo-an," I singsong. "Girls' trip, remember?"

"You have to have a piece," Ruby says, swallowing. "This is excellent."

Hannah bats her eyelashes at Joan.

Joan uncovers her eyes and sneaks a glance at the bread, then tenaciously reaches out and takes the smallest piece left.

She moans as she bites into it.

I grin. "Ladies, Joan has officially fallen off the wagon. A round of applause, please."

We clap for her.

She swallows, closing her eyes. "Laurie, you breathe a word of this to your father, and I'm sending you to boarding school in Tibet." She grabs another piece.

"I'm too old for boarding school, and that is such a stepmother comment." I grin cheekily.

She rolls her eyes and swallows another piece.

Chapter Nine

I get back to the hotel late the next day and fall flat on my bed, groaning. My feet ache, my head hurts, and my wallet has lost some serious weight.

And this after our first day at the malls.

I never realized how much Joan, Hannah, and Ruby like shopping. The four of us would go into a store, I'd find something in a few minutes, try it on, buy it, and be ready to go, and they would have just gotten started sorting through the racks.

"Tired, Laur?" Joan smiles, coming in the room, hefting several huge bags behind her.

"Mm." I sigh.

"Better change clothes, Honey, we have a dinner reservation in thirty minutes."

"Mm." This time I moan it.

"You need to wear the black dress for this one."

I roll to my back and blink up at her. "Do I have to fix my hair?"

"You're funny." She laughs.

I'll take that as a yes.

Here's what I hate: Fixing my hair in the morning, and then redoing it at night. What a waste of hairspray.

I peel my body off the mattress and stumble to the bathroom mirror.

Ponytails have been seen frequently at Hollywood premieres lately, right?

Right.

I comb my hair back into a ponytail, spray it, and change into the black dress.

———— ❦ ————

Forty minutes later we all sit around a table in a nice, dressy casual restaurant. A fire roars in the fireplace behind Ruby's chair, and the blue lighting is, quite frankly, making it difficult to see.

But it is nice, probably as nice as we could get with a baby in tow.

We order our drinks.

Joan leans forward, resting her hands on the table, smiling across at me.

It isn't a friendly smile.

"So," she says, drawing out the word.

I suddenly realize that both Hannah and Ruby have leaned forward as well, also wearing that same "ha-ha-let's-get-her-now" smile.

I squirm. "So?"

"Let's talk about Ryan," Joan says.

"Let's not," I say.

"Laurie, it's been a year and a half," Hannah says.

"Since what?" I ask.

"Since you and Ry started dating," Ruby replies.

I sigh, schlumping back in my chair. "That's what this whole trip is about, isn't it?"

They keep smiling.

I cover my face.

How could they do this to me?

"Look, it's not that I don't appreciate the concern," I start.

"Laurie, this is more than concern," Hannah interrupts sternly. "If someone doesn't push you forward, you will never get married."

"So?" I protest. "What's wrong with that?"

"You know you want to get married," Ruby says. "You told us you did."

"I'm twenty-four! I'm hardly approaching spinsterhood." I inhale harshly, fidgeting in the uncomfortable dress. "Guys, I have plenty of time," I tell them.

They exchange a look.

"Ryan is twenty-six," Ruby says.

"I know."

"So he's getting to the point where he wants to settle down, buy a house, start a family," she continues.

"And he wants to settle down with you, Laurie," Hannah says, flipping her shimmering hair behind her shoulder.

"How do you know that?" I fold my arms over my chest.

She rolls her eyes. "Don't be so dense, Laurie."

"Listen, maybe it's just me—" I start.

"Probably," Ruby interrupts.

"But I've always thought it was the guy's job to initiate this kind of thing," I finish. "You should've kidnapped Ryan instead of me."

"Laurie, we brought you here because we think you're missing the obvious," Joan says, redirecting the conversation. "Ryan has so many great qualities you don't have, and you have most of the qualities he doesn't." She spreads her hands. "To me, that says *matrimony.*"

I remember something Joan told me a long time ago, about how she arranged both of her kids' marriages, and I hold back a sigh.

But wait a minute.

I am Lauren Emma Holbrook, right? I believe God is sovereign over my future husband decision, right? And not only sovereign, but He's promised to give both Ryan and me wisdom about this decision.

I let the sigh out and hold up my hands. "All right, okay, I accept that statement," I say.

Maybe if I just agree to everything, they'll let the issue go.

Joan's eyes brighten. "For example," she says, "Ryan is a great provider, and you're a great supporter of him."

Ruby reaches down and pulls a few sheets of paper from her purse, grinning at me self-consciously. "I had extra time on my hands while Adrienne was taking a nap one afternoon."

She spreads the pages on the table. I lean over.

Reasons Laurie Should Marry Ryan.

I have to laugh. "Oh brother!" I shout.

"Laurie, we are in a public place. Keep it down," Hannah shushes.

I read the first reason out loud. "'Both are strong Christians.'"

"Very important," Joan says.

I keep reading. "'Both have a good sense of humor.'"

"Also very important," Hannah says. "I think I'd die of boredom if Brandon couldn't catch a joke."

"I wouldn't have let you marry him if he couldn't get a joke," I tell her.

Oh. No.

I blink repeatedly and then my mouth drops open. "Hey . . ." I say slowly.

Ruby and Hannah grin cheekily.

"Just repaying the favor, Dear," Hannah says, batting her eyelashes.

"This is not how this is supposed to work!" I protest.

"You practice matchmaking on us; we do it to you." Ruby nods.

"Girls, the matchmaker isn't supposed to be matched. That's not the natural order of things," I try to explain. "I'm supposed to grow up to be the nice, older, unmarried woman who everyone goes to with their problems."

"Well, we're making you the nice, older woman with five kids and a husband whose kids go to her with problems," Ruby says, pastor's wife voice back. "Marriage is a biblical concept."

"Preach it, Sister," Joan says, eyes twinkling.

"And you want to get married!" Hannah exclaims, reaching over and grabbing my hand.

"To quote my father—"

"I know, I know, you don't get everything you want." Hannah sighs. She squeezes my hand. "But I distinctly remember a conversation at work where you admitted to wanting a husband."

This is exactly why I need to be confiding in a diary and not in friends. I know what my next purchase will be.

"Laurie, why are you so hesitant?" Joan's voice is quiet.

I look at my hands, at Adrienne, at the tablecloth, and finally at her. "I don't know," I say finally.

"What's number three, Ruby?" Joan asks, once again redirecting the conversation.

The waiter comes then. "Are you ready to order?"

They drop the subject for the evening, but I'm not holding my breath that it won't be brought up again during the next two days.

— ❖ —

That night I change into my pajamas and go into the living room/kitchen to get a snack before bed. Joan is already under the covers, asleep.

Hannah sits curled up on the couch, phone to her ear, the room dark, save for one streak of moonlight filtering through the curtains.

"Mm-hmm. It was good. I miss you too," she says quietly.

Brandon.

She looks up, sees me, and smiles.

I pull a few cookies from the bag Ruby brought. Ruby makes good cookies.

"The what? Oh, it's in the vegetable drawer. Why?" She listens for a minute and chuckles. "Good luck with that one. I'll talk to you tomorrow. Okay. Love you too." She hangs up and stretches.

"What's he making?" I ask, settling into the chair beside the couch.

"He was trying to make nachos." Hannah grins.

"That's Brandon for you."

"One time he tried making barbecue chicken for me. I figured it would be an easy meal for him to make. You know, put everything in the Crock-Pot and wait." She giggles. "He put garlic marinade on the chicken instead of barbecue sauce."

I wrinkle my noise. "That's disgusting."

"I have no idea how he got those two confused. The house smelled like garlic for a week."

"That's why?" I grin.

She shakes her head. "A gourmet, Brandon is not."

"I'd agree with you there."

She pulls her knees to her chest and wraps her arms around her legs. "So are you liking the trip?"

"Depends. Was the whole point to talk to me about Ryan?"

She smiles. "That had a lot to do with it."

"Hannah . . ." I look over at her, nibbling on a cookie. The room is dark and peaceful. I'm finally in comfortable clothes, and the chocolate is soothing my nerves.

"What?"

I let my breath out. "I like Ryan."

She nods, rubbing her chin on her knee. "I know."

"He's nice."

She nods again.

"And funny. And polite. And he brings me coffee." I smile, feeling a little sappy. "He takes care of me. I really like it when he gets all protective."

Hannah looks at me. "There's a *but* coming."

"But . . ."

She grins.

"I mean, if he asked . . . I'd definitely consider it."

"What's holding you back, Laurie? It can't be your dad anymore. He's married. He wants you to get married now."

"It's not Dad."

She waits, watching me expectantly.

I let my breath out. "Ryan and me . . . Ryan and *I* . . . we're really good friends beyond the fact that we're dating. . . ."

Hannah purses her lips. "Right. Exactly."

"But if I love him, I love him the way I love you."

She frowns. "What?"

"You know. As a friend. As one of my best friends. It's kind of like how I love Brandon."

"Like a brother."

"Sort of, yeah."

She stays quiet for a minute, tipping her head at me. "Maybe that's because a friend is the only way you've looked at him."

I shrug, pulling out my ponytail and rubbing my hair where the elastic had been. This conversation is rankling my nerves, and the chocolate is gone.

"Well. Think about it, anyway. Want to see if there's a late-night movie on?" She reaches for the remote. "Ruby and Joan are both sacked out."

"I know. We're the only ones who understand what a vacation is, Hannah."

"Late nights and later mornings?"

"That's it."

She flips on the TV, scrolling through the channels.

"Hey!" I shout.

"I see it!" She grins.

Bill Pullman steps out of his old truck and opens the front door of his parents' house.

I settle back in my chair. "Good. We're still toward the beginning."

"I love *While You Were Sleeping*." Hannah sighs.

A plaintive cry drifts from Ruby's room, and I look at Hannah. "Should I?" I ask.

Hannah shrugs. "Why not?"

I push the door open and peek into the dark room. Adrienne's crib is right next to Ruby's bed. The baby is shifting around restlessly, blowing bubbles and telling her mother something in baby speak.

"Gotosleep," Ruby mumbles, her hand appearing from the covers.

"Hey, Ruby, I got her."

"Mmm. Thanks, Honey." She rolls over, still asleep.

I bend over Adrienne's crib, and she blinks big Shirley Temple eyes at me, sticking her thumb in her mouth.

"Buh-buh," Adrienne says, puckering her bottom lip out.

"Come with Auntie Laurie," I whisper, reaching down and lifting her out. I carry her into the living room and settle back down on the chair, laying her on my chest, facing the TV.

Adrienne keeps her fingers in her mouth, staring at Bill Pullman, wide-eyed.

"I think she's thinking about boys," I whisper to Hannah.

She grins. "Won't Ruby be happy?"

I rub Adrienne's stomach. "Poor baby hasn't gotten used to her new bed yet," I coo, nuzzling her hair. I kiss the top of her head. "I'm adopting her."

"I think you might want to discuss that with Nick and Ruby first."

"Hmph. Maybe I'll just kidnap her."

"Look at her cute little cheeks!" Hannah squeals quietly. Adrienne frowns at her, sucking loudly on her fingers.

"She likes me better."

"Believe what you want. I'm the one who gave Adrienne her favorite teddy bear." Hannah leans over and tickles the baby's chin.

Adrienne pops her fingers out of her mouth with a loud *thwock* and a lot of spit. "Kuh, kuh nnn," Adrienne tells Hannah.

"Go away!" I say for her.

"I think she wants me to hold her."

"Watch the movie, Hannah."

Adrienne falls asleep twenty minutes later. I hold her until the movie ends. Hannah stands, stretching. "Good night, Laur." She yawns. "Sweet dreams."

"Mm. You too." I can't move from the chair. "Take the baby?"

She gently pulls Adrienne off my chest and cradles her against her shoulder. "See you in the morning."

"Late in the morning." I stand and stumble toward my room, crawling into the bed next to the window.

Joan stirs. "Mmph?"

"It's just me, Joan. Go back to sleep," I whisper, pulling the covers up around my head.

I shouldn't have bothered telling her. She is asleep again before I finish.

I blink up at the ceiling.

Lord, is Ryan the right guy? And if he is, wouldn't I know this? Isn't there supposed to be some big enchanted moment when I just know? You told me to ask for wisdom. God, this is me asking for wisdom. You know who I'm supposed to marry or if I'm even supposed to get married.

Relaxation takes over. I smile. *Thanks, God.* And I go to sleep.

Chapter Ten

My eyes flutter open slowly, sunlight singeing my corneas. I jerk back and cover my face.

"Why did you open the curtains?" I shout.

"Good morning, Darling," a deep male voice says, a smile lurking in his tone.

I keep my eyes closed. "You should shut the curtains. My doctor told me I should have nothing but artificial light until noon."

"Funny, Laurie," he says dryly. "Wake up, Honey. I have a surprise for you."

I cup my hands around my eyeballs and glare at Ryan through my eyelashes. "Please close the curtains?"

Ryan sighs. "Fine, fine."

I shut my eyes again, relaxing in the darkness. "Thank you."

"Don't you care about the surprise?"

I look up at him, smiling and stretch. "Yes, I do."

He grins his little-kid smile. "Good! Come on, get up."

I moan and toss the covers over my head. "Can the surprise wait?"

He sounds muffled through the covers. "Nope."

Something jabs me in my ribs and I squeal. "AUGH! Stop!" I start laughing, twisting away from his fingers. "That tickles!"

"Get up!"

I throw the covers off and sit up, huffing. "Fine! Good grief, Ryan!"

I trudge to the bathroom, brush my teeth, and come back out, rubbing my eyes. "There'd better be coffee involved with this surprise."

He grins at me and hands me a pair of jeans and a T-shirt. "You have to get dressed first."

"I hate this T-shirt."

"Get dressed," he singsongs.

"This is the T-shirt we got at that art festival a year ago."

"Get dressed, Laurie."

"I hate art."

"Laurie!"

"Fine!"

I yank off my pajamas, tossing them on the floor, and jerk on the T-shirt and jeans. Ryan watches me, rolling his eyes. "You take such good care of your clothes."

"Thanks."

He leans over and kisses me, cupping the back of my head, pulling me close. "Are you ready, Mrs. Palmer?"

"Coffee?"

"Later."

"Now."

Another kiss. "No."

"Please?"

"Laurie . . ."

"Laurie?"

I jump, gasping.

Joan stands over the bed, frowning. "Are you okay, Sweetie? Having a nightmare?"

I blink at her, my mouth open, my eyes wide. "Wh—what?"

"Are you having a nightmare?" she asks, louder and more distinctly.

I try to regulate my breathing and sit up, clutching my pajama shirt. It was just a dream?

"Joan," I wheeze. "I just had the weirdest dream ever."

"You always have the weirdest dreams ever. I'm convinced it's because of all the caffeine you drink. Honestly, Laurie, five cups last night? How do you sleep?"

I take in a deep breath and drop my head into my lap. "Not well," I moan.

"Well, what did you dream about?"

I open my mouth to tell her and then stop.

At this point, telling my stepmother I dreamed I was married to Ryan is probably not the smartest idea.

"Um . . ." I fidget, crawling out of bed. "I don't remember all the particulars."

Joan shakes her head and follows me into the bathroom. "Better get dressed, Laurie. Ruby and Adrienne are raring to go and starving to boot."

"What about Hannah?"

"I haven't seen her yet."

I shower, dry my hair, dress, and slap on mascara. Ruby is sitting on the couch in the living room, Adrienne in her lap, when I walk out.

"See, Precious? Red. That's red," Ruby says, waving one of those squishy baby books in front of Adrienne's face.

Adrienne chews on her fingers in thought.

Ruby looks up. "Oh my gosh, Laurie, are you up? It's only ten thirty." She grins sarcastically.

"I had a late night with Bill Pullman."

She chuckles. "I don't want to know."

"Is Hannah up?"

"She was doing her makeup last time I checked." Ruby looks at her watch. "I'm starving. Joan said we'll get breakfast out, seeing how you two slept right through the free continental breakfast." She arcs her eyebrows at me.

I smile an apology. "Sorry?"

She shakes her head and goes back to the book. Adrienne looks up at me, grins toothlessly. "Puh puh," she says, overannunciating.

"Aww!" I squeal and lean over the couch, rubbing noses with her. I make coffee in the miniature coffeemaker, and it has just started gurgling when Hannah comes out of the room.

"Morning, all," she mumbles.

"Coffee is being made as we speak," I tell her.

"Good." She yawns. "Where's Joan?"

"In here!" Joan yells from our bedroom.

"Joan, could we go to the outlet mall today instead of tomorrow?" Hannah calls to her. "I want to go there before I have no money left."

I hear Joan laugh. "Sure."

We arrive at the mall an hour later. Joan immediately goes for Clarks/Bostonian Outlet, and Ruby disappears into Gymboree.

I look at Hannah. "Which one do we follow?"

She frowns. "I'm not inclined to follow either one."

"Want coffee?"

"Yes."

I laugh at her immediate response. "Look. Starbucks."

She sighs with relief. "May the Lord bless them and keep them."

"Walk while you're quoting the benediction."

I go into the little store, inhale the sweet aroma, and smile at the kid behind the counter, who encompasses the Starbucks look. Nerdy black glasses, curly hair, skinny as a telephone cord, and wearing the worst clothes known to man.

"Thank you for choosing Starbucks," he says.

"You're welcome, I— "

He holds up his hand to me, pointing to the earpiece in his ear. "Drive-through," he whispers. "One minute."

I nod.

"A Venti Caramel Macchiato. Will that be all? Four sixty-seven at the window, please."

He looks at me. "Sorry, miss, we're a little short staffed today."

"Not a problem. People order macchiatos here?"

He blinks at me behind his thick glasses. "Should they not?"

"It's one hundred and thirteen degrees outside," I tell him.

"Ah. You're an out-of-towner, then." He grins. "This is cool. Wait until it's August."

Hannah *tsks* behind me. "I feel for the people who settled here before air-conditioning was invented."

"I imagine that anything romantic in nature didn't happen until the winter." The guy laughs. "Sweat stench and all that."

"That is disgusting," I tell him. "And I'd like a Grande Mocha Frappuccino."

Hannah holds up her fingers. "Two, please."

"You two are easy," he says. He punches the order in and gives me the total.

I hand him a ten and tell him to keep it, and we gather our drinks and step back into the quiet mall.

"Thanks for the drink, Laur."

"Sure. So where do you want to go?" I ask again, slurping my drink.

"I need to find Brandon a birthday present," she says.

"Best of luck with that."

"Thanks," she says dryly. "He's the hardest person to shop for ever in the history of modern civilization."

"So get him a T-shirt that says that."

"That says what?"

"'I'm the hardest person to shop for in the history of modern civilization.'"

She frowns in thought, chewing her straw. "That could work," she says after a minute.

"See? I'm a genius!"

"And he has been saying he needs more weekend T-shirts," she continues.

"So get a pack of T-shirts and we'll paint slogans on them."

She grins and waves her free hand. "No, no, no!" she laughs. "I've got it. Claire at the studio, she's got this software that can print iron-ons for clothes. We'll use that. We can make him five T-shirts. Start coming up with more slogans."

"'Chocolate, Coffee, and Candy: Taste and see that the Lord is good.'"

She laughs. "How about, 'Well gee, Wally!'"

I grin. "I like it, I like it."

Ruby sees us and comes our way, holding the baby, her purse, three heaping bags from Gymboree, and a bottle of water that

Adrienne is eyeing jealously.

"Here, take the baby," she says, handing her to Hannah.

"Hi, Baby," Hannah coos.

"You take the bags, please," Ruby says, giving them to me.

"Good grief!" I yell, my arms jerking from their sockets with the weight. "What did you buy?"

"Everything the store had." She sighs and drains the rest of the water, looking at Adrienne, who is making hard *g* sounds. "Baby, you'd better be worth this."

"Hey!" I yell, looking at Hannah.

"That's a good one!" she agrees, chucking the baby on her elbows.

"What?" Ruby asks.

"That was good," I tell her, patting her shoulder. "If you come up with more, let me know."

"More what?"

"Hello, girls," Joan says, holding one bag. "Look, I found the most adorable sweater."

"It's one hundred and twenty degrees outside. And you bought a sweater." I stare at her oddly.

"You know, the temperature goes up an average of seven degrees every time you tell it," Hannah says. "I think you're prone to exaggeration." Her eyes widen.

"Yeah, that would be another good one," I tell her.

"Good what?" Joan asks.

"I've tried already, Joan; they're speaking in code. Can we see the sweater?" Ruby asks.

Joan pulls a black-and-white-checked, long-sleeved cotton blend from the bag. The three of us nod. "Cute!" I say. "Looks like you."

"Meaning what?" Joan smiles. "Old?"

"Not old," I tell her. "Mature."

She laughs.

"Let's get lunch," Ruby says.

"It's eleven o'clock," Hannah states. "It's barely past breakfast time. Brandon's probably still eating breakfast!"

I shift the weight of Ruby's bags. "Yeah, and if I know him, it's probably instant waffles."

"Not cereal?" Joan smiles.

"Are you kidding? That's two ingredients. Cereal and milk," Hannah says.

Joan chuckles. "I'm amazed he didn't die of starvation before he got married."

"Why do you think he was over at our house all the time?" I ask.

"Lunch, ladies, lunch," Ruby says, tossing the empty water bottle into the trash and taking her baby back.

"There's the food court, or we can go somewhere," Joan says.

"Food court," Ruby votes. "Fast and cheap. And I don't have to strap the baby back into her car seat."

We start walking in that direction, Hannah and I still slurping our Frappuccinos. "So what are you getting for lunch?" I ask her, the two of us lolling behind Joan and Ruby, who are power walking to the Chinese place.

"I feel like we just ate breakfast."

"We did," I say, sucking down the last of the whipped cream.

"I'm not hungry at all," she says.

"Me neither."

I toss my cup away and my nose suddenly jolts awake.

What is it? I ask my nose.

My nose doesn't respond. It is too busy smelling. Which I guess is better than it being too busy talking. People look oddly at people whose noses are talking.

My nose jerks my head around, and I stare at a little corner bakery in the food court.

Paradise Bakery.

My nose smiles.

I look at Hannah. "Ever heard of Paradise?"

She gives me one of those "What's this I hear about you and Kramer from *Seinfeld*?" looks. "Uh, yeah," she says slowly and in that you-should-know-this tone.

"Is it good?"

"Well, I haven't been! But hang on! Let me ask my great-grand-mother." She rolls her eyes.

I frown at her.

"What?"

"Paradise *Bakery*, Hannah."

"Oh!" she yells and is all smiles again. "Nope, never heard of it."

I shake my head. And people wonder about my reduced mental creativity. Look at what I get to deal with.

"Let's go see what they have," I say.

"Let's not. I'm not hungry."

"But something smells good and my nose said it was Paradise."

"Yeah? Well, my stomach says it's full of whipped cream, ice particles, and about four thousand calories from that Frappuccino you bought me!"

"You make it sound like I forced you to drink it, Hannah Curtis Knox. I will not accept responsibility for that one."

I start toward Paradise.

Funny. I never thought I'd say *that* particular comment for another fifty some-odd years.

Hannah *hmpghs* behind me. Which is Hannah-speak for "yes, you're perfectly right, Laurie Darlin', I just can't admit it."

"It's just that I'll have to run like seven hundred miles when I get home to work all of this off!" she complains behind me.

"Hey!" I say, whirling. "Girls' trip! You can't count!"

She sighs. "Fine, fine. I'll go see what they have."

We walk over to the Paradise counter.

"Cookies!" I yip like one of those little terriers. "Yay!"

The lady behind the counter laughs at me. "And they're good," she says. "My grandkids swear by them."

"Which one is the best?"

She purses her lips as she thinks. "If you want to be classic, go with the tried-and-true chocolate chip cookie."

"What if I want to be unique?" I ask.

"Then I'd suggest the macadamia nut white chocolate."

I'm not the biggest nut fan. Nuts contain protein. Protein should not be allowed in any kind of junk food.

"Can I have three chocolate chip cookies?" I order.

She punches the numbers in and gives me the total. Hannah crosses her arms over her chest and just watches.

I pay the woman, give her a tip because I'm nice, and take my bag of cookies.

"Have a nice day," the woman calls after me.

"You too!"

Hannah sighs and follows me to where Joan and Ruby are setting out their wonton chicken salads and chopsticks.

"I hope I know you in thirty years, Laurie," she says, sitting across from Joan.

"Thanks. I hope I know you too." I beam.

"I want to see how big your waist is then."

I open the bag of cookies, inhaling. "What can I say? I was blessed with a high metabolism. Let me enjoy it while it lasts."

Ruby pushes the chicken around on the lettuce with her thumb until it is in an arrangement suitable for Rachael Ray on the Food Network. She licks the sauce off her thumb and looks at me.

"As a pastor's wife, I should tell you to appreciate what God has given you and not take undue advantage of it," she says seriously. Then she grins. "But I won't. You're young. You're marginally active." She pats my hand. "Eat your cookies and be happy."

I brighten. "Hey!"

Hannah starts laughing. "You're right; you're right. There's another one. Does that make five?"

"More than, I think. Why are we just settling for T-shirts? Let's make a book of modern-day proverbs!"

Joan exchanges a sigh with Ruby, but they both keep their mouths shut and concentrate on their chicken.

Hannah looks enviously at the cookies, and I give her one of them.

"I'll give you this, Laurie," Joan says, swallowing a mouthful of lettuce. "My life has not been boring since I met you."

I believe I'll take that as a compliment.

Chapter Eleven

I hold up a black sleeveless top on Saturday afternoon, the last full day of our girls' trip, and show it to Hannah. "Sweet or sexy, Hannah?"

She squints up at it, using her thumb to mark her place in the rack she is sorting through. "Boring," she says and goes back to flipping articles of clothing.

I sigh. "Black is classy."

"Black is *boring*. You know, for having such a colorful personality, you dress downright monotonously. Get a life, Laurie!" She holds up a blinding lime green number.

I shield my eyes. "Too much life."

I hear Joan squeal from across the aisle. "Let me see that!" She runs over and snatches the top from Hannah. "How *adorable*! Oh, this is my favorite color. What size is it?" She digs through her purse to find her bifocals, which happen to be hanging from the beaded string around her neck.

Now the question. Do I be nice and tell her where her glasses are? Or do I enjoy the entertainment and keep my mouth closed?

Hannah spoils it. "Around your neck, Joan," she says sweetly.

Joan grins. "Laurie's father got this for me. Can you tell I haven't gotten used to it yet?" She shoves her glasses on her nose and peers through them. "A six? Perfect!" Adding the shirt to the ones already over her arm, she marches back across the aisle to join Ruby in the misses section.

"As I was saying," Hannah says, going back to her sorting. "You should buy at least one thing that you wouldn't normally while we're here."

"Why? So it can sit in my closet and stare at me?"

"So you can wear it. Shock Ryan."

"I shock Ryan enough as it is. Leave me alone."

She pauses in her sorting again and stares at me. "Look at yourself."

"What?"

"Jeans and a T-shirt. And not even one of those cute pink T-shirts I packed for you!"

I grin. On our first day shopping, I bought enough shirts to last me for the rest of the trip.

Here's what I am: Smart, Successful, and Skilled at all things.

"All you wear is jeans and T-shirts," Hannah continues her tirade.

I hold up a hand. "Not true! During the winter, I wear sweaters."

"Whatever! My point is, T-shirts or sweaters, you don't change colors!"

"I like primary colors! I don't like pink, I don't like neon, and I don't like anything in pastel." I shrug. "Sorry."

Hannah sighs. "You are a fashion train wreck. Can I at least plan your wedding?"

"Well, let me think about it. No."

"Please?"

"Lexi has already asked, and, no, you two are to stay as far away from me and Ryan as possible."

My mouth drops open and I slap a hand over the lower half of my face as I realize what I just said.

Hannah's eyes gleam evilly. "Ha!" she shouts victoriously. "You do love him!"

Here's what I am: Daft, Doomed, and Ducking for cover.

I slip into the nearest dressing room with a mumbled excuse about trying the black shirt on and clasp my hands against my chest.

Oh my. Did I really say . . . ?

Granted, I miss him right now. He's got a cute laugh, and I like hearing it on a regular basis. But even so!

An older lady with a mountain of white hair and nice brown eyes is standing in front of the three-way mirror in the dressing room hall wearing a black, long-sleeved fluttery dress.

"Something wrong, Dear?" she asks, looking at me in the mirror.

I sigh and slump down on the little sofa behind her, comfort of strangers and all that.

"My friend is trying to set me up with someone I don't . . . think is . . ." I let my breath out and sink further into the sofa. "Never mind." I smile weakly. "Nice dress."

"Do you like it? You don't think it makes me look bottom-heavy?"

"Well, seeing as how you aren't bottom-heavy to begin with," I say, "I think it looks great."

She smiles elatedly. "Oh, this is wonderful! I've been looking for a dress for three days! And this one is even 40 percent off!"

"What is the dress for?" I ask, like the nosy person I am.

"My granddaughter is getting married."

"Oh. You don't like the groom?"

She turns and looks at me with confusion. "What?"

"You're wearing black."

She laughs. "My granddaughter loves black. She's having all the women wear it."

I spread my hands in amazement. "I'm not the only one who thinks black is classy?"

She laughs again. She has a nice, Judy Garland–like laugh. It makes me think about yellow brick roads and munchkins popping out of flower petals.

"I like your laugh," I tell her.

She grins. "You're a direct one, aren't you?"

"I've been called worse."

"So who is this friend trying to set you up with?"

"A guy I've dated for about a year and a half."

"You've dated for *a year and a half*? And you're surprised someone's trying to get you married?" She frowns. "Honey, my husband and I courted for one month!"

"One *month*?"

"You kids today," she *tsks*. "You think it takes years and years to get to know someone well enough for marriage. You only need to know three things about a man before you marry him."

She motions with her hand and I scoot over on the couch. She sits down with a slight huff and turns to face me, ticking the points off on her fingers.

"One, how he treats his mother. Two, how he treats his pastor. Three, how he treats himself." She waves her hands. "See? Nothing that you can't find out in less than a month."

"How long have you been married?" I ask.

"Forty-five years."

I feel my eyebrows go up. "Wow. Congratulations."

"Listen, Honey. My husband treated his mother with love. He treated his pastor with respect. And he took care of himself. See? I knew Earl was loving, respectful, could listen to authority, and would take care of me." She pats my hand. "How does your young man treat people?"

"Well, his mom lives out of state. I've never met her. But he treats his sister very nicely."

She nodded. "A sister will work."

"And he listens to our pastor."

"Excellent."

"And he's in construction. Builds houses."

She smiles. "Meaning?"

"Well, he hasn't nailed his thumb to a wall yet, so I guess he takes care of himself." I grin.

She laughs her Judy Garland laugh again. "See? What else do you need to know?"

"Well, *his* feelings on the subject wouldn't hurt."

She *tsks* again. "That's the other thing with you kids today. Feelings, feelings, feelings. That's all Jessica talked about in regard to her fiancé."

"Jessica is your granddaughter?"

"Yes. I'll tell you the same thing I told her, and you can do with it what you like." She smiles gently, keeping her hand on my arm. "Marriage, love . . . they aren't about feelings. There have been *many* mornings that I've gotten up and not felt like loving Earl. But I did. Because it's not about how you feel. It's not about romance." She shakes her head. "Don't misunderstand me, Honey, romance is nice. But marriage isn't romance." She looks me in the eyes. "Can you respect and honor this young man for the rest of your life?"

I squirm under her gaze. "If I say yes, are you going to make me go tell my friend out there?"

She laughs. "No."

"Okay. But isn't there a point when it's the guy's responsibility to initiate?"

She smiles. "He's dated you for a year and a half?"

"Mm-hmm. Well. Almost."

"Has he mentioned marriage at any point?"

"A couple of times, I guess. Not seriously."

She squeezes my hand and stands. "I wouldn't worry about that then."

Hannah comes in then and sees me. "There you are! Geez, Laurie, I've been through three dressing rooms looking for you!"

"Sorry," I say. I look up at the lady. "This is Hannah."

"Hi," the lady says.

"Hi." Hannah smiles. "Nice dress."

"Thank you," she responds, eyes twinkling. "I'm going to change out of it now. It was a pleasure talking to you," she says to me.

"Thanks for the advice," I say as she disappears into a stall.

Hannah grabs my arm. "Joan and Ruby are ready to move on to another store. You're not getting that ugly shirt, are you?"

"Guess not."

"Come on then. Adrienne's starting to get fussy, and if we stick together several yards behind Joan and Ruby, maybe we won't get the job of pacifying her."

I laugh. "You're priceless, Hannah."

She dimples. "Thanks for recognizing it. And just to keep you on your toes, I haven't forgotten that great little sound clip you gave me a few minutes ago, and I will love dangling it over your head someday soon."

"I hate you."

She laughs.

We leave the dressing room. I hang the black shirt on the rack for restocking and follow Hannah out of the department store.

"Where to next?" I ask her. "Gymboree?" We've only been to one in every single mall. Adrienne has more pairs of denim shorts than I do, and I'm the Denim Queen.

Hannah grins at me, flipping her shimmering hair over her shoulder. "No, actually, I think we were supposed to meet them at Macy's."

"More department stores?" I groan. "How can any mall have this many stores this big?"

"And here I thought you liked shopping."

"I do. When it's for one afternoon in one store and I have end-less cash at my disposal. Then I like shopping."

"That's not called shopping, Laur; that's called daydreaming. This way." She points down a hall, and I follow her mindlessly.

Here's something I will never understand: Hannah has never been to this mall, yet she knows her way around it instinctively. I got lost finding my way out of the bathroom.

"So let's think of how we can expand your color palette," she says as we walk.

"Let's not. I like my closet the way it is."

"I'm thinking that a baby blue would look great with your eyes."

"I'm thinking no."

"Pair it with stonewashed jeans, Laurie."

"I don't wear stonewashed jeans. I wear faded, worn jeans. Comfortable jeans."

"You know, baby blue looks fab with black. We could get you in a short black skirt."

"I don't wear short skirts."

Hannah rolls her eyes. "Knee-length, Laurie. You make it sound like I want you in a miniskirt."

"With you, you never know."

We walk through the entrance to Macy's and I grin at her. I love Hannah; I really do. She's one of my closest friends, and I was her maid of honor. And I think she is a great dresser.

For her.

Not me. I would look pretty strange in some of the outfits she can pull off.

We go past the hygiene products and find Joan bending over the perfume counter, talking to a salesperson.

"What are you doing?" I ask, smiling and stopping beside her.

"Smell this." She sighs and holds up her arm.

I inhale. *Oo.* Strong stuff! I clear my throat, somehow tasting it on the back of my tongue.

"Isn't it great?" Joan gushes.

"Mm." I smile, swallowing. *Blegh!* I feel like sticking my tongue out and wiping it off with the little tissue papers on the counter. I don't think the perfume lady would like that.

Hannah does not have the same reaction I have.

"This smells wonderful! What is it?" she asks, her eyes sparkling.

The perfume lady smiles, a sale in her sight. "Curious, by Britney Spears," she says.

I want to laugh. I *really* want to laugh. I bite my bottom lip hard and clench the strap of my backpack.

My father *hates* Britney Spears with a passion. He is convinced that everything that is wrong with America's youth today is her fault. In his mind, she single-handedly tossed our nation into the dumpster with her blonde, high-on-the-cleavage persona.

Not that Dad used those actual words, you understand.

I can't help grinning at my stepmother buying the paltry 1.7 ounces of Britney's kingdom.

"What?" Hannah asks me.

"Nothing," I singsong.

Joan takes her package and leads us upstairs to the children's department. "Ruby's meeting us up here."

I hear her before I see her.

"No, Precious, you can't have that," Ruby says. "That's Mommy's water. Let Mommy get you your cup."

Question: Do *all* first-time parents refer to themselves in the third person?

Ruby looks up as we join her. "Hey, guys. Hold on a second." She unlocks Adrienne's seat to get to the stroller and hands the car seat to me, since I am the only person without a bag. I nearly drop it.

"Wow. Adrienne's gained some weight since I last held her."

Ruby sighs, digging the baby's cup out of the diaper bag in the bottom of the stroller. "Nick just had to get the top-of-the-line car seat. He didn't even care that the thing weighed forty pounds. He heard 'safe in cars' and bought it."

Joan nods. "My first husband was like that. Safety first."

"For the children," Ruby says. "Heaven forbid I be able to walk upright." Joan chuckles. Ruby takes the baby back, sticks her back on the stroller, and holds the cup up to Adrienne. "We're learning to drink from the sippy cup slowly, aren't we, Precious?"

"You didn't already know?" I ask sweetly.

Ruby sighs and rolls her eyes, but laughs. "Oh, Laurie."

We sit down to dinner at Claim Jumper to split two huge orders of ribs.

"So, Laurie, I hope you had a good trip." Joan smiles across the table at me.

"I did."

Ruby licks her fingers. "Let's talk about why we're here."

"At Claim Jumper?" I ask, flinching.

"No. About Ryan."

I sigh. "We've talked! I've heard this discussion from you, from Hannah, from the old lady in the dressing room. . . ."

"What?" Hannah laughs.

"Remember that lady in the black dress? She gave it to me too!"

"Good." Ruby nods. "Listen, Laurie, I love my brother with all my heart, and I want him to marry you. Is that so hard to accept?"

"It's not the acceptance that's hard," I mumble.

Hannah clears her throat. "Laurie accidentally told me something this afternoon."

"You wouldn't dare," I say slowly and threatening. "Best friends don't tell each other's secrets."

"This isn't a secret, Laur, and even if it were, secrets are meant to be told."

"I feel like I've been transported into the Ya-Yas! Quick, tell me, when does the date-rape drug come out?"

Joan looks at me soothingly. "Laurie. Honey. We love you. We want to see you happy."

"I appreciate that. So why can't—"

"And lucky for us, we happen to know that God's plan for your happiness includes Ryan," she continues.

"How do you know that?" I demand.

"God told me," she says sweetly.

"What?"

"It's the rule for being a parent. God starts telling you things about your children."

"Is that true?" I ask Ruby.

She nods. "Remember when Adrienne got a hold of that gum wrapper?"

I nod slowly. She'd almost choked to death.

"I think God told me to go check on her."

"Okay, I'll believe that." I sigh. "But could we put this stuff about Ryan to rest? You've done your job. If he asks, I'll definitely consider it."

"We've failed!" Hannah moans.

"No!" I yell. "No, no. I meant, I'll definitely say yes!"

Hannah bangs her head repeatedly on her fist, Ruby rubs her eyes, Joan sighs loudly, and I swear Adrienne starts babbling *tsk, tsk, tsk*.

I blow my breath out.

"Laurie," Hannah starts again.

"Okay, I get it. All right? I understand that you want me to marry Ryan. If he asks, I'll accept. Okay? Can we put this to rest now?"

"How will you get him to ask?" Hannah says.

"What?"

"How are you going to convince him to ask you?" she rephrases.

"What are you talking about?" I ask, staring at her blankly over my plate of ribs.

"Half the fun is getting the man to ask you to marry him," Ruby says.

"Ruby, I hate to tell you this, but *I* told Nick to ask you," I say.

"But who convinced him?" she shoots back.

Adrienne pops her fingers out of her mouth with a loud *twock!*, as if to say, *Yeah! So there! Tell her, Mom!*

Joan reaches across the table and pats my arm. "Let's discuss how we can get Ryan to propose, shall we?"

"No," I say.

"Yes," Ruby and Hannah say together.

"Good," Joan says brightly. She digs in her purse and comes out with the small notepad she carries for grocery lists. "Number one."

"Laurie needs to be more upfront with her feelings," Ruby says.

"Good one, Ruby, thank you." Joan writes it down.

"You want upfront? I can be upfront. Why are you doing this to me?" I moan loudly, covering my face.

"Number two. She needs to be quieter," Hannah says, motioning to me with her fork.

"Amen," Joan says under her breath.

"I heard that."

"Number three," Ruby starts. "She needs to employ the tried-and-true Smile-Slowly-and-Stare maneuver."

"I'm sorry?" I ask.

Ruby looks at me, softening her pretty brown eyes and smiling sweetly, holding my gaze.

"That is not called the Smile-Slowly-And-Stare. That's called The Look," I say.

"Whatever," Ruby says. "She needs to do that. Worked for me."

"And me," Hannah puts in.

Joan smiles cheekily.

"You too, hmm?" I ask, rolling my eyes.

"Works wonders, Dear. I have number four. We need to establish an outing that the two of them can go on where Ryan will feel protective of Laurie."

"Oh, that's a good one," Ruby croons.

"How about they go hiking?"

Joan nods. "Maybe in the hills behind the house?"

"That sounds good. Laurie can trip on a rock or something and fall," Hannah says.

Ruby bursts, "Oh! Oh! Oh! And Ryan could catch her!"

"And have to carry her back!" Hannah adds.

"Where he could patch up her scrape!" Ruby finishes.

Through all this, Joan nods agreeably. "We'll plan it."

Hannah points at Joan. "Without their knowing."

"Hello? I'm right here." I wave. "The whole point of planning things behind someone's back is to actually do it behind someone's back. Not in front of her face."

"Shh, Laurie," Joan says, scribbling madly. She keeps talking to Ruby and Hannah. "Okay, I'll make sure that Laurie's father and I are out of the house. What else?"

"Fire," Ruby says slowly, nodding. "There has to be a fire in the fireplace."

"It's July, Ruby," I say.

"Laurie, be quiet," Hannah shushes. "And, Joan, mark down that there needs to be first-aid supplies in the house."

Joan nods. "Got it. Anything to eat?"

"Strawberries!" Ruby shouts.

Hannah gasps. "Chocolate-dipped!"

I lean forward and bang my head on the table, narrowly missing my BBQ ribs, giving myself a nice welt on my forehead.

The only one who notices is Adrienne, who coos at me.

"I'm dead, Adrienne," I say.

"Laurie! Quiet!" Ruby lectures, not even sparing a glance.

By the end of the evening, it is arranged for me to make Ryan propose in exactly one week so I can plan a wedding and be married by October to beat the holiday rush.

I'm curled up on the little sofa, my Bible perched right under the lamp. James and I have gotten out of the habit during this trip. It's hard to have daily devotionals on vacation!

"But the wisdom that comes from heaven is first of all pure; then peace-loving, considerate, submissive, full of mercy and good fruit, impartial and sincere."

Wisdom.

Gee, Lord, could You be trying to make a point or something?

Chapter Twelve

I walk into The Brandon Knox Photography Studio at exactly 8:58 on Monday morning and stretch.

Claire, my psychologist-turned-photographer coworker, watches me, one brow raised.

"So, have a fun trip?" she asks.

"Yeah. Mostly."

"Mostly?"

"Long story that can wait."

She regards me with that cock-headed look that shrinks typically have and nods slowly. "You were confronted, weren't you? I didn't think they'd actually pull it off."

"What?"

"About Ryan. About marriage. About your reservations, which we'll discuss in a minute."

"Claire, I . . . they . . . we . . ." I stutter.

My nine o'clock walks in.

"We're here for Lanny," the woman says.

"Laurie," I correct.

"We're trying," she says and hustles a little kid in the door.

"What?" I ask.

She blinks. "Didn't you say hurry?"

"No, I said *Laurie*. My name is *Laurie*."

"Oh!" the woman says, drawing the word out, stopping.

Claire's eyes are twinkling madly.

"Right this way," I say. "We'll be in Studio Two." I look at Claire. "We'll talk later." There is no room for argument in my tone. I knew Joan, Ruby, and Hannah planned the Ryan talk, but they told Claire?

"I'll be here," she says gleefully.

This woman likes confrontation.

I escort the lady client and her son into Studio Two and proceed to photograph the snotty-faced boy for the next forty-five minutes.

After they leave, I disinfect and go back into the lobby.

Hannah sits at her desk, holding her head in one hand and a huge cup of coffee in the other.

"Wild night last night?" I ask her.

She sighs and looks at me bleary-eyed. "I have the worst headache known to man, and it is all your fault."

"What?"

"You're the one who pumped me full of caffeine the entire four days we were there! Who knew your body could get addicted to it so fast?" She moans, sipping from the cup.

"Well, it is a potent drug."

"Potent? Potent?" she gasps. "Laurie, I feel hungover! My eyeballs feel like they got suctioned out of my head, fried in a vat of corndog batter, and plopped back in!"

I blink. "Good analogy."

She sighs loudly and keeps sipping her coffee.

Claire appears from Studio One. "Thanks for coming," she says soothingly to a sobbing young woman.

The woman turns and embraces her tearfully. "Thank you," she blubbers. "You've helped me so much."

"Anytime. You have my card?"

The woman sniffles, nods, smiles raw-eyed at us, and quietly leaves.

Claire watches her go, shaking her head slightly. "Poor thing. Her husband left her for a garbage woman. It's been a big blow to her self-esteem."

I look at Hannah, who wears the expression I imagine I have.

"You're counseling your photography clients?" I ask.

"Laurie," Claire says slowly. "Psychology is more than a job; it's a way of life."

Creepy.

I feel for Claire's future kids.

"So is matchmaking, I guess," I say.

Claire brightens. "Speaking of which, I believe we had an appointment to discuss your feelings regarding the ambush?"

Hannah shoots Claire a glare that makes dry ice seem hot.

"Claire, we talked about this," Hannah hisses.

Oo. And this particular secretary has major sway with the boss.

"Stick a fork in her, she's done!" I yell, raising my fist for emphasis.

Hannah and Claire both look at me curiously.

"I've always wanted to say that." I grin.

Hannah closes her eyes, rubbing her head. "Keep the volume down, you psycho caffeinated uncolorcoordinated oddball," she mumbles.

I raise my eyebrows. "You're mean when you're not high, Sister."

"Laurie," she threatens.

"Well, I just remembered that I had an out-of-the-office session today, so if you'll excuse me," I say, grabbing my backpack from behind Hannah. I pat her shoulder. "Don't work too hard now."

I duck out quickly, hopping into the Tahoe, leaving Claire, bless her heart, wide open for Hannah's attack.

I drive the familiar path, park, and open the front door of Merson's, inhaling deeply.

"Laurie?" Shawn questions from behind the counter. "Is it you? Or a mirage?"

I grin. "Nope, it's me."

"Thank goodness! My daily totals have fallen in the last several days. What happened to you?" he asks, rolling his eyes at his sarcasm.

"I got kidnapped."

"Really."

"Yup. By power-hungry mongrels who wanted to steal my idea of a quick-serve coffeemaker that takes a mere seven seconds to nuke the water, absorb the coffee, and speed into the cup!"

Shawn rubs his hands on his ever-present towel. "Well. If they succeed in making it, let me know. It will help with serving certain patronage whose name starts with *L* and ends with *E*."

"Lance?" I ask.

A guy at the bar looks up from his book, squinting at me. "Do I know you?"

"What?" I say.

"You called my name. Lance. Lance Barton. Do we know each other?" he asks again, smiling flirtatiously at me.

Eek. This guy is twice my age.

Too much *Emma* going on for me.

"Sorry," I say, waving my hand. "We don't know each other. I was talking about . . . um, someone else."

"Oh. Okay." He goes back to his book.

Shawn, meanwhile, eats his fist through all of this.

He looks at me, teary eyed. "Hallie is going to murder me for missing that one." He laughs.

"How is Hallie?"

"She's fine. Today's her day off."

I grin cheekily. "She wearing a ring yet?"

He angles his brows at me. "I could be mean and ask you the same thing."

"You could. But you won't. You're nice."

"Are you wearing a ring yet?"

I glare at him. "An extra-large coffee. To go."

"Hey, I heard about the ambush. Tough luck," he says, pulling a paper cup from the stack.

"It was terrible."

"I can imagine. Know how?"

"How?"

"Because oddly enough, it happened to me!" Shawn says, eyes big. "This girl came in here every day and started pushing this other girl on me, leaving me no choice but to date her." He finishes filling the cup and turns to the sugar to doctor it for me.

"And what do you know?" I say. "The other girl won your hard, cold heart. Lucky her." I bat my eyes sardonically.

Shawn grins. "Yeah. Well, let him know I feel for him."

My chest freezes into one big lime green popsicle. "I beg your pardon?"

Shawn pops the lid on my coffee concoction and passes it over. "Let him know I feel for him," he says slower.

"Feel for who?"

Shawn looks behind me. "Hi, can I help you?" he asks, smiling proprietarily to the man behind me.

I take my coffee and go out the door, eyes narrowed.

Him? Him who?

Shawn is not talking about Lance, of that I am certain.

They couldn't have.

I march over to the Tahoe, hitting the keyless entry button.

"Hey, stranger."

I turn, watching Ryan climb out of his beat-up truck. He grins oddly at me, and I manage a tight smile. I haven't seen him yet since I got back late last night.

"Hi."

"You don't look happy," he says slowly, approaching even more slowly. Anticipating an attack, I guess. "Did Shawn give you decaf again?"

"No."

"Oh." He stops in front of me, frowning. "How was your trip?"

"Fine." I stare up at him, eyes narrowed. "How was yours?"

He angles his head at me. "What trip?"

"You didn't get kidnapped?"

His frown deepens. "Nooo," he says, drawing the word out. "Was I supposed to be kidnapped?"

I tap my nails on the Tahoe, thinking.

Him had to refer to Ryan, didn't it?

I sigh. When it comes to my stepmom, who knows? I'm not about to ask Ryan if someone cornered him into proposing to me.

Talk about awkward.

I sigh again and smile tiredly. "Hi, Ryan," I say, this time more genuine. I grin up at him. His hair is curling under his baseball cap, and his brown eyes are twinkling at me. Stepping closer, he kisses me lightly on my cheekbone.

He shakes his head. "You're one odd duck, Laur, but I have to say I missed you over the weekend."

"What did you do?"

"I went to Nate and Lex's mostly."

I smirk. "What did you build this time?"

"Shelves for the guest room closet."

"I thought Lexi didn't want shelves in the closet."

"She changed her mind."

"You're kidding," I say, incredulous. "Lexi's nothing but hard-headed when it comes to how she keeps her house."

"Yeah, well, when it was that or installing a new kitchen sink, she was quite happy to have shelves," Ryan drawls, grinning.

I laugh. "You two are ridiculous." Nate and Ryan have built something nearly every weekend for the last year and a half.

Lexi is losing her mind.

Ryan nods to me. "So where are you going now? Back to work?"

"Yeah. I have a ten thirty appointment."

"When are you off today?"

"Three? I think."

He smiles at me. "Want to hang out this afternoon?"

"If I have to," I say, opening the driver's door. I wink at him. "I'll meet you at my house."

"Sounds good." He reaches over and pulls me close for a few minutes before disappearing into Merson's.

———❖———

I walk back into the studio a few minutes later. Hannah is nowhere in sight. Claire is halfway through a deli sandwich.

"Laurie! Come. Sit." She smiles, patting the chair beside her.

I stare at her, wide-eyed. "You live?"

She chuckles. "Hannah's more into lecturing than actual violence."

I sit.

"Would you like to talk about the trip? Tell me about your initial feelings. Were you scared? Nervous?"

"Uh . . . just confused, really."

"Ah." Claire nods, dabbing the corners of her mouth with a napkin. "Confusion. It's a hard emotion, yes?"

"Mm. You knew about the talk?" I ask.

"About Ryan? Of course I knew." She says this like she of course knows everything, including the inner workings of my brain, which are now thinking she's an extraterrestrial come to Earth to analyze the daylights out of all of us, return back to the mother planet, and then annihilate us all.

"Something wrong, Laurie?" she asks, apparently noting my freaked-out expression.

"What?" I gasp.

She smiles placatingly. "You still haven't lost the hunted look." She suddenly jerks, sets the sandwich down, and digs into her pocket, pulling out a pager that is vibrating.

She stares at it for a moment, then smiles again at me. "Excuse me, Laurie. I need to phone home."

"Phone home?" I echo.

She goes around to her cubbyhole, yanks out her purse, finds her cell phone, and goes into Studio One, shutting the door behind her.

I stand slowly and go down the hallway to Brandon's office, slamming open the door, not bothering with knocking.

Brandon looks up from his desk and sees me, and a grin spreads over his face. "Hey, Nutsy!" he yells, jumping up. "You were gone when I got in. How are you, Kid? Like the trip? What a surprise, huh?" He claps me into a hug and then steps back, grinning a self-satisfied smile. "I knew a long time ago."

"You can keep a secret now?"

"Why do you think I was avoiding you? Here. Let me look at you."

"Brandon, it was five days, not five decades." I laugh, then sober quickly. "Something really weird just happened. See, I was—"

"Someone on the phone wanting inappropriate pictures?" he interrupts. He waves his hand dismissively. "Don't worry about it. Happens all the time. Here. I'll talk to them."

"No, that's—"

He picks up his receiver and then looks at me confusedly.

"They must've hung up."

"Brandon, I—"

"Dial tone. Hey, so we need to catch up!" He slaps my shoulder.

I wince. It's starting to hurt physically to talk to Brandon. "That sounds great, but I need—"

"How about sometime next week, huh?"

"Brandon!"

He doesn't look at me but grabs his keys. "Look, I'd love to chat, but I've got a meeting."

"With who?" I demand.

"Gotta run!" he shouts, kissing the top of my head and high-tailing it out of the studio like Wile E. Coyote is chasing him.

Here's what I am: Not totally clueless.

Something fishy is going on, and after a month-long fishing trip awhile back, my ability to sense fishiness is stellar.

Chapter Thirteen

I get home a little after three. I walk in the front door, jerking my key out of the keyhole.

"Hey!" I yell. "Who stole my garage opener?"

No one answers.

Come to think of it, Darcy isn't even here doing his usual greeting. After I arrived home from my kidnapping, I explained everything to him, and he accepted my apology for the early morning. So we're pals again.

Or at least we were.

"Hey!" I shout again.

I go into the kitchen. Empty.

Dad isn't in his chair in the living room. Joan isn't organizing her files in the study. Darcy isn't camping out on my bed.

There is not a note explaining their absence.

This is not like my father.

I pick up the phone, dialing his cell.

He answers on the second ring. "Hello?"

"Dad?"

"Hi, Honey."

"Where are you?"

"Buying groceries."

"Oh. Well, why didn't you leave a note?"

"I did. It's on the refrigerator."

"Dad, I'm looking at the fridge, and I'm telling you. No note."

"Well, that's odd. Could Darcy have . . . ?"

"Darcy's not here, Dad. You didn't take him with you?"

"No," Dad says slowly. "I'm grocery shopping. He would have had to stay in the car. It's hot. That's cruel."

Now I'm getting worried. Not just about my missing puppy, but about my father's sanity. And where on earth is Joan?

My heart starts pounding. I just know a terrorist has swiped my stepmother and my dog to try and hold them for ransom until we give into their demands like in *Air Force One*.

Or worse! Maybe Claire *did* phone home and some of her alien cronies are brainwashing Joan and Darcy to get them to help with a presidential assassination!

I knew I shouldn't have watched *The Manchurian Candidate*!

My breath starts coming faster, and my fingers begin to shake.

"Honey?" Dad says.

"What?" I gasp.

"Joan probably just took the dog for a walk. Relax."

Relax? Did my father just tell me to *relax*?

I did not even know that word was in his dictionary. My father is the worrywart of the family! Why isn't he getting more anxious?

"She does this frequently, Laurie-girl."

"Who does what?"

"Joan. She takes Darcy for a walk every afternoon while you're at work. Helps her to clear her head. Now, I really need to go, Honey. We're wasting minutes."

He hangs up.

I stare at the phone in shock.

The doorbell rings, and then the front door opens. I clench the kitchen counter in fear, my fingers turning white.

"Laur? Laurie?"

I let my breath out, my energy diminishing from the sudden lack of adrenalin.

Ryan.

"In here," I call weakly.

He walks in, swinging his keys over his finger. "Hey, your front door is unlocked." He stares at me. "Are you okay?"

"You just scared me, that's all. And Joan isn't here, and Darcy's disappeared, and I'm having a nervous breakdown because they've been abducted, and meanwhile my father is blissfully grocery shopping!"

He stands blinking at me for a few minutes. "That was quite a run-on sentence," he says finally.

I cover my face, moaning. "I need caffeine!"

"And you think your heart is racing now . . ." Ryan says quietly.

"What?"

"Nothing. Let's go for a walk."

I drop my hands from my face, staring. "What did you just say?"

"Uh. Let's go for a walk?"

I gape at him. "A walk," I repeat dubiously.

He grins his little-kid smile. "Yeah. Come on, Laur, it will be fun." He reaches over and pushes my hair off my shoulder. "It's gorgeous out there. Go put on a tank top. You can start tanning."

"Dad has prohibited me from tanning."

"Okay. Then wear long sleeves and die of heat stroke." He shrugs, still grinning.

I give him a careful once-over and then climb the stairs to my room.

I change out of my work clothes (jeans and a black sequined top) and into denim shorts, a white T-shirt, and flip-flops, since I can't find my sneakers.

I come back down five minutes later, using my fingers to comb my hair into a ponytail.

Ryan grins. "Nice T-shirt. What happened to the tank?"

"It's where I keep my goldfish."

He laughs. "Nice." He dangles his keys in front of my face. "I stole your house key so we can lock up after us."

"Okay. Hey, maybe we'll run into Joan," I say brightly.

"Stop worrying."

"I'm not!"

"You are too." He pushes me out the front door and locks it behind him. "So," he says, grinning at me. "Shawn told me about your new boyfriend."

I stop, eyes wide. "He told you?" I gasp. "Who is it?"

"I believe his name was Lance."

"Oh," I say, shoulders drooping in disappointment. *Shoot.* I manage a smile. "Yeah. Sorry about that. I meant to break it to you easy."

Who did Shawn mean by him?

Ryan shakes his head. "I guess I always knew you liked older men."

"It's the Jane Austen coming out in me."

"Right, right. I figure we can still be friends though." He casually reaches for my hand and entwines his fingers with mine, smiling at me.

I smile back, my stomach turning just a tiny bit off-kilter, like it generally does when I'm around Ryan.

I think I'm allergic to him.

"So where are we walking?" I ask.

"I don't know." He looks around. "Let's go that way."

We start up the street toward the back of my house.

"You know, Nate's cousin Dave is coming into town this week," Ryan says.

I brighten immediately. "Hey! We're supposed to match him up! You promised to help!"

"Sadly, yes, I did."

"This is great!" I feel the tension melting off me, and I grin widely. "Yay! Just think! Something to do with myself!"

"Just don't know what to do with myself," Ryan sings off-key.

"Don't make fun. I didn't. I was actually thinking about teaching my dog one hundred words," I tell him seriously, quoting the title of the cute children's book.

"Oh yeah? When do you think you'll start? Tomorrow?" He grins.

"You've read the book?" I ask.

"Of course. Any emotionally secure child has read that book."

"What are we going to do with Dave?" I ask, pulling my hand free and rubbing my hands together in ecstasy.

He watches me, frowning. "Stop that. You look like a crazed miser."

"A miser of love instead of money." I sigh.

He gags.

I grin. "So what are we going to do? Who are we going to introduce him to? When will we start?"

"Well," he says slowly, "seeing as how you are the only single girl left in the singles' class . . ."

I laugh. "You forgot Hallie."

He waves his hand. "She's basically engaged."

"Ah."

"Who else hasn't said the vows?" he asks.

"What's wrong with me? You said it yourself, I'm the only one left."

He looks down at his hands for a long minute before turning and meeting my eyes. He stares at me, his eyes softening.

The Look.

I break the gaze, glancing away and taking a deep breath. There's a weird skittering feeling deep in my stomach.

Oookay.

Ryan clears his throat, back to looking at his hands. Then he takes my hand again.

We pick our way along the walking path that leads up through the hills behind our house, thinking.

"Well, Claire's not married," I stutter.

"I thought you said she was engaged," Ryan says.

"She wears a ring. I've never actually seen the guy."

"But she told you she was engaged."

"Well, sure, if you want to be technical."

He grins, and everything is back to normal. Good. I am not built to be on the receiving end of all this emotional guessing.

"What's his name?" Ryan asks.

I blink. "Who?"

"Claire's fiancé, Laurie."

"Oh! Um . . . I don't remember. So it was obviously something forgettable, meaning that the person could be as well."

He raises an eyebrow. "I don't understand your logic."

"Not many people do."

He laughs.

"Hey!" I shout. "What about—*AUGGGH*!"

My sandal catches on an upturned rock, my foot suddenly slides out of my flip-flop, and I go crashing to the ground.

Well. Almost.

Ryan catches me under my arms just as my rear end is grazing the rocky, dirt-caked path.

"Whoa!" he yells.

I start laughing, which is a bad idea considering that Ryan barely has a hold on me.

I lean my head back and grin at him upside down. He smiles but then reverts into lecture mode.

"I should've let you fall. Maybe it would've knocked some sense into your head," he grouses, lifting me up. "Sheesh, Laurie. Who wears sandals to go on a walk?"

I keep laughing, brushing myself off.

"Look, are you okay?" he asks, taking me by my shoulders.

"I'm fine, I'm fine!" I shout, pushing his hands away. "Thanks for catching me."

"You're welcome."

I stop brushing at my shorts. "Hey, where's my shoe?" I yell.

"What? You lost your shoe?" Ryan says, incredulous.

"It was right here!"

I hop on my sandaled foot around in a circle, looking. Ryan turns around and searches farther down the path.

"Uh, Laurie?" he calls a minute later. "You need to see this."

I hop over and my mouth drops open. "Darcy!" I shout. "Bad dog! Bad!"

Darcy looks up guiltily, licking his chops, the remnants of my bright red sandal between his paws.

Ryan's eyebrows climb on his forehead. "I have never seen a dog demolish something so quickly," he says, his voice ringing in amazement. "Wow. You'd think your shoe was basted in barbecue sauce by the way he attacked it."

I stop dead in the middle of the path, my jaw going slack, the rocks in the path digging into my foot, staring at my dog.

"*Number four*," I hear reverberating in my brain. "*Establish an outing . . . hiking . . . Laurie can trip! . . . Ryan can catch her . . . carry her back . . . I'll plan it . . .*"

"Laurie?" Ryan asks, touching my shoulder. "Hey? What's wrong?"

"Darcy ate my shoe," I say dully.

"That's an Old Navy flip-flop," Ryan tells me. "I'll buy you another one. They're five bucks at the most."

"No, I mean, Darcy ate my shoe!" I screech. "He's never eaten anything of mine! Heck, he's never eaten anything domestically created, period!"

I hop toward my dog and snatch a remaining shred from his paws. Darcy shudders, not looking at me. I inhale the foam and gag. Aside from smelling like really bad dog breath, I don't detect any other substance, and I'm sure not going to taste it to make sure.

I stare at Darcy and then turn to Ryan, who is looking at me like I need to be put immediately into solitary confinement.

"Hey!" I shout. "I couldn't find my sneakers!"

"What?"

"My sneakers were missing!" I rant, waving the shred of red foam in front of Ryan's nose.

He grimaces and pushes my hand away. "I have no idea what you are talking about, and to be perfectly honest, I don't want to know." He looks down at my feet and sighs. "Look, let's just go back to your house, I'll help you look for your sneakers, and we can try this whole walk thing again."

I nod, but my brain is working overtime.

I start down the path after Ryan but immediately stop, yelping. "Ouch! Ouch! Ouch!"

He turns. "What?"

I sit down on the rocky path, examining the bottom of my foot. "There's a sticker in my foot!"

"A sticker?" Ryan tries to cover a grin but fails miserably. "Like a smiley face one?"

I have to smile, regardless of how mad I am. "Funny, Ryan," I say dryly. "No! Like a pokey thing."

"Ohhhhh, a pokey thing." Ryan draws the words out.

"Ryan!"

He laughs. "Sorry, Kid. All right. Let me look." He bends down and stares at my foot. "Huh. You're right. Want me to pull it out?"

"No!" I shriek, cuddling my foot close to my chest. "Are you a doctor? Are you a nurse? Are you a first-aid graduate? No, no, no!"

"If it helps, I took health in eighth grade," he grins.

I rub my forehead. "Look. Could you just go back to the house, find me another shoe, and bring it back?"

He stares at me. "And leave you here alone?"

"Hey. Darcy's here."

"Yeah, and I saw what he just did to that sandal!"

"I don't think he'll do the same to me."

"Weren't you the one who told me your dog was going to kill you for that early morning walk?" he asks.

I look over at Darcy, who still won't meet my eyes, and grimace. "Um, yeah. But we talked! I thought he was over it!"

He lets his breath out. "I'll just carry you back, okay? Solves everything."

"No! No! No!" I shout. That would be exactly what my sadistic stepmother would want! "No!" I add for good measure.

Ryan looks surprised. "Why not?"

I sigh, groping for an excuse. "Your back!" I shout. "I wouldn't want you to hurt your back."

"Laurie, I lift boards and tools all day that are heavier than you. Just shut up and let me get you back home."

There isn't room for argument in his tone. I sigh dejectedly.

He grabs my hands, pulls me to my feet, and hefts me up.

"See?" he says, starting back down the path. "Not a big deal."

I *hmph*, but I don't protest. He carries me easily, like I weigh nothing, and I have to admit: I like feeling all small and protected. I have both arms wrapped around his neck, and I relax long enough to smile at him.

He catches my expression. "What?" he asks, grinning at me.

"Nothing." I lean over and kiss his cheek gently. "Thanks for carrying me."

"Sorry about your sandal."

Darcy slinks along behind us, tail between his legs, nose rubbing the ground.

⌖

Five minutes later we are back at my house. Ryan sets me down on the front porch and uses my key on his key ring to open the front door.

He inhales, frowning. "What's that smell?"

I sniff. "I don't smell anything."

Darcy creeps past us into the house.

Ryan follows him in, forehead creasing, motioning for me to stay on the porch. "If something's on fire, I don't want you inside."

"Ryan, if something's on fire, I don't want *you* inside!"

He disappears from view.

"How come I have to be the one cooling my heels on the porch?" I shout in after him. "And I do mean cooling! This porch is in the shade and my foot is cold!"

Ryan comes back a few minutes later, the frown more deeply etched into his face. "Get in here," he says, grabbing my hand and yanking me into the living room.

A huge fire roars in the fireplace.

I want to cry.

"Oh man!" I cover my face.

Ryan turns to look at me. "You know how this happened? Your dad and Joan aren't anywhere around here! So unless Darcy started it and then came after your sandal . . ."

He rakes his hands through his hair, looking at me confusedly.

I sigh and fall onto the couch. Time for confession.

"Joan did it," I tell him.

He sits down beside me, staring at me. "Joan did it?"

"Yeah. And if it wasn't her, it was Ruby or Hannah."

"Ruby or Hannah?"

"They planned this on the girls' trip in front of me."

"They planned this?"

"Are you going to repeat everything I say?" I ask, a small smile sneaking onto my face.

He lets out his breath, also smiling, and leans back against the couch.

"So what was the plan? For Darcy to eat your sandal?"

"That and for you to carry me home and for there to be a big fire in the fireplace, and I'll bet you next week's salary there's a big plate of strawberries in the fridge."

I groan and cover my face again. "I'm sorry, Ryan."

He pulls my hands away. "Why are you sorry? You didn't do this. I know how you do things, and you're not quite this . . ." His voice trails off as he stares at my shoeless foot and the fireplace.

"Tacky?" I suggest.

"I was going to say obvious, but tacky will work too."

I sigh and look at him.

"Actually, I have a confession too," he says guiltily. "It was Brandon's idea for me to take you on a walk today."

"Brandon!"

"Yeah. They uh . . . sort of took me out to dinner while you were gone." Ryan looks down at his hands.

"Who's they?"

"Uh, your dad, Brandon, and Nick."

"Wait. Can I guess what they said?"

"Sure."

"You need to propose to Laurie soon?"

He nods. "Yep, that was about it."

"When did Brandon tell you to take me on a walk?"

"This afternoon. He called when I was on my way over. He said that you'd protest, but the fresh air would be good for you after all that germ-infested air in the malls."

"And you believed him? Brandon doesn't even know what a germ is!"

Ryan shrugs. "It sounded like a good idea. It's a gorgeous day, and you're my favorite girl, and we're rarely alone." He grins suddenly. "Hey," he says slowly, a mischievous gleam in his eyes.

"Uh-oh. I know that look."

"Still got that coffeemaker upstairs?"

I brighten immediately. "Carl, yeah."

He smirks. "Carl? You named your coffeemaker Carl?"

"It fit him."

"And you got on me for naming my truck?"

I wave my hand. "Totally different."

"Not different!"

"Anyway, what about Carl?"

He grins again, his eyes twinkling. "You go get *Carl*. I'll go get the strawberries. We'll make coffee and prop our feet up, and when Joan and your father get back, follow my lead."

I return the grin and rub my hands together again. "I smell justice."

"Revenge anyway."

I laugh.

Chapter Fourteen

I clench my teeth together, shielding my eyes with one hand.

Ryan rolls his eyes. "It's not surgery, Laur."

"Just get it over with," I plead.

"I haven't even bent down yet, and look at you. You look ready to have a stroke, you're so tense."

"Please, just do it!" I shout.

He laughs. I feel him hold my ankle, and he lifts my foot off the ground.

With difficulty.

"Laurie, for Pete's sake," he mumbles.

Metal tweezers press against my heel.

"Ouch!" I shout.

"Hold still!"

"That hurts!"

"Aha!" he shouts, dropping my ankle. "Got it. You are sticker free. I'd kiss it and make it better, but it's your foot and it's not clean."

I sigh and uncover my eyes. "Thanks."

"You're welcome. Is the coffee done?"

"Probably. It doesn't take long to make four tiny little cups," I say, examining my foot. "Nice job."

"See? Eighth grade health comes in handy."

"I wouldn't know. I had health in seventh grade." I grin.

Ryan pulls the pitcher out of the coffeemaker and pours two cups of coffee.

"You either need smaller mugs or a bigger coffeepot," he says.

"I'm voting for the bigger coffeepot. You know, I really thought Joan had fallen off the health wagon on the trip, but she jumped right back on it when we got back."

"Still eating tofu?"

"With a side of sprouts, yes."

Ryan makes a face. "Sounds good and gross." He stirs sugar and milk into my coffee and hands it to me. "Now. Follow me to the living room, if you please, my lady." He grabs the plate of strawberries from the fridge that I knew would be there.

I stand from the kitchen chair, sipping. "Hey, you gave me coffee with the perfect amount of sugar and milk!"

He grins back at me. "What can I say? I know all things."

I bow, holding the coffee carefully. "Your wish is my command, Yoda."

We sit on the couch, the strawberries between us.

"So what exactly are we going to do?" I ask.

"I'm working on it."

"Meaning what?"

He holds his finger to his lips. "Shh. I'm thinking."

"About what?"

"Laurie!"

"Sorry, sorry."

I drink my coffee in silence.

He finally looks over. "Okay. We'll sit like this."

I stare at him. "It took you five and a half minutes to decide that?"

"I didn't finish. Joan and your dad will come in. I'll be in the middle of feeding you a strawberry—"

"Okay, whoa, time out," I interrupt, setting my coffee on the table beside me.

"What?"

"Don't take this offensively, Ry, but the thought of you feeding me anything makes me worry."

He grins. "I'll be nice."

I throw my hands up. "Ryan! Remember when I wanted to taste your ice cream cone at that Fourth of July party last year?"

His grin grows, which means yes, he does remember.

"You shoved it in my face! I had ice cream in my hair!"

"And it rained later, so you turned out fine."

"That's because we have a merciful God, Ryan."

He spreads his hands, trying to look innocent. "I promise I won't shove the strawberry at you."

"You promise."

"Laurie, if I did, it would spoil the whole plan. Chill, Girl!" He tosses a pillow at me, laughing.

I smile.

"Okay, continue with the plan," I say, picking my coffee up again.

"So there's a fire in the fireplace, we're on the couch, I'm feeding you a strawberry. Accounting for their recent activities, the odds of Joan and your dad interrupting aren't high," Ryan goes on.

I nod. "No. They'll probably stand in the kitchen and watch."

"Right. When you're done with the strawberry, I'll lean over and take your hand like this," he says, picking up my free hand.

"Then what?"

"We smile sappily at each other."

I grin. "Ryan, this is starting to affect my gag reflex."

"That's the point, Laurie."

"How is this revenge?"

"I haven't gotten to that part yet," he soothes. He squeezes my hand. "It'll be worth it to see their faces, I promise."

───◈───

They don't get home for another three hours. By now it is dark, I am starving, the strawberries look wilted, and the fire has burned down to a few orange pieces of wood that flicker in the near darkness. We haven't moved all day just in case Dad and Joan walk in.

I hear the garage door squeak and look at Ryan, grinning.

He stops midsentence about something he and Ruby did growing up and picks up a strawberry, winking at me.

"Be nice," I whisper, giggling.

I hear footsteps in the kitchen and Ryan casually scoots closer, wrapping his arm around my shoulders, holding the fruit in front of my face.

"Here, Laurie, this one looks good," he says, his voice deep. His hand is under my hair, cradling the back of my neck, his fingers lightly drawing little circles there.

I smile sweetly at him. The orange glow reflects in his brown eyes. He presses the strawberry against my lips and I bite into it.

And try very hard not to gag.

Not only is it mushy and warm from sitting out all day, it is *tart.*

My eyes start watering and I swallow the piece I'd bitten off whole. "That's enough," I say, my voice an octave higher. "They're sour!"

Ryan's mouth works hard not to burst into laughter. He puts the rest of the strawberry down and takes one of my hands instead, lightly kissing my palm.

I stare at the orange flecks shimmering in his eyes and let a slow smile work across my face.

I hear someone in the kitchen—I assume Joan—stifle a gasp.

"Did you have a good time today, Laurie?" Ryan asks deeply, slowly running his hand down my cheek.

"Mm-hmm," I sigh. "I'm glad I changed my plans. . . ." My voice trails off and my eyes widen. "Um . . ."

"Changed your plans with who?" Ryan asks, dropping his hands from my face.

"Well, it doesn't matter now. Say, want to watch a movie?"

"No. Who did you have plans with?"

I smile tensely, shifting away from him. "We bought *The Fugitive*, did I tell you that? Want to watch it?"

"Laurie," he says sternly.

I sigh and crumple into the sofa, covering my face. "Keller," I whisper.

"What did you say?" he gasps.

"Keller! I had plans with Keller!" I shout at him. "Now leave me alone."

He sits there blinking at me.

I look at him like I imagine a beagle would.

"I see," he says slowly.

"No, Ryan, it's not—"

"Look, Laurie, if you love Keller, why didn't you just say so?" he demands, standing, keeping his back to the kitchen.

"I don't love him!" I stand as well, grabbing his shirt.

He rips my hand away. "You like him!"

"But I like you too!"

"Well, sorry! I'm not the kind of guy who doesn't mind if his girlfriend goes out with other people!"

I recoil. "What do you mean?" I whisper.

"I mean we're through! Consider this our last night together!" He stomps off in the general direction of the front door.

"Wait, you don't mean that," I plead, following him, half-skipping to keep up with his stride.

He stops, whirling, and laughs evilly in my face. "Oh yes I do," he growls. He jerks the front door open and marches out.

"Wait, Ryan!" I yell, charging after him, closing the door behind me.

He stops at his truck, turns around, and scowls at me just in case anyone is watching, but his voice is tinged with laughter. "Well, Honey, I think we deserve an Oscar."

I keep my expression one of pleading and heartbreak. "Golden Globe."

"Emmy."

"All three," I say, wiping at my eyes.

He frowns harshly. "Don't look behind you, but I think that's Brandon's car."

I use my shirt sleeve now, tucking it in the corner of my eye. "Wouldn't surprise me, I guess."

"What are you going to do when you go inside?"

"Tell them it's over, I don't want to talk about it, run upstairs, and lock my door."

He rips open his truck door. "Call me from your bathroom."

"This is great." I grin at him, since my back is to the front door.

He slams the truck door with a bang that makes me jump. I run for the front door, jerk it open, and fall inside.

"Laurie! What on earth just happened?" Joan bursts.

I look up to see Ruby, Hannah, and Dad right behind her, eyes wide with shock.

I cover my face, sucking in my breath. "I don't want to talk about it!" I yell. "It's over! Just leave me alone!"

I scamper through the kitchen, up the stairs, into my room, and slam the door closed with a crash, snapping the lock in place.

I duck into the bathroom, pulling my cell phone out of my pocket.

"Ryan?"

He laughs outright now. "Did it work?"

"Are you kidding?" I say quietly. "They're probably downstairs blaming each other for this."

"You realize how mean we are, don't you?"

"We're very mean."

"You and me? We're a good pair, Lauren Holbrook."

"Yeah." I grin. "Oh, but wait," I say, getting serious. "Where does Keller fit into this pair?"

He chuckles. "I liked your touch with *The Fugitive*. We should watch that sometime."

"Yeah, right. Not any time together in the near future, thanks to you."

"I'm only taking half the blame."

I smile. "So how do we make up?"

"I don't know. I came up with the breakup; you get to create the makeup."

"Okay. You'll come over, we'll watch *Runaway Bride*, *The Prince & Me*, *Ella Enchanted*, and *While You Were Sleeping*—"

"Why is this sounding like an attempt to get me to watch these movies?" he interrupts.

"You can fall on the floor in apology, I'll sob a little, you can take me in your arms, and then all will be right."

I can hear the grin in his voice. "Well, the last part doesn't sound too bad."

"When should it happen?"

"Tomorrow?"

"Too soon. Give them a week to try and get us back together."

He laughs. "We could just let them arrange the makeup."

"Could."

"Have I mentioned how much I like you, Laurie?"

"Not anytime lately."

"I like you."

"Mm. It's mutual."

"Go sob for a little bit now."

"You go eat a frozen pizza in your dark apartment."

"Guess I'm stopping at the grocery store first."

"You don't have frozen pizza?" I ask, incredulous. "That's the staple of bachelorhood!"

"Well, not in this bachelor's hood."

I snort. "Terrible joke. Bye, Ryan."

"See ya, Kid."

I hang up, lay my cell on my desk, and throw myself on my bed, burying my face in the covers.

Darcy tries to sneak out from under the bed.

I look at him and smile.

His tail wags slowly as if to say, *I'm forgiven?*

I pat the bed, and he jumps up, lying down beside me. "You're an innocent bystander in all this," I whisper to him. "We're good."

He licks my forehead.

"Other thing is, you need to start brushing your teeth more," I mutter. "Yucky dog breath."

Someone knocks on the door.

"Laurie?" Joan calls.

"What?" I sob.

"Can we come in?"

"No! Go away! I don't want to talk to anyone!"

"What happened?"

"Leave me alone!"

I hear her sigh.

I grin at Darcy, who stares at me confusedly.

"It's all a joke," I whisper to him. He nods in understanding.

"Laurie? It's Hannah," she calls loudly, like I can't recognize her voice. "I made you a mocha!"

I raise my eyebrows. Carl is safely back in my bathroom cabinet. Where did Hannah get the coffee to make me a mocha?

"I don't want coffee!" I screech.

I never thought I'd hear those words come out of my mouth.

Apparently, neither did they. I hear mumbling outside the door.

"Want Merson's?" Ruby yells.

My mouth starts watering. When dinner is just a tart strawberry, anything sounds good, but Merson's?

I dab the drool off my bottom lip.

"No!" I shout.

Darcy raises his eyebrows at me like, *Are you stupid?*

"Well . . ." I hedge, sniffling loudly.

"Well?" Ruby jumps on it.

"I don't want to leave my room!" I cry.

"We'll bring something back! You have to eat!"

I sob loudly. "No! Just let me die! I've lost him!"

"You haven't lost him! We'll fix it!" Joan calls.

I mash my comforter into my mouth to keep from laughing out loud.

This is so much fun!

That passage I read in James earlier catches my eye again. Something about wisdom being "sincere."

Uh-oh.

I rub my cheek. *Lord, I'm sorry. We're being really mean to my family. It's uh . . . their just deserts?*

Silence.

Not good. I swallow. *Okay, You're right. We'll fix it. I promise.*

Chapter Fifteen

I wake up early Tuesday morning when something rattles on my window.

Darcy jumps off the bed, runs to the window, and starts barking deeply and ferociously.

Good guard dog.

I climb groggily out of bed and tiptoe to the window, rubbing my curling-out-of-control hair.

I lift one slat in the blinds.

Ryan stands a floor below, digging around in Joan's garden, coming out with a few pebbles. He is dressed in faded jeans, a bright red T-shirt, and a baseball cap smashing down his curly hair.

I pull up the blinds and open the window.

A rock sails past my head and lands smack in the middle of the bed. Darcy yelps and dives for cover.

"Ryan!" I hiss. "The window is open!"

He starts laughing.

"Shh!"

"Sorry," he says. He squints up at me. "Wow. You look awake."

"What time is it?" I moan.

He shrugs. "Around seven, I think."

I yawn. "Ryan, the whole throwing-rocks-at-the-window is really a clichéd action. What happened? Did you drop your cell phone in the bathtub?"

He grins up at me. "This is romantic."

"It's not romantic. It scared the living daylights out of my dog." All I can see of Darcy is his tail. I turn back to Ryan. "And what if Dad or Joan sees you?"

"Then you start sobbing, and I'll tell them I was trying to make up the old-fashioned way, but I forgot my ladder."

I grin then, rubbing my face. "Making up the old-fashioned way involves broken windows and a ladder?"

"And a justice of the peace."

"Ah." I yawn again, blocking it with my wrist. "Well. Thank you for the history lesson. Good night." I start to close the window.

"Whoa, Laurie, not so fast."

"I thought you said it was seven. In the morning."

"Well, it is."

"Mm. My doctor told me I can't wake up until nine on my days off."

He grins. "You babysat way too many kids."

"Tell me about it. 'No, but my doctor said' was the number one line all of them used."

"I'll believe that."

"Good. See you later."

"Hey! Don't you want to know why I'm here this early?" he protests as I again start shutting the window.

"It wasn't just to see my morning hair?"

He snorts. "Uh, no."

"Why are you here, Ryan?" I ask dutifully.

He spreads his hands, looking up. "I came to ask you out to breakfast."

I frown in thought. "Well, I don't know. Is a justice of the peace a stop along the way?"

"If you're a good girl, we can maybe fit that in." He grins.

"I don't know, Ryan. Dad and Joan would probably be worried if they discovered I wasn't in my room."

"They're both on a walk," he says.

"What?"

"Yep. Left about six thirty. I even gave you an extra thirty minutes to sleep!"

"Ryan, stalking is illegal in all fifty states."

He grins. "But I'm nice. I even waited so you didn't have to climb out your window."

"And pull a *Pollyanna* on you?"

"Exactly. Just go brush your teeth, throw on some jeans, and meet me outside your front door in five minutes."

I rake my hand through my hair, thinking. "What about Dad and Joan?"

"Leave a note saying you went to get coffee. I think they'll understand." He waves his arm at me. "Go!"

I close the window, go into the bathroom, change into jeans, a T-shirt, and my sneakers that mysteriously reappeared in my closet, brush my teeth, and try to tame the curls. I end up looking like a country music star gone psycho. *Au natural* is going to have to be my makeup choice. I start past the mirror and then stop.

Well. A little mascara never hurt anyone. Plus, it's good to make Ryan wait. Isn't that like the First Law of the Female Dating Code?

I open the front door a minute later. "Totally clichéd," I tell him, accepting the bouquet of roses.

"I know. Which is why I also got you these just to off-balance the flowers." He hands me a bag of Twix bars.

I give him a smile and a kiss on his fuzzy cheek. "You're the best, Ry."

"I know," he says again, cockily.

We have to take two cars so the note I wrote would be believable, and he drives straight to Callahan's, another little café in town not half as good as Merson's. But we can't go to Shawn's place. By now he would have heard about the breakup.

The restaurant is mostly empty. We sit at a little table, and a woman in a white apron comes over and gives us menus.

"What are you going to get, Laur?"

"I want to get pancakes, but I know I'll just be saddened that they can't make them as good as Shawn, soooo . . ." I stare at the menu. "I'll get eggs. It takes a very untalented person to destroy eggs."

"You do realize that eggs are healthy." Ryan grins across the table at me.

"Actually, they're high in cholesterol, so my reputation is okay."

He laughs. "Eggs sound good. Same for me. I'll order the eggs, you order the coffee."

"Two coffees with room for lots of milk, not cream, and about sixteen of these little sugar packets." I yawn, flicking the box in the middle of the table, cupping my face in my hand.

"*One* coffee like that. I want mine black."

"I've never understood why all coffee places can't do the sugar and milk like Shawn does."

"What do you call it?"

"The doctor's station."

"Right." He smiles and rubs my hand that's playing with the sugar packets. "So are you glad I came?"

"Are you fishing for a compliment?"

"Yep."

I laugh. "Yes, I'm glad you came. Even though you just about killed me with that rock through my window."

"It was a *pebble*. You make it sound like I was heaving boulders at you."

"David killed Goliath with just a tiny pebble. Hit him smack in the forehead, just like you would have done to me if you had better aim."

"Laurie, I've read the story. And I have to say that I think God's power was working in that particular battle scene."

I gasp. "You don't think David had good aim?"

Ryan rolls his eyes, and the white-aproned waitress reappears.

"Know what you want?" she asks.

"Two orders of scrambled eggs," Ryan says.

"And two coffees. One with room for *milk*. And can I have more sugar packets please?"

She eyes the half-full box on the table and frowns. "More sugar?"

"Please."

Her frown deepens. "Be right back."

I watch her go. "Not as good service as Merson's either."

"You're just prejudiced."

"No, I'm not," I protest. "Shawn's place has just been blessed, that's all."

Ryan chuckles.

"So why are you so happy this morning?" I ask, stretching.

He smirks. "What are you talking about?"

"You haven't stopped smiling yet."

He rubs his mouth as if he were checking the accuracy of my words. "Sure, I have."

"No, you haven't. What happened? Did you bump into Brad Pitt or something?"

His forehead creases. "Why would that make me smile?"

"Because you could then hold it over my head."

He thinks about it and then nods. "Okay, yep, that would make me smile."

"So? Where did you bump into him?" I ask excitedly.

"I didn't meet Brad Pitt, Laurie."

"Oh man!"

"Get a life." He grins.

"Seriously, Ryan, why are you so smiley?"

"I'm having breakfast with the most beautiful woman in the world. Why else?"

I roll my eyes, but I feel myself blushing. "Thank you for the compliment, but I don't believe you. Look at me."

"I have been," he says cheekily.

"Okay. You can be quiet now." I cover my hot face with my hands and look away.

He laughs.

The waitress brings our coffee out. "One black?"

"Here," Ryan says, raising his hand like a third grader.

I grin. He shoots me a warning glance.

"One with cream?"

I sigh. "Here," I say dully. She sets the teeny cup in front of me, and my eyes start watering from the overwhelming half-and-half scent.

Milk. What is so hard about putting in *milk* instead of cream?

"Um, I asked for milk?" I say politely.

She looks at me. "I know."

"In the coffee." I point. "I asked for milk in the coffee."

She nods. "It's in there."

"This smells like half-and-half."

"Right. Half milk, half cream. So I put in two. Now there's a full serving of milk in there." She sets down two extra sugar packets and leaves.

I stare at the coffee and then at the waitress's back as she goes into the kitchen.

Ryan has his fist over his mouth, and his eyes are squinched up and twinkling in a full-fledged silent laugh.

I look at him, open-mouthed. "I'm scared to drink this," I say slowly.

He loses it. His shoulders start shaking and he leans forward, his face reddening as he laughs. "Oh, Laurie, you should have seen your face!"

I lift the little cup and stare at it. The thing can't be bigger than a mosquito and weighs about as much.

"And this is not a coffee *cup*," I state, setting it back down.

"What is it?"

"It's a coffee teaspoon. Two containers of half-and-half? Look at this! It's not even tan!"

Ryan starts laughing again. "Want mine?"

I reach over and take a sip from his thimble-sized cup and gag. "This stuff is nasty!" I exclaim, choking.

"Shh," Ryan says, taking his cup back. "Keep it down, Laur.

Not everyone here has been spoiled with good coffee their entire lives."

I lower my voice but keep talking. "You mean you can develop a taste for that pond scum?"

"Laurie!"

"Sorry!" I hiss. "Ryan, can we please go to Shawn's? Please? We can go in separately and then eat together somewhere else. *Please?*" I clasp my hands in front of me and lean across the table, blinking big, sad eyes at him.

He chuckles. "Okay. To be honest, I am a little worried about what they're doing to the eggs if that's what they do to your coffee."

"Thank you, thank you, thank you!"

He waves to the waitress. "Excuse me, ma'am? We've actually got to run." He hands her six bucks for the meal.

"Want change?" she asks.

"Keep it," I tell her. "Use it to buy higher quality coffee filters."

Ryan kicks my shin.

"Ouch," I tell him.

He smiles placatingly at the waitress. "She just woke up. She's always cranky this early in the morning."

"Mm," the waitress huffs.

Ryan hustles me out the door and shakes his head. "You need a lesson in manners."

"Ryan, it's not even eight o'clock yet." I drop my head into my hands. "I promise I'll be nice when I get caffeine."

He looks at me and smiles yet again. "Follow me to Shawn's."

I wrap my arms around his neck. "God bless you."

"You're such an oxymoron, Laurie. To calm down, you drink coffee. Most people get wired up from caffeine." He hugs me around my waist.

I pull back a little bit and meet his eyes. "I'd hate to be predictable."

"I wouldn't worry." He grins, pulling me in tightly.

I suddenly realize how close we are standing. His hands are on my waist and there is a distinctive spark in his eyes. I feel him sigh even before I hear it.

Four hundred and thirteen bouncy balls dump into my stomach.

I drop my hands from his neck.

"Laurie," Ryan says gently, keeping his eyes on mine. He brings one rough hand up and lightly traces my face.

I jump back like he set a waffle iron on my cheek.

"What time is it?" I gasp.

He stares at me confusedly then looks at his watch. "Almost eight."

"We should go!" I shriek, breathing hard. "Shawn makes a fresh pot of coffee every hour! We want to get the fresh stuff!"

He angles his head and rubs my shoulder. "Hey, are you okay?"

"Yes!" I squeak. "I'll . . . I'll follow you."

I dive for the Tahoe and hop in the driver's seat. Ryan watches me curiously but climbs in his truck.

I wait for him to crank his engine, resting my forehead on the steering wheel, forcing myself to take long, deep breaths.

What on earth is wrong with me?

Could I have reacted any more ridiculously? *Probably not.*

I slap my leg angrily. *Good grief, Laurie!*

I shift into reverse to follow Ryan out of the parking lot.

This always looks so easy in the movies.

Well, news flash, Lauren Emma Holbrook! This isn't the movies!

I turn right, tailing Ryan's rust-bathed Chevy, sighing, sinking lower into the driver's seat.

I'm not sure whether it was the lectures from the girls' trip, God revealing something, the gallons of coffee he's brought me, or just him. . . .

Oh, Lord. What's going on?

Here's what's happening: I think . . . I think I love Ryan Palmer.

Chapter Sixteen

I walk into my house a little after nine thirty after sharing breakfast with Ryan at the park by the elementary school.

Joan sits at the kitchen table, hands folded, expression tragic.

"Laurie, I am so sorry!" she bursts when I come through the doorway.

I toss my keys on the table, sighing, sliding into the chair beside her. "It's not your fault, Joan," I say dully, cradling my head in my hands.

"I feel terrible!"

I chattered nonstop through breakfast, staying at least a foot away from Ryan the entire time and leaving with a friendly but entirely unromantic wave.

"I feel terrible too," I tell Joan. *Terrible* might be the wrong word. Try *unnerved*. Beyond that, there's the dozen guilt guppies swimming around in my stomach.

"We have to do something, Laurie. You and Ryan belong together. I know it!"

I force my lips together in a sad smile and look up at Joan. "It's no use," I say. "He never wants to see me again."

"He only thinks that, Honey!" Joan grabs my hand. "We need to make him rethink that."

"Yeah?" I say tiredly. "How?"

She looks at me for a long minute. "You should run into him again. And soon! He loves you; I know it!"

I blink at that. "No, he . . ." My voice trails off. "I don't think he . . ." I pull my hand away and rub my face. "Wouldn't that be dumb?" I mutter finally.

"Why?" Joan wails. "You two were created by God for each other! We have to get him back, Laurie. Listen. I have a plan."

She leans forward and starts talking, but I can't concentrate on what she is saying for the life of me.

My head pounds, and my hands are trembling. If this is love, then I'm echoing that eighties song: Love stinks.

Of course, this could have something to do with the three extra-large coffees I ordered, telling Shawn they were for me, Claire, and Hannah and then drinking all three of them at breakfast.

The lies just keep stacking up.

Joan finishes and leans back, smiling in relief. "Don't you think that will work?"

"Mm-hmm."

"Great! We'll do it tomorrow. I'll call Hannah right now!"

She bounces up from the table and runs for the phone.

I stand and climb the stairs to my room. Darcy is sacked out on my bed. He lifts one eyelid when I open the door, sees it is me, and promptly goes back to sleep.

"Don't go overboard with the welcome, Darce."

His tail thumps once as I fall down on the bed next to him and bury my face in the soft scruff around his neck.

"Sometimes I'm glad you can't talk."

He licks my ear.

Joan knocks on the open door. "So it's all set, Laurie. Hannah's on her way over. Ruby would've come, but the baby's sleeping."

"Come where?" I ask, rolling over and accidentally squishing Darcy's nose. "Sorry, Pal."

He sighs.

Joan frowns at my dog. "Sometimes he's more human than he should be." She looks back at me. "Shopping, Laurie! Remember? The plan?"

"Oh yeah." I nod. *No, I do not remember the plan.*

Honestly, more shopping? Didn't we just get home from a long weekend at three different malls?

"And Lexi's coming."

Oh no.

My older sister might be the most gullible person in the civilized world, but she can see through me like I'm Saran Wrap.

"Lexi?" I squeak.

Joan nods, holding the phone. "She's worried about you, Honey. And plus, she has a great sense of style."

"I guess I can't argue with that."

"No. So do whatever you need to do to get ready to go because they'll be here any minute."

"Okay," I mumble.

Joan leaves.

I look at Darcy. "Think I need to put on some makeup?"

He gives me a look that says, *Uh, yeah!*

I slide off the bed, add some eyeliner, and go downstairs. Lexi is in the process of pouring a big mug of Soyee.

I keep my mouth closed and creep back up two steps, watching her add a little sugar and take a big swallow.

She hacks and starts choking, setting the cup down, barely making the counter.

I step into the kitchen, grinning.

She wipes tears away. "Something's wrong with the coffee-maker, Baby," she whispers.

"The coffeemaker's fine, Lex."

She fills a monster-sized plastic cup from Smith Valley Barbecue with water and drains the whole thing.

"What is that stuff?" She gags, backhanding her tongue. "It's not washing out of my mouth!"

"Soyee. Naturally caffeine free," I say, like one of those sales-people on HSN.

"Soyee?"

"Oh, good, you're here, Lexi," Joan says, coming in from her bedroom. She looks at me. "Are you ready, Laurie?"

"Is Hannah here?" I ask.

"I just saw her pull up. Let's go, girls."

I follow meekly. Lexi stumbles after me, wiping her tongue on her shirt sleeve.

That's Lexi for you.

She comes up behind me and wraps her arms around my shoulders. "Don't worry about what happened with Ryan, Sweetheart," she whispers in my ear. "He loves you too much to let you go that easily. Though I am a little curious about this Keller person." She turns me around. "What exactly were the plans you had with him?"

Lauren, the female arachnid, viciously spins her web of dripping deceit.

"Uh, we were just going to get coffee," I fib.

Lexi frowns at me.

"Don't look at me like that, Lex," I moan. "He asked me and . . . well, you know how I am about using the word *no*."

"Baby! How could you do that to Ryan?"

"It's not like I meant to! And I was going to see if he wanted to come with us!"

Who am I? I'm Spider-Woman.

I will owe quite the apology. My fingernails are hurting from the guilt.

She rolls her eyes. "Oh, that would be good. Knight in Shining Armor and Count Dracula both having coffee with my sister."

I frown at her description. "You've never met Keller, have you?"

"No and I don't want to." She pushes me into the garage after Joan. "What does he look like?" she asks after a pause.

"Do you remember what Nick looks like in *The Princess Diaries 2*?"

She gasps. "Are you kidding? Oh my lands, that guy is cute!"

"Well, add a great voice, a guitar, and two inches in height. . . ."

Lexi's eyes get big. "Wow," she says. "Can I start coming to Bible study?"

"May I remind you that you're married?"

"And that we're trying to keep Laurie with Ryan?" Joan says, sounding slightly ticked at my sister.

I hide a grin.

Hannah comes into the garage, shoving her keys in her purse. "I parked in front of the house, Joan, but let me know if I need to back up some."

Joan goes to look. Hannah leans over and kisses my forehead. "It'll be okay, Laurie," she says gently.

I smile sadly at her.

"You're parked fine, Hannah," Joan says.

We climb in my stepmother's car. As the local mourner, I get to sit shotgun.

"So black is what I heard," Lexi says to Joan. "Right?"

"Right. Think a Chanel knockoff."

"The perfume?" I ask innocently.

"The dress," Hannah says, rolling her eyes.

"Whoa, whoa, whoa," I start, waving my hands as Joan pulls out of the driveway. "A dress?" I shriek. "I have to wear a dress?"

"Yep." Lexi grins.

"I haven't worn a dress since . . . since . . ." My mind goes blank.

Joan remembers. "Since dinner out, Laurie."

I catch my hands around my throat. "Another black dress?"

"Correction," Lexi taunts. "A *little* black dress."

"But why?" I plead.

"Because it's a surefire way to win Ryan back," Joan says. "The boy hasn't ever seen you in anything fancy, save for bridesmaid dresses."

"Which were pretty fancy!" I argue.

"He needs to see that you'll dress up occasionally for him," Hannah says.

"But I do! I wear nice shirts when he's around!"

Lexi laughs. "Ah, for the days when a nice shirt was dressing up for my husband." She sighs.

"Ryan is not my husband!"

"I'm thinking something good and lacy," Hannah muses.

"Lacy?"

"Definitely sleeveless," Lexi joins her.

"Oh, definitely. Laurie has pretty shoulders," Joan says.

"And a nice waist. Look for an empire cut waist," Lexi says.

"With beads!" Hannah chimes.

"Beads?!"

"And it should be knee-length," Joan says.

"Sure. She's got nice calves."

"All right, that's it," I burst. "I feel like I'm being auctioned off! Just cut it out, all of you. I will find a nice shirt."

All three of them start in at once.

"A shirt? Laurie, for heaven's sake!" Joan says.

"A dress, Laurie, it has to be a dress," Hannah says.

"You want to win my pal Ryan back? It's got to be a dress, Kid," Lexi says.

I shut my eyes tightly and slink down in the seat, listening to them decide what neckline would look best with my face shape and bust size.

I think I love Ryan.

Is it possible to love someone and want to kill him at the same time?

———— ❖ ————

I come out of the dressing room for the sixty-seventh time three hours later. Joan, Hannah, and Lexi all stand in a half circle outside the fitting rooms, arms crossed, eyes narrowed.

"Ta-da," I say without enthusiasm.

"Mm." Lexi frowns. "Too low cut. We're going for classy, not trampy."

"Try the satiny one, Laur," Hannah says.

Joan nods. "Boy, that black is slimming. Do they have one

in my size?"

I turn and go back into the dimly lit dressing room and sort through the fifteen or so dresses hanging on the hooks around the square room and sigh.

Satiny . . . satiny . . .

I find the dress underneath two chiffon, full-skirted disasters-in-the-making for my hips.

Tugging off the other dress, I climb into the satin dress and give myself a cursory glance in the mirror before heading to the door.

Hold on.

I go back to the mirror, feeling my eyebrows arc.

The dress is a V-neck, sleeveless, above the knee, with a fluttery hemline, and unlike the other twenty-something dresses I have already tried on, this one doesn't make me feel itchy anywhere.

Plus, it does something very nice with my hips.

I walk out, and Lexi, Hannah, and Joan all start nodding.

"Perfect!" Lexi exclaims loudly. "I love it!"

"That's the one!" Hannah says, raising a fist in triumph.

Joan smiles at me. "You look perfectly sweet, Laurie."

"Thank you," I say, trying to curtsy.

There's a reason Grace is not my middle name.

I half-fall, catching myself on the wall and nearly spearing my side with the rack for clothes that didn't fit. I double over laughing.

Lexi shakes her head. "I'm thinking the heels might be a problem, girls," she says to Hannah and Joan.

"Heels?" I stand upright. "Um, I can't walk barefooted."

Hannah grins evilly. "Ha! What about something strappy with a stiletto heel?"

"Oo!" Lexi coos. "In silver!"

"With chandelier earrings," Joan says.

"Also in silver!" Lexi adds.

"And one of those dainty dangling bracelets," Hannah says, staring at my wrist.

"And a silver clutch purse," Joan says.

"And a tattoo that says *Ryan*," I squeal, jumping up and down.

Lexi gasps, clasping her hands at her heart. "In silver!" She grins.

"And a big silver rose in my hair," I tell her, eyes big.

She studies my head and nods. "Perfect!" She sobers and adds, "With a haircut."

"Ryan likes my hair long," I say.

"What about silver sunglasses?" she suggests.

"No, no, no," I tell her dramatically, holding my hands up. "What do you think about this?" I lower my voice. "Silver *contacts*."

"Bingo!" Lexi yells.

Joan and Hannah exchange a look. "Sometimes I wonder how their father managed to raise these two together," Joan tells Hannah.

"I'm guessing a lot of prayer," Hannah responds.

"Where on earth am I going to go in this dress?" I ask seriously. "Don't get me wrong, it's beautiful, but I already have a black dress."

"A *long* black dress," Joan says.

"You can go out to dinner, Laurie," Hannah says.

"Yeah, but where? Unlike Phoenix, this town has one nice restaurant. Vizzini's. I go there once a week. In jeans."

"You lie," Lexi says. "What about The Golden Sea? It's a beautiful restaurant! And you have to wear a dress like that to get in!"

I sigh, fingering the dress.

"Come on," Joan says. "Go change. We'll buy the dress, get some accessories, and set up an appointment for you to get your hair trimmed."

"Sheesh! It's not that bad!"

"Laurie? Yes it is," Hannah says, no room for argument in her tone. "Go change."

I go into the dressing room, come out in my jeans, holding the dress, and follow the Mall Monsters to the jewelry counter, where they find nice, albeit cheap, earrings and a bracelet.

I nearly break my ankle trying on the shoes they buy, but they tell me all I have to do is practice, practice, practice.

We don't get back home until four o'clock.

"Okay, so I'll have Laurie ready by five tomorrow night," Joan tells Lexi and Hannah as they unload our purchases.

"Excuse me? How are we going to get Ryan dressed as nice as I am? You forget he's a construction worker," I say.

"Fear not." Lexi grins.

"And what about Bible study? It's tomorrow night. I am not going to Bible study dressed like this!"

"Look, will you relax?" Hannah bursts.

"We've taken care of it, Laurie. Don't worry," Joan says soothingly.

Don't worry.

Yeah, right.

Chapter Seventeen

(Scene: Daylight, five o'clock Wednesday. The house, decked out with tiny white Christmas lights, glows in the warm July evening. Our heroine, Lauren Emma Holbrook, gently swings back and forth on a hand-hewn wooden plank swing set high in the ancient ash tree, dressed to kill in a long, fluttery, white lace dress)

LAUREN: *(humming)* Someday my prince will come. . . .
    (Suddenly, a footstep is heard upon a twig)
LAUREN: *(stilling)* Harken! Who goeth?
RYAN: *(taking foot off broken twig)* It is I! Your prince!
LAUREN: *(frowning)* But where is your horse? Where is your sword? Where is your richly ornate clothing? Answer me at once, sir!
RYAN: *(confused)* I thought you liked me as a construction worker.
LAUREN: *(shakes head slowly)* I do not. Think of how dangerous your occupation is! What if you were killed?

RYAN: No more dangerous than riding a horse! Laurie, my love, please!

(A horse's cantering is heard)

LAUREN: *(brightening)* Harken! Horse steps! It is he! My prince!

RYAN: But I am your prince!

(A glistening white horse appears in front of the ash tree. Lauren's pulse is visible on her slim throat, her excitement spilling from her rapturous eyes. From the horse climbs a richly dressed prince. Keller Stone)

KELLER: *(in an English-accented voice)* Lauren Holbrook, I have finally come.

LAUREN: *(gasping, catching hands in front of her)* My prince!

RYAN: But he's not your prince!

KELLER: *(stepping forward, gently pulling Lauren from the hand-hewn wooden plank swing set high in the ancient ash tree)* Come, my love, let us ride away to Happily Ever After.

LAUREN: *(sighing)* Yes, of course!

(Keller leans down and places a kiss on Lauren's lips and leads her by her right hand to the panting horse. Ryan grabs her left hand and yanks)

RYAN: Laurie! What are you doing?

LAUREN: I'm going with my prince!

RYAN: With Keller? *(laughs mockingly)* Keller Stone? He's your prince? You'll have to explain the punch line of every joke to him!

LAUREN: It doesn't matter! Look at him! He's beautiful and plays the guitar and sings like that blind Italian opera singer! In short, he's perfect!

RYAN: *(in amazement)* You want to live with perfection?

LAUREN: *(stubbornly)* I think I could stand it.

RYAN: You want to wake up next to perfection? You want to make him a perfect breakfast every morning and listen to his perfect voice twenty-four hours a day? All the while knowing that you can't play the guitar and your singing isn't Italian opera material?

LAUREN: Well . . .

RYAN: You don't! You know you don't! You're happy with imperfection! With me! *(Pulls her closer to him)*

KELLER: *(jerking her back)* What are you listening to him for? I am the one you've been waiting for! This stuff about wanting imperfection is nonsense! Lauren? Lauren, are you listening to me?

———— ❖ ————

"Laurie?"

I blink and shake my head, staring at Lexi. "Huh?"

Lexi sighs. "Turn around, Baby, I need to see the back of your hair."

I turn, hands perpendicular to my sides, feeling like that little girl in *The Secret Garden*. Cleaned, dressed, and powdered by my own three personal servants.

"Can I please get coffee now?" I ask.

"No," Hannah says to me. "Maybe we should try pulling just the sides of her hair up," she says to Joan and Lexi.

Okay, so servant is stretching it.

I stare at myself in the mirror, frowning. The hairstylist, a chatty little blonde wearing a shirt that was not much more than a bra, did a decent job on my split ends, but not such a decent job on the actual styling.

Hannah fingers the back of my hair. "It just looks weird up."

"Probably because Laurie never wears it like that," Joan says. "Down and scattered is a good description."

"Hey," I protest. "The bedhead look is in! I take good care of my hair!"

"I know!" Hannah says, the three of them completely ignoring me. "Let's put curlers in it and go with a wavy-curly style like Kelly Clarkson!"

Lexi and Joan express praise for that suggestion and six hands start winding hot metal rods into my hair.

"Good grief, how many people does it take to help me get ready for a date?" I grouse, winking uncontrollably as Joan tosses a section of hair in my eyes.

"We're all in this together!" Lexi starts singing from *High School Musical*.

"Oh my gosh, I love Troy." Hannah sighs.

"You're married," I tell her.

I sneak a look at the clock. Four forty-five.

The curlers will never be cool in time.

"Hey! Let's smear one of those avocado masks on my face and get my bathrobe and then I could really impress him!" I say.

Hannah looks back at the clock. "Oo, Laurie's right." She frowns. "Okay. We need to delegate tasks here. Lexi, you finish with the curlers—"

"Aye, aye." My sister grins.

"I can do her makeup," Hannah says.

Joan nods. "I'll get her dress, shoes, and purse laid out."

Exactly fifteen minutes later, the doorbell rings.

"I still can't figure out how you got him to come," I say to Hannah and Lexi, slinking into the satin dress while Joan runs downstairs to let him in.

"It's very simple, actually." Lexi smirks, pulling another curler out of my hair. "Ryan loves me."

I grin.

She leans down close to my ear. "Plus, I figure if you and Ryan are together, I'll just knock off my husband and go for Keller, who would automatically be fair game."

"You know, your ulterior motives are so innocent. That sounds just like something Shirley Temple would do." I grin.

Hannah comes at me with a tube of lip gloss, and Lexi starts attacking my hair with hairspray.

"Okay, shoes on, and you're done," Hannah says.

"Finally." I choke on the sticky particles floating around the room.

Hannah kisses my cheek. "We'll be praying for you, Honey," she says.

Lexi hugs me, careful not to touch my hair. "You look beautiful."

Here's how I'm feeling right now: Guilty, guilty, GUILTY!

I manage a nervous smile, sure that if lightning doesn't strike me and Ryan tonight, we will probably get electrocuted by a runaway subway car or something.

I hear Ryan standing in the entry, talking quietly with Joan. Gripping the banister with a Darth Vader clench, I carefully make my way down the stairs in the shoes I still don't know how to walk in.

I feel my eyebrows go up when I see Ryan. Suit, nice tie, and are those possibly loafers on his feet?

He stares at me, not smiling. "Laurie," he says unemotionally. His voice is flat, but his eyes are sparkling.

"Ryan," I mutter, glaring at him.

Joan smiles overcheerfully, hands clasped. "Well, now, you two have a wonderful night, okay?"

"Okay," we say dully.

I step onto the wood-floored entryway and grab Joan's shoulder to keep from pitching to the floor.

"Bye now!" she trills, shoving us out the door.

I do mean shoving.

I lose my footing the minute the door hits my rear end and feel myself falling.

"Wh . . . whoa!" I scream.

Ryan grabs me around my stomach, and if I'd been chewing gum, he would have had to do the Heimlich.

He starts laughing. "What is with the shoes, Laur?"

"I think . . ." I gasp, righting myself. "I think Joan, Hannah, and Lexi are subtly trying to kill me."

He helps me stumble to Joan's little BMW in the driveway.

"She says we should take her car." He grins, unlocking the doors. "Something about you not being able to get into a truck in that dress."

I look down, nodding. "Yep. Very probable."

"By the way," he says, smiling, "I like the dress."

"I like your suit. Nice tie."

"Thank you."

I take off my shoes and fall into the passenger's seat.

"You do realize that The Golden Sea requires those shoes, right?"

"Shut up, Ryan."

He slides into the driver's seat, laughing.

"So when are we going to reveal our deceit?" I ask.

He looks over at me as he pulls out of the driveway. "You been watching soap operas lately?"

"No. Why?"

"I don't know. That last comment sounded really soap opera-ish."

"How would you know? Have you been watching them lately?"

"Sometimes they show previews of them during baseball games."

"Oh, that's a novel idea," I say, rolling my eyes.

"Yeah. I'm thinking the guy in charge of that idea was a few pieces short of a puzzle." He makes a right. "And to answer your question, I'm thinking a long time from now. I repented. What about you?"

"Well, yeah, but still." I raise my eyebrows at him. "You're not paying for this dinner are you?"

"Nope. Joan and your dad are."

"So tell me, oh Estranged One. How did they get you to come?"

He grins at me and pulls two tickets from his pocket. I take them.

"Colorado Rockies tickets?"

"Two of them," he says, holding up his fingers like a six-year-old.

"Ryan, we don't live in Denver."

"Forty-five minutes and we're there."

"We're? As in you and me?"

"As in." He grins.

"And that's forty-five minutes when you're in an ambulance, Ry."

He grins wider. "And it's pro baseball, Kid."

I settle back in the seat, watching the cars beside us. Ryan presses the gas pedal down, and his eyebrows go up.

"What? Shocked because the whole contraption didn't get left in the street behind us?" I ask.

"Pretty smooth." He whistles.

"How long are we playing this pretending thing?"

He stops at a red light and looks at me. "We've gotten free clothes, two Rockies tickets, a meal at the most expensive restaurant in town, and you obviously got a haircut, Laur."

"And my fingers are pruney from swimming in the guilt!" I shout.

He laughs. "If it's storming when we're driving home, I'm camping out at the Marriott. Getting struck by lightning seems a fairly likely occurrence." He pats my hand. "We'll tell them tonight. Okay?"

"Promise?"

"I promise. I'm not keen on this whole lying thing either, Laur."

He parks at the restaurant a few minutes later and comes around and opens my door. A tux-encased waiter stands at the door, holding a clipboard.

"Name, please."

"Ryan Palmer."

He checks the list and nods once. "Right this way, please."

We are seated at almost the same table we were at when we watched Nick and Ruby get engaged. Left side of the restaurant, right behind the wall of fish tanks.

"Good evening, I'm Gloria. Our specials this evening are broiled lobster, grilled salmon, or coconut shrimp. What beverages can I get you?"

Ryan squints at the waitress. "Could I get iced tea?"

"Absolutely. We have raspberry, strawberry, peach, or mango."

"What about just plain?"

"We don't have that."

"Okay," he says slowly. "Coke then."

"Is Pepsi okay?"

"Um, actually, I'll have the peach tea instead."

She looks at me.

"Dr. Pepper."

"We don't have that."

"Mr. Pibb?"

She shakes her head. "Sorry."

I lay my elbows on the table. "Maybe it would be easier if you'd tell me what you have."

"Nonalcoholic?"

"Yes."

"Pepsi, Mountain Dew, Diet Pepsi, or iced tea."

Blegh.

"I'll have water," I tell her.

"I'll give you a few minutes to look over the menu."

She leaves.

Ryan watches her go, smirking. "Most expensive restaurant in town and they have four drink choices. And I hate Pepsi."

"I'm sure most people get wine."

"Or whine because there's just wine."

"Pitiful joke."

"I couldn't resist."

I shake my head. "See, my family is all concerned that I've lost you forever. Little do they realize that if I hadn't lost you, I'd have to listen to those little one-liners the rest of my life."

"Ah, to be so lucky." He grins.

The waitress comes back and sets Ryan's tea in front of him. "Let me know if I can add more peach syrup," she says sweetly.

"Wait a second," he says, holding up his hand. "You added peach syrup to this?"

"Yes," she says, setting my water in front of me.

"So what was it before you added syrup?"

"Iced tea."

"Plain?"

She angles her head at him. "I guess so. Yeah." She smiles that polite waitress smile at us and spreads her hands. "Have you decided what you want?"

"Coconut shrimp," I say.

"Okay. Comes with a side of either asparagus spears or baked zucchini."

I sigh. "Um. Zucchini."

"And for you, sir?"

"Prime rib."

"Okay. Comes with a baked potato or a salad of summer squash."

"Potato."

She nods and leaves.

Ryan takes a sip of his tea. "Mm," he says, his face creasing in a grimace. "This is like drinking just the syrup."

"Try stirring it."

He does, sips more, and grimaces harder. "Worse. Much worse."

"I'm thinking this place is slipping from their five-star rating."

He rubs his forehead. "Rockies tickets are worth this."

The waitress reappears. "Sir? We're out of potatoes. I can offer you a side of summer squash or potato soup."

He covers his face.

I smile nicely at the waitress. "That means he wants the soup. Thanks."

Chapter Eighteen

Ruby opens the door before we have a chance to knock.

"Hey, guys. Here," she says, unloading Adrienne into Ryan's arms. "I have to go make coffee."

Ryan watches her go. "Don't worry, I can hold the baby," he says dryly.

We'd gone back to my house and changed quickly, and it is now five minutes until Bible study is supposed to start. Definition: Bible study won't start for another thirty.

Ryan follows his sister into the kitchen, and I set down Ryan's and my Bibles on the sofa.

Someone touches my upper arm. "Hey, Laurie, how are you?" Keller asks.

"I'm good." I smile. "How are you?"

"Well. I like your hair like that. Can I get you something to drink?"

"Coffee sounds great, but I don't think Ruby's finished making it."

"I know that Holly brought cookies."

"Oo!" I squeal. "Her white chocolate chip peanut butter cookies?"

Here's the thing: I *hate* white chocolate chips. I have no idea how they manufacture white chocolate, but it seems like a worthless waste of white food coloring. Just use regular chocolate for gracious' sake!

Holly's cookies are the only white chocolate cookies I'll eat.

Keller laughs at my excitement. "Actually, Laur, I think she brought just plain chocolate chip cookies this time."

I nod. "Sounds good anyway."

"I'll be right back then."

He squeezes my arm again, smiles, and leaves.

Hannah walks over right then. "Lauren Emma Holbrook, how could you?"

"How could I what?" I protest.

"You just made up with Ryan, and now you're talking to him?"

"To who?"

"Keller!"

"What am I supposed to do? Ignore him completely?"

"Yes!" she shrieks.

Nick comes by then, holding the music stand he uses to set up his notes. He looks at Hannah thoughtfully. "Amos 5:13," he says slowly.

"What?" Hannah asks.

"'Therefore the prudent man keeps *quiet*,'" he says, raising his eyebrows on the last word.

Hannah tips her head, staring at him. "The prudent *man*, Nick. Nothing is said about the quiet woman."

"First Peter 3:4," Nick starts.

Hannah throws her hands up. "All right, all right!"

Keller comes back then, holding two napkin-shrouded blobs. "Hi, Hannah. I saw you walk over and got you a cookie too."

He hands us our cookies and Hannah smiles at him politely. "Thanks, Keller."

"Thank you very much," I say, crumbs landing on my chin. "Oops."

He grins at me. "You might need a couple of napkins."

"Coordination doesn't run in my family." I smile at him. "These are great cookies."

"Holly is a great chef."

"Luke's a lucky guy."

"She's pregnant, you know."

I almost spit out the cookie. "What?"

Keller nods proudly. "I just heard from Lacy, and she's Holly's best friend. Five weeks along, whatever that means."

Hannah sends me a closed-mouth, eyebrows-up expression that says, *And yet another one.*

"That's great," I say.

Keller leans forward and squeezes my shoulder. "Save the bright stuff for Holly, Laur." He winks at me and goes back into the kitchen.

Hannah swallows. "It would be a lot easier to hate him if he weren't so darn nice," she mutters, crunching her empty napkin into a ball.

"Holly is my age!" I whine.

"I know."

"She gets married, and now she's pregnant?"

Hannah sighs and gives me a look. "Well, that's generally the proper order, Laurie."

Ryan comes over and hands Adrienne to me. "She keeps swiping for my cookie. Hold her for a second?"

I cuddle the baby close. "I can hold her for longer."

"No, actually, you can't." He takes a bite and then brightens. "Hey, did you hear about Holly?"

"Uh-huh," I say, kissing Adrienne's hair.

"We're feeling a little green around the gills, Ry," Hannah says.

"Ah." Ryan grins. "You want a baby now?"

Hannah sighs, smiling. "I want ten kids now."

"I want this baby," I declare. "I'm taking her home with me. She's officially mine. Adrienne Holbrook has a ring to it."

Holly walks over, all smiles, eyes shining, her blonde hair shimmering. "Laurie, Hannah, I haven't gotten a chance to tell you!" She presses her hands together, face glowing. "I'm pregnant!"

"Oh, Holly, I'm so happy for you!" I grin. I am happy for her. Honestly. I've known Holly since we were in kindergarten. I *have* to be happy for her.

Nick calls everyone into the room and starts his opening chat. "Tonight, I'm reverting back into singles' pastor mode, and we're going to talk about waiting for God's timing," he starts.

I crane my head, looking around. Shawn and Hallie aren't here, so there is a grand total of three singles here. Me, Keller, and Ryan.

Nick sends me a grin, obviously seeing my look. "Minorities are still important," he says to me.

"Thank you, President Amery," I say in CNN broadcaster tones.

"Everyone, flip in your Bibles to 1 Corinthians 7," he says, ignoring me.

Ah, the should-we-or-should-we-not-marry passage. A personal favorite of mine, seeing as how I am a matchmaker.

I can't help the smile.

"Cut the smirk, Laurie," Nick says.

I grin cheekily at him instead.

He shakes his head and starts reading. "Verse seventeen. 'Nevertheless, each one should retain the place in life that the Lord assigned to him and to which God has called him.' Keller, you're up, Buddy."

"Thanks, Nick." Keller settles in front with his guitar and puts his pick between his teeth as he does a quick tune-up.

Twung . . . tweng . . . twang!

He pops the pick out and grins his gorgeous smile at the crowd. "Evening."

We sing six songs, and Nick is back, watching me warily. I hold up my hands surrender-style.

"Let's talk about your place in life. I said this would be for the singles, but there is excellent truth for the marrieds here as well. Where are you in life?"

I sneak a glance at Ryan. *Lord, where am I in life? Is he going to be a major part of it?*

It's tough being twenty-four, I tell you.

───◈───

Ryan walks out with me two hours later.

"Sorry you had to give Adrienne back, Kid." He grins, slipping an arm around my shoulders.

"You noticed she wanted to stay with me."

"Until she saw her mother."

I wave my hand. "Semantics."

He laughs. "Yeah, sure."

I stop beside his truck, and he keeps walking. "We're walking back, Laurie."

"You're just trying to get me to start exercising."

"Possible." He grins. "Come on. You're two blocks away. That's not far enough to even start the car."

"You mean it's not far enough to *try* to start the car," I say, rolling my eyes.

"You are so funny," he says dryly.

"Thanks. I thought so."

We start walking, and I take a deep breath, feeling myself relax.

"Hey, Ryan?"

"Hey, Laurie."

"I'm glad we're back together."

He turns and smiles at me. "Me too."

"Now maybe I won't get nearly killed by rocks tomorrow morning."

"Anyone ever told you that you exaggerate terribly, Laur?"

"Yeah, well . . ." I grin at him, reach over, and take his hand. "My job in life is to keep you humble."

He squeezes my hand. "And my job is to keep you away from other guys. Honestly, Laurie. I'm going to have to have a serious talk with Keller about bringing you chocolate."

I laugh at his expression. "You're cute when you're jealous."

"You're flirting."

"Yeah, but I'm trying to quit. Hey, did you hear that Dave came into town today?"

"Finally, huh?"

"Lexi's been counting down the days, you know." I grin.

"Cringing?"

"I think that's a tame word."

Ryan laughs. "Poor Lex. I'll try to drop by after work tomorrow and check up on her."

"You mean check out Dave."

"Right."

"Fear not. I think Lexi's planning a 'Save Me from Dave' party. You'll meet him."

"Are gifts appropriate for this occasion?" Ryan smirks.

I return the grin. "Appreciated but not necessary."

"Maybe a sympathy card would be better."

We walk around the corner onto my street.

He's lightly rubbing his fingers on my hand and we are walking very slowly. I can feel my pulse start to speed up, and I bite my bottom lip, hearing that corny David Cassidy song playing in my brain.

"Laur?"

I think God created me to be single. Single and getting my fill of all this emotional musical chairs by watching chick flicks and setting up other people.

"Laurie?"

I take a deep breath, trying to calm my erratic heartbeat. *Sheesh.* How come this never happens in the movies? Like *Sweet Home Alabama*, for instance. Melanie loves Jake, and yet she's completely calm around him.

Yeah, right.

"Laurie!"

I yelp. "What? What is it?"

Ryan shakes his head. "You're off in La-La Land."

I press my free hand to my now-definitely racing heart. "Why did you yell?"

"To get you out of La-La Land."

"For the love of Mike, Ryan! I thought I was about to step on a snake or something!"

He grins. "What were you thinking about?"

Uh, a member of the Partridge Family.

"Nothing." I smile. "Stuff. Life."

"Me?"

"Now you're flirting."

"I'm trying to quit," he echoes.

I smack his shoulder. "Come up with your own material, Buddy."

He walks me up to my front door, smiling, his face partially shadowed.

"So this Rockies game is on Monday," he starts.

"Okay."

"Can I pick you up at four?"

"Four? What time does the game start?"

"Seven."

I gape. "I thought you said it took forty-five minutes to get there!"

"I thought if we were early, we could get dinner before the game."

I spread my hands, mouth open. "Now I'm expected to go to dinner *and* a football game?"

Ryan frowns. "It's baseball, Laur."

"Same basic idea."

He starts laughing. "There's a huge difference, Laurie."

"Two teams trying to outscore the other."

"Yeah. But one is with a baseball on a diamond, and the other is with a pigskin on a field."

"Both trying to outscore the other."

He rolls his eyes. "There's a Cheesecake Factory right down the street from the stadium, you know."

I smile brightly. "I love football!"

"Baseball! Baseball, Laurie!"

I grin. "Right!"

He laughs. "You don't know anything about baseball, do you?"

"I do too," I say, hands on hips.

He raises his eyebrows mockingly. "Really. Tell me something."

"The Yankees are a baseball team," I say proudly.

"Who is their manager?"

I squirm and say the first name that pops in my head. "Gary Cooper?"

Ryan closes his eyes. "I'm feeling the need for serious prayer. . . . So who made you watch *Pride of the Yankees*?"

"Is that where Gary Cooper came from?"

He grins. "And I repeat. You know nothing about baseball."

"You can't know everything."

He shakes his head. "Yeah, but baseball, Laur. That's up there with apple pie and Wal-Mart. It's un-American to not know anything about baseball."

I raise my hand in a pledge. "I promise to pay attention on Monday."

He smiles. "Promise, huh? You'll be ready for the quiz on our way back?"

"Completely prepared." I wrinkle my nose. "What kind of quiz?"

"About the game, Laurie."

"Like who scored the first touchdown?"

He closes his eyes and mumbles something under his breath.

I start laughing and smack his arm. "Just playing with you, my friend. I know touchdowns are in basketball."

"Laurie!"

"I'm kidding!"

He laughs and grabs me in a hug. "Very funny," he says into my hair.

I pull back a few inches and grin up at him. "Did I have you going?"

"You had me going."

"Good. Someone needs to keep you on your toes."

"I assume you're claiming that job as well."

I nod. "I am."

His mouth curves in a smile and my pulse starts hammering again when I realize he still has his arms around my waist. My arms somehow ended up around his neck. He leans down and kisses my forehead.

Is it bad that I'd rather debate with Ryan than deal with all of this stuff?

"So I'll probably see you tomorrow," I say, trying to keeping my voice light, but instead it cracks on the last syllable of *tomorrow*. I start to step back.

Ryan tips his head at me and locks his fingers together behind my back. "We need to talk, Laurie," he says, no jocularity in his tone.

Eek.

"Oh?" I say, trying to twist out of his hands. No avail. "What about?"

"You and me."

Good grief, how clichéd can we get here?

"Can we sit down?" I ask, nearly pleading.

He gives me a look and then nods.

I collapse on the bench. He sits beside me, angling a little so he doesn't have to turn his head so far. He still isn't smiling. Instead he looks . . .

Confused? Depressed? Nervous? I can't read his expression.

"Laurie, we need to talk."

"You already said that," I say, like the honest person I am.

He looks at his hands, then at me, and half-smiles. "I did, didn't I?" He blows his breath out. "I've never . . . never actually done this . . . uh, before . . ." he stutters.

I smile slightly at him in encouragement.

He rakes his hand through his hair. "We've been going out for a while," he says in a rush.

"Yes, we have." I nod.

"And um. Well, I feel like I've gotten to know you pretty well." He pats my hand awkwardly, and I bite back a huge smile.

Thank goodness! I'm not the only one on edge here.

I turn my palm over and squeeze his fingers. "Go on."

"See, I think that . . . well, I was thinking . . . actually . . . I um . . . well, I was hoping *you* were thinking that . . . see, maybe we should . . ."

He stumbles through more words and I try, I honestly try, to pay attention, but there are so many pauses and commas and no periods, that I start having trouble.

This never happens in the movies.

The heroine never, *never!*, gets lost during the "I Like You" speech.

Here's what I think: It is sad that I base my view of reality on movies.

Well, except for *Pride and Prejudice*. I think that one is grounded in reality.

Ryan is still stuttering, and I keep squeezing his hand, trying to get him to say a complete phrase.

In some movies, they don't even have the "I Like You" speech. Sometimes they just kiss and the audience knows that the speech doesn't even need to come because the characters are so in tune with each other's thoughts.

And again I say, yeah right.

Ryan stops talking and takes a deep breath, staring into my eyes. I smile at him. He uses one hand to cup my cheek.

"I love you," he says quietly.

Screeeeech! And just like that, my brain stalls.

Chapter Nineteen

"You what?" I gasp like the eloquent romantic heroine I am.

He suddenly grins, and the Ryan I know comes back, leaving the weird, stumbly worded, quiet-speaking guy I don't know behind him.

His face splits in that cute little-kid smile he has, his plain brown eyes lighting up, and he grabs my other hand, holding both of them tightly.

"Now that was romantic," he says, laughing. "You'd think for a girl who watches *Pride and Prejudice* on a weekly basis, you'd be a bit more practiced in this, Laur."

My chest feels tight. I can't breathe. I decide I contracted a deadly lung disease at Ruby's house.

Probably from that cookie Keller gave me.

"Hey," Ryan says more softly, shaking me slightly.

"What?"

"You okay? You look . . . shocked."

I blink repeatedly, staring at the nonchalant Ryan and wondering if I've slipped back into Neverland and dreamed the whole thing.

"You just said . . ." I cough, unable to finish.

"I love you?"

"Yeah. That . . . we . . . I didn't . . . um, that is to say . . . I wasn't expecting . . . you could've . . ."

And on and on I go. Ryan keeps watching me, frowning slightly, squeezing my hands, and nodding.

I stop about five minutes later, totally out of breath and completely out of my monthly allotment of commas.

Ryan dropped my hands about three minutes into the monologue and is now carefully watching his own hands, bottom lip between his teeth.

I stare at him, noting his curling-out-of-control hair, the lines by his eyes because he doesn't wear sunglasses and smiles all the time, his flannel shirt and jeans that he wears every day. . . .

"Um, Ryan?"

"Mm-hmm?" he mumbles, not looking up.

"I love you too," I say softly.

His head jerks up. "Really?"

"Yeah. Really."

He suddenly is all smiles again. "I'm glad."

I have to laugh. "I guess . . . that's good." I grin.

He returns the smile and picks up my hands again. "It's good."

This is the part where we are supposed to kiss.

Ryan's eyes warm into The Look as he smiles at me, and I watch him, waiting, feeling jittery.

"So, uh, what's next?" I ask a few minutes later, when he hasn't moved.

He squeezes my hands. "I think, traditionally, marriage comes next."

"Oh. I actually meant, um, like right now."

Either a kiss or a proposal, one of those two is supposed to come next.

He lets me go and gently brushes one hand through my hair. "I could talk to your dad tonight."

"Ryan!"

He blinks. "What?"

"You haven't asked me anything yet! I haven't agreed to anything yet!"

He raises his eyebrows. "You said you loved me."

I cover my face. "And I do!" I need coffee.

I hear him sigh and he pulls my hands away from my face. "Calm down, Laur."

I guess I shouldn't be surprised. I mean, Ryan's not romantic and I've known this, but . . .

I try pinching myself. What happened to liking debating with Ryan more than romance?

He rubs my leg. "Wait here?"

"I'll wait," I mumble.

He takes off running down the street.

Apparently, in Ryan's mind, romance occurs after a marathon.

I sigh and lean my head back against the bench, closing my eyes. No kiss, no ring, no proposal.

Lord, what is happening?

I sigh again. All I ever have are questions for God.

When Brandon proposed to Hannah, it was very romantic. He took her to a park, they had a picnic, he gave her a bouquet of her favorite flowers, a diamond ring, and a question. Then they kissed.

Even Nick and Ruby's was romantic!

I'm seeing a trend here.

I open my eyes, staring up at the black sky void of stars, and suddenly I know.

I am the common denominator!

I coached Nick, and I coached Brandon. *I* am the reason for their romantic proposals!

Coaching Ryan, though, seems like poor form to me.

I hear the front door squeak. "You can come out, Joan," I call.

She steps out, looking chagrined. "How'd you know it was me?"

"Like stepmother, like stepdaughter."

She grins and settles down in the place Ryan vacated. "So I watched you two, I just didn't hear anything. Care to elaborate?"

I turn and look at her. She rubs my shoulder in a motherly gesture, her eyes kind.

I love this woman.

I look down at my hands, breaking eye contact. "Uh. Joan?"

"Yes, Laurie?"

"So, um, well . . ." I bite my bottom lip. "You know the whole breakup with Ryan that happened?"

She suddenly starts laughing, and I turn to look at her. "What?" I ask.

"Oh, Laurie-girl, you didn't really think you fooled me, did you?"

"What?" I am aghast.

"You were trying to get back at us for the weekend confrontation trip, huh? I figured it out when I saw him before the date tonight. No man looks at a woman who just broke his heart like Ryan looked at you." She pats my leg. "I let you get away with it. But let's just keep this between us, hmm?"

I close my eyes and drop my head into my hands. I will never outsmart my amazing stepmother. Never. I look up and sigh. "Thanks for dinner out, then. And the dress."

"You're more than welcome. Someone needs to spoil you, Laurie-girl."

I like that Joan has picked up my dad's nickname for me.

"Joan, how did Dad propose?"

She blinks at the change in subject and then grins an evil smile. "He botched it. Badly. I felt so sorry for him, I said yes."

I smile. "Now that's romantic."

"Mm. He tried to propose while we were here, actually. He was drinking his lemongrass tea—"

"Blegh," I interrupt, gagging.

Joan smiles. "I was sipping a Diet Coke, and he managed to spill both drinks as he got down on one knee."

I start laughing. "That's awful! Poor Dad!"

"Pity *me*, my dear. I'm the one who had both drinks spilled down my shirt." She pushes my hair over my shoulder. "Why the questions, Honey? Did Ryan propose?"

"Um . . . no . . ." I squirm. "He told me he loves me."

"And?" Joan prods.

"And that's it."

"That's it?"

I sigh.

Joan frowns. "Doesn't he know you never tell a woman you love her unless there's a 'will you marry me' attached?"

"Apparently not."

She pats my shoulder. "It's okay. He'll get around to asking it."

"He didn't even kiss me!" I burst.

"Honey, you have to face the fact that Ryan isn't Brad Pitt or one of those squishy guys you watch in movies," Joan says, the maternal voice of wisdom.

"Squishy?" I parrot.

"Soft. Spongy. Sort of . . . squashy-like in nature."

By now I am laughing.

"All right, Laurie, you can stop," she says, rolling her eyes. "My point, Sweetheart, is that there are more unemotional Mr. Darcys in this world than . . ." Her voice trails off, and she waves her hands around, trying to find the word.

"Squishy ones?" I suggest, grinning.

She rolls her eyes again, but smiles. "Yes. Squishy *Prince & Me* men."

"Someone should write a manual about this kind of stuff."

"Such as, *Life Ain't the Movies*?"

"I think that's the first time I've ever heard you use the word *ain't*, Joan."

"Well. Since it ain't a word to begin with . . ."

"Terrible joke, Joan."

She smiles. "Come inside, Honey. Don't tell your father—he's in bed right now—but I hid some regular coffee in the back of the pantry behind the waffle iron."

"Regular coffee?"

"French roast, to be precise."

"I love you! I love you!"

She stands, laughing, and I almost stand before I remember.

"Joan, I can't. Ryan told me to wait here."

"Jewelry stores are closed at this time of night, Laurie."

I snort. "I don't think a jewelry store is where he's going."

Joan smiles. "I'll brew the coffee then, and we'll sit out here to drink it. Sound okay?"

"Sounds fantastic, Joan."

She comes back out ten minutes later carrying two mugs of coffee in her hands and a magazine under her arm.

"Here we go. One creamed and sugared to an inch of its life for you, straight up and black for me."

"Yummy." I sigh, inhaling. "You're the best, Joan."

"Remember that." She looks at me sheepishly. "I was in Barnes & Noble the other day and I couldn't resist. . . ."

She shows me the magazine, and I groan. "Joan . . ."

"I couldn't help myself!"

A curly-haired, way-too-white-to-be-real-toothed woman in a white lacy wedding dress carrying a bouquet of some flower I don't recognize smiles up at me from Joan's lap.

White Wedding Wonders.

"What a name." I sigh.

"See, I remembered your penchant for alliteration."

Double sigh.

She hands me the magazine along with a big grin. "Turn to page seventy-three," she says giddily. "There is such a great article on how flowers impact the whole ceremony."

"How flowers what?"

"Affect the wedding," Joan says again, flipping the magazine to the right page and starting to read it to me. "'For Carol Macy of Rhode Island, a floral arrangement of red poppies and June lilies had been her lifelong dream. But the imagination can make things much more beautiful than reality.'"

Already, this is worse than Dad's favorite magazine, *Medical Mysteries and Common Occurrences.*

I hold up my hand. "Whoa, okay, stop. I want to carry Hershey bars down the aisle."

Joan looks at me like I've suggested camping out in the

Putt-Putt parking lot for my honeymoon.

"You what?" she bursts.

Tires crunch on the gravel at the end of our driveway, and headlights bounce crazily on the front of the house.

Joan stands and pats my head. "We'll talk later, Dear."

She disappears through the front door.

I sigh and look over at the driveway, where Keller is climbing out of his Mercury sedan.

Wait a second.

What is Keller doing here?

He climbs up to the porch, and I gape at him.

"Hey, Laur. You left a little early. I was just making sure you were okay," he says, shoving his first and second fingers into the pockets of his jeans and smiling at me.

I nod. "I'm fine."

"Watching the stars?"

"Uh, no. Not really."

Here's what I would like to know: How do you say *get lost* to someone that gorgeous?

His grin widens and he sits down beside me on the bench.

"So how did you like Nick's teaching today?"

"It . . . it was good," I fumble.

"Nice to have a lesson directed toward us instead of how to properly rear your children," he says.

I grin. "Discipline, Keller. All it takes is discipline."

"What's that, Laurie?"

I study him for a second and then shake my head. "Never mind."

Keller leans forward, rubbing his fingertips together. "So, you left early. You missed the big announcement."

"Holly's pregnant. I heard."

"Shawn and Hallie are engaged."

My mouth drops open. "What? They announced it? I missed it? They weren't even there!" I shout.

"Whoa, calm down, Laurie," Keller says, patting my hand. "Didn't you put them together? You knew this was coming, right?"

I sink lower into the bench, disappointment flooding my ribcage. "Yeah, but the announcement . . ." I mumble, rubbing my head. I suddenly have the worst headache known to the human race.

"Laur? You okay?"

"My head hurts."

"Well, have you had any water today?"

Meet Keller, my personal dietitian.

"I had coffee," I say.

"You need to drink more water," he says seriously.

"There is water in coffee," I say, matching his tone.

He sighs. "Laurie, Laurie, Laurie . . ."

I smile close-mouthed at him.

He grins. "So are you and Ryan still a couple?"

"Keller—"

"Okay, just asking," he interrupts. He pats my hand again. "I'll let you go get some water. Have a good night, Laurie."

He stands and walks back to his car, slides in smoothly, and backs out.

No Ryan in sight.

Joan opens the front door wide, her mouth wider. "What was he doing here?" she asks.

"I don't know, Joan."

"Well, I do!"

"Then why did you ask me?"

"Ryan called. He's not coming tonight. He said he'd come tomorrow afternoon."

"Swell," I say dully. I sigh and stand, my head pounding. "My hopes and dreams have been shattered. I'm going to bed."

Joan mashes her lips together as I pass her. "Okay," she croaks. "Sleep well."

I climb upstairs, open my door, and flounce down on my bed, landing right beside the little black dress I'd hurriedly changed out of earlier this evening.

Darcy pads into the room and cocks his head at me as if to say, *You're still here? I thought you were out with Ryan.*

"So did I, Boy. Come on, get up."

He jumps on the bed and settles down beside me. "Darce, I have a logistical question to ask you."

He blinks solemnly at me.

"Is there a rational reason that Mr. Darcy didn't grab Elizabeth and kiss her after he proposed the second time?"

I swear my dog shrugs.

A lot of help that dog is.

I sigh and burrow into the covers, burying my face in my pillow. Like it or not, I've given my heart away to an unemotional construction worker who is better at pounding nails than speaking sentimentally.

My faith in romance has been shaken. Are there really guys out there like Freddie Prinze Jr.'s character in *Summer Catch* or not?

I blindly grope for my Bible and grab it when I feel the soft leather. I turn my face on my pillow to my right cheek and open the Book.

Instead of getting James, however, I open to 1 John.

"Dear children, let us not love with words or tongue but with actions and in truth."

I close my eyes. *Okay, God, I get it.*

Things I Am Currently Learning:

- *Tell the truth!*
- *Loving Ryan apparently doesn't mean romance. But I still love him, right?*
- *I should've changed into my pajamas before falling on the bed because now I don't want to get up. And my dad told me that sleeping in jeans constricts blood flow, and that is just not good.*

Lord, I guess I need even more wisdom. Now that I know how I feel about Ryan and what I want to happen, give me patience, God, please!

Chapter Twenty

I wake up Thursday morning with that day-old-hairspray-clogging-my-scalp-pores feeling. It's not a nice sensation. Rather grosses me out.

Joan is pouring milk into a cereal bowl when I get downstairs. "Hi, Honey. Breakfast is ready," she croons, her nails clinking on my hair as she tries to ruffle it. She frowns.

"You used too much hairspray yesterday," I tell her matter-of-factly, scrunching into a chair at the table. Dad looks up from his newest edition of *Medical Mysteries and Common Occurrences*.

"Aerosol hairspray or nonaerosol?" he asks, frowning.

"Non."

He starts *tsking*. "Not good, Laurie-girl, not good. Aerosol hairspray damages the environment, yes, but nonaerosol hairspray is a liquid form and can seep in through your skin." He taps on his magazine. "Says so right here. Read the bottom of page seventeen."

He passes the magazine over and takes a huge swallow of his gunky tea.

Blegh.

I clear my throat. "'Heartache. Sorrow. Loss of —'"

"No, no, no, Laurie. The *bottom* of the page," Dad clarifies.

"That is the bottom of the page."

"Let me see."

I slide the magazine back over. Dad squints through his bifocals at it and nods. "You're reading an ad, Laurie. Read the article."

"That's an ad? For what, funeral homes?"

"Processed cheese. Go on. Read the article."

I pull the magazine back. "'To spray or not to spray: forty-one reasons to just say no to hairspray.'" I look up, gaping. "Forty-one?"

"They're short, I promise. Keep reading."

"'Number one. Spraying causes injury to the cornea by administering tiny microscopic beads of alcohol that ooze through the soft tissue of the conjunctiva and adhere to the zonular ligament, instigating irritation, tenderness, and ultimately blindness.'"

Dad listens to me, nodding, holding his glasses. "There. You see? I would say that right there would be reason enough to not use hairspray."

I look at Joan, who nods in agreement, calmly spooning her triple-bran-twice-the-vitamins cereal into her mouth.

"So what should I use to keep my hair the way I want it?"

Dad smiles. "Skip to the end."

"'Wanting the healthy way to keep your hair looking like perfection? We suggest following the Randy Johnson approach: Wear a hat.'"

I put the magazine down and stare at Dad.

"What if I just closed my eyes when I sprayed?"

Dad strokes his chin thoughtfully. "I didn't consider that. . . ."

I walk through the door to Merson's one hour later.

Shawn looks up from the counter and frowns. "You okay? You look a little . . . frizzled."

"My father has restricted me from using hairspray," I say, sitting on one of the bar stools.

Shawn starts laughing. "Your family, Laur, I swear."

"So I heard you made an announcement last night," I start.

He winces.

"You couldn't have the decency to wait for the person who set you up in the first place?"

"Laur, I'm sorry. We just stopped by because Ruby had a book Hallie wanted to read and she was wearing her ring and you know how those girls are with diamonds. . . ."

I laugh. "Okay, I'll give you that one."

He smiles. "Thank you. Usual?"

"Yep. So how'd you do it?"

"Do what?" he asks, pulling an extra-large mug from the counter.

Men.

"Propose, Shawn!"

He grins. "Oh. That. I asked her as we pulled up to her folks' place for dinner."

I blink at him. "And she said yes?"

"Sure. Why wouldn't she? She loves me; I love her." He starts pouring coffee into the mug.

"Well, did you at least have the ring?" I ask.

He shakes his head. "We picked it out after we left her folks' house."

"Wait, wait, wait," I say, waving my hands. "You proposed in the car, you didn't have the ring, and why do you keep calling it her folks' place? Hallie lives there too, you know!"

He doesn't give me my coffee. "What is wrong, Laurie?"

"Nothing, I'm just shocked that Hallie was okay with all of this."

"Why?"

"Because it's the opposite of romantic! Honestly, Shawn, the car?"

He shrugs. "It wasn't like I was intending to propose there. It just happened."

"What did you say?"

He shrugs again. "I don't remember."

Then I spaz. "You don't remember?" I freak. "What is wrong with you guys? Don't you understand anything? Like a woman's basic desire for romance?"

"Laurie, calm down!" Shawn shouts. "You are disturbing my other customers."

I quiet, grab my coffee, and start inhaling it.

"Laurie? Hey, Laurie?"

I set the cup down when I reach the bottom. Shawn stands there staring at me openmouthed, eyebrows high on his head.

"That was black coffee," he says slowly and distinctly.

"Oh."

"No, Laurie, I mean that was straight-up black. There was no sugar in it." He gapes. "You downed it like—"

"I know, Shawn, all right? I was here, thank you." I rub my static-clung hair and sigh. "Sorry for the outburst."

"It's okay," he says, still frowning. "Do you want to talk about it?" he asks, shifting uncomfortably.

I look up, hopeful. "Really, Shawn?" He really does care!

"Hallie's in the back."

Then again . . .

"What is she doing?"

"Washing muffin pans. I'm sure she'd like company."

I hop off the bar stool and go around behind the counter and through the doorway that leads to the kitchen.

Hallie is in front of the sink using a gigantic hose, whistling.

"Hey, Hal."

She turns and grins, eyes squinching up in her classic cute smile. "Laur! Hey, Girlfriend, how are you?"

Exhausted. Depressed. How are you?

I decide to duck the question. "So I heard something last night," I start.

She dimples and blushes. "Really?"

"Mm-hmm," I hum, leaning up against the stainless-steel counter beside the sink.

"What did you hear?"

"Ruby's thinking of redoing the baby's room to green."

She blinks several times in succession. "Oh, well, that's great, I guess," she stutters.

I grin. "You're engaged?"

Her smile speeds back and she holds out her sudsy left hand. "Crazy, isn't it?"

"Completely."

"Your fault, you know."

"I know," I say smugly.

She laughs. "You're just begging for a lesson on pride, Laur."

"When's the wedding?"

"We've talked about sometime in March," Hallie says, drying her hands on a paper towel. "I've always wanted to get married in March." She sighs wistfully. "Just as the snow is melting and new life is beginning . . ."

I frown. "You mean when the sidewalks are lined with muddy sludge and dandelions are popping up everywhere?"

She rolls her eyes. "You are so unromantic, Laurie Holbrook. Hey," she brightens. "Be my maid of honor?"

"I thought you had a sister, Hal."

"She's getting married in January. You're the only unengaged girl I know. Please do it?"

"Sure, I'll do it," I say, trying to keep the *oh boy* tone out of my voice. I have become a robotic maid of honor. Walk down the aisle, hold the bride's flowers, hand over the ring while juggling flowers, watch the kiss, smile sappily, walk back down the aisle with the usually married best man.

What fun.

Hallie looks at me and shakes her head. "You've got that look again."

"What look?"

"The classic when-is-it-my-turn look."

"I do not," I protest.

"You do too. Honestly, Laur. Are you and Ryan ever going to tie the knot?"

"Probably. Maybe. I don't know."

She *tsks* at me. This is the second time today I have been *tsked* at. "You're not getting any younger, and Ryan's twenty-six and has a good job *and* wants children, and you know you want them too."

"Hallie, I'm twenty-four years old, for heaven's sake!"

Here's what I think: Christendom inspires single girls to go ballistic if they are not married before the age of twenty-two.

She shrugs. "I'm just saying . . ."

"Well, thank you for your concern, but I think I have many

good years left."

She gives me a *mm-hmm* look, sighs wistfully again, and twists her engagement ring around and around her finger like newly engaged girls do.

"I want to carry June lilies down the aisle," she says breathily.

I shake my head. "Bad idea, Hallie."

"Why? I like June lilies."

"So did Carol Macy and look what it did to her wedding."

Hallie frowns. "I don't know a Carol Macy."

"Read this month's issue of *White Wedding Wonders*."

Her mouth drops open. "You're reading bridal magazines? Laurie! You and Ryan must be serious!"

I hold up my hands. "Correction. *Joan* is reading bridal magazines. She made me read the Carol Macy article."

She sighs again, not listening to me. "Shawn will look so handsome in a tux!" she squeals. "Oh, Laurie, I've been dreaming of this day my entire life."

─ ❖ ─

I walk through the door of The Brandon Knox Photography Studio a little later, frowning.

Florence looks up from where she was crouching over the calendar on Hannah's desk. Hannah appears scared to death with Florence that near to her.

"What's eating you?" Florence barks at me.

"Huh?"

"You look depressed."

"Oh. Nothing."

"Take a pill, will you? You'll frighten all the clients." She goes back to the calendar.

I'm not entirely sure that estrogen runs through Florence's veins.

"Lexi's called every four minutes," Hannah says. "Please call her back."

I grin. "Suffering from Dave-ism?"

"And hysterics."

Florence looks up again. "Who's Dave?"

"My sister's cousin-in-law. He's in town. Lexi can't stand him."

Claire walks in, pushing her designer sunglasses up on her head, her brown hair bouncing around her shoulders. "Hi, girls."

"Hey, Claire," Hannah and I chime.

"Hello," Florence says stiffly.

"Florence, I've been meaning to tell you. You look positively svelte," Claire croons, putting her purse in her cubbyhole.

Florence blinks and then *smiles*.

Smiles!

The corners of her mouth lift up! Her lips spread! I see teeth!

I am shocked, to say the least.

"Why, thank you," Florence says gleefully. She rubs her calico-covered stomach. "I've been dieting for two weeks now."

"The North Shore diet?" I pipe up.

She shoots me a glare. "Yes, actually." She turns back to Claire and smiles again. "You really notice a difference?"

"A huge difference, Flo—may I call you Flo? You look amazing."

Florence blushes now, and Hannah and I both gape in absolute astonishment.

"My mother used to call me Florrie," she offers Claire shyly.

Florrie.

No wonder Florence is such a living nightmare.

Claire nods, grinning. "I like that. Listen, I noticed that Penney's was having a major sale this week. We should go together."

Florence keeps smiling. "I'd like that. I'm just leaving today, but I'm off tomorrow."

"It's a date then," Claire says. "Have a great afternoon, Florrie."

"You too, Claire."

Florence leaves.

Claire sits regally in one of the chairs in front of Hannah's desk. "And that, ladies, is how it's done," she says.

"She smiled," I say incredulously.

"And she *blushed*," Hannah says, mouth still open.

Claire takes a sip of her iced decaf and smiles cheekily. "We'll get her in some fitted, stylish clothes and get rid of that hair tower. . . ." She starts ticking the points off on her fingers.

"Don't forget makeup," I say.

"Right, of course." Claire sighs. "Oh, I just love projects!"

"Think she could be done by dinner tomorrow?" I ask thoughtfully.

"Honey, I'll have her done by lunch."

"Excellent. Because I have someone I'd like her to meet."

Hannah covers her face. "Oh no."

"Quiet, Hannah."

Claire lifts her eyebrows as she looks at me. "Matchmaking again, Laurie?"

"Florence needs someone like Dave in her life."

"What is Dave like?" Claire asks.

"Loud, unorganized, a practical joker, basically a big kid."

A smile splits Claire's face. "Opposites do attract, don't they?"

"It's been my experience, anyway." I lean over and grab Hannah's phone, dialing.

"Hello?" someone whines.

"Lex?"

"Baby! Thank God!" she whispers. Then in a loud voice, "I'll be right back, boys." A moment later she is back on the line, moaning. "I have been around that man for only two days, and I'm turning into a psychotic!"

"Lex, surely you're exaggerating."

"Surely I'm not! He brought ducks!"

I press the phone closer to my ear. "What?"

"I mean geese!"

"He brought geese?" I repeat in disbelief.

Hannah snorts and whirls around so all I see is the back of her chair shaking. Claire tips her head quizzically.

"Four of them," Lexi says. "This morning, they woke me up at five thirty, honking!"

"Five thirty?"

"In the morning! Apparently, this is normal. Dave said that they're morning birds."

"He drove to your house."

"He's driving *across the country*. We just happened to be one of the lucky stops along the way."

"He's driving with geese in the car?"

Lexi moans.

"I'll take that as a yes," I mutter. "Wow. Geese."

"Look, just come over soon, please? You can say you're taking me shopping, and I won't go home until next week."

I laugh. "I'm sure that will work."

"Dave brought duck food. I mean geese food. They can live

on that."

"Geese have to eat special food?"

"Wheat."

"Oh."

"Or, better yet, I'll let the geese in the house, they can kill my husband and his sick cousin, and I'll go marry Keller," Lexi says dully.

"Lex, it can't be that bad."

"I went outside to water my plants this morning, and Meeny attacked my ankles. If I hadn't been wearing rubber boots—"

"Wait a second, hold on," I say. "Dave named the goose Meany?"

"Meeny. As in Eeny, Meeny, Miny, and Moe."

I try really hard to stifle a laugh.

"Stop it, Baby."

Apparently, not hard enough.

"Oh, Lexi, I'm sorry, but this is hilarious."

"It is not," she protests. "I can't even go outside anymore. And Moe has some weird fascination with standing in front of the screen door and just staring at me with his beady little eyes. It's creepy!"

I sigh. "Okay, all right. I'm off at two today. I'll come over for a little bit."

"Stay for dinner. Please? Ryan's here. I'm getting barbecue. And ask Brandon to come."

I have to smile. "Okay. I'll ask Brandon, though."

"Thank you! Tell him to say yes. You're my favorite little sister!"

"Mm-hmm. I'm your only little sister. Bye."

I hang up and shake my head at Hannah, who has both hands covering her mouth, her eyes watering from held-in laughter.

Claire purses her lips. "Geese," she says shortly.

"Four of them."

She narrows her eyes and stares thoughtfully out the front windows. "Perfect." She grins. "I'll have Florence ready by five tomorrow night."

"And you chide me for matchmaking," I say airily, my ten thirty coming in.

Hannah swipes at her eyes. "Poor Lexi."

"I'm sure she'll appreciate your sympathy."

She nods, snorts, and starts laughing hysterically again.

The Crandells, my clients, shoot her an odd glance and then smile at me. "Hi, Laurie."

"Hey."

Rob and Julianna Crandell are both in their midforties and just got married. Neither had been married before. Two Christian people proving that Christian girls can actually wait until later to get married without losing their minds.

I like the Crandells.

~⊛~

I fish my backpack out of my cubbyhole a few minutes after two, waving good-bye to Hannah, who is on the phone, and walking down the hall to see Brandon.

I slam open his door and he looks up. "Hey, Laur."

"Hi, Brandon."

I climb up on his desk and sit down, lips pursed. He leans back in his chair, fiddling with a pen, grinning.

"How you doing, Kid? I haven't seen you in a while," he says.

"Well, you're married."

"So?"

I smile sadly at him. Brandon was my best friend since second grade, but marriage changes priorities. I knew things would change.

I just didn't count on it being so *complete*.

"Lexi's dealing with geese," I say.

Brandon chokes. "I'm sorry." He hacks. "I thought you said geese."

"I did."

His eyebrows climb. "Geese?"

"Four of them."

"Wild geese? In this part of the country?" He frowns. "I thought geese mostly resided in the northern part of the U.S."

"Not wild. Dave brought them."

A grin splits his face so wide I can hear his cheeks pop against his gums.

"So Dave's in town, hmm?"

"Lucky Lexi."

"Her car still running?"

"I didn't ask. She's a little freaked out about the geese."

Brandon sighs thoughtfully. "What was he into last time we saw him?"

"Cooked rice, apparently."

"No, it was an animal."

I shrug. "I try not to spend any more time than necessary with him. He's weird."

"I'm thinking it was turtles. Or maybe it was emus."

I open my mouth and then close it. "Uh, Brandon, there's a big difference between a turtle and an emu. Regardless, now it's geese. Know anything about taming geese?"

He shifts farther back, grinning. "She could always pull an *I Love Lucy* and walk around squawking so the geese think she's their mom."

I laugh.

"Heading over there now?"

"Pretty quick. She's invited Ryan to dinner. Want to go watch?"

He levels a look at me. "You're mean."

"No, I'm not. I'm a nice person."

"You're looking forward to watching your sister be tortured."

I hide a smirk. "Am not. Poor Lexi. See? I pity my sister."

"You're just inviting a sermon on sympathy, Laur."

Preachers must love me. Apparently, I invite a lot of sermons.

"Yeah, well. You and Hannah can go to dinner too, if you'd like. She's serving barbecue."

Brandon nods. "I'll check with the wife."

I hop off the desk, grimacing. "I'd take a piece of advice and not call her 'the wife' anymore."

He laughs and shoves me out the door. "Be nice," he says before slamming it.

Hannah is off the phone when I get back to the lobby. "Heading out?" she asks, not looking at me as she scrawls a note on a yellow legal pad.

"Yeah. You and Brandon might go to Lexi's tonight for barbecue."

Hannah looks up then. "I'm allergic to geese."

"Yeah, right."

"Cole slaw, then. I barely even get around the stuff and my sinuses fill up."

"You handled it all right the last time you ate barbecue. With cole slaw on the bun, I might add."

"I'm on a diet."

"You're in better shape than Chuck Norris, Hannah!"

She blows her breath out, aggravated. "I'm going to kill my husband," she mutters.

"Can I watch?"

"He always gets us in situations like this! I would rather not meet this Dave character." She rubs her head, her hair shimmering in blonde waves.

I watch, fascinated. It's like staring at a lighter-colored version of Jennifer Aniston's hair. "You know Brandon. He hears free food and jumps on board," I say.

She growls and lets go of her hair. "Well, he's going to hear it from me." She stands. "Brandon!" she yells.

His door opens a minute later. "You called?" he says, poking his head out.

"We're not really going to Lexi's tonight, are we?"

"Sure are," Brandon says cheerfully.

"I do not want to meet Dave."

"So don't introduce yourself." His door closes.

Hannah sits and moans. "Woe is me," she mutters.

I pat her shoulder. "I think you'll live. I won't, though, if I don't get out of here. I'm surprised Lexi hasn't—"

My cell rings, interrupting me.

I look at the caller ID, grinning. "Called," I finish, answering the phone. "Hey, Lex." I wave at Hannah and leave.

"Where are you?"

"Leaving the studio. Brandon and Hannah are coming tonight."

"Good. Ry's here."

"He's there already?"

"He's been here all day. He has to work on Saturday, so he's here today. Sheesh, Laur. Don't you two ever talk?"

"We talk a lot," I say, miffed, climbing into the Tahoe.

"Sure, whatever. Do me a favor and stop by the grocery store and get me a package of M&Ms."

She hangs up.

I stare at the phone, eyebrows raised. Lexi must be going out of her mind, because she does not eat chocolate.

She thinks it's unhealthy.

To quote Cher from *Clueless*, "As if!"

I park in front of the local grocer's, run in, grab a package of M&Ms for Lexi and three monster-sized Milky Ways for me.

It's not good to eat chocolate alone.

I drive the few miles to Lexi's, my chest tight.

This is what I'm wondering: How do I act around Ryan after his botched proposal last night? And, most importantly, after I know he loves me?

I pull up behind Ryan's pile of scrap metal that he calls a truck a few minutes later, taking a quick breath.

"Lex?" I yell into the house, walking in through the front door.

She attacks me from behind.

"AUUUUGH!" I scream.

"Thank you, oh, thank you," she gasps, cutting off the circulation in my lungs and snatching the grocery sack from me.

"What, just plain M&Ms?" she harps, ripping open the bag with her teeth and pouring the contents into her mouth.

"Lexi?"

She looks at me, wiping the slobber off her lips with the back of her hand. "Wha id it, Bwaby?" she mumbles around the melting candy globs.

"You are gross."

"Ank oo."

I sling my backpack on the couch and walk into the kitchen.

Ryan stands at the island counter, polishing off a bag of potato chips. He looks up and his eyes brighten. "Hey, Babe. Want some chips?"

"My appetite just left, thank you, though." I lean against the counter next to him. He has grass particles packed into the creases of his jeans, his flannel shirt sleeves are rolled to his dirt-marred biceps, and a backwards baseball cap is mashed on his sweaty head.

Ick.

At least his hands are marginally clean.

He grins self-consciously. "What?"

"You're dirty."

He wraps an arm around me and kisses the side of my forehead. "I love you too."

"Yuck!" I shout, jumping away.

I hear Dave before I see him.

"Holy cow!" he yells. I turn and squint a smile at Dave, who lets out a long wolf whistle. "My lands, Cuz, you've grown up!"

Ah, Dave.

If the compliment came from anyone else, I would have been flattered. Alas and alack, it came from Dave.

It's like being told you're beautiful by Mr. Collins. It makes you want to run for the shower hollering, "I want my life back!"

"Hi, Dave," I say. Dave has gained some weight since I last saw him, and he was overweight to begin with. Nate's side of the family isn't small.

"Whoa," he says again, coming around the counter and wrapping his squishy arms around my shoulders.

Eww, eww, eww!

I prefer Ryan's dirt-caked perspiration.

I scoot out of the hug and half-hide behind Ryan, gripping his forearm. "You've met Ryan, right?"

"My PK? Sure have!"

"I'm sorry, PK? Ryan's not a preacher's kid."

Ryan looks at me, and I can tell he is hiding a huge smirk. "Practically kin."

Dave smacks Ryan flat on the shoulder blade. "That's right. Once you two are hitched, that is! Hey, I am invited to the wedding, right?" He grins devilishly.

I hesitate before answering. "We haven't really gotten a chance to talk about the wedding yet," I say slowly. Talk about uncomfortable subjects.

"Oh, come on!" Dave exclaims and this time wraps one arm around me and the other around Ryan. "You two look so dang cute together!" Now he smashes me against Ryan. "Go ahead, PK. Kiss her!"

Ryan blushes seven shades of red and one shade of purple. "Well, uh, I'd kind of like to be clean before I . . ." He clears his throat. "Kiss her," he whispers.

Dave *tsks*. "If you don't snatch her up quick, PK, I will."

By now I am praying for deliverance from Dave-isms.

"You know what, I think I heard Lexi calling. Excuse me, boys," I say quickly, diving for the living room and hightailing it for the hall.

Lexi is spread-eagle, flat on her back on her bed, moaning.

"Lex?" I say quietly, tiptoeing in.

"Why did you buy me those M&Ms? You're a horrible sister, and you can no longer have custody of my kids when I die." She groans.

"Lex, you don't have any kids," I point out, like a nice person.

"Shut up."

"Sorry."

"Is Dave still here?"

I snort and fall on the bed beside her.

She opens one eye and sighs at me. "I'll take that as a yes."

"That's a definite yes."

"I've been trying to kill him with kindness, but so far all it's done is make him rethink living so far away from me."

I roll to my side. "Maybe you should try poison."

"He's already eating my cooking. I think he's immune to poison."

"Electrocution?"

"Where would I find enough volts?"

"Drowning."

"Bathtub's too small, and I don't have a pool."

"Slit his wrists?"

"I'm not strong enough to hold him down."

"Lexi?"

"Yeah?"

"You know what Jesus said about murdering someone in your heart?"

"Uh-huh."

"Well, I think today is giving me a lot to own up to on Judgment Day."

She starts laughing. "Oh, Honey."

"Where's Nate?"

"Buying barbecue."

"And Dave didn't go with him?"

She moans loudly.

"Why not?" I pester.

"Because he wanted to stay and spend time with lucky me." She sighs and rolls over, smiling slightly. "Thank God for Ryan. I'm going to make him all his meals for the next month just to say thanks."

I purse my lips. "Maybe you should just give him a gift card to Merson's."

She flicks my arm. "Meany."

I brighten. "Hey! Speaking of which . . ."

"You haven't seen the geese," Lexi finishes my sentence.

"Where are they?"

"Dead, I hope. Eaten by rabid dogs amid a spray of white feathers."

"You're getting morbid, Lexi."

She sits up, groaning. "It's that man's fault."

I join her on the edge of the bed, patting her arm. "Well, I may have a solution."

"Speak, Beloved One."

"Remember that lady I work with?"

She gasps. "Yes! Oh, I had completely forgotten! When is she coming over?"

"I was going to see if you wanted to help me set the two of them up for dinner tomorrow night."

She hugs me tightly. "You are so sweet! I will throw you the best engagement party ever known to man!"

"But, Lexi, I'm not—"

She vaults off the bed and is out of the room before I can finish.

I fall back on the bed and close my eyes.

My life would be *so* much nicer if it involved scene markers and a soundtrack.

Chapter Twenty-One

"So these are the geese."

I stand on the porch next to Ryan, watching four white birds waddle from one side of the yard to the other.

"These are the geese." He nods.

Dave and Lexi are inside debating the ever-important question of whether cole slaw or potato salad goes best with barbecue.

Needless to say, Ryan and I stepped outside to avoid the bloodshed. It's about five o'clock, the air is cooling, and the huge trees lining Lexi's yard are casting long shadows on the grass. Her flowers are in full-bloom around the yard.

I look around. Ryan and Nate have done a lot to the backyard. I haven't paid that much attention before. Lexi and Nate live on about two acres, all grass and trees and trails. There's a little honeysuckle arbor in the back corner now, roses surrounding the benches inside.

It's gorgeous out here!

I look over at Ryan, who showered since he was finished cutting their grass. He's got on a clean pair of jeans and yet another flannel shirt. His hair is drying curly.

The lead goose turns and honks something to the other three, and they all start waving their wings as they waddle across the lawn.

I grin.

"They're kind of cute," I say.

"Now don't go and say something like that." Ryan moans. He jerks up one pant leg and points to a mark. "Moe gave me that shiner."

"Is it technically called a shiner if it's not on your eye?"

"Regardless," Ryan says, rolling his eyes. "Geese are mean and stubborn. Plus, Darcy would eat them alive, so you can't have any." He reaches for my hand and leads me off the porch.

"But maybe I'd get one that lays golden eggs," I say cheerfully.

"What would you do with golden eggs?"

"Go to Australia. Marry a cute Australian boy. Live among kangaroos."

Ryan keeps walking toward the archway in the back, my hand still securely in his. "Sounds like you have a plan. Did you see the new benches we installed?"

"Um. No."

"Want to?"

"Mm." The geese are running around us, and I kind of feel like I got transported back in time somewhere.

He gets quiet and I can feel the tension in my fingers, which is not a good place to feel tension. According to Dad's magazine, that leads to serious arthritis and sensitivity in the distal phalanx.

We stop under the honeysuckle, and he looks around at the benches and roses. There's a little path they laid in there.

I look around. It's all shaded and cool. "Wow, Ryan! This looks amazing!"

"Thank you."

Ryan abruptly blows out his breath and whirls to me. "Laurie, will you marry me?"

I respond with the first thing that comes to my brain. "What?"

He steps forward, holding my hands, his eyes sparkling. "Will you marry me?" he says again.

I blink at him, my mouth slightly open in shock.

He swallows, brushing one hand down the side of my face. "You know I love you," he says huskily.

"Yeah, but . . ."

"I want to spend the rest of my life with you, Lauren Holbrook."

He smiles softly at me, keeping his hand on my face.

"You're proposing," I mumble after a minute, trying to clear my head.

He grins. "Uh, yeah, I am."

"In my sister's backyard."

"Mm-hmm."

"With . . . geese."

Ryan starts laughing then. "So I am." He brings his other hand to my face, cupping my cheeks. "Please say yes," he says seriously.

"Ryan," I start, closing my eyes. "You can't just . . ." I shake my head. He doesn't let go of my face.

"I can't just what?" he prods.

"You don't just *propose*," I stutter. "There should be a plan, or a direction or something!"

He brushes his thumbs on my cheekbones, eyes soft as he looks at me. "Shh, Laurie."

I clamp my mouth shut, the backs of my eyes burning.

He drops his hands from my face. Slowly he kneels down on one knee.

"Why do you think Lexi stayed inside?" He grins.

"She knew?"

He smiles.

"Oh," I say quietly.

My heart pounds, my hands shake. I can hear my breathing and try to regulate it.

Here's what's happening: I am being proposed to!

Ryan smirks at me and pulls a package of Oreos from underneath an upside-down pot.

"And you thought I hadn't planned this." He smiles, handing me the Oreos.

I start laughing. The first time I met Ryan, I was hiding Oreos under my shirt.

"Payback," he taunts.

I stick my tongue out at him.

"Open it."

I rip into the package and pull out the plastic tray. Neatly lined chocolate cookies parade around a black box right in the center. I roll my eyes, laughing. "This is so corny."

"Hey, you're the chocolate freak."

I pick up the box, swallowing, opening it slowly.

Ryan grins at me, still on one knee.

"Uh, Ryan?"

"Hmm?"

"The ring's gone."

His eyes get huge with horror and his mouth falls open. "What?" he gasps. My stomach drops. I show him the empty box, hand shaking.

"It's not here."

He stares at me wide-eyed for a full minute. Then he grins teasingly. "Good thing I kept it in my pocket."

I narrow my eyes at him. "You're asking for one heck of a marriage with a proposal like this."

"What can I say? I like challenges."

I laugh.

He scoots closer, reaching for my hand. "You haven't answered my question."

"What question?" I smile.

"Will you marry me?" he asks quietly, all traces of a smile gone.

I look down at him, noting the jeans, the flannel, the curling, out-of-control hair. He looks at me warmly, and I smile. Ryan couldn't have proposed in a nice restaurant or dressed up in a tux.

This is Ryan just as he is.

I squeeze his hand. "Yes."

"Really?"

I laugh and—what is this?—tears start building in my eyes. He grins, his little-kid smile blooming hugely.

He slides the ring on my finger, and my mouth drops open.

"Lexi, Laney, Ruby, and Joan helped," he says, still grinning.

I start laughing at *that* mental picture, swiping at my eyes. "It's gorgeous!"

He stands and pulls me into his arms. "I love you, Laur," he whispers into my neck, his whiskers tickling. "I can't believe God brought someone as amazing as you into my life."

Now I am seriously blubbering. "I love you too." I sniff.

Cupping the back of my head, he bends down and kisses me.

Funny, in my daydreams I never had mascara running down

my cheeks during this scene.

I wrap my arms tightly around his neck, and his hands settle on my waist. I pull away a few minutes later, sighing contentedly.

"Happy?" Ryan smiles, pushing my hair behind my ear.

"Mm-hmm." I turn my head against his chest and hold out my left hand. White gold, three round-cut diamonds—simple but beautiful.

"Hannah actually found this one on the Internet. I liked it, but the other girls insisted that they see it for themselves before I bought it."

I laugh. "Sounds like them."

"Lexi spent thirty minutes staring at it in the store. Asking all kinds of questions like carats and clarity. Stuff I don't have a clue about."

I twist my hand around so the sun glints off the diamonds.

"Do you like it? Honestly? Because if you don't, we can get another one," he says, worry creeping into his voice.

I look up at him, wide-eyed. "Are you kidding?"

"No." He reaches out and grabs my hand, touching the ring.

"Hey!" I yell, closing my fist.

He starts laughing. "I wasn't going to take it, Laur."

"Good. It's never coming off."

He smiles sweetly. "You like it then?"

I kiss his chin. "I love it."

His eyes warm into The Look, and he lowers his head again, stroking the sides of my face. I close my eyes.

Something brushes past my leg right at that moment.

I scream.

"Laurie! Laurie, calm down!" Ryan yells.

One of the geese squats next to my leg, staring at me with a beady, narrowed-eye, evil look. I grimace and grab Ryan's shirt.

"He's going to bite me," I whimper.

"No, he's not. That's Eeny."

"So?"

"So Eeny doesn't bite."

"Says who?"

"Dave."

"Why is he looking at me like that, then?"

"Like what?"

"Like I'm Brutus and he's Popeye."

Ryan grins. "You have quite the imagination, Laurie. What happened to thinking the geese were cute?"

"Let's just go inside." We walk back across the yard, hand in hand.

I pull him in the door and Lexi stands there, arms crossed over her chest, a smug look on her face.

"Go ahead and say it," I say.

She smirks. "I knew it, I knew it, I knew it," she singsongs. Then she suddenly tears up and grabs me. "Oh, Baby, I'm so happy for you."

"Don't, Lexi. You'll get me started again." I sniffle, hugging her back.

"Let me see the ring!"

"You helped pick it out!" I protest, jerking my hand back.

She rolls her eyes at me. "Yes, but I didn't see it on you." She yanks it back. "It looks just like you!"

"Uh. I guess that's good."

She grins, backhands her eyes, and kisses my cheek before reaching for Ryan. "Come here, Honey. I'm so excited I get you for a brother!"

Ryan laughs and hugs her back.

"I would have adopted you even if she had said no," Lexi declares, pulling away.

"What time is it?" I ask.

"Wear a watch," Lexi responds, walking through the kitchen to the living room. I watch her go, sighing.

"Ask a simple question . . ."

"Almost five," Ryan tells me.

I squeeze his hand. "I didn't think you'd propose today. At Lexi's house. With geese."

He laughs. "I'm never going to live that down, am I?"

"No, actually, you're not." I suddenly remember something and my mouth drops open. "Oh no!" I shout and run for the back door.

Too late.

I skid to a stop on the porch, staring at the shredded package and the chocolate-frosted poultry in front of me.

I hear Ryan gasp behind me. "Uh oh."

The geese waddle around, pecking at the few remaining Oreos scattered across the yard, chocolate coating their beaks, their heads, and their feathered bodies. Mo squawks at us, raising his wings and glaring.

"Man, they made time!" Ryan whistles.

"Do you think chocolate is as bad for geese as it is for dogs?" I ask, half-whispering.

"I don't know." Ryan shakes his head. He sets his hands on my shoulders. "You go distract Dave; I'll get them cleaned up."

I turn around and run smack into the aforesaid Dave. His jaw has dropped to rest on his left big toe, his eyes look like Frisbees, and his hands clutch his face.

"What on—" he sputters.

"Okay, Dave, before you get mad," I start.

"AUGGGHH!" he shrieks.

"Are geese allergic to Oreos?" Ryan asks, wincing.

Dave swipes Moe off his feet, and the bird lands with a resounding *uumph* on his rear.

He is taking out his wrath on the birds!

"Dave!" I yell, running to grab him.

He grabs Moe by the beak and rips him off the porch. "How could you?" he bellows at the bird.

Moe goes still.

"How could you destroy her engagement present?"

My eyebrows take the elevator up on my forehead.

The other three geese quake on their webbed feet. Dave sets Moe down and glowers at all of them.

"Bad boys! Bad!"

He straightens immediately and grabs my shoulders. "Laurie, I am so sorry." He has a tortured look on his face. "I'll make it up to you! I'll buy you a new package! I'll buy you three packages! Forgive my geese, please!" he shouts, dropping his head on my shoulder.

Ooff. I about fall to the deck.

"Dave, Dave, Dave," I soothe, awkwardly patting the back of his head. "Uh, don't worry about it."

Ryan pulls him off me. "She would have just eaten them anyway, man. It's not a big deal."

Dave lets his breath out, hand at his heart. The geese hightail it to another part of the yard.

"Look, let's just all go inside and calm down," Ryan says, smoothly pushing Dave inside with one hand, reaching for mine with the other.

"Yeah," Dave says breathlessly. "Just calm down."

"Right. Calm down."

"Is Nate back?" I ask.

"Been back for a while, Honey," Dave huffs.

"Where is he?"

Dave shrugs and goes to the kitchen, pouring a glass of water.

Ryan clears his throat, which is his way of hiding a laugh.

"Don't you dare start laughing," I hiss.

He coughs and forces a half-serious look on his face. "What are you doing for dinner tonight?"

"Hmm. Probably spending time with my fiancé." I pull him close again and kiss him.

"Let's go drop your car off at your house first, okay?"

I nod. "Okay. Bye, Lex!" I yell.

Her bedroom door opens an inch. "See ya, Babe!"

Ryan opens the front door and walks over to the Tahoe with me. "So I'll follow you over," he says, opening my car door.

He kisses me again, pulling me very close, then helps me inside and closes my door, walking over to his car.

I start the ignition and wave as Ryan disappears inside his truck.

The diamonds catch the light filtering through the window and I freeze, hand in midair.

Wow, Lord.

"I'm getting married," I say softly to the empty car.

Chapter Twenty-Two

My father has always told me that a wedding is for two people: the bride and the bride's mother.

Apparently, no one else cares.

I open my eyes Friday morning and roll over in bed, stretching. After dinner, I got home and found Dad at the kitchen table, drinking a cup of tea. He spent the whole time talking about the dangers of using moth balls.

He didn't even notice my ring.

I shouldn't have been so disappointed. Dad doesn't detect much unless it involves germs or finances. Still . . .

Joan was in bed with a headache when we got home, so shortly after we got back, Dad kissed me good night and joined her.

There I was, nine thirty on the eve of my engagement with no one in my family to tell, save for my loyal mutt, Darcy, who licked my ring suspiciously and then washed my kneecap.

What happened to entire villages celebrating someone's engagement?

Ryan and I stayed up talking about our wedding and the future and why we knew God's plan was for us to get married until one o'clock in the morning.

I love him. A lot.

I sit up in bed, yawning, rubbing my morning hair. My ring catches the light again, and I hold out my left hand, studying it.

Yesterday was a long day, beginning with me spazzing to Shawn about men in general and then ending up engaged.

I half-fall downstairs a few minutes later and pause on the fifth step.

Ruby, Hannah, Laney, and Joan are all sitting around the breakfast table, which is heaped high with books and magazines galore. Hannah has a laptop. I hear Lexi talking in the kitchen.

"She's really more of a summer complexion," Lexi says, going to the table with a mug of coffee, sniffing it suspiciously.

"Don't worry, that's regular. I tossed the Soyee," Joan whispers. "It started gagging me."

Lexi grins appreciatively.

Hannah lays her hands on the book she was reading. "I don't understand this conversation. She has to wear white! It's her wedding!"

I sit down on the stair, mouth open.

Ruby looks up then. "Ladies, I think we have an eavesdropper." She grins.

Laney climbs the stairs and has her arms around me before I can fully process it. "My baby sister," she says sappily into my hair. "I can't believe you're even old enough for this!"

Ruby reaches in between us, grabs my left hand, and starts squealing. "It looks so precious on you!"

Joan pushes teary-eyed Laney aside and hugs me. "You and Ryan." She sighs. "I knew it from the first time I met you two."

I get all teary again too. Then I start jumping up and down and screaming with Laney and Ruby.

"What's going on here?" I ask, looking at the table.

Lexi looks up from the table, sipping her coffee, squinting at the clock. "Baby, Ry's going to be here in fifteen minutes." She gives me a once-over. "Not that I don't love this tousled pajama look, but you may want to save it for after the wedding."

Hannah pushes her way in, wrapping her arms around me. "I'm so excited! Come on, Laur, I'll help you change."

Suddenly I am an invalid.

I hug Hannah back and look at the five of them. "You wouldn't be planning my wedding for me?"

"We would." Lexi nods, grinning.

Laney sighs and gives Lexi her classic older sister look. "No, we're not. We're just trying to get some options so you don't have to comb through all this yourself." She points to the wreck on the breakfast table.

"We know you too well, Darling," Joan says, going back to her chair. "You would take one look at this and decide to elope."

I go down the remaining stairs, Hannah clutching my left hand, and gape at the table.

At least fifteen magazines and thirty books are on the table.

I pick one up. *You May Now Kiss the Bride: How to Get Here Without Losing Your Mind.*

I flip it open with difficulty, since Hannah is still cooing over my ring.

"'Chapter Nine. When to Call It Quits and Head to Vegas,'" I read out loud.

Lexi snorts.

Joan rolls her eyes. "Honestly, Honey, you would have to pick up that book. Here. Look at this one."

She hands me a thick spiral-bound book titled, *Weddings Can Work!*

"Look in the back," Joan instructs. "There are some wonderful lists and worksheets for everything you could possibly need."

"'Checklist for Registry,'" I read. "'Formal dinnerware, casual dinnerware, flatware, crystal, additional serving pieces, pots and pans, linens, appliances, kitchen appliances . . .'"

By the time I finish reading just the titles, I feel exhausted.

"You need all of this stuff to get married?"

Laney nods, swallowing her coffee. "Tragic, isn't it? Most important thing on that list is a cheese grater. I could not live without mine."

Hannah gives my oldest sister a look. "I think the most important things are electronics. TV, DVD player—those are expensive. Let the guests buy them."

Ruby starts laughing.

"Here we go," I say weakly. "Cookie jar. Coffeemaker. Ice cream maker."

Joan chuckles. "Funny, Dear."

Lexi squints at the clock again. "I was serious about Ryan, Honey. He'll be here in ten minutes."

"Why?"

She snorts. "You should never ignore the groom, Doll-face. They care about wedding details too."

I have doubts about this, but I am not going to argue with five females armed with wedding manuals.

"I'll go get dressed," I say, sighing.

I'm halfway up the stairs when Joan says, "Laurie?"

"Yeah?"

She smiles at me, tears pooling in her eyes. "Congratulations,

Sweetheart."

I feel myself getting foggy, smile a thanks, and hurry upstairs. I change into jeans, brush my hair into a ponytail, and go back downstairs just as the doorbell rings.

"I'll get it!" I yell, scooting out of the kitchen.

Lexi snickers. "You bet you will."

I open the door and Ryan grins at me. "You know what I love about you most, Laurie?" he says, not coming inside.

"My amazing analogies?"

"Nope."

"My stellar vocabulary?"

He shakes his head.

I rub my cheek, thinking. "Picture-taking skills?"

His grin grows. "No, it's your elegant taste in clothes."

I roll my eyes. "You're one to talk. Two outfits. This . . ." I point to his jeans and flannel shirt. "And your church clothes."

He steps inside. "Then I guess we're even."

"I guess so." I smile up at him. "Hi."

"Hey." He kisses me and then frowns at the avid debate coming from the kitchen. "What's going on in there?"

"They're deciding whether we want the classic scroll formal dinnerware or the flower motif."

"What?"

"How does Vegas sound?"

Joan comes into the entry then and grabs him. "Ryan! Bless your heart, I am so excited about you two!"

He grins self-consciously. "Yeah, me too." Subtly, he yanks his shirt out of Joan's hands and wraps an arm around me.

"Tell me what you two think about this," she starts. "Yellow daffodils and baby's breath."

"What's baby's breath?" Ryan asks.

"For what?" I say at the same time.

"Your bouquet, silly!" Joan says.

"Joan!" Ruby yells from the kitchen. "It's red tulips and baby's breath!" She comes in, kisses her brother's cheek ecstatically, and then turns accusingly to Joan.

"I like yellow flowers better." Joan shrugs.

Hannah walks over and congratulates Ryan with a hug. "Do you have plans on the eighth of November?" she asks him.

He blinks. "Uh, no, I don't think——"

"Great!" She turns and heads back to the kitchen, yelling, "Go ahead and mark it down, Lex!"

"Hey, Laur?" Laney yells.

"What?"

"Do you like oak or pine better?"

"Oak or pine what?"

"Cabinets."

Joan perks up at that. "You found one?"

"Live and in person!" Laney yells back. Joan leaves.

I look at Ryan and sigh. He squeezes my shoulder. "What were you saying about Vegas?"

"Can we go?"

"Sure," he drawls. "When?"

"Now?"

"I'm free. Get your shoes."

I find a pair of flip-flops by the entry closet, shove my feet in, and follow him outside.

He opens the passenger's door of his truck for me, and I grin at him.

"What?" he asks as I climb in.

"Can we have Elvis at our wedding? Because I've always wanted to get married to an Elvis impersonator, so having one at the wedding would be a good alternative, don't you think?"

He shakes his head. "No Elvis at our wedding."

"Rats."

"If it makes you happy, I'll sing 'Jailhouse Rock' as we're leaving the ceremony, though."

"How thoughtful," I say, rolling my eyes.

He leans in and kisses me. "My thoughtfulness is one of the reasons you love me, right?"

"Uh-huh. Just get in the car."

He laughs, shuts my door, and slides into the driver's seat. "I was thinking breakfast sounded nice."

"You didn't get to eat either?"

"Lexi called at eight this morning to tell me to come to your house right away."

I frown. "Ry, it's ten thirty."

"Right. I knew you weren't up and I figured this had something to do with wedding planning, so I stalled."

I hold up my hand. "Let me guess. Did it involve staying under the covers?"

"You're a genius."

"I know."

"Humble too. Merson's?"

"Drive on."

The truck suddenly jerks and makes a loud *huuuurrrumph*, sort of like one of the R.O.U.S. characters in *The Princess Bride*.

I gasp.

Ryan cradles the steering wheel in his palms. "Shh, shh, Alice. Calm down," he soothes.

As Yoda would say, "Flat-out weird, my fiancé is."

"Why don't we take my car?" I suggest, nervously picking at my knuckles.

"Have a little faith, will you?"

"A little faith in what?"

"Alice. My car-handling skills. God." He looks over at me. "Just to name a few."

"I do not trust Alice. And last I understood, you still hadn't heard back from *The Italian Job* producers about your role as a driver. And of course I have faith in God."

"Good. Then show it."

"I just don't like taking risks."

"This from the girl who has watched *Pride and Prejudice* forty-three times."

"What is that supposed to mean?"

Alice reduces the growl a few decibels, and Ryan sighs contentedly. "There you go, there you go," he croons, mashing the gas pedal down.

He glances over at me and grins. "What were we talking about?"

"Would you be terribly upset if I carried Hershey bars down the aisle?"

He shrugs. "No. It would give us something to snack on if Nick starts to get carried away."

I laugh. "See, I knew there was a reason I liked you."

~ ❖ ~

We pull up to Merson's a few minutes later, and Ryan comes around and opens my door.

"So how do we tell these two?"

"You're assuming they haven't already heard."

"True."

I shrug. "How do you want to tell them?"

"Loudspeaker?"

I grin. "I'm thinking that would cause a disturbance with his other customers, and I get warned about that every time I come in."

He laughs and holds open the glass door leading to Dessert Heaven, the sweet smell of gingerbread wafting out.

Shawn looks up from wiping off the counter and waves. "Hey, guys."

"Gingerbread, Shawn? Isn't that kind of a Christmas thing?"

"Hallie had a taste for it." He grins at us. "You two want coffee or the full morning meal?"

"Can I have chocolate chip pancakes?" I ask.

"With or without whipped cream?"

I give him a look.

"With, of course," he answers himself. "Ryan, what will you have?"

"In four months? Laurie. But for now, I'll have an omelet."

I lay my left hand oh-so-subtly on the counter.

Shawn starts laughing, comes around, and wraps both of us in a hug. "You finally asked her?" he says, clapping Ryan on the back.

"Finally asked her." Ryan nods, smiling his little-kid grin at me.

Shawn hugs me again. "And you actually said yes to this guy?"

"He proposed with Oreos! I couldn't say no."

Shawn snorts and starts laughing all over again. "That's a classic." He steps back a few inches and grins proudly at us. "To think, I watched this whole thing play out right in front of me," he says sappily. "Wait right here, you have to tell Hallie." He disappears into the back.

Ryan wraps his arm around me, kisses my forehead, and leans down close to my ear. "I am starving."

I giggle.

Hallie runs in from the kitchen. "You guys!" she shrieks. "You're engaged, right? You have to be engaged!" She grabs my left elbow and jerks me forward.

"Ow," I say.

She sees the diamonds and starts screaming. "Oh my gosh, oh my gosh!"

I laugh as she yanks me into a hug.

"I knew you two would get engaged," she says, reaching for Ryan. "I just knew it."

"We seem to be somewhat predictable, Babe," Ryan says.

"This is what being predictable feels like?" I ask, eyes wide.

"Not all it's cracked up to be, is it?"

Shawn pulls Hallie into a hug, and they stand there smiling sentimentally at us. "You said four months, Ryan?" Shawn asks.

"According to Hannah," he answers.

Hallie starts laughing. "Oh no. Are they planning everything?"

"Right down to the last monogrammed dishcloth." I sigh.

"I'm sorry. I know what it's like. Shawn has two sisters, a mother, and a grandmother, and I've got a sister and a mom, and all of them have decided we're getting married in January by Franklin Graham."

"Best of luck with that," I say dryly.

She grins. "You just have to take it all in stride."

Shawn shakes his head. "It's when they're coming at the inside of your leg with a tape measure that it starts to get a little uncomfortable."

Hallie brightens. "Speaking of which, Laur, I need to talk with you. Got a second while Shawn's making your breakfast?"

I nod and she pulls me over to an empty table.

"Hey, what am I supposed to do?" Ryan calls.

Hallie turns halfway in her seat. "Actually, if you're dying for something to do, you can finish scrubbing the last of the crepe Shawn burned off the pan."

"The crepe that who burned?" Shawn demands.

Hallie smiles a brilliant grin at him and settles into her seat across from me. "I have tentative plans to check out that bridal store on Third tomorrow. Think you can make it?"

"I don't know why not. It'll give you a chance to try on brides-maid dresses too."

Hallie grins. "I thought about that." She adds in a whisper, "Don't tell my mom or sister about it."

I smirk. "So this is a *secret* search for a wedding dress."

"They think they've already found the perfect one," Hallie says, rubbing her cheek. "It's strapless. And beaded. And lacy. And all the other things that just don't look anything like me."

I tip my head as I study her. Hallie is adorable. Shoulder-length, shiny red hair, sparkling green eyes, a perfect complexion, and a figure that broadcasts she's a runner.

"You need a slip dress. Long, form-fitting, and only detailed on the bodice."

Hallie hits the table with her palms. "Why couldn't you have been there when my family was planning my dress?"

"Sorry. I was kind of being proposed to."

She grabs my hands. "I am so excited for you, Laurie! Finally, right? You two are such a cute couple."

"Why, thank you." I grin.

"I mean it, Laurie. I can so picture your wedding too."

I tip my head at her, curious. "Yeah? What's it look like?"

"I'm thinking daisies. White ones. The bridesmaids wear blue, and your dress is very simple, very elegant. At the church. Reception outside on the lawn."

I grin, cradling my chin and balancing my elbows on the table. "Sounds pretty. According to Joan, though, I'm carrying yellow daffodils and baby's breath."

Hallie gasps. "Yellow?"

"Yep."

"How horrible! You are not a yellow person, Laurie." She shudders. "When I think yellow, I think liver failure."

I smirk. "That's good and romantic."

"So tomorrow? I'll pick you up about two?"

"Sure. Pick me up at the studio, though. I have to work until then."

She nods and stands. "Sounds great. I need to go finish that crepe pan. You two have a good breakfast, all right?"

"Thanks, Hal."

She comes over, bends down, and wraps her arms around me. "Congratulations, Laur."

Ryan sits down in her empty seat a minute later. "Hey, Darlin'." He leans across and flicks a curly strand of hair that hadn't quite made it into my ponytail. "I'm assuming you didn't get a chance to fix your hair?"

"It's that haircut they made me get. Too many layers. Now it curls all weird."

He grins. "I like it curly."

"I'll wear it curly for the wedding if you'll let us get married by Elvis."

He rolls his eyes. "I already told you, no Elvis."

"Please, Ry? We don't even have to get married by him. He could just be in the audience."

"Laurie, I do not want to have to explain to our grandkids what the man in the tacky white costume with big hair was doing at my wedding."

"*Whose* wedding?"

He grins.

"And I happen to prefer younger Elvis. Hey!" I brighten. "How about you pick the honeymoon, and I'll handle the wedding?"

"No Elvis."

"Fine. You handle the wedding, and I'll take care of the honeymoon."

"I do not want to spend my honeymoon gawking at Elvis in Las Vegas."

I groan. "Will you get off Elvis already?"

He points at me. "It's what you were thinking, wasn't it?" He must read my expression because he pounces. "It was!"

I bat my eyelashes. "I tell nothing."

"Yeah, right."

Shawn sets a big plate of chocolate chip pancakes with a mountain of fluffy whipped cream in front of me. "You realize I feel completely ridiculous serving this to a woman who's on the verge of matrimony," he says.

As is my custom, I stick my fork in the middle of the concoction, pull it back up, and lick the chocolate off the end of it. "I think you'll live, Shawn. I like the consistency, by the way."

He shakes his head and puts Ryan's omelet down.

"You do know that by marrying her you have to spend the rest of your life in the same house with her," he tells Ryan.

"I did know that," Ryan answers. "I think I can survive."

"Don't be so sure," I say, waving my fork at Ryan and in the process spattering Shawn's apron with tiny flecks of whipped cream.

He looks at me for a long minute. I smile hopefully. "Sorry?"

He leaves, muttering under his breath.

I lick my fork and look over at Ryan, whose head is so low it's nearly touching his steaming omelet, shoulders shaking.

"Hey, Ry?"

Ryan looks up, in a full-fledged silent laugh.

"I saw this wedding special on TV once. What do you think about us coming into the ceremony on elephants?"

He scoops a forkful of egg, still laughing. "Oh, Laurie."

Chapter Twenty-Three

I ring the doorbell, the muscle right below my left eye twitching.

Bad sign.

The door opens, and I am face-to-face with my engaged psychologist coworker, Claire.

"What are you doing here?" I ask.

Claire steps out onto the porch, pushing me back a few feet. "She was nervous. Promise me you'll be nice, Laurie Holbrook."

"I promise, I promise." I crane my neck trying to see through the half-open door. "What does she look like?"

Claire huffs and then grins. "I think you'll be surprised."

"I'm more concerned with Dave being surprised. Speaking of which, we need to go. Ryan's waiting in the car."

Claire suddenly smiles and grabs my left hand. "So . . . ?"

"He proposed."

"Laurie, how exciting! I love it. Okay, wait here. We need another diamond ring in the studio. And I'm convinced tonight will clench it."

"Claire, you've obviously never met Dave."

She disappears into Florence's house, and I lean around the wall to wave *just a second* to Ryan.

He gestures to the clock on the dashboard.

"Laur? Ready for the new Florrie?"

"Born ready, Claire."

The door swings open dramatically, and I swear I hear a drumroll.

Florence stands in the entry wearing a soft, flowing, silky skirt that lands near her model-thin knees, a baby blue three-quarter-length sweater, and . . . her hair!

I gasp and cover my mouth. "Oh my gosh!"

The hair tower is gone! Someone has bleached the daylights out of her drab brown hair, and now it curls gently down to her shoulders in blonde waves.

Florence smiles shyly. "What do you think?"

"Holy cow!"

Claire comes up behind Florence and wraps her arm around her shoulders. "I think that means she likes it."

"I love it! Turn around," I command.

She does, frowning, and I see a bit of the old Florence come back. *Good.* I think it's just weird when the person changes personalities as well as clothes on those makeover shows.

"Wow. Claire, kudos. Florence, you look amazing. And if we don't run, we'll completely miss dinner."

Not necessarily true. Lexi is not what you would call punctual.

Florence nods once, turns to Claire, and gives her a hug. "You're such a sweetheart," she murmurs in her ear.

Claire hugs her back. "Have a good time. Flirt, Florence, you hear me? It's all in the eyes."

"The eyes, right." Florence nods somewhat nervously.

Claire winks at me and shoves Florence out of her own house. "I'll lock up. Get going, guys."

Ryan hops out of the driver's seat in my car and holds the back door for Florence. "Hi there." He smiles nicely.

"Hi," she says, blushing.

By the time she is in and the door has been closed, I'm settled in the passenger's seat.

⸻ ❖ ⸻

Exactly seven minutes later we pull to a stop at Lexi's. Seven minutes of zilch conversation.

At least with Dave there's conversation. Scary conversation, but talking nonetheless.

Florence takes a quick, timid breath and follows Ryan and me up the walk to Lexi's front door. I open it without knocking.

Nate stands in the entryway, licking a Popsicle. "Hey, Bro," he says loudly, grinning and grabbing Ryan in a one-armed hug.

"What's with the Popsicle?" Ryan asks.

"It's grape."

"What?"

I laugh and motion Florence forward. "Hey, Nate, this is Florence, my coworker. Florence, Nate."

Florence nods to Nate.

Nate grins his lopsided grin. "Hey. Want a Popsicle?"

"Um, no thanks," Florence twitters.

"Where's Dave?" I ask. No use putting off the inevitable.

"Getting more Popsicles with Lex. We ran out of cherry."

"What is it with you and Popsicles?" Ryan bursts.

Nate slurps the artificially flavored grape juice dripping down the wooden stick and cocks his head as he thinks. "They're good?"

"Is that a question? Because personally, I prefer toffee ice cream bars," Ryan answers, the two of them moving toward the kitchen.

"Oh, those are good. So are fudge bars."

"And frozen Snickers bars."

"Ever tried putting a bowl of Frosted Flakes in the freezer?"

Ryan stops, halfway through the open doorway. "No. Is it good?"

"Aw, man. The best. Kind of gives new meaning to the word *Frosted*."

"Hmm."

I turn to look at Florence, who wears the same expression I imagine I have. "Ah, the depth in that conversation," I mutter.

She raises her eyebrows and nods.

"So Dave is . . ." Florence stops, clears her throat, adjusts her skirt, rolls her shoulders, and then continues in a whisper, "Lexi's brother-in-law?"

"Oh, heavens no," I say, not bothering to lower my voice. "No, no, no. That would make us more than distantly related. No, Dave is Nate's cousin."

Florence suddenly shrieks and dives behind me.

"What? What?" I yell.

Nate and Ryan come running from the kitchen.

"There's a . . . a . . ." She points to the back door, wordless.

Nate looks out the window and lets out his breath. "I nearly swallowed my Popsicle stick. It's just Moe."

"Who is Moe?"

"Dave's goose," I tell her.

Florence gapes at me. "Dave has a goose?"

"No, Dave has geese. Plural. Four of them, to be exact. They devoured my engagement present."

I hear the door to the garage slam and Lexi's and Dave's raised voices. "Look, we got them. We're home. We can stop arguing now," Lexi shouts.

"I just think we should have gotten the cherry-banana-root beer combo instead," Dave argues.

They come into the kitchen, completely oblivious to us. Lexi slams a plastic-bag-enshrouded box on the counter and turns to Dave, hands on her hips. "First, we're *home*," she enunciates. "I am not going back to the store now. Second, it was my money and my husband who wanted the Popsicles. I think I know him best. And third, and most importantly, anyone—*anyone*—who considers watered-down soda crammed into a mold and frozen to be a Popsicle has serious mental problems."

"I like root beer Popsicles," says Dave.

Lexi spreads her hands. "Then I rest my case."

Nate clears his throat. "Uh, Babe?"

She whirls, sees Florence, and spreads a polite smile on her face. "Hi there. How are you? I'm Lexi."

Dave sees Florence, and his eyebrows go up. "H-hi," he stutters.

She blinks several times before muttering back, "Hi."

Hmm. Not the best first exchange I've ever witnessed.

Dave looks at me, at Ryan, at Nate, at Lexi, at the counter, at his shoes, at his hands, and finally back up at Florence. "You like geese?" he says.

Florence is still blinking. "Um. I've never . . . actually . . . that is to say . . ."

"Want to meet them? They're very friendly."

"Uh, well, I think dinner is soon."

Dave waves his hand. "Not for another fifteen minutes at least. Lexi's a slow cook."

Lexi slams a saucepan on the stove at that comment.

"I think we should go outside now." Dave grabs Florence's forearm and drags her out onto the porch, where she immediately starts squealing. Either with fright or flirtatiousness, I'm not sure.

After the door closes behind them, Nate purses his lips and looks at me. "This was your idea, Laur?"

"Well—"

"Because I'm not sensing much, uh . . ." His voice trails off and he squints at me.

"Chemistry?" Ryan suggests.

"Right." Nate nods. "Not getting that vibe, Sis."

"Just give them a few minutes. Maybe they'll warm up to each other," I say.

Lexi looks mad enough to bite the lid off the can of barbecue beans, but she restrains herself and uses a can opener. "Personally, I think any woman who finds that man appealing should have more than her head examined," she seethes, jerking the lid off.

"I take it the grocery shopping didn't go well," Ryan says.

She clenches her hands. "I offered to go in the first place just to get away from him. But no-o-o. He had to come with me. Then we stood there arguing in front of the freezer section for twenty minutes!"

She starts banging the can upside down in the saucepan, trying to get the last few beans out.

I slip over and grab the can out of her hands. "Whoa, Lex. Calm down," I soothe.

"I can't! He's still here! He may never leave!" Her voice keeps rising octaves.

"Nate, take your wife out to dinner, please," I beg. "Ry and I can get this dinner ready."

Nate stares at his hysterical wife and nods. "Yeah, I think that might be best."

He escorts her out of the kitchen.

I sigh.

Ryan comes over to the stove, rubbing his mouth.

"You are not a nice person," I say, snatching a mixing spoon from Lexi's overcrowded drawer.

"What?"

"You're laughing."

He keeps his hand over his mouth, his eyes sparkling. "Am not."

"Are too."

"I'm not!"

"You are, Ryan!"

He pulls his hand away, grinning ear to ear. "You have to admit, this is beyond ridiculous, Laur." He smirks.

I allow a tiny smile on my face and then quickly sober up. "We can't laugh, Ryan," I say under my breath. "At least not until Lexi's gone."

"Right."

"Hand me the pepper, please."

"What are we making?"

I look around. "Well, I thought she was picking up barbecue, but by all appearances, that never happened." I purse my lips. "What's in the fridge?"

He opens it, stares at the contents for a few minutes, and rubs his cheek. "Um. Cheese, lettuce. A couple of sad-looking tomatoes and a gallon of orange juice."

"That's it?"

"Well, we know there're Popsicles." He grins.

"So she apparently hasn't been grocery shopping either." I stir the beans and sigh again. "Is there even a meal you can make with cheese, lettuce, and tomatoes?"

"Don't forget the orange juice."

I frown in thought. "Any eggs?"

He opens various drawers and hideaway places before he finds them. "Yep. Five."

"And we have cheese."

"Going to make omelets?"

"Thinking about it."

He pulls his head out of the fridge, smiling. "Do omelets go with barbecue beans?"

I wave the spoon at him. "Hey. You're supposed to be the helpful encourager here, Ryan."

"My apologies, Madam Cook. Beans and omelets are fantastic! You should just put the beans straight into the eggs and cook them all together!" he shouts.

I close my eyes, trying to keep from grinning.

Nate comes into the kitchen and hands Ryan forty dollars. "Here. Lexi said to tell you guys that she forgot to get the barbecue and so you can get that or go get burgers somewhere."

Ryan pushes the money back. "You do not have to pay for my dinner, Bro. We got it covered. Laurie's making bean and cheese omelets."

Nate's face scrunches and he swallows. "Oh."

"You and Lex want some to go, Nate?" I ask innocently, stirring the beans.

"Uh, no. Thanks." He smiles and grabs the back of Ryan's neck, pulling him out of the kitchen.

Ryan comes back a few minutes later. "They're gone," he announces.

"What was the little meeting about?"

He walks over and stares into the beans. "Oh, just explaining a handy little thing called takeout. For future reference."

I laugh.

"Seriously, what are we going to make?"

I hand him the spoon and find my backpack, pulling out my wallet. "I've got thirty-two dollars," I say. "How much do you have?"

"About forty, I think."

"Should we send Dave and Florence to Vizzini's and you and I can go get Merson's or something?"

He grins, kisses my forehead, and nods. "Good idea."

"Why, thank you. Can you put the eggs back?"

"Hey, Laur, so I've been thinking," Ryan says, closing the fridge.

"Always scary with you."

"Funny. Listen. What do you think about getting married on August twelfth?"

"August twelfth? That's in, like, four weeks."

He nods. "Good math skills."

"Why August twelfth?"

"Well, September and October are notoriously busy months at work. The last part of August, my little cousins start school, and I'd really like them to be at the wedding. We could put it off until November, but I would, if at all possible, like to be married before the holidays."

I stop stirring and look over at him. "Why?" I ask again.

"The holidays are the most romantic part of the year, Laur." He grins.

"Uh-huh."

"Well . . . and I think my mom and Joan would pretty much go ballistic if we had a wedding right before Thanksgiving or Christmas."

I laugh. "That sounds more like you."

He gasps. "You don't think I'm romantic?"

I shake my head slowly. "Not really, no."

"Why not?"

"You proposed with geese," I say, pouring the beans into a Tupperware bowl.

He starts laughing, comes over, and wraps me in a hug. "Will you just forget about the geese?"

"Nope. Never. I'll hold it over your head until death do us part," I say, smiling up at him.

"Now that's romantic."

"Isn't it though?"

He kisses me gently and then lets me go.

I seal the lid on the Tupperware. "So, about August?"

"What do you think?"

I shrug and put the Tupperware in the fridge. "I think it sounds fine. I mean, honestly. Buy a dress. Buy some flowers. Reserve the church."

Ryan nods. "Sounds easy."

"Exactly. How hard can it be?"

Chapter Twenty-Four

I slam the book on the table and cup my forehead in my palms, wanting to scream but not able to because little Adrienne is napping in the guest room.

Ruby balances her chin on her hand and looks at me sympathetically. "Overwhelming?"

"Who would have thought?" I say. "You have to get a dress, then you have to get it fitted, then you have to find shoes and a hairstylist and a makeup artist and someone to make the garter, and then there's flowers—"

"More periods, please," Hannah says, setting my favorite Minnie Mouse coffee bucket on a coaster in front of me.

It has been exactly a week since Ryan suggested the twelfth of August, and all that has taken place is brain fluid leaking out my ears.

Three weeks. Three weeks until our wedding, and the book I have been reading says to mail the invitations three months in advance.

If someone sent me something that didn't happen for another three months, I would definitely forget about it before then.

Hannah, Ruby, and Joan had gathered around the table earlier this morning, passing out legal pads and mechanical pencils and stacking phone books beside them.

Hannah sits down beside me and taps her pencil on her legal pad. "Okay. Three weeks, guys. Laur, you didn't find a dress when you went with Hallie, so why don't you try that other bridal shop on Maple today?"

I drink half the cup of coffee before answering, feeling myself start to calm down. "Okay," I tell Hannah.

"As far as invitations go, I have a great friend in Colorado Springs who does absolutely beautiful cards. I can ask her to do it," Joan says.

"Nothing fancy," I warn.

Joan nods. "Nothing fancy."

The three of them had become much more understanding about my personal wishes after I'd told them Ryan and I were getting married in four weeks.

They just made one stipulation: no Hershey bars down the aisle.

The front door opens, and Lexi comes into the kitchen, pushing her sunglasses up on her head, blonde hair rippling around her shoulders. "Hey, guys." She bends over, kisses the top of my head, and hands me a Butterfinger bar.

"Thanks." I sigh and look up at her. "You look better."

"Well, Dave's gone, Honey."

"I know. I don't think Florence will miss him."

"Your first failure. It was bound to happen." She squeezes my shoulder and sits down beside Ruby. "So I called the florist Nate and I used. He'll give you a 25 percent discount just because he likes me."

Joan, Ruby, and Hannah exchange looks. "Sounds great, Lex." Hannah nods.

Ruby makes a notation on her legal pad. "Okay, we'll do that then. Did you order anything, Lexi?"

"No, because I couldn't remember if we'd agreed on white daisies or stargazer lilies."

Hannah looks back at her notes. "It was lilies, right, Laur?"

I nod, slurping the last of my coffee. "Yeah. I think lilies won't blend into my dress as much."

"Hand me the phone, Hannah, and I'll call him back," Lexi says.

"Oh!" Hannah brightens as she gives Lexi the phone. "I talked to Sherry at the church. It's booked for you and Ryan from ten thirty to five on the twelfth."

"Thanks, Hannah. Ruby, Nick is going to marry us, right?"

"He said he would, if only because then he could do your premarital counseling."

"Our what?" I ask, half-choking on the Butterfinger bar.

She looks up, brushing her curly hair behind her ear nonchalantly. "Premarital counseling. You have to cram ten weeks' worth of sessions into the next twenty-one days."

"What?" I gasp.

"You have to cram—"

"I heard what you said, Ruby." I look around the table. "Why didn't anyone tell me about this before?"

"Counseling?" Hannah questions. "You knew Brandon and I were having premarital counseling."

"Yeah, but I didn't know it was required. I just thought you two were doing it because you hadn't known each other very long."

Ruby waves her hand. "Anyhow, it needs to happen, and Nick

said he's free tonight. Want me to call Ry?"

"Sure," I say tiredly.

Honestly, a test before marriage?

Ruby starts dialing as Lexi hangs up. "Okay, Baby, all set with the flowers. We're meeting him at ten thirty at the church on Wednesday for a consultation."

"Have you two discussed the housing issue?" Joan asks.

"The housing issue?" I echo.

"Yeah. Where are you two going to live? Because it's not here." Joan grins.

Hannah looks up. "There's a house down the street from us that's for sale," she says excitedly.

"Really?" I ask.

"Yeah! Oh, Laur, that would be so much fun!"

"Well, what's the house look like?" I ask.

"We could borrow cups of flour from each other and babysit someday down the road—"

"The house, Hannah. What's it look like?"

"And carpool and have each other over for dinner and a movie—"

I set my pencil down and stare at her. She winces and rubs the back of her head.

"Okay, remember that Ryan is a carpenter," she starts.

"Pretty good one too." Lexi nods.

"He actually builds houses for a living," Hannah says.

"I know what he does, Hannah," I say. "How big is this house?"

She bites her bottom lip. "You know our guest bathroom?"

"You're kidding!" I burst. "It's that small?"

"Just the living room. The bedrooms are bigger. Of course, the bathroom is the size of my kitchen sink. . . ."

I wave my hands. "How big is the whole house?"

She hedges. "You could easily add on. The yard is big."

"Hannah."

"Eight hundred." She sighs.

"Eight hundred what? Yards?"

"Square feet."

"Oh my goodness."

Joan shrugs. "I don't see a problem with that, Laurie. Eight hundred feet is a nice size for two people. And it's bigger than Ryan's apartment."

Ryan's apartment has less storage space than my Tahoe.

Lexi looks up from one of the wedding books. "So go check it out, Laur. That's a nice area of town."

"You'll love the yard, Laur," Hannah says. "It's gorgeous. Huge, old trees and a lot of grass. Plus, there's a guest house on the back of the property."

"How big is the guest house?"

"It's small," she admits. "A bedroom, a bathroom, and a tiny living area with a little kitchenette. But it would be great if Ryan's parents came to visit or something."

"Why wouldn't they stay with Ruby? She's got a huge house."

"And a grandchild." Ruby grins, off the phone. "I think I'm officially the favorite as far as your in-laws go, Laur. Better face it now."

"You've met the Palmers, right?" Lexi says.

"Once briefly, right after Adrienne was born."

Ryan's dad owns a major construction business in Dallas. He builds factories and office buildings for big names like Pepsi and Frito-Lay. Ryan's mom went back to school when Ryan left for college and is working as a nurse now.

And that is the extent of my knowledge regarding Ryan's parents.

Sad, isn't it?

Ruby stands to get coffee and ruffles my hair as she passes me. "Don't worry, Laur. Mom and Dad love anyone who loves their kids. And we're not a close family, never have been actually."

Lexi smirks. "And then poor Ryan met us."

Joan nods, eyebrows raised. "You guys are definitely the closest family I've ever met."

"And apparently you liked that," Lexi says.

"It's almost as if you just adopt anyone who comes along," Joan continues.

"Like Brandon?" Hannah suggests.

"Right. Brandon, Ryan, Ruby . . . you, me. Shawn, Hallie, Nick—"

Lexi and I start laughing. "We get the picture, Joan." I grin.

"Actually, forget the eight-hundred-square-foot house. With all the company they have over all the time, I think we need to look at five hundred *thousand* square feet," Joan says dryly.

"I guess we can look at this house," I say.

Hannah grins. "Good. It would be so much fun to be neighbors."

"Hey, let's go check out that bridal store now," Lexi suggests, standing. "My feet are falling asleep, and I'm tired of writing mundane details. I want to see lace!"

I laugh and stretch.

Ruby sends Lexi a look. "Thanks. I just poured a huge cup of coffee."

"Put it in a thermos, Dear," Joan tells her. "When Lexi gets an itch, it's best just to follow."

Hannah stands and tears off a few sheets of yellow paper, folding them eight times so they'll fit in her Polly Pocket–sized purse.

"It's always good to have paper handy," she says, noticing my look.

The front door opens, and Ryan comes into the kitchen. "Hey, girls. Ma'am." He nods to Joan. He kisses the top of my head and then rests his hands on my shoulders.

"Hey, what are you doing here?" I ask, leaning my head back to look up at him.

"Lunch hour. I thought I'd eat here."

"Good timing. We're just leaving," Lexi says, passing Ryan and flicking his bicep.

"Where are you going?"

"Dress shopping," I say, rubbing my face.

"Uh-huh. I could just come with you."

"Absolutely not," Joan says, horrified. "You are not allowed to see this dress until you're standing at the altar, Dear Boy."

Ryan grins. "I'm kidding. You really think it's bad luck to see the bride in her dress beforehand?"

Lexi and Hannah exchange a look. "Yes," they say together in a *duh* tone of voice.

Ryan nods. "Okay then."

"A friend's cousin's roommate saw his bride before the wedding and they had like the worst honeymoon ever," Lexi says, big-eyed and tragic. "First, their flight got cancelled because of bad weather, so they decided to rent a car and make a road trip out of it, but then they got stranded in this awful snowstorm, and they spent an entire week in this little sedan eating Grape-Nuts because that's the only snack they had, and when they finally were found, the groom had gotten frostbite on three of his toes, so they had to amputate them, and now he can't ever wear flip-flops."

Everyone is quiet for a second. Soaking in the moral of the story, I guess.

Hannah finally shakes her head. "No one in this house uses periods."

"Honey, it seems like if their flight was cancelled for bad weather, they'd realize it would be bad weather on the ground too," Joan says.

Lexi shrugs. "If they were stupid enough to look at each other before the wedding, I guess they were dumb enough to try to out-drive a blizzard."

Ryan squeezes my shoulders. "So I won't go today. Uh, where's your dad?"

"In the study," Joan answers for me.

"I'll go see if he wants to have lunch with me. Hey, did you hear about this counseling thing, Laur?"

"Yeah. Scary, isn't it? We have to go through therapy to get married."

He laughs. "Guess I hadn't thought about it like that before. I'll pick you up at seven, okay?"

"All right."

Ruby comes over and kisses Ryan on the cheek. "Do me a favor and get Adrienne up for me?"

"Hey!" I yell, jumping out of my chair. "You told me I could get her up."

"Don't you need to get ready to go?" Ruby asks.

"I am ready to go."

"Baby, you're wearing sweatpants," Lexi says.

"So?"

"So you don't wear sweatpants to try on wedding dresses," she says. "I wore that cute summer dress with the sunhats on it. Remember?"

Yes, I remember. She made me wear something only Brittany Murphy in *Uptown Girls* could pull off.

"Hey, is Laney going to come?" I ask, by way of getting the attention off my clothes.

"She said she could meet us there," Lexi says. "I called her this morning on my way over here. Her sitter could come any time after noon, and it is three minutes after."

"And we need to call Hallie," I add.

Hannah nods. "Done."

I frown. "She knows what time?"

"Twelve fifteen," Hannah says, grinning.

Ryan chuckles, kisses my forehead, and backs out of the kitchen.

— ❖ —

Exactly fifteen minutes later we walk through the frosted glass doors of Vicki's Bridal Shop. I had been forced to put on jeans. Ruby is hefting Adrienne on one hip, Laney meets us at the door, and Hallie steps out of her car right as we pull up.

Racks and racks of white fluffy dresses line the walls. A woman with long blonde hair and a business suit comes over, smiling. "Hello," she says.

"Hi," Hannah says, shaking her hand. "We're here for Laurie Holbrook's appointment?"

"Oh, yes," the woman croons. "I'm Sharon, the assistant manager here."

"Hannah, Laurie's maid-of-honor. This is Laurie." She grabs me by my elbow and jerks me forward.

"Hell-o-o-o," Sharon says, drawing the word out like she is talking to a preschool class. She looks at the five women milling around behind me and Hannah. "This is your wedding party?"

Joan raises her hand. "I'm the mother."

"Wonderful!" Sharon squeals.

"Her wedding is the twelfth," Hannah says, businesslike.

"The twelfth of what?"

"August."

Sharon just about swallows her saliva glands. "August?" she repeats, an octave higher. "That's like . . ." Her voice trails off, and she looks up at the ceiling.

"Three weeks," Hannah supplies.

"Exactly." Sharon puts a hand to her temple and takes a deep breath, closing her eyes.

I look at Hannah, eyebrows raised.

Hannah sends me a *behave* look.

"Okay, we can do this," Sharon says finally. "You'll have to content yourself with a dress off the rack, though, because we don't have time to order one."

"Works for me," I say.

"Lovely. First, can I offer anyone coffee or tea?"

Ruby holds up her thermos. "I'll take a refill on coffee."

Laney, looking harried—and who wouldn't with a know-it-all six-year-old, twin four-year-old boys, and twin year-olds?—raises her hand. "Coffee," she says. "Much coffee."

Everyone nods. Hannah smiles at Sharon. "Coffee all around."

Sharon nods. "Okay. Laurie, what size do you wear?"

"A six."

"Will everyone please follow me to the dressing room, and I'll get you all situated," Sharon yells to the people behind us, who are busy ooing over dresses.

We follow her into a huge room decked out with a massive three-way mirror, four couches, coffee tables, magazines, and huge pictures of brides on the wall.

Hallie wraps an arm around my shoulder as we walk in. "I hope you don't mind, Laur, but I have the appointment after you. It made sense to me. We're all already here."

Sharon disappears, and everyone makes herself comfortable on the couches. Joan, Hallie, and Laney take one couch, Ruby and Adrienne take another, and Lexi, Hannah, and I take another one. Ruby lays Adrienne against her chest, and the baby blinks big Shirley Temple eyes around the room.

A few minutes later, Sharon reappears with a rack of dresses and an assistant who hands out cups of coffee to everyone but me.

"Okay, Laurie, here is the first of our size-six racks," Sharon starts.

"How many do you have?" I ask weakly, looking at the seven-foot-long hanging rod crammed with dresses.

"Ten."

I try very hard not to grimace.

"But you might find that you should skip down to a size four," Sharon goes on. "You have a small bust size, and so a smaller dress might fit better. I understand that you want to avoid alterations."

"I do?" I ask, looking at Hannah, who nods vigorously.

"It'll cut down on the price," she says.

"Sounds good to me, then." I finger the first dress. "I have to try all of these on?"

Sharon laughs. "Of course not. Only the ones that fit your

particular desires."

"My particular desires? Okay. Do you have any wedding-themed T-shirts?"

"Laurie," Lexi warns.

"Right," I say. "Okay. I would like a——"

"Sleeveless," Lexi cuts in. "She should try a sleeveless gown."

"With lace," Laney adds.

"And lots of little flowers," Ruby says, chucking little Adrienne on the chin.

Sharon holds up her hand. "Laurie, may I suggest that you try on a variety, see which cut flatters your figure the best, and decide from there?"

"Good idea," Hannah says.

"Okay, sure," I say.

Sharon pulls out four different dresses and hangs them on a separate rack. "Go ahead and start trying on."

I look around at the five women who know me best, the perfect stranger, and the cherubic baby staring at me, waiting for me to strip down, and pause.

"Only gets worse, Lauren," Laney says, guessing what I was thinking, tiredly running a hand through her shoulder-length brown-blonde hair. "Wait until childbirth, when the whole world gets to see everything. And I do mean *everything*."

I shrug. "True." I pull off my tank top and jeans and slip into the first dress, a lacy, strapless number with a full skirt and lots of beading. Hannah comes over, helping with the many zippers and buttons.

Ick.

"Now, this one does come with a handbag and a matching shawl," Sharon says.

Hannah pushes my bra strap into the dress and tilts her head, lips pursed, as she looks at me.

"Mmm," Joan says, squinching her face. "You look . . . not normal."

"I don't like it," Lexi says, her typical tactless self.

"Next," Ruby says.

The next gown has three-quarter sleeves and a long train.

"That makes you look bulky," Hallie says.

A halter-top dress, eyelet lace, and a form-fitting skirt is after that.

"I like the bottom of the dress," Hannah says.

"That V-neck is awfully low," Laney says. "The point is to save that for your honeymoon, not flaunt it in front of five hundred guests and a pastor."

"My husband, I might add." Ruby grins.

"How many guests?" I gasp.

"Next dress, Honey," Joan says.

I pull on a sleeveless, A-line gown with just a smattering of detail on the top of the dress and hardly a train, and turn to look in the mirror.

"Wow," Joan says, leaning back. "That is very slimming, Laurie."

"I love this one," Hannah declares.

"That's beautiful," Ruby says. Adrienne coos.

Lexi tilts her head. "Pull your hair up, Baby, I can't see the back." I pile my hair in a bun on the top of my head and she nods. "Very nice. But I like your hair down."

"What do you think, Laurie?" Hallie asks.

I look at my reflection in the mirror and ruffle my hair back. The dress does emphasize my good points.

"It's nice," I say, smoothing my hands over the silky fabric.

"Look at that smile," Laney says softly.

"I think she likes it," Joan answers, also smiling.

I turn around and grin at the women in front of me. "Guess what?"

"What?" Lexi asks.

"I'm getting married!" I squeal excitedly.

Hannah bursts into laughter. "Want to look at the other dresses, Laur?"

"Nope. This is it."

Sharon comes out of the background then. "That is the quickest decision I've ever seen," she declares.

"Well, Laurie's nothing if not decisive when it comes to trying things on," Lexi says, sprawling back on the couch.

"How much?" Joan asks.

"Well, like I said, these are our off-the-rack dresses, meaning they're last year's styles." Sharon looks at me. "Trust me, in thirty years, no one will have a clue when they're looking at your wedding album."

"True." I nod.

"So these are half price. I think this one is two hundred."

Joan raises her eyebrows, pleased. "Wonderful. Let's try on veils. And then, Honey, you need to pick out bridesmaid dresses."

Sharon hangs the first three dresses back on the rack and pushes it out of the room.

"What color are you thinking for the bridesmaids?" Hannah asks, pen in hand.

"How about orange?" Joan suggests.

I tame my expression and shake my head. "I'm really not an orange person, Joan," I say nicely.

Orange. *Blegh*.

Sharon reappears with a selection of veils. "When choosing a color for the bridesmaids, try to think about what color would look best on everyone," she says. "For example, this young lady has red hair and very fair skin, yet your maid of honor has blonde hair and darker skin. So a deep blue would look nice on everyone, or a purple. But stay away from reds and pinks."

I nod and take the veil she hands me. "Veils have gone somewhat out of style. Most brides opt for a tiara instead," she says.

"I like the idea of a veil, though," I say. "If I wore a tiara, I'd feel like I was dressing up as Cinderella for Halloween."

Sharon nods. "Perfectly acceptable. Do you want a veil with a blusher?"

"Does that mean it applies blush for me? Sure."

She laughs. "No, that's a shorter veil that covers the face during the processional and sometimes until the kiss."

"Oh. Why can't they call it the shorter veil that covers the face during the processional and the kiss?"

Sharon regards me for a minute.

"She's kidding," Hannah says. She takes the gauzy piece of white from me and deftly sticks it on my head.

"Ick," Lexi declares, now taking up the entire couch and lounging on her stomach. "Looks like someone dumped a container of frosting on your head. Which is actually making me hungry." She looks up at Sharon. "Do you have cookies or something?"

"I'll get Connie to bring them right in."

Connie, the silent assistant, appears with a tray of every kind of cookie imaginable, sets it on the rolling table by the coffee, and leaves.

"Hey, there're Oreos," I say, squirming as Hannah tries to get the veil off.

"Hold still, Laurie."

"I'm hungry."

She wrestles it off and promptly sticks another one on. "You'll have to wait."

"But we didn't get lunch," I whine.

"We're taking you out afterward," Joan says.

Lexi makes a big show about biting into the Oreo, a shower of crumbs falling on her shirt. "Mmm." She sighs. "These have to be the freshest Oreos I've ever had."

"Shut up, Lexi."

Hannah fluffs the veil. "There. Look at that one."

Laney finishes chewing a mint-flavored cookie and squints at me. "It looks marshmallowy."

"Could we stop referring to this using food items?" I ask.

"Well, it does!" Laney argues. "Don't you think, Joan?"

"It does look marshmallowy," Joan admits. "Sorry, Honey."

Hannah puts a slinky, sheer veil on and smiles. "There. What do you guys think about that one?"

"That's pretty. Maybe with a lily behind her ear?" Lexi says.

I shake my head, the veil rippling. "I don't think so. I'm not going to look like a Hawaiian hula dancer at my wedding."

"For the reception then?" Lexi asks.

"Right, at the reception." I grin. I look back at the mirror. "You know, I'm not feeling this blushing thing."

"Blusher, Laurie."

"Whatever. Can I just get a veil without the front part?"

Sharon nods. "Absolutely." She sets a long, one-tiered veil on my head and steps back. "What do you think of this one?"

I fluff the veil and grin. "Perfect."

"Great!" She claps her hands and pulls in a huge rack of bridesmaid dresses in every color under the sun and announces that it is now time to pick them out.

"Laurie, you're the big decision maker on this one, so go ahead and get changed."

The girls all crowd around the rack. Joan holds up colors on Hallie and gives her opinion. Lexi and Laney argue about designs, and Adrienne squeals.

I turn and look in the mirror again.

Wow, Lord. I'm in a wedding gown.

Chapter Twenty-Five

Ryan rings the doorbell at seven. I finish pulling on a pair of hiking boots and open the door, grinning. "Hey, future husband."

"Hi, future wife." He kisses me, winks, and looks at my shoes. "I think you should tie those laces, Hon."

"I was just getting to that. So can we make Nick regret having us take this therapy?"

"No, that's not nice, Laurie."

"Please? Just in the beginning?"

He sighs. "How'd the dress shopping go?"

"We decided on a hula theme, so I'll actually be wearing a bikini."

He snorts and laughs. "Uh-huh. What do I get to wear? Board shorts and a lei?"

"You can even have a flower behind your ear, if you'd like."

"Sounds charming."

"Dad and I will hula down the aisle and toss paper umbrellas instead of flower petals. What do you think?" I ask, finishing with my boots.

"I don't know. Will we serve Hawaiian Punch afterwards and

limbo?" he asks seriously.

"Hey!" I shout. "We could even canoe race!"

Dad comes through the room, sipping a mug of lemongrass tea.

Blegh.

"Laurie-girl, I don't like the idea of you canoe racing," he says, frowning. "You got your mother's coordination, bless your heart. Anything that requires that much control you should probably avoid, Honey."

He goes into his study and closes the door.

I look up at Ryan, who grins unrepentantly, and I shake my head. "Let's go. Time for therapy."

He snickers and follows me out the door.

⎯◈⎯

Ten minutes later Nick sits down opposite us in the very empty church office. "All right, guys, let's get started."

I hold up my hand.

"What, Laurie?"

"Why are we meeting here?"

He looks around. "Because this is my office."

"Churches are creepy at night," I declare.

"Deal with it," Nick says, handing us each a spiral-bound note-book. A picture of a couple walking hand in hand barefoot on the beach decorates the front, the words *A Harmonious Life* above the couple.

"Premarital counseling is a time for you as a couple to get to know each other better," Nick says, half-reading from the leader's guide.

"And thus live harmoniously?" Ryan asks, straight-faced.

I cover my mouth.

Nick shoots both of us a warning look and goes back to the guide. "The first question I want to ask you, the engaged couple, is why are you getting married?"

"Tax benefits," Ryan says immediately.

"And yet you call yourself romantic," I say to him.

He grins.

Nick sets the guide in his lap. "Guys, you're going to have to be honest if these sessions are going to work."

"Sorry," Ryan says. "I love her. I've loved her for a long time. And I know that she's the one God created for me."

I smile sappily and squeeze his hand.

"Laurie?" Nick asks.

"Well, I love him. I know I want to spend the rest of my life with him," I say. Ryan squeezes my hand this time.

Nick smiles. "Okay. Good. Now, a big thing in marriage is the compatibility of dreams. Ryan, you have a job. Is this where you want to stay?"

Ryan purses his lips and nods. "In town you mean? Yeah. I'd like to own my own construction business someday, but I want to stay here."

"Laurie? What about you?"

"My whole family lives here, Nick. Of course I want to stay here."

He nods once. "Okay, good."

"Um, Nick?" I say, half-raising my hand.

"Yes, Laurie?"

"This is premarital counseling?"

"Yes, Laurie."

"Oh. Okay, then. Go ahead."

He flips to the next page in the guide. Ryan raises his hand.

"What is it, Ryan?"

"Nick, sorry. Just curious. This is a required course here?"

"To be married by one of our pastors, yes."

"Oh."

Nick sighs and looks up at us. "Most couples are more communicative. Particularly the would-be wife."

I blink. "I'm not communicating enough?"

"That's a first," Ryan says.

Nick ignores us. "The next part of the session involves personality tests, so if you'll flip to page three in your workbooks, you can start."

I raise my hand again, meekly.

Nick lets his breath out. "What, Laurie?"

"I don't have a pencil."

───❖───

I'm nearing the end of James. I block a yawn and flip the page over, finding where I am. "The Lord is full of compassion and mercy."

I lean back on the pillows and smile. Compassion, mercy, and a sense of humor. Who would have ever thought that I, the matchmaker, would have my own match someday?

Not me.

God is very good!

───❖───

I am woken up Tuesday morning by someone grabbing my foot from under the covers and pressing something very hard against it.

"Hey, whamsipgh?" I mumble, putting my arm over my eyes.

"Shh," Joan whispers. "I'm just getting your foot measurement, Laurie. Go back to sleep."

"Foot measurement?"

"For your wedding shoes. Shh."

"Mmpgh. What time is it?"

"Seven thirty, Dear."

"In the morning?"

"Go back to sleep."

The hard thing removed, I roll over and drift back off.

— ❖ —

I go downstairs at nine, ruffling my freshly fixed hair and blinking repeatedly because a fleck of mascara had dropped in my eye when I was applying eye shadow.

Joan and Hannah are sitting at the kitchen table, drinking tea and coffee. Hannah is eating a bagel.

"I always wanted another sister," I say sleepily.

"Hi, Laur." Hannah grins.

"Don't you ever work?" I yawn, filling my mug.

"I could ask the same thing about you."

"My first client isn't until ten. I love having my part-time job back."

Joan laughs. "It is good. Think if you'd been trying to plan the wedding before the studio hired Claire."

I groan and sit down at the table. "So what was with the early morning foot massage, Joan?"

Joan rolls her eyes. "I told you, Laurie. I was measuring the width of your foot so we could go ahead and order your wedding shoes."

"My wedding shoes," I repeat.

Hannah nods. "They're adorable. Strappy, high-heeled sandals. I would wear them after the wedding too."

"Strappy?" I moan.

"Sandals. You need something elegant to match the dress."

"You know, you can't see my feet underneath the gown, ladies." The dress, safely sealed in a temperature-regulated and humidity-safe bag, hangs in my closet.

"Still, you should *feel* elegant. It is your wedding, after all."

"So it is."

"Oh, we're receiving your invitations in the mail today," Joan adds, sipping her tea. "I'm having the girls over to address them, and we'll get them mailed by tomorrow. We're really pushing the clock with those."

"And your registry needs to be done by tomorrow too," Hannah says. "Once people get their invitations, they'll go buy you stuff. It helps to be registered where the invites say you are."

I raise my hands. "I have tomorrow off. We'll get it done. Now. About these sandals . . ."

"Gotta go, Laur. I'm very late as it is," Hannah says, swallowing the last of her bagel and kissing the top of my head. "See you there in a minute."

I wave good-bye and look over at Joan, who is calmly flipping through a white-washed magazine titled *Bridal Dreams*.

"Don't forget that we're all going over to look at the house this afternoon, Dear," she says.

"Who's we?"

"Ryan, Hannah, me, your father, and I think that's it."

"Think we'll all fit inside?"

"Probably."

"And the flower guy is tomorrow," I say.

"Ten thirty." Joan nods. "Do you want candles in the wedding?"

"As what? Bridesmaids?"

She rolls her eyes. "In the background. Candelabra. It gives such an ethereal glow to everything." She sighs.

I frown, cupping my coffee mug with both hands. "Considering that I'll be in strappy high-heeled sandals, it sounds dangerous."

"Oh, nonsense," Joan rebuffs. "You'll have your father to hold you up down the aisle, and Ryan to hold you up when you get there. They'll be beautiful, Laurie. And if you're using lilies, candles would add so much."

"I'll think about it," I say, standing, swallowing the last of my coffee. "Got to go, Joan, or I'll miss my client."

"Who's on your plate today?"

"The Mayberlys, the Peters, the McHardys, and Tina and Kyle . . ." The last names I say with a groan.

Joan smiles. "Have a good day, Dear."

⚬⬧⚬

I arrive at the studio at exactly ten o'clock and the Mayberlys are already there waiting.

"Hi, sorry for the wait," I say, slinging my backpack into my cubbyhole.

Mrs. Mayberly shrugs, pets her four-year-old blonde daughter, and says not to worry.

The morning goes by quickly, and I have a twenty-minute break before the Queen of Beauty and her perfect husband show up.

I slam open Brandon's door and he gives me a cursory look up. "Hey, Kid."

"Hey."

I climb on his desk and sit in front of him. He leans back, grinning. "How's the wedding prep?"

"Preposterous."

"Well. You did name my wife for your matron of honor."

"We're reducing her marital status and calling her the maid of honor, Brandon. Matron sounds like she's overweight."

He frowns. "You know, it does."

"I know. That's why I said it."

"So, uh, how much longer?" he asks, trying unsuccessfully to hide a grin.

"How much longer until what?"

He clears his throat, grinning. "Perkiness."

"You did it!" I screech, jumping to my knees, crunching papers beneath me.

He leans back farther, laughing. "I told them they had a free session for being the cover couple." He smirks, dodging my fist. "Hey!"

"You are so mean, you know that?"

"I just wanted to give you a good dose of marital joy before your happy day," he says.

I scald him with my pupils, vault off the desk, and stomp out to the waiting room, where the couple in reference stands.

Kyle and Tina Medfield have been married for a year and a half. Four months ago baby Sophie was born.

Miraculously, as some have called it, she lost her pregnancy weight the week after giving birth. She still has a figure like Mischa Barton. Kyle, muscular and handsome, is the perfect specimen of an American husband.

Two years ago I took their engagement pictures, and now a larger-than-life beauty shot hangs above Hannah's desk.

"Hi, guys," I say, forcing a smile to my face.

Tina flashes a gorgeous smile at me, tugging on Kyle's ample bicep. "Hi, Laurie. How are you? I brought the baby because I couldn't find a sitter. Hope that's all right."

"You don't want her picture?"

"No, we're just getting our free couple picture."

"Oh," I say, frowning.

Here's the thing: It's not that Tina and Kyle are not nice people; it's that I always feel inferior after they leave.

Tina, with her long, silky black hair, chocolate skin, huge coffee-colored eyes, perfect cheekbones, and graceful figure, makes me feel clumsy, plain, and boring.

I snap their pictures as quickly as possible, baby Sophie lounging in her car seat behind me, making little sucking noises on her fingers.

They leave forty-five minutes later, passing Hannah's empty desk. Tina pauses as she is halfway out the door. "Laurie, please feel free to say no, but do you think you could watch Sophie tomorrow night during Bible study?"

My jaw drops.

She hurries on. "I mean, since it really is a couples' Bible study now. Most of what Nick talks about isn't relevant for singles."

I blink at her.

It's happening! My premonition is coming true! Me, single girl, babysitting for my own singles' Bible study.

"Uh, I'd love to," I lie, "but I'll be very busy planning floral arrangements probably right up until the study starts." Throughout this little speech, I've been flashing blinding light from my ring into Tina's eyes.

"Oh, are you working at that new Hallmark florist as well?" she asks, sliding her sunglasses on.

Arg.

"For my wedding," I say. Insert fake smile here. "I'm engaged."

"Aw!" she squeals suddenly, making baby Sophie jump. "Laurie! You and Keller? Oh, I am so glad you two are tying the knot!"

"Me and Ryan, Tina."

"Ryan? Ryan who?"

Oh, that's right. You wouldn't know who he is because he doesn't fit into your mold for perfectly chiseled men.

Immediately I feel bad. *Okay, sorry, Lord. That was mean.*

"Ryan Palmer? We've been dating for almost two years."

Tina's perfectly lip-glossed lips fall open. "No way," she says. "Oh, I had no idea! What's he look like?"

"Moderately tall, curly hair, pretty brown eyes."

"I guess I just haven't noticed him," she says, tossing her shiny sunlit hair.

"He's a really sweet guy."

"What a pity, though," she says, ignoring my statement. "I honestly thought you and Keller had something there."

I shake my head, lips smashing together tightly.

"Well, congratulations, Laurie. I hope the flower arranging goes well. You know, you really should hire a wedding consultant to handle all that. I did, and my wedding was beautiful—well, you were there. Wasn't it gorgeous? Trish did such a wonderful job," she croons.

"I'd rather do it myself," I say sweetly. And what kind of name is Trish, anyway?

Tina shrugs her delicate shoulders. "Most weddings that are hand done look a little simplistic. But maybe that suits your tastes better."

No comeback for this one.

"Well," she says, smiling again. "See you tomorrow night!"

I watch her hips sway as she walks to the metallic green Mustang convertible that Kyle is standing by. He takes the baby, fastens her into the backseat, opens the driver's door, where Tina takes charge, and then slides meekly into the passenger's seat.

What a life.

I never had brothers, but I did have Brandon, and it would seriously offend him if I offered to drive, whether it was my car, his car, or his parents' car.

It's a control thing.

Simplistic?

I turn around and nearly run into Hannah, who is coming out of the boss's office, shaking her head. "Sorry about that, Laur."

"What?"

"Tina and Kyle. You should swat my husband."

"Hannah, you're my best friend, and as such you have a responsibility to be perfectly honest with me," I start.

She sits down at her desk and steeples her fingers together. "I will be perfectly honest. What's up?"

"Do I have simplistic tastes?"

"This from the woman who wanted the *Calvin and Hobbes Anthology* for Christmas."

"Does that mean yes?"

She smiles at me. "No, Laurie, it means you vary between simple and extremely complex. Take, for example, when you go to Merson's. Do you ever get just a brownie?"

"Occasionally."

"What do you get otherwise?"

"If he has it, I get Shawn's German chocolate brownie topped with pecans, caramel sauce, and whipped cream."

"See? Case in point." Hannah makes a face. "And that sounds way too sweet."

I frown and look up at the ceiling in thought. "I'm sorry, I'm not familiar with the term *way too sweet*. What's that mean?"

"Funny, Laurie."

Chapter Twenty-Six

Dad pulls to a stop in front of the For Sale sign and looks back at me. "Is this it, Laurie-girl?"

"I guess so," I say, looking out the window.

A white picket fence surrounds the whole property, which in this part of town is usually at least an acre.

Ryan leans across the seat to look out my window. "Yard's nice," he murmurs.

I open the door and step out, catching sight of the house.

"Where's Hannah?" Joan asks, hands on her hips, looking around. "She said she'd meet us here at two."

Dad comes over and stands next to me and Ryan. "No garage," he notes.

"There's a carport," Ryan says. "We could easily enclose that. Make it a garage."

The house is a white ranch-style and has a cute little front porch with two white wicker chairs and a table set up on it. Huge massive trees shade the grass, and a little brick walkway leads around to the back of the house.

Joan looks over at me. "First impression?"

"Has potential."

Hannah comes running down the sidewalk just then. "Hey, sorry I'm late. Brandon called right as I walked into the house." She turns to the house and waves her hand. "So? Cute, right? The realtor, Nancy, and her husband are the couple who mentored Brandon and me when we were engaged. She's inside, I guess, because that's her car in the driveway."

We follow Hannah up the walk to the little house. She rings the doorbell and squeals at the chairs. "How cute are they!"

Ryan leans over. "If we buy the house, the chairs go."

I grin.

A classy-looking brunette opens the door and immediately envelops Hannah in a hug. "Honey, I am so glad you called. Look at you!"

Hannah pulls back and waves her hand at us. "This is Ryan and Laurie and Laurie's parents, Mr. and Mrs. Holbrook."

"Hi," Nancy says, smiling at us. "Please come in."

I step into the tiny living area. All the furniture has been moved out, and orange shag carpet covers the floor. Huge windows take up almost all the walls.

Immediately to the left is the kitchen, barely big enough to hold a refrigerator and a microwave. The breakfast nook off of it is small but cute, again surrounded by windows overlooking the side yard, which is overrun with giant sunflowers.

"There are two bedrooms," Nancy says, leading us down the hall toward the back. "One on the right, one on the left, and a central bathroom."

The bedrooms are each the size of the living room. The bathroom is nice and has obviously been remodeled.

Nancy smiles at me. "The guest house is my favorite. It's perfect for an office or a workshop."

The back door comes off the living room, and the brick walk-way meets the other one leading from the front door.

The guest house is basically a miniaturized version of the actual house.

"So what do you think?" Nancy asks, hands together, tour complete.

Ryan rubs his chin and forces his backwards baseball cap far-ther down on his hair. "I'd like to look at the structuring. Mind if I do some measurements?"

"Not at all," Nancy says.

Ryan looks at Dad. "Want to help, sir?"

Dad nods. "Sure, Son. We should look at the carport first," he says, the two of them walking back to the house.

I hear Ryan laugh. "You read my thoughts."

Nancy smiles at me. "Hannah tells me that he's in construction."

"Yeah, houses."

"This would be a great house to add on to. There is so much room."

"How big is the lot?" I ask.

"Two and a half acres. The house itself was built in 1934. The guest house was added around 1976, if I remember right," Nancy says.

"When were the bathroom and kitchen remodeled?" Joan asks.

"About two years ago. The water and gas lines were both redone then too."

"Why are the owners selling?" I ask.

Nancy sighs. "The wife died of a heart attack not too long

ago. They didn't have any kids in town, so the husband moved to California, where he could be closer to two of his daughters."

"How sad," Joan says.

Nancy nods.

I excuse myself and go back into the house.

Small, but livable.

Ryan passes me on his way from the second bedroom. "Hey, Babe, what do you think?"

"I think we could live here," I say slowly, turning around in a circle. "The kitchen's tiny, but that's an excuse not to cook."

He laughs and slings an arm around my shoulders. "I have an idea for this living room. That wall between here and the second bedroom isn't a load-bearing wall. We could knock it and the wall between the bedroom and the hall down and then we would have doubled our living space."

I nod. "That would be nice."

"We don't really have a need for a second bedroom right now," he says, grinning at me.

"Change of subject. I like the nook area."

"Yeah. But I would take out that cabinet toward the end there and push that side out some so the kitchen would be bigger and we'd still have eating space."

"Mm." I nod. "I like the fact that there's a fence too because Darcy's coming with us."

"Exactly. And about our bedroom," he says, steering me down the hall. "It's kind of dark, so I'd add some of those marbled glass blocks and that would kick up the lighting."

I watch him as he talks, using his hands animatedly, his eyes sparkling with the thought of a new project, and grin.

"What?" he asks, looking at me.

"You're cute when you're excited."

He smiles self-consciously. "Is it that obvious?"

"You love this house, don't you?"

"It's got a lot of good features and a lot of things we could make better. Plus, it's very close to Brandon and Hannah, and I like that we'd have people we could call who could be here in thirty seconds if we needed them."

I nod. "And it's like five minutes both to Ruby's house and Dad and Joan's house."

"Right. And you know I want to start my own business someday. We could revamp the guest house, and it would be a perfect office for me."

"It's on two and a half acres. That's a lot of yard work."

"So we get a riding mower." He grins. "Put it on the registry."

"Problem. I'm not registering at Home Depot. Sorry."

He laughs and pulls me back against his chest and rests his chin on the top of my head. "I think it would work, Laur. I really do."

I look at the empty room and squeeze his arms. "Okay. We'll do it. On one condition."

"What's that?"

"First home improvement project is ripping up that orange carpet."

I feel him laugh. "Deal. I'll go tell Nancy."

Wednesday morning I wake up with a sticky, envelope-flavored taste in my mouth and gag. I had to have licked at least forty invitations before Joan suddenly remembered that we had an envelope wetter in the study.

"Blegh." I shudder, sitting up in bed.

Darcy rolls over from his position on the foot of the covers and blinks sleepily at me.

"Envelope residue," I explain to him.

He sighs sympathetically.

I smile and knee-walk across the bed, leaning down and wrapping my arms around his neck. Poor guy. With all the prewedding frenzy, he's been getting a little neglected.

Darcy licks my elbow, and all is well.

"Come on, Baby. Bacon for breakfast for you."

He perks up at that and follows me downstairs, after I've brushed my teeth and pulled on a pair of jeans. No telling who'll be waiting in the kitchen these days.

Ryan stands by the table, holding a box of Krispy Kreme doughnuts. I gasp, race down the stairs, and wrap him in a hug.

"I love you, have I told you that?" I ask, grabbing for the box.

"I hope you love me for more than the doughnuts," Ryan says dryly.

"Sure I do! Sometimes you bring me coffee." I grin cheekily.

He laughs and looks at Darcy. "Hey, Bud."

I lift a still-warm ring of heaven out of the box and smile at Darcy. "Our first child, Ry."

"What?"

"You know how newlyweds treat their pets. He'll be our baby. Then we'll get pregnant, and poor Darce will be shoved out into the cold."

Ryan rubs Darcy's ears. "Sorry about that one, Pal."

"It's his destiny," I say, tossing him a bit of my doughnut. I smile at Ryan. "What are you doing here?"

"Nancy has more papers for me to look over, and I asked her to meet me here rather than my apartment."

"Got it."

"What about you? You're up early."

I sigh. "Today is going to be a very long day. Joan set up a consultation with some cosmetologist at nine fifteen today to figure out my makeup, the flower guy is meeting us at the church at ten thirty, we're setting up the registry right after that, I have a haircut scheduled for four o'clock because according to Hannah, you should not cut your hair directly before the wedding, and then at six we've got that wedding cake sampling."

Ryan blows his breath out. "Wow. Hannah's right. No one in this family uses periods."

I sigh again.

He leans down and kisses me. "You'll make it. Just think about the cake."

I smile. "Cake."

He kisses me again and then straightens. "Don't let them cut too much off your hair. I like it long."

"Trust me. I do not want short hair for my wedding."

"Good."

"Hey, did you make sure Friday works for all the guys to get their suits picked out?" I ask, taking another bite of the doughnut. Ryan's best man is Brandon, and the groomsmen are basically all the bridesmaids' husbands: Nate, Adam, Shawn, and, since Nick is performing the ceremony, Ryan asked a friend from college I hadn't met, Tony Garcia.

Ryan nods. "All of them in town can. Tony e-mailed me his measurements. He'll be in town the Tuesday before the wedding."

I brighten. "Hey, does he have a girlfriend?"

"Honey? You have obviously never met Tony."

"Tony doesn't want a girlfriend?"

"Girlfriends don't want Tony."

I grin. "You're not a nice friend, Ryan Palmer."

"At least I'm honest." The doorbell rings, and he winks as he leaves.

Dad walks into the kitchen then, holding his ever-present mug of lemongrass tea. "Laurie-girl, Joan said something about a cosmetologist appointment?" he says, shoving his mug into the microwave to reheat it.

"Yeah, in about an hour."

Dad *tsks*. "I don't like the idea of you putting toxic chemicals on your face like that, Honey. Do you know what's in makeup these days?"

"Dad, I wear makeup every day."

"You're kidding," he says, truly shocked. He leans against the counter, mouth open. "When did you start wearing makeup?"

"In the fifth grade?"

"You've been wearing makeup since the fifth grade?" he asks. "Why?"

I polish off another doughnut before answering. "Well, because right around there is when Lexi started wearing makeup, and she was convinced she wanted to be a makeup artist, and like most younger siblings, I got to be the guinea pig."

Dad just blinks at me.

"I just heard my name, and whatever I did, I didn't mean to," Lexi says, coming in and going straight for the coffeepot. She pours a cup, then leans over and kisses Dad's cheek. "Morning, Dear Father. You look a mite bit appalled."

I send her a look.

"I watched *Sense and Sensibility* last night. The English hasn't faded yet," she explains.

The microwave beeps and Dad throws up his hands. "I don't know how I survived raising the two of you."

"Easy. We're very self-reliant." Lexi grins, stirring cream into her coffee.

"Self-reliant, my foot," Dad gripes. "You wrecked the car three times in high school, Lexi."

"All of which were not my fault," Lexi says calmly.

"You didn't even have your license yet!"

"Well . . ." Lexi says, drawing out the word. "Technicalities."

Dad shakes his head, walks over, and stands two inches away from my face. I lean back.

"Way in my circle of space, Dad."

"Do you have on makeup right now?" he asks.

"Yeah."

He stares a minute longer and then walks out of the kitchen, muttering, "Amazing."

Lexi sips her coffee and looks at me. "What was with that, Baby?"

"Dad didn't think I wore makeup."

"I am astounded. How utterly negligent in his concentration."

I roll my eyes. "Hey, are you coming to the cosmetologist appointment?"

"Of course, yes! I am inquisitive as to if I chose the proper career."

"Lexi?"

"Yes, Dear?"

"Cut it out."

Chapter Twenty-Seven

"You really should put this waffle iron on the registry, Laurie."

I look up from the list I am reviewing and blink at Joan. "Joan, when I want waffles, I go ask Shawn to make them for me."

She turns to Ryan, clutching the shiny appliance. "Ryan, what do you think?"

"Sorry, Joan, it's the same for me. I'm not much of a waffle guy, anyway."

"So what are you?" I grin as Joan stalks away to put back the waffle iron. "A muffin guy?"

"A cereal guy," Ryan corrects, smiling.

"Ah, puffed and crunchy."

He sighs. "What's next?"

We've been wandering around the department store for the last two hours and have already decided on sheets, towels, and a few plastic cups and plates, and now we are looking at appliances. First on the list? Definitely the restaurant-sized coffeemaker.

I never realized that by getting married you could order so many presents. If I had known, I would have gotten married a long time ago.

"Do we need a blender?" I ask.

"Do we like milkshakes?" Ryan counters.

I check it off on the complimentary list of everything in the store. "One blender."

Ryan chuckles.

"We should've measured the inside of your oven," Joan says, coming back. "What size pans will fit in there?"

"I thought all ovens were the same size," I say.

She shakes her head. "When was the kitchen updated on the house?"

We both look at Ryan, who frowns, staring up at the brilliant florescent lights. "Um . . . five years ago? Six?" he says to someone beside Joan's left shoulder.

"Over here, Ry," I say.

"Sorry," he apologizes, blinking repeatedly.

Joan watches him, one eyebrow slightly bent. "Didn't your mother ever teach you not to stare directly at bright lights? Never mind. I wouldn't ask for any pans bigger than a nine by thirteen or you may have problems."

"Nine by thirteen, got it."

"Also, while I was putting the perfectly beautiful and functional waffle iron away, I found this." She holds out a miniature incubator.

Ryan and I both stare.

"What is it?" I ask.

"It's an egg cooker, Dear."

"You can make eggs in that thing?"

"Yes. Soft-boiled, hard-boiled, over-easy—"

"Omelets?" Ryan suggests.

"No omelets. Those you have to use either a skillet or an

omelet pan."

Ryan shrugs. "I only like eggs in omelets."

"And I don't particularly like eggs," I say. "But I like egg salad sandwiches."

"This is what you would use to boil the eggs, Laurie."

I look at Ryan, who shrugs again. "Okay, sure," I say, checking the egg cooker off. "We'll get an egg cooker."

"We need a toaster," Ryan says.

Joan glances at her watch. "We have another hour and a half to pick out dishes, place settings, and pans, Honey. Let's get a move on."

⎯⎯◈⎯⎯

We finish right at three forty-five. I hand the employee my list, kiss my fiancé, and get smashed into the car. Fifteen minutes later I plop into a twirly chair with a curly haired woman behind it.

"I'm Veronica. I'll be cutting your hair," she says.

"I'm Laurie. Not too much off," I say.

"She's getting married in two and a half weeks," Joan says.

"Oh, how exciting! Who are you marrying?" she asks, I guess expecting that she knows him.

"Um, Orlando Bloom."

Her mouth drops open, and Joan drops her head into her hands.

"Oh my goodness, how did you two meet?" Veronica gasps.

"Well," I start.

"She's just kidding," Joan interrupts quickly. "Her groom's name is Ryan Palmer."

She flicks the back of my head. "You're a funny girl. You totally had me going."

"Yeah. I know." Fake smile. "Not too much off."

"Of course not. You appear to have layers." She lifts a chunk of my hair and sifts it through her fingers.

"Lots of them. I don't like them."

"How are you wanting to fix your hair for your wedding?"

"Probably down and curly."

"Is your hair naturally curly?"

"No, it's naturally wavy."

"Very wavy," Joan adds.

"When is your wedding?" Veronica asks.

"August twelfth."

Veronica nods and bites her bottom lip as she riffles through my hair. "Okay," she says, finally. "I'm just going to shape up the ends, which shouldn't take long. Wedding day morning I'll have you come back in. I'll curl your hair and put the veil on, and that will make your morning so much easier."

Joan beams. "Thank you so much."

"My pleasure. Laurie, you have beautiful hair."

I lean forward and dig around in my backpack for my cell phone. "Would you mind repeating that for my friend Hannah?"

Joan shakes her head. "Ignore her. She has five bridesmaids. Could we get their hair done the morning of the wedding as well?"

"Of course," Veronica says. She turns and shouts into the din of hairdryers and chatter. "Hey, Lisa!"

A blonde woman turns. "What's up, Ver?"

"Come here for a second."

Lisa comes over. "Hi," she says to me and Joan.

"This is Laurie and her mother, Joan. Laurie's getting married on August twelfth, and she has five bridesmaids."

Lisa nods, also runs her fingers through my hair, and listens as Veronica explains the wedding day morning.

"Sure," she says when Veronica is finished. "I'm free and I know for a fact that Debbie is because she said something about sleeping in on the twelfth. Between the three of us, we can handle it."

"Poor Debbie," I say.

—⊕—

I receive my first gift exactly six days later on the first of August. We'd just closed on the house that morning. Ryan and I are scrambling to figure out which home improvement projects need to be done first so we can start moving furniture.

"Laurie! Laurie! Laurie!" Lexi screams, running into the living room, where Joan and I are discussing menu options.

I jump up from the couch, sure that she'd scalded herself on the coffeemaker, sliced open her hand, or something else life-threatening, since she only uses my name in emergencies or when she's mad.

She grins, grabs my arm, and jerks me to the front door, where two hulking delivery guys are trying to wrestle a box the size of a large pony into the house.

"What's this?" I ask, mouth dropping.

Shoving the box in, one of the guys looks up, backhanding his forehead and gazing appreciatively at my sister. "Addressed to Laurie Holbrook and Ryan Palmer," he says.

Lexi fakes a yawn, blocking it with her left hand, her ring sparkling.

The delivery guy raises his eyebrows and grins. "Smooth."

"Thank you," Lexi says to him. She whirls to me. "Quick! Open it, Baby!"

"With what, my bare hands?" I ask.

Joan and Dad come into the entry then. She gapes at the box and smiles at me. "Ah, the first present."

"We should wait for Ryan," I say. "It's addressed to him too."

"Is he the guy with the backwards hat who pulled up behind us?" the second delivery man asks.

"Matches his description." I nod.

Ryan's big shoulders come into view. He sees the delivery guys, grins, and keeps sauntering up to the house, swinging his keys on one finger.

"Hurry, you dolt!" Lexi shrieks. "We're opening it!"

"Better move it, man," Delivery Guy #1 says. "These women do not look patient."

"Hey!" Lexi protests. "Did we ask for your opinion? We did not. Besides, you're done delivering. You can go."

"The last time I delivered a box this size, it was a rare African sloth," he says. "I'm sticking around."

"I don't think a sloth would get along too well with Darcy," Dad says.

"Yeah, what if it's a masked marayder and he's out to getcha?" Delivery Guy #2 drawls.

"That's marauder and get you," Joan corrects.

Ryan squeezes around the box, kisses my cheek, and cocks his head at the vacant return address. "From anonymous?" he asks.

I nod. "Do you have your work knife with you?"

He spreads his hands and shakes his head. "Nope. I didn't come from work."

Delivery Guy #2 hands me a box knife. "That is a very sharp

knife. Cut with carefulness."

"Care," Joan says.

"Whatever." Delivery Guy #2 rolls his eyes.

Ryan takes the knife from me. "You're not allowed to use sharp objects, remember?" he says. He slices the tape cleanly and hands the knife back to the owner.

"Open it, open it, open it," Lexi squeals.

I pull up one flap, and Ryan takes the other.

Styrofoam peanuts fill the box.

"This box weighs more than my great-aunt Colleen, and she's ninety pounds overweight," Delivery Guy #1 says. "There's more than peanuts in there."

"Poor Colleen," Dad says. "That is not healthy at all."

"Don't worry too much, sir," #1 says. "She's on Atkins now."

Ryan nods to the delivery guys, and the three of them dig into the box, looking for a shape to try to pull out.

"I found the bottom!" Ryan yells, his voice echoing from inside the box.

"Got the top," #2 grunts.

"Okay, count of three," #1 says, hands halfway in the box. "One. Two. Three!"

Amid groans and huffs, a humongous TV is lifted out of the box and set carefully on the entry floor.

I stare at it, my chin grazing my toes.

Ryan steps back next to me, whistling. "Wow."

The two delivery guys grin. "Now that is a TV," #1 says, dusting peanuts off his sleeves.

Lexi starts laughing. "Oh my gosh," she says after a minute. "That has got to be the hugest TV I have ever seen in all my life."

Delivery Guy #2 fishes a tape measure from his pocket, hands one end to #1, and pulls it across the face of the TV. "Eighty-six inches," he announces.

"Who needs an eighty-six-inch TV?" Dad asks, eyes locked on the screen.

"I cannot fathom," Joan answers him.

"Can you imagine how big Colin Firth would look on that screen?" Lexi whispers in my ear.

I grin, then sober. "Why would you send something this big and not tell who you are?"

"Maybe there's a note or something still in the box," Ryan says.

The two delivery guys, Ryan, and I all start going through the zillion peanuts and come up with four John Wayne DVDs, six romantic comedies I have seen but do not own, two Rodgers and Hammerstein musicals, and a plain white shoebox.

Ryan frowns, opens the shoebox, and holds up a gift certificate for three hundred dollars' worth of furniture at Furniture Mart.

No note.

I pluck a peanut out of my hair and sit down in the middle of the entry floor, brain in overload.

Ryan joins me, balancing his arms on his kneecaps.

"You guys have no idea who sent this?" I ask the two delivery guys.

"We just ship the boxes, miss. That's it," #1 says.

Ryan leans back, staring at the TV. "I have an idea," he says slowly.

"What?"

"My parents."

"Why would your parents send us a TV that's bigger than our future living room?"

"They haven't seen our future living room. They're the only ones I can think of who would remember to send John Wayne movies."

"Honey, everyone knows you love John Wayne movies," I say.

"And my mother's favorite movie is *Oklahoma!*," Ryan adds.

Delivery Guy #1 nods. "Well, it sounds awfully suspicious to me."

Lexi kneels down on the floor next to my ear. "Baby, I was just at that big electronics warehouse on Fifth," she starts. "You know, because I was looking for that automatically adjusting cooler dealie—"

"Lexi."

"Right. Anyway, a TV this size costs at least three thousand dollars," she tries to whisper, unsuccessfully.

Delivery Guy #2 whistles.

"You really think your parents would send us a three-thousand-dollar TV, a gift certificate for furniture, and a collection of movies?" I ask Ryan, mouth still open.

Ryan shrugs and then nods. "Yeah, it sounds like them."

"Ryan, I don't even know your parents!"

"Well, they've always given us extravagant gifts to make up for the fact that we're not close," he says. "Remember when Adrienne was born? They basically gave Nick and Ruby their baby room."

I blow my breath out. "Wow."

Delivery Guy #1 pulls a gadget out of his pocket and tells me to sign on the electronic screen. I do and hand it back to him.

"Hey, if you want, we can move this to your new house," he says.

"Really?" I ask.

"Where's your new house?"

I tell him the cross streets and he nods.

"Yeah, we can move it. Free of charge, just 'cause I like you guys."

"And we're shippin' some other dude's sofa over in that direction this afternoon," #2 says.

Delivery Guy #1 grins. "Right. And that."

Ryan stands and shakes his head. "Here, I'm parked behind you anyway. I'll lead you to the house, all right?"

"Sounds great, man. Nice meeting you folks. Good luck with the wedding, miss," Delivery Guy #1 says to me.

"Thanks for your help," I say.

They lift the TV back into the box, the two delivery guys hustle it out to the truck again, and Ryan kisses my cheek. "I'll be back in fifteen minutes."

"Oh, Ryan, I have a quick question," Joan says as he starts to leave.

"Sure, ma'am."

"Do you prefer fresh salmon or chicken?"

Ryan blinks, then looks at me. "Is this a trick question?"

"No, silly," Joan chuckles.

"Chicken."

"Ha!" I yell.

Ryan winks and leaves. Joan sighs. "And I was counting on him to choose fresh salmon."

Lexi makes a face. "Yuck."

"Salmon is very healthy," Dad says. "Lots of omega-3 fatty acids in salmon." He looks at us, waiting for our reaction.

When Lexi and I don't respond, Dad sighs and continues. "It's good for your heart. It helps keep platelets from sticking together."

"Do we have to serve a meal?" I ask. "Can't we just have cake?"

"Your wedding is at three, Laurie," Joan says. "It's customary to serve something."

She leads the way to the sofa, where we again pick up the wedding books. "See? Says at least a tea reception for an afternoon wedding," Joan says.

"Meaning what? Cucumber sandwiches?"

"Sure, or scones or little savories . . ." She looks down at the book, reads a few lines, and shakes her head. "I wouldn't serve anything sweet. Your cake is sweet enough."

I grin. I'd compromised and picked a white angel food cake, but a ripple of chocolate mousse runs through the layers.

Joan had told me that not only would a chocolate cake be a pain and a half for whatever poor baker got to ice it, but it would also stain my dress terribly if Ryan decided to smash the cake in my face.

Knowing Ryan, I chose the white cake.

Ryan has been put in charge of the honeymoon and the groomsmen. Hannah and Joan are basically in charge of everything else.

Occasionally, I get asked for my opinion.

The phone rings right as Joan and I finish deciding on scones and cream, crackers and cheese, and lots and lots of sparkling cider.

"It's for you, Laurie-girl."

I take the phone from Dad. "Hello?"

"Laurie?"

"Yes?"

"Hi, this is Wendy."

Here's the thing: I do not know a Wendy. I run for the invitation list.

"Ryan's mom," the woman says after a long pause.

I set the list down. "Oh, hi! Sorry, I've been referring to you as Mrs. Palmer."

She laughs gently. "I figured as much. Please, call me Wendy. Or Mom. Or whatever suits your fancy, really."

Hmm. Nice lady.

"I was calling, actually, for a couple of reasons. Ryan told me that you two found a house."

"We did. It's tiny, but cute."

"I don't know if you know this or not, but before I became a nurse, I worked as an interior decorator."

"I did not know that."

"I'd love to help you with your house, if you need it."

"I would love help."

"Also, since Ryan's father and I live too far away to really be of any help with the wedding, we'd like to contribute to the honeymoon."

Note to self: Ryan's parents did not send the TV.

"That would be wonderful, Mrs. Palmer—"

"Honey, please. Call me Wendy. You're making me feel much older than I am."

"Right. Wendy. That's great. Ryan's actually handling the honeymoon, since my stepmom and best friend are going ballistic with the wedding and he didn't want Elvis there."

Long pause. "I don't quite get the connection," she says slowly.

"Long story. I'll tell you when you come. Speaking of which . . ."

She laughs. "And that was the final reason I called. Ryan's father has a major meeting that week. We won't be able to get there until Thursday. Also, we sent a gift that should have gotten there already or will be there soon."

"Oh, wow! Thank you for the TV! It's amazing. And too much," I exclaim. "You're coming Thursday?"

"I'm glad you like it. Does that throw a huge kink in the plans?"

"No, not at all. Ryan got his dad's measurements for the suit, and all I need to tell you is that the mothers are wearing midnight blue."

"Midnight blue," Wendy repeats slowly, like she is writing it down. "Okay. Any specifications on what the dress should look like?"

Someone taps my shoulder. Joan stands there, holding out her hand for the phone. "Let me give you to my stepmom," I say.

Joan takes the phone. "Wendy," she croons. "It's so good to talk to you!"

They end up talking for almost an hour about me, Ryan, houses, grandchildren, plain scones or raspberry . . .

Right then is when my cell phone rings.

"Hey, Babe. Want to come over to the house and look at this?"

"Uh-oh. That sounds bad."

"It's not bad. It's just, um . . ." He clears his throat. "Come on over, all right?"

I drive over immediately, jump out of the Tahoe, run up the walk, and open the front door.

And stop dead in my tracks. "Oh my goodness," I say.

Ryan stands from where he is kneeling in the kitchen and grins. "Doesn't it look great?"

The TV takes up at least half the living room, leaving us a grand four feet to cram some sort of seating in.

"I think it adds a lot to the house. Like weight. When we finally got it through the door, I was concerned for our foundation."

"It can't stay here!"

Ryan laughs. "I know. Brandon's coming over. We're moving it to the guest room for now."

I feel like Ricky Ricardo. *Aye-ei-aye-ei-aye.*

"Hey, I just talked to your mom. She gave us the TV."

"Very neat. We need to send a note."

"She also said that for our other gift, she wants to give us our honeymoon."

Ryan raises his eyebrows. "Wow. That's nice. Tell them we're going to Europe for a month."

"Too late," I say, running a finger along the top edge of the TV. "I told her we were going to Graceland."

"Oh, Laurie, you didn't," he moans.

"Gotcha."

"Good grief, Kid, life with you . . ." He doesn't finish his thought. He just looks at me and slowly shakes his head.

Chapter Twenty-Eight

There are just twenty-four hours until my wedding.

My wedding!

I trip over three boxes while racing to get the door. The UPS guy, a tall, chunky man with a shock of graying hair, whom I have come to know very well, hands me a clipboard.

"Afternoon, Laurie," he says.

"Hey, Bob. Been to church yet?"

He sighs.

"I'll take that as a no and tell you again."

He holds up a hand. "No need, no need. Sheesh. Between you and the missus, I'm getting more church talk than anything else."

"Good." I give him back the clipboard and level a look at the stack of boxes by his feet.

"I'll say this for you, Laurie. You sure have a lot of friends."

"Too many." I sigh, taking half the stack and following the tiny path we'd carved out after two wedding showers.

Bob grabs the bottom boxes and follows me into the living room, whistling. "Is it me, or have they multiplied since yesterday?"

"I had my last shower yesterday. And Ryan's friend Tony keeps buying us huge, ridiculous presents like exercise trampolines and Christmas trees."

Bob grins, sets the boxes down, winks, and leaves. "Hope your wedding goes well."

"Me too."

Hannah digs her way to the living room and grins unrepentantly at me. "Wow, Laurie, I have to say this. People took your list and expounded on it."

"In more ways than one. I will never get all the thank-you notes written. Ever. And there is no way this will all fit in our tiny little house."

She looks around, hands on hips. "Well, let me worry about that. Your job is to be gorgeous and relaxed tonight."

"I haven't even seen Ryan in three days," I gripe, ripping open the latest boxes.

"He's busy working on the house, Honey. I haven't seen Brandon for three days, and I live with him!"

Ryan moved into the house last Saturday.

I pull out a huge teddy bear the length of my torso and shake my head, trying not to laugh. "Tony!"

"Not another one."

"Another one. Good grief. I'm sending these gifts back with him. He sent a package of fortune cookies yesterday."

Hannah grins.

Joan walks in, smoothing her hair. "Ken and Wendy are on their way over, Laurie." She gives me a once-over. "You might want to change."

I look down at my track pants and Tinkerbell T-shirt. "I'll be beautiful tonight, Joan. I think it's appropriate that we meet again in my natural form."

"Her hair's fixed at least," Hannah offers.

Joan smiles. "True."

Dad comes in, carrying his mug of tea. He hasn't looked at me all day today. Instead, he's been going over and helping Ryan on the house and fiddling around in his study.

I smile at him, my nose stinging, which is a good sign of oncoming tears. Hannah must've seen my look because she joins me, wraps an arm around my collarbone, and kisses the top of my head. "Five minutes away, just remember that," she whispers.

"Yeah," I say quietly and squeeze her arm.

The doorbell rings, and Joan opens it.

"Wendy!"

"Joan!"

They hug like they'd been college roommates, Dad and Ken shake hands, slap each other's backs, and shake hands again.

Joan puts her arm around Wendy's shoulders and escorts her into the living room. "Laurie," Wendy says, opening her arms.

I pick my way around the gifts and give her a hug. "Hi."

"Oh, you're even more beautiful than I remembered. Ken, Darlin', come here."

Ryan looks absolutely identical to his dad. Brown curly hair, broad shoulders, sparkling eyes. Ryan's dad has more gray than brown in his hair, but that is the only difference.

"Hi, Honey," he drawls, hugging me as well. "So good to see you again!"

"I so wish we could come out here more often, but Ken's work just keeps him busier than a little worker ant, and I hate to travel alone." She looks at Joan. "I brought my dress. It's in the car so we can compare."

Joan and Wendy were bound and determined to buy

identical dresses so they could add to the conformity in the wedding pictures.

"We saw the house," Ken says. "Y'all have done a lot, even in just the few days you've been there."

I nod. We'd stripped the ugly wallpaper and ripped up the carpet, and for the last three days, Ryan and Brandon had been covering the entire house with a woodlike floor.

"Ryan's a hard worker," Dad says to Ken. "He's a good kid."

"Yes, he is. Makes me proud, if I do say so." Ken grins at me, and I blink at the resemblance to Ryan's smile. "Found a right nice girl too."

"Why, thank you." I smile. Hannah taps my shoulder. "Oh!" I say. "This is my best friend and maid of honor, Hannah Knox."

Hannah shakes both their hands. "If you were just at the house, you probably met my husband, Brandon."

"He the tall, dark-haired guy with the weird sense of humor?" Ken asks.

Hannah grins. "Yep, that would be him. He and Laurie have been friends since second grade. He owns the photography studio where we work."

"Oh, okay," Wendy says slowly. "I got it now." She squeezes my arm. "By the way, I apologize for Tony. Bless his mother's heart, he's such a rascal. Ryan said he's been sending you the oddest gifts."

"A teddy bear today," I say.

Wendy shakes her head. "You should have seen it when he and Ryan graduated."

The rehearsal starts promptly at five, and Hannah, Ruby, Adrienne, Joan, and Wendy drive me to the church. I wear a sleeveless, ruffly, knee-length dress.

Laney, Adam, and her troop are there when we arrive.

"Hi, Honey," Laney says, kissing my cheek. "You look beautiful."

"So do you."

Dorie prances over. "So, Auntie Laurie, do I throw the flowers like this or like this?" She flicks her wrist first and then just drops imaginary petals.

I shrug. "Personally, I like the first one. It's a little more aggressive."

"What's aggressive?"

"Forceful."

"Oh. Okay then."

Jack and Jess, the four-year-old twins, are the ring bearers.

Nick arrives next, hugs me, kisses his wife and daughter, and ruffles a hand through his hair. "All right, let's get this rehearsal started."

"We're missing a groom," I say.

"Let's wait," Nick says.

Hannah hands me a silk flower arrangement that I distinctly remember seeing in their living room. "What's this?" I ask.

"Your flowers. Pretend ones."

"Oh."

Ken and Dad arrive next. Then Lexi and Nate. Hallie and Shawn walk through the door a few minutes later. Brandon, Tony, and my fiancé finally arrive.

I grin at Ryan across the room as Nick tries to explain how we are going to have Dorie and the twins come down the aisle.

Ryan has showered, put on a collared shirt and khakis, and is not wearing a hat. This makes three times I have seen him without one. He winks at me.

Nick turns to see what I am looking at and sighs. "Finally." Then in a loud voice, "Okay, everyone, gather around the stage, please!"

He gives us a twenty-minute instruction list, then has everyone but Joan, Ryan's parents, the groom, and groomsmen go to the back.

"Okay, Dorie Honey, you're up," Hannah says, smoothing Dorie's hair.

Dorie flashes me a smile and skips down the aisle, tossing invisible petals in the air.

Jess and Jack walk shyly down, grinning self-consciously.

Hallie is next, then Ruby, Laney, and Lexi. Hannah turns and grins at me. "You have exactly twenty-one hours of singleness left."

She sways down the aisle, and I look over at Dad, who still isn't meeting my gaze.

"Dad?"

"Hmm?"

"It's, uh, time for us to practice the walk."

"Oh! Okay."

We walk down, his gaze on Nick the entire time. I send Ryan a look, and he smiles sympathetically, reading my mind.

We reach the front, Ryan takes my hand, and Nick takes center stage. "Okay, now I'll do my dearly beloved speech, we exchange the rings, Ryan kisses Laurie—"

He leans over at that and does as Nick says.

Everyone chuckles as he pulls away. Dorie giggles. "Wooo," she squeals.

Ryan winks at her.

"Right, and as I was saying, I pronounce you two husband and wife, you leave to the courtyard out front, and everyone else follows."

"Sounds pretty easy," Ryan says.

"Pictures will follow the ceremony," Hannah announces. "So directly after we leave the sanctuary, I need everyone on the front lawn. Also, girls, all of you need to be here by ten thirty so we can get hair and makeup squared away. Guys, if you make sure you're here by two, we'll be good. Any questions?"

❖

The rehearsal dinner passes in a blink, Ryan kisses my cheek and wishes me a happy last night of singleness, and all the bridesmaids gather at my house.

I grab Joan's arm as she heads to the kitchen. "Joan, Dad's acting really weird," I whisper.

Joan looks at me, smiles sadly, and squeezes my hand. "You're his last daughter, Honey. Of course he's acting weird."

"But he has *you* now! I didn't think this would be a big deal! Particularly since he's been pushing for this every since he met you."

Joan sighs, pours a cup of coffee, and hands it to me. "Laurie, you and your dad . . . it's always kind of been the two of you since Laney and Lexi are so much older. Just give him time, Honey. He'll make it through this." She smiles, her eyes wet, leans over, and kisses my cheek. "I love you, Sweetheart."

I set the coffee down and pull her into a hug. She holds me tightly, then inhales harshly and pulls away. "Okay, now see to your guests."

Between the seven of us, we get all the gifts organized, and they stay until well past midnight, chattering about Ryan and me, guessing where Ryan is taking me for our honeymoon, since he hasn't told me, and deciding what our future kids' names should be.

———— ⊕ ————

My suitcases for the honeymoon are stacked against my wall, and most of my stuff is boxed up and ready to be moved or is already at the new house.

I fall into bed at one thirty. I'm ending James tonight. "The prayer of a righteous man is powerful and effective." I save my place in James with my finger and flip over to 1 Thessalonians. I thought I remembered reading something about prayer in one of the last chapters.

"Be joyful always; pray continually; give thanks in all circumstances, for this is God's will for you in Christ Jesus."

I look over at Darcy, sleeping soundly. At my suitcases and the near-empty closet. At Ryan's picture on my desk. At my room, where I've slept every night since I was eight years old.

How could I not be thankful always?

"Lord, You're amazing," I whisper in the silence. "Thank You for everything. I can't even wait for tomorrow."

———— ⊕ ————

I close my eyes.

Don't fall asleep.

I roll over and close my eyes. Still don't fall asleep.

I try lying on my back, on my stomach, on my side, under the covers, over the covers, with a pillow and without.

Nothing.

My fingers feel itchy.

Lord, please let me sleep!

Apparently, I am not supposed to sleep. I sit up, take a deep breath, slide out of bed, and pad down the stairs to the kitchen, where I guess we'd accidentally left the light on over the table.

Dad sits at the table, holding a cup of tea and a photo album.

Dad is never up this late. Usually he goes to bed at nine.

I feel myself start to tear up, take another breath, and step into the kitchen. "Hi, Dad," I say softly.

Dad looks up, the first time he's looked at me all week. "Laurie-girl," he says, swallowing.

I sit down beside him and lean over to look at the album. Me as a third grader smiles a crooked smile back at me.

Dad angles his head at the picture. "Remember those days? Laney was fourteen and obsessed with getting a dog, Lexi was nine and obsessed with Barbies, you were eight and all you wanted was a Cabbage Patch Kid."

I laugh, trying hard not to cry. "Yeah, Mom had just died like four months before that picture," I say quietly.

"Mm-hmm."

We sit in silence for a long minute, me trying to hold it all in, Dad staring at the picture, his thumb rubbing the edge of the album.

"Hard to believe, huh?" I say softly.

"Very," Dad says, voice deeper than usual. "I am happy, you know."

"Are you, Dad? Really?"

He looks at me and smiles shortly. "It's just a little more difficult than . . . than, uh, I thought it would be," he stutters.

I smash my lips together and blink, but it is too late. The first tear falls and I rub it away. "I love you, Dad."

"Oh, Honey," Dad says and pulls me into a hug. "I love you too, Laurie-girl," he whispers into my hair. He holds me for a few minutes and then pushes me away. "Now. Go to bed. We have a long day tomorrow."

"Yeah," I sniff, backhanding my face.

Dad frowns and hands me a Kleenex. "Sometimes it's very hard to believe that you're really my daughter."

I laugh, blow my nose, and kiss his head. "Good night, Dad."

"Sweet dreams, Laurie-girl."

Chapter Twenty-Nine

I wake up slowly, yawn, stretch, and lie in bed for a minute, staring at the ceiling, trying to remember something vaguely important that I have forgotten.

OH MY GOSH!

It's my wedding day! I'm getting married this afternoon!

A huge grin splits my face and I stretch my arms back behind my head, still grinning like an idiot at my ceiling. Sunlight filters through my blinds.

Thanks, God. Suddenly I am teary again. God has been so good to me. For giving me my family and my friends, and definitely for giving me my future husband.

Future husband. I grin again, roll out of bed, and hop to the bathroom to brush my teeth and take a shower.

I come out wearing my robe and find Hannah standing in front of my closet, sorting through my shirts.

"Hey," I protest.

She turns, looks at the robe and dripping hair, smiles broadly, and then frowns at me. "I thought you said you had a button-up shirt."

"I do. Or did. It's red plaid."

"A farmer's shirt."

"What?"

"I call red plaid shirts farmer's shirts."

"Oh. Well, then, yeah. It's not really a button-up, exactly, it's a snap-up."

"That works too." She riffles through again and turns to me. "It's not here, Laurie. Are you sure you had a shirt like that?"

"Hannah."

"I'm just asking."

Joan comes in, grins cheekily at me, and hands Hannah the red plaid shirt. "I ironed it."

"Ha," I tell Hannah. "Morning," I tell Joan. "Guess what?"

"What?" she asks.

"It's my wedding day!" I shriek, making Hannah jump.

"Good grief, Laurie, warn someone before you start screaming," she complains, but the smile doesn't leave her face.

⁓◈⁓

We get to the church exactly at ten thirty. All of my bridesmaids are there, all wearing the customary button-up shirt. Veronica, Debbie, and Lisa of the hair salon had been talked into fixing our hair at the church by means of a healthy tip, and they immediately sit us down and start curling.

Veronica blows my hair dry, combs a mousse in, and slowly works around my head with a curling iron.

Next is makeup by Teri, the cosmetologist. She goes around applying blush, mascara, eye shadow, and lipstick to the brides-maids first, then Joan and Wendy, then me.

When they finally finish, Hannah hands me a mirror and tells me I look gorgeous.

My hair curls down past my shoulders in shiny, perfectly placed curls, my eyes are spotlighted by the excellently applied eye shadow and mascara. The veil, instead of precariously balanced like I had imagined, attaches securely and flows flawlessly with my hair.

I hug Veronica and Teri.

The flowers arrive at noon, and I sneak into the sanctuary to watch Hannah, her hair and makeup worthy of the Oscars but wearing sweatpants and a button-down shirt, argue with the florist about where the flowers should go.

Dorie grabs my jeans. "Auntie Laurie?"

"What's up, Baby?" I ask, bending down to her eye level.

"Can I wear makeup?" she whispers in my ear.

"What's your mom say?"

"She said to ask you." Dorie smiles angelically and clasps her hands together. "Please, Auntie Laurie?"

Teri has left already, but I smile. "I'll put it on you myself."

"Yay!"

I use my fingers and spread a tiny bit of sparkly blush on her still-baby-round cheeks and kiss her forehead.

By the time the flowers are arranged in a way that Hannah is happy with and the bouquets are in a box, ready for us in a few hours, things start to get fuzzy.

And I suddenly realize that I have not had a chance to get coffee this morning.

This is bad.

I grab Hannah as she waves good-bye to the florist. "I need coffee," I gasp.

She tears my hands off her arm. "Calm down, Laurie. Didn't

you get some this morning?"

"No, you shoved me in the car before I could!"

"Okay, don't panic. Laurie, don't panic! Listen, I'll get someone to go get you coffee, okay? Try to calm down."

"I can't, Hannah!"

"You'll have to!"

Someone clears his throat behind us and we both whirl. There stands Shawn, two hours early, wearing jeans and a sweatshirt and carrying a huge takeout cup.

"Shawn!" I shriek. I barrel across the hallway and wrap my arms around his neck. "Is that coffee? Is it for me? Please say it's coffee and it's for me," I beg.

Shawn levels a look at me and glances up at Hannah. "Pitiful, isn't it?"

"Yes, it is."

"Funny, you guys. It's coffee, right?"

"Fixed to perfection. Now please tell me that I know you better than you know yourself."

"You're wonderful. I should've married you." I sigh happily, grabbing the cup from him, and begin to inhale it.

"I don't know that we make a good match, Laurie," he says, shaking his head as I drink, but smiling. He pats my arm awkwardly, winks, and leaves. "I'll be back in a few hours."

"You'd better be on time!" Hannah yells to his back. "Hey! Did you hear me?"

"I heard you, I heard you. Hey, where's my girl?" he asks, turning the corner to the room we are using.

Hannah freaks. "Augh! No, Shawn, you can't go back there! Shawn! Don't kiss her! Her makeup's perfect!" She runs down the hall, chasing him.

I finish the cup in record time. Inhaling, I close my eyes and let my breath out.

Today is my wedding day.

I smile and open my eyes, just as the beautifully decorated cake comes wheeling in the door. "Hi," the guy pushing it says to me.

"Hey."

"I need to talk to Hannah."

"She's about to murder one of my groomsmen. This'll be a good distraction," I say, looking around for a trash can and not finding one.

The delivery guy's eyebrows go up as he processes my statement. "She's what?"

"I'll go stop her. Hey, could you throw this away for me?" I hand him my coffee cup and start down the hall.

"I don't know where a trash can is," he calls after me.

"Hey, neither do I!" I yell back.

Hannah has saved Hallie from Shawn's affections, I guess, because her makeup still looks great.

"Hannah, the cake's here."

"Oh, wonderful!" She smiles, running down the hall back the way I came.

Hallie grins at me. "You're the best, Laur. I'm so happy for you. I'd hug you, but Hannah would get mad."

I laugh and we squeeze each other's hands instead.

Ruby comes over and rubs my shoulder. "You'll be such a great sister," she says, smiling. "I'm so happy for you, Laurie. And I'm really happy for Ryan."

I blink and suddenly it is two thirty and we are pulling on my wedding gown.

"Okay, Laur, arms up," Hannah says.

"You realize that I put this on by myself at the dress shop," I say.

"Well, today's different." She smiles, helping me step into the dress and looping the straps over my arms.

Lexi gently holds my hair back, and as soon as Hannah has the buttons closed, she carefully lets it down.

"There. Still looks perfect." Hannah sighs. "Okay, everyone else, in your dresses."

Lexi turns me around, hugging me tightly despite Hannah's restrictions. "I love you, Baby. You're going to knock Ryan's boutonniere off."

"Hey," I say, lowering my voice. "Did you get—"

"It's all set," she interrupts, her eyes sparkling at me. "Your bouquet was in a separate box, so it was really easy."

"Thanks, Lex."

She leaves to go get her dress on.

We decided on fabulous creamy cornflower blue dresses for the bridesmaids with soft, flowing fabric that complements my gown. The girls are wearing their hair half up and curly, revealing long blue chandelier earrings. Dorie is wearing midnight blue like Joan and Wendy's dresses. Jess and Jack are in suits that match all the guys'.

Lexi hands out the bouquets, Hannah checks everyone's hair and makeup, Joan and Wendy recheck everyone again, and then we line up.

And everything starts to shift into lightning speed.

Dad comes over, smiles at me in my dress, and rubs a finger

along my veil. "You look beautiful," he says, eyes shimmering.

"Thank you, Dad," I half-whisper.

Can't cry, can't cry, can't cry.

"Hey," Hannah whispers back to me as we wait.

"What?"

"The cosmetologist used waterproof mascara. You still can't cry, though. Your eye shadow will smear, and you'll look like an iridescent koala bear."

I grin. "Oh, Hannah."

The doors open, and Ken walks Wendy and Joan down to their front row seat. Dorie is next, lightly stepping down the aisle, flinging rose petals in all directions.

Jess and Jack match to a fault, hide smiles, and trip over Dorie's flowers.

Hallie looks back at me, grins widely, and starts the very slow walk down the aisle.

Ruby follows, babyless, tendrils of brown hair curling around her face. Laney and then Lexi step down the aisle, both grinning widely to their husbands.

Hannah turns, looks me over once more, and grins, her eyes glistening. "Congratulations, Laur. I love you."

Then she whirls and is gone.

I look at Dad, who smiles at me, squeezes my arm, and starts walking as the wedding march begins. I turn, and there he is.

Ryan's smile is so wide his eardrums are probably hurting. His eyes sparkle, his hair curls just so, and the suit fits him very nicely.

I grin back at him. It takes forever and no time at all to reach him. Dad claps Ryan's shoulder, then kisses my cheek before lowering my veil again and taking his place beside Joan.

Ryan squeezes my free hand, still grinning, and Nick's voice booms from somewhere to my left.

"We are gathered here today to witness the marriage of Ryan William Palmer and Lauren Emma Holbrook," he starts.

I hold my bouquet tightly in both hands, smiling at Ryan, only half-hearing the short teaching Nick has prepared. We asked him to do it for Ryan's unsaved friends from college. Ryan glances down at the flowers. His shoulders shake once and he mashes his lips together, his eyes sparkling with the little-kid smile that's completely his.

I grin widely.

"Ryan, do you take Laurie to be your lawful wedded wife?" Nick asks a moment later.

Ryan nods once. "I do."

"Laurie, do you take Ryan to be your lawful wedded husband?"

I smile at him, suddenly feeling teary again. "I do."

"May we have the rings please?"

Jess and Jack jump from where they are standing in front of Brandon. "We forgot to get them!" Jack shouts, panicking, his chubby little fingers trying to rip the plastic rings from the pillow.

I start laughing.

"It's okay, it's okay," Brandon soothes, whispering. "Those are fake rings, remember?"

"Oh yeah." The boys sigh.

Ryan rubs his mouth; Nick clears his throat. The girls twitter, and Dorie flat-out giggles.

Hannah hands me the ring, and I hand her the bouquet. She takes one look at it and closes her eyes, smashing her lips together.

I smile at Ryan, his ring securely in my fist.

"Laurie, place the ring on Ryan's finger and repeat after me.

With this ring, I thee wed."

I slip the shiny white gold band on his left hand and look up at him, holding his hand tightly. "With this ring, I thee wed."

"Ryan, place the ring on Laurie's finger and repeat after me. With this ring, I thee wed."

He places a gorgeous white gold ring with tiny diamonds set all around on my finger and squeezes my hands. "With this ring, I thee wed."

"Ryan, Laurie," Nick says, a huge smile on his face. "It is my honor both as your pastor and as your friend to pronounce you husband and wife. Ryan, you may now kiss the bride."

He pulls me close, eyes shimmering, his hand cupping the back of my head, and smiles at me for a long minute before kissing me.

I hug him tightly as the crowd applauds, and he bends down next to my ear. "Honestly, Laurie, you put a plastic Elvis in your bouquet?"

I laugh loudly and hug him even more tightly. He slips his arms around my waist, twirls me around, and then leads me down the aisle and out the door.

"So, Mrs. Palmer," he says as we move toward the front lawn for pictures.

"Yes, Mr. Palmer?"

"What do you say to a romantic week on the Northern California beaches?"

"I don't know," I say, tipping my head as I study my very good-looking husband. "Think you can stand all the romance?"

He looks me over and grins.

I blush.

"Okay then," I say.

He laughs, slings an arm around me, and kisses my temple.

"Oh, Laurie, life with you is going to be very interesting."

Here's what I think: In the words from—what else?—*Pride and Prejudice*, "God has been very good to us!"

Oh, and by the way, Elvis is *not* present on our honeymoon.